Mary pulled off the road and slowed to a stop.

Cindy kept beeping repeatedly that she needed to talk to them from the second jeep.

Henry jumped out of the first jeep before it even came to a full stop, climbing over Sue in the passenger seat to do so. "What's the matter? We don't have time for breaks right now. We need to keep moving. "

"I know that, Henry," Cindy snapped, her voice filled with concern. "But Jimmy's been shot—and Henry; he's not moving!"

ANTHONY GIANGREGORIO

DEAD WATER

DEAD INVASION

WHAT HAS COME BEFORE

Many years ago, a deadly bacterial outbreak escaped a lab to infect the lower atmosphere across America, unleashing an undead plague on the world.

With rain clouds filled with a killer bacterium, to venture outside in the rain was tantamount to suicide.

To get caught in the rain and exposed to the bacteria would be instant death. But that wasn't the end. Once dead, the host body would rise again, becoming an undead ghoul, wanting nothing more than to feed on the flesh of the living.

Time passed, and eventually the bacteria burned off in the atmosphere. But mankind still wasn't safe. The virus then mutated inside the host, and to be bitten by one of the living dead was a death sentence. Sickness followed by a painful death, only to return as one of the undead.

The United States was torn asunder; civilization collapsing like a house of cards in the weeks after the dead began to walk.

But mankind survived, eking out a dreary existence, always keeping one eye open for the attacking dead.

At least, that is until suddenly, for no known reason after years of existing, the walking dead collapsed and the threat was over.

But though the dead are gone, the world is still a very dangerous place, fraught with peril.

Gone are cell phones, the internet, restaurants, and shopping malls; now all lost relics of a culture slowly fading into history.

In this new apocalyptic world, a man follows the rules of the gun, where the strong are always right and the weak are usually dead. Major cities are nothing but blackened husks, nothing but giant tombs filled with the rotting corpses of the fallen dead.

Across America, towns have become small municipalities with makeshift walls protecting them from attackers. Strangers are not welcome and are either shot on sight or made to move on, that is, if they are not exploited by the rulers of the towns.

Through the destruction of what once was walks a man, crushing death beneath his steel-tipped boots. Before, he was an ordinary man, living a quiet life with a wife and a career, but the rules have changed and, so too, has he adapted, becoming a warrior of death who wields a gun with an iron fist, but shows mercy and wisdom when it is needed.

His name is Henry Watson, and with his fellow companions, Mary, Jimmy, Cindy and Sue by his side, he travels across a blighted landscape, searching for someplace where he and his friends can lay their heads down in safety.

Though life is fleeting, each breath means the possibility of one more day of survival, and a better future for all.

Chapter 1

The zombie's head seemed to implode from the force of the blow of the makeshift weapon, blood and brains squirting out in all directions. Most of the brain matter struck the wall behind the body, splattering the chipped plaster, to then slide down the wall, the design resembling a Rorschach painting on steroids.

The headless body slumped to the side as dark-red blood squirted from the jagged neck stump, arterial spray shooting off in all directions.

That was an oddity that Henry Watson always found strange. How can a zombie squirt red blood if its heart didn't pump anymore? Conjecture had been that the body built up gases, and that those gases had to go somewhere when the body was pierced; much like a balloon being popped. Still, seeing blood shoot from a zombie was always a weird sight.

The body had slumped completely to the floor, blood quickly saturating the filthy wall-to-wall carpeting; the arms and legs continued to twitch, a few remaining synapses still firing, the origin of those synapses, which had come from the brain, now nothing more than pulped meat and fragments of bone.

Footsteps sounded from the second floor of the house Henry was presently in, and a second later, his companions came charging down the stairs.

First was Jimmy Cooper, his pump 12-gauge Browning shotgun in his right hand, his sidearm in his left, a .45 pistol. Right behind him was Mary Roberts, her .38 held firmly in her right hand, her long brown hair blowing behind her from the wind of her haste. And taking up the rear of the little parade was Cindy Jansen, her flowing blonde hair also waving in the breeze of her rushing down the stairs, her beautiful face now wearing a mask of worry.

"Relax, guys, the trouble's over," Henry said while gesturing to the prone and headless corpse. As he took in the body in more detail, he realized it wasn't a zombie at all, but rather was a lone brigand, or looter, who had crept into the house unawares. But then, it couldn't be a zombie, for the walking dead had become extinct a little over a month ago. In the shock of the attack and the gloom of the dark room, Henry had gone into reflex mode, and had assumed his attacker had been a zombie, but now with clarity replacing the adrenaline that had flooded his system, he wondered how he had even thought his attacker had been of the reanimated dead kind.

Still, from even a cursory glance, the dead attacker had the appearance of a zombie. The dead man's clothes were tattered and filthy, as were the exposed arms. As for the face, well, there wasn't much of the visage left to get a clear picture of what the man had looked like. That it was a man there was no doubt, but other than that the rest would remain a mystery. A foot away from an outstretched hand was a baseball bat with nails driven into the tip to make a lethal-looking weapon of carnage. Henry took all this in a matter of seconds, the others not even fully down the stairs yet. "This guy got in here somehow, but I took care of him," Henry explained. "But it's good you came down. Where there's one there might be more, we need to make sure he's alone."

Mary went to Henry and wrapped her arms around him. She was the daughter he'd never had and the two were as close as a father and daughter could be. He would die for her if necessary, though he'd prefer not to if given a choice.

"When we heard the crashing and you yelled out we all feared the worst," she said, separating herself from him and looking up into his eyes.

"Shit, old man," Jimmy said as he inspected the squashed head of the corpse. "You really went to town on this guy. Look at the mess. Who's gonna clean this shit up?"

Henry shrugged; something he did often when he didn't really care about something one way or another. "No one. We'll be leaving here in the morning and I doubt the long-dead owners of the house will care if we leave that here." He pointed to the corpse with his makeshift club, which had been a piece of a chair leg he'd made the previous night when the companions had taken refuge within the four walls of the single-family home on the outskirts of Las Vegas.

After the death of Lazarus and his zombie army, the group had stayed in the area, resting and just enjoying a world where the living dead no longer existed. In truth, they had nowhere to go, so instead, took what in the old world would have been called a vacation. For the past few weeks, all they'd done was relax and enjoy the peace and quiet of not having to deal with deaders, which had been the nickname the group had used for zombies. Of course, they all knew the quiet wouldn't last, and it had finally been broken tonight, in a way they expected to eventually occur, but had hoped to put off for as long as possible.

"Yeah, the owners of the house aren't gonna complain about a damn thing," Jimmy said. "Especially seems they're nothing but beef jerky upstairs in their bedroom."

"Jimmy, don't be so insensitive," Cindy said from the stairs. "Respect the dead."

The owners of the house, a man and woman, were lying on the floor in the master bedroom, long dead from gunshot wounds to the head. There was a story there no doubt, a sad one, but there were a million more just like it since the dead first began to walk.

"Sorry, babe, I didn't mean nothin' by it; just makin' a joke," Jimmy said.

Henry smiled. Jimmy had always been a wiseass, but Cindy now kept him on a rather tight leash. But Jimmy was still Jimmy, only now he had a conscience and was a hell of a lot more mature than when Henry first began traveling with him. That seemed like a lifetime ago, and in fact, it was. The world before the dead began to walk was like a dream now, a dream where things like TV and fast food restaurants were as common as death was now.

"Is everything all right down there?" Sue Anders called down from the second floor. Less than thirty seconds had passed since the others had gone barreling down the stairs after hearing crashing from the first floor.

"It's all good, Sue," Henry replied, his voice loud in the otherwise quiet house. "But stay up there till I give the all clear."

"Okay, as long as no one's hurt," Sue said and then went quiet, only the sound of her shuffling feet as she returned to the bedroom she had been occupying carrying down through the ceiling of the thin-walled home.

Henry pointed to the two exits leading from the room he was in, which had once been the living room of the small, two-story house. He gestured to Jimmy and Cindy. "You two go to the kitchen and check the backyard, while Mary and I check the rest of the house. If this guy isn't alone were gonna have company."

"Henry!" Sue screamed from upstairs, as if on cue, her voice filtering down the stairs, the panic in her tone apparent. "There are people outside carrying torches!"

Henry opened his mouth to respond when the large picture window overlooking the front yard and street suddenly shattered, something large and burning flying into the room to crash against the far wall, the curtains on the window, as well as the other flammable items in the room, immediately becoming consumed.

Henry dropped his makeshift club and reached for the Glock on his hip, but before he could even pull it from its holster, the room exploded into violence, as bodies began flooding into the room through the broken window, swarming over him and the others like a tidal wave.

Chapter 2

The flames were already out of control, and as Henry fought the surge of attackers coming through the window, he figured an accelerant had been used in the object tossed into the house.

The once-dark living room was now as bright as day, flames licking up the wall to cover the ceiling. The temperature had shot up to over a hundred degrees in a matter of seconds, and already the fire was getting inside the walls to surge throughout the home, making sure no room would remain untouched for long.

Sounds of combat came to Henry's ears as he fought with the two men that had come at him. Through brief glimpses at the other companions every few seconds, looks quickly cast when bodies shifted to create openings, he could see Jimmy, Mary and Cindy in battles of their own.

A total of eight coldhearts had swarmed into the house, four via the shattered front window and four more by using the entrance from the kitchen, which was how the first man had snuck in after forcing the door open, despite the barricade Henry had put in place before settling in the living room.

Two-to-one odds weren't the best in a life-or-death fight, but the companions had been in worse scrapes and come out alive and intact.

As he fought the two coldhearts trying to kill him, Henry took in their appearance in the blink of an eye. Like the one he'd just killed, who was no doubt a scout, the two men before him looked the same. Both unshaven, with filthy clothes and a mad gleam in their eye that spoke death to any they came across. There would be no mercy given to any of the companions, only a knife to the throat or a spear to the heart.

Henry only managed to get off two shots from his Glock before it was knocked from his hand by a slashing blade. It was only dumb luck that the knife struck the barrel of the Glock and not his wrist. The pistol went flying to strike the floor and roll, the dirty carpet protecting it from damage.

The blade came back again after striking the Glock, the serrated edge heading directly for Henry's forehead. Moving fast, only his battle-honed instincts from years of fighting zombies allowing him to react so quickly, he raised his arm and deflected the blade, his forearm striking the attacker's wrist, the man's arm then sliding across Henry's raised arm until it reached the end, where the blade continued past Henry's face to swipe empty air.

Henry used his free hand to reach down and grasp the hilt of the sixteen-inch panga strapped to his leg, then snapped it free in one fluid motion, while he simultaneously kicked out with his right foot, his heavy combat boot connecting with the second attacker's groin. Henry felt the man's testicles become crushed under his heel, and a high-pitched scream of agony filled the room. A dark-yellow fluid mixed with blood ran down the man's leg to pool on the floor, the coldheart crumpling to the carpeting before curling up in a fetal ball, his high-pitched shrieks getting ever higher.

The second man was rebounding from Henry's kick, and he came in fast and low, tackling Henry around the midriff, so that Henry could do nothing but exhale the wind from pummeled lungs. Both men toppled onto the couch, as all around them flames licked at anything that would burn.

Hands like a vise, the man having unbelievable strength in his berserker rage, he wrapped them around Henry's throat and began squeezing.

Henry's hand along with his panga were trapped under his body, the pain from his stretched arm socket causing white spots to flash before his eyes. Or was that the first sign of losing consciousness as the feral coldheart squeezed the life from his body?

A few feet away, Jimmy was dealing with his own problems as two more coldhearts tried to take him down. One was a woman, but she was no less fierce than her partner, a man with a scraggly beard and a hole where his nose should have been, but was now just a gaping maw where phlegm forever dripped out of the opening.

"Gonna kill and eat cha," the man said, his voice high and nasally thanks to his missing honker, his weapon of choice a slim dagger-like knife. His eyes were wide, his pupils dilated. Jimmy could tell the man was high on something other than bloodlust; PCP or some other drug that would let the host ignore pain or their wellbeing.

The woman held a crowbar, and in the firelight Jimmy saw the dried, dark-brown coating that covered the tip of the weapon. He highly-doubted it was dried ketchup. Her eyes were glassy as well, the pupils tiny: she as high as her partner.

"Nah, guys, you don't wanna eat me," Jimmy quipped as he tried to back away to get some fighting room. "I'm all gristle." He leveled the shotgun at the man, and just as he was about to fire, the coldheart lunged for the weapon, his abdomen pressing up tight to the double barrel. The expected 'boom' of the shotgun was muffled as Jimmy squeezed the trigger, but the devastation to the man was no less damning, despite the almost silent report. A fist-sized hole blossomed out his back, taking with it large coils of greasy, purple-yellow and pink-frothed intestines, along with a few organs, such as the spleen, appendix, and half a kidney.

Jimmy looked into the man's eyes, expecting to see shock and pain, but all he saw was the same manic look as before. The man didn't even feel the hole in his body. Bloody spittle ran down his beard to coagulate with the mess of a beard, his tongue flicking out like a snake's. "Gonna eat cha," he hissed, the knife poised to strike. Behind him, the woman moved in as well, ready to attack.

Something grabbed Jimmy's right leg around the ankle, and he glanced down to see the man with crushed testicles doing his best to grab Jimmy. Henry was now forgotten to the man, and he was going for the next available target—Jimmy—who could see the same gleam of drug-induced madness peering up at him as the man slobbered and wailed.

Jimmy realized his situation had just gone from bad to worse.

Near the entrance to the kitchen, Mary and Cindy stood back to back while four of the coldhearts attempted to kill them.

One woman in the group was so frail she looked like a toothpick, but despite her thinness, there was still strength beneath the taut skin. Cindy found this out first-hand when the frail-looking woman attacked, a small dagger held in a raised hand, the goal to slash Cindy's throat open.

Cindy had tried to fire her M16 but it was knocked to the side, so that the barrel was aimed at the floor. Pulling the trigger, Cindy sent bullets into the filth-covered linoleum, the wood beneath the vinyl tiles soaking up the abuse without complaint.

Cursing a blue streak for her mistake, she tried to get the weapon up and aimed at a target when the frail woman lunged, wrapping a free hand around the hot barrel while the other hand wielded the dagger.

Realizing the M16 was useless in such tight quarters, Cindy's left hand went to her side and pulled a hunting knife of her own from its sheathe—a seven inch Bowie—and began fighting for her life, as the thin woman's partner—a man with wild eyes and a thick beard covering so much of his face, the beard so filthy and filled with muck and filth that it looked like a large mask — came at her as well, a short, makeshift spear in his hands.

She managed to block the first attack, the tip of the spear missing her by no more than an inch, but the man was adroit at using the weapon, and before Cindy could move, he swung the spear around and jabbed the blunted top into her abdomen, knocking the wind from her chest. The man hadn't struck her with the blunt top of the spear on purpose, or for any sense of mercy, he had just spun the weapon around so as to make up for his first blow.

Cindy bent over and her face turned red from the blow, and for a second she was all but helpless. The frail woman was going to use this to her advantage and slice Cindy's throat, when she was accidentally struck by another of the coldhearts, who had been fighting with Mary. The blade missed Cindy's flesh, only managing to slice off a few stray blonde hairs instead.

Recovering from the spear handle blow, Cindy punched the frail woman in the face, then managed to avoid being impaled for the second time by the man's renewed attack. Backing away, she could see Mary wasn't doing any better than she was, but there was no way to help her friend. Cindy knew she had to help herself first, but as the two coldhearts moved in simultaneously, their weapons before them and ready to draw blood, she knew it might be harder to do than she would have liked.

Cindy had been correct about Mary, who was the worst off of the beleaguered companions. Though over the years she had learned to fight, she was still the weakest of the group when it came to hand-to-hand combat.

Two men attacked her, entering through the rear entrance and charging through the kitchen. One man grabbed her in his arms and threw her roughly to the floor, while the other man dropped down and sat on her chest. The foul odor of his unwashed body was overwhelming, and it was all Mary could do not to retch.

"Gonna have some fun with ya first, little missy," one of the men hissed. Mary couldn't see who had spoken, as she had one of the men's open jackets in her face. The zipper kept swatting her on the cheek, the stinging pain more of a nuisance than anything else. Then there was a weight on her legs as well as the other man pinned her firmly to the floor by sitting on her thighs. The two men were straddling her like two friends riding double on a horse. The man on her chest began fumbling with his belt with his left hand, and a moment later his semi-hard penis was hanging out of his open pants, lying on her chest between her covered breasts like a sleeping snake. His right hand brought up a large Bowie knife, the edge more than sharp enough to slice her throat. He placed it at her jugular, the threat clear: do as I say or you're dead.

The aroma of unwashed privates flooded her senses and Mary had to fight not to vomit. The man leaned forward, his member getting harder the closer it came to her face.

"Gonna suck it good, missy," he cackled. "If you do a good job and swallow it all, maybe I won't kill ya right away."

"I want to have a turn, too," the other man said as her tried to get Mary's pants off, but was having difficulty as his partner was sitting on Mary so that she was flat on the floor, her prone body hindering the clothing-removal process.

Mary couldn't move, her arms pinned to the floor beneath her. The top of her head was hot, really hot, and the odor of singed hair came to her, the smell powerful enough to override the scent of the unwashed dick an inch from her mouth and nose. She struggled to get free, and though frightened, a voice inside her wanted to yell at the two men for being such fools. They were so desperate to have her they didn't seem to care that the house was burning down around them, and that if something wasn't done soon, they would all burn to death, both attackers and attackees.

She opened her mouth to say just that, to yell at her attackers, to tell them what was painfully obvious to her, but the instant she parted her lips, the man on top of her leaned forward and shoved his now rock-hard member into her mouth.

He forced it deep into her mouth, the tip of his penis striking the back of her throat, causing her to gag in response. The man moaned in pleasure as her head bucked forward. He thought she was trying to take him deeper, not realizing she was gagging.

Meanwhile, the other coldheart had managed to unbuckle her BDU's and was pulling them down slowly, his hands caressing her inner thighs. Tears welled up in her eyes as she fought to breathe.

The man pushed into her mouth even harder, moaning with delight.

But he thought he had a trapped woman beneath him, one that was entirely in his power. What he didn't know was that Mary wasn't a normal woman, one who would cower in terror, even while being face-fucked by a killer.

A little more than a year ago, Mary had been taken hostage by a gang of cannibals, and she had been tied to a hospital bed to be raped.

But when the rapist had climbed on top of her, he had made the mistake of getting too close to her face, thinking she was submissive. Mary had torn out the man's throat with her bare teeth, chewing and gnawing at the man's jugular until he had bled out on top of her, then she had made her escape.

If the coldheart had known this, he might have made sure Mary had been knocked unconscious before sticking his dick where it didn't belong.

Now, as he slowly withdrew his member a little, readying for yet another thrust, he pulled out just enough so that only two inches was still in Mary's mouth. This gave her a chance to swallow, and to reposition her tongue. Just as the man was about to thrust forward again, this time wanting to force his dick as far as it would go down her throat, Mary slammed her teeth closed and began to saw at the hunk of meat in her mouth like it was a large piece of beef jerky.

At first the man let out a soft moan, thinking she was being playful with her teeth, but then his eyes went wide and he began to scream—long and high.

The blade at Mary's throat was withdrawn, as the man was in so much pain the last thing he could do was focus enough to slice her throat. Mary hadn't planned this, but was certainly glad it had worked out in such a way. She had simply reacted, not thinking about her own life, when given the choices she'd been offered, which was be raped and killed, and not necessarily in that order.

She'd seen the other companions go down as they were attacked by their own enemies, and she knew if she was going to survive, that it would be herself that did the saving. No one was coming to her rescue this time.

The coldheart on top of her reeled back to the point he almost fell backwards. Blood squirted from his severed dick, his left hand still wrapped around the base. He looked down in horror, seeing two inches of his pride and joy gone, blood squirting everywhere with each beat of his heart. His mouth fell open, his yellow teeth flashing in the reflection of the fire, his scream taking on a fevered pitch, getting ever higher until he mimicked a woman.

The second man still wasn't aware what was happening to his partner. His hands were between Mary's legs, fondling her roughly, as he prepared to rip off her panties. All around him was the cacophony of battle and the crackling flames consuming the house, so his partner's shrieking barely registered. The front of his trousers jutted outwards, showing off his own excitement.

The first coldheart, his bleeding-wound-of-a-dick still clasped in his left hand, the Bowie knife having fallen to the floor, finally slid off Mary to begin rolling around and screaming on the floor. That was when his partner figured out something was wrong.

He looked up, pulling his gaze away from Mary's creamy thighs, and was shocked to see Mary sit up, a menacing grin on her blood-covered face. In fact, she looked like a she-devil straight out of Hell itself.

Her face was entirely coated in blood, her eyes two bright orbs floating in a sea of crimson. Behind her, the flames licked upwards, over the walls to cover the ceiling, an inferno in its own right. The tableaux made her look unearthly, a spawn of Hell come to claim a soul to return with it from whence it came.

But that wasn't the part that made the man really take a step back, or slide back off of Mary's legs.

Mary's lips were closed, her teeth clamped tight like a vise, but as the man watched, she opened her mouth, and spit out what she was holding inside her mouth.

Two inches of severed penis went flying through the air, flipping end over end, looking for all purposes like it was in slow motion, as if a movie was being played out and the director thought it would be extra special to let the dick move from woman to man extra slow. Blood flew off from the jagged bottom, small droplets going off in different directions. There was a coating of spittle on the tip, the bloody-globules coating it so that there was a bright sheen the firelight caught and reflected.

When the severed dick struck the second man in the forehead, leaving a dark red circle there before falling into his lap, at first he didn't know what to make of the object, still unsure what it was.

He opened his legs and it slid between his thighs to end up perched at the juncture to Mary's closed legs. It had landed upright, so that it looked like the member belonged to her, was a part of her anatomy. Jutting there above her panties, she resembled a she-male who was about to give her new lover the surprise of his life. That was when the second coldheart realized what had hit him on the forehead, what had been in Mary's mouth. Glancing at his still-shrieking partner, he finally put two and two together. "You fucking cunt!" he screamed and growled simultaneously.

"Kill the bitch!" Dickless shrieked from the floor beside his friend. "She bit my fucking cock off!"

"Uh-uh. Me first," Mary hissed. With her arms finally free, and her gun hand especially, she brought up her .38 and fired one shot at the second man, who was still astride her legs.

The bullet entered his face slightly above his lips, on the right side of his face. It entered at an angle so that it ricocheted off his cheekbone, then went sideways, tearing up his mouth, shattering teeth, slicing his tongue in half, before then ricocheting yet again upwards, where it tore up his cheek and exited just below his left eye.

The man's mouth opened and a bloody wail issued forth, but before he could suck in a second breath to let out more wails, Mary shot him again, this one going almost directly between his eyes. The coldheart took on an odd expression, his eyes turning inwards, as if he was trying to look at the entrance wound. The back of his head was missing a good-sized chunk, and a decent portion of his brains now decorated the small table behind him. Mary kicked up with her legs and the body toppled off her, only the man's legs remaining on hers to keep her trapped.

The briefest of glances over her shoulder showed her that Jimmy and Henry were still fighting for their lives, as was Cindy, who was off to her right. Mary hoped to extricate herself from her attackers so she could give aid to her friends, following the same thinking as Cindy had moments ago. The only reason the companions had survived for so long, when so many others had perished, was that they had long ago learned to fight as a team. Though not related, they were still family, the ties to one another forged in spilled blood.

"You fucking bitch!" Dickless hissed from the floor, causing Mary to turn her attention on him.

With his left hand still cupped around his bleeding genitals, his right hand went to an axe hanging from a loop on his belt. Ripping the axe free, the loop snapped. Though the coldheart's clothes and appearance may have been shoddy, the way the man cared for the axe was apparent. It was polished to a high sheen, the firelight dancing off the surface. The edge looked razor sharp, the hand holding it still strong. Evidently, the shock of becoming a eunuch had faded, to be replaced with a need for revenge.

Mary didn't care one bit how much the man desired revenge, and shifting her aim with the .38, she began squeezing the trigger of the revolver to take out the threat, but before she could, the man threw the axe at her, the spinning head aimed right for her face.

She was still partly trapped under the man she'd shot in the head so all she could so was try and fall back, her hands going upwards as her head went down to the floor. The gun was struck by the flying axe, the sound so loud it penetrated the din filling the room. The revolver went flying from her grasp, her hand stinging from the blow. Her entire arm went numb in an instant.

The coldheart looked around and spotted a hunting knife on his dead partner's hip, and reached out and pulled it free, then with one hand holding his bleeding crotch and one with a new blade, he crawled on his knees towards Mary, who was only now realizing her time had just run out.

Mary reached down to the hunting knife she carried on her hip, one similar to what Cindy carried, but before she could pull the blade free, she saw the coldheart raise the knife to begin bringing it down, the sharpened blade going straight for her face.

Chapter 3

There was nothing Mary could do to save herself and she knew it, the premonition of her coming death flashing past her eyes in a fraction of a second. Deep in the back of her mind, she wondered how much it would hurt. Would it be the briefest hint of pain when the knife penetrated her face, to then go deeper into her brain and silence her forever? Or would the blow not do the job immediately, and she would end up not dying quickly.

The speed it took for neurons to fire was how fast she contemplated her own doom.

The knife was about to come down, the coldheart's face a mask of hate and pain, when suddenly his head snapped to the side and he tumbled to the floor, the blade landing three inches from Mary's thigh. The tip stuck in the carpet for a brief moment before falling over and remaining still; the hand that had clenched it a moment ago was still twitching, the fingers spastic.

Mary looked up, past the fallen killer, to see Sue standing at the stairs leading to the second floor. In all the commotion of the attack, Sue had been forgotten.

Which was a lucky thing for Mary, for it was now Sue, alone and standing on the third stair, her arms propped on the railing for support, her hands holding the small .22 she carried, who was free to shoot the coldhearts attacking her friends.

Though the .22 she used didn't have much stopping power, in the hands of a skilled marksman the small caliber weapon could still do some damage to an opponent, or even kill if the shot was well-placed.

Sue had become quite proficient in using the small gun since she had been given it more than six months ago. When time and extra ammunition allowed, Henry would take her someplace where she could practice. Most of the time she had used the walking dead for targets, Henry teaching her how to anticipate the zombies' movements so that fewer bullets would be wasted on missed shots.

Shooting an animated corpse in the torso would do nothing to stop it, and unless it was shot in the knees to cripple it, the ghoul would never stop coming. So Sue had learned to aim for the head, and even now, with only human opponents to deal with, she did what she'd learned, which was to go for head shots only.

Safe from harm for the moment, Mary watched Sue shift her aim, then glanced over her shoulder to see where Sue was aiming.

Cindy was being pressed against the far wall, and Mary could only stare in horror as her friend was kicked hard in the abdomen by the man she was battling, while beside him, a frail-looking woman laughed and tried to slice at Cindy with her weapon.

Cindy let out a whoosh of air and bent over, the blow hard enough to make her vomit. The frail woman laughed with glee and raised her arm to slice Cindy's throat, but two quick pops of Sue's .22 stopped the woman in her tracks. The first bullet struck the woman in the throat on the left side, only to exit out the right side an instant later.

Blood jetted from the wound, and the woman reached up with her free hand to try and staunch the squirting blood. The bullet had struck the carotid artery, destroying the voice box simultaneously. Blood landed in the nearby flames to hiss and steam, the odor of boiled blood filling the room.

Already dead but not knowing it yet, the woman stumbled away, only to be knocked into the roaring flames a moment later by a coldheart who was battling Henry. She screamed and fell face-first into the fire, her clothing catching immediately. Her hair was the next to go, the straggly moss of hair curling up and smoking, puffing into fire and then vanishing as if it had never been there. Her flesh began to bubble next, her eyes exploding from their sockets from the shear heat. The fat in her body, though little due to her thinness, nevertheless allowed her to keep burning. Mary could only watch in amazement from where she lay on the floor, as the woman turned into a human candle, the flesh blackening and then cracking. It only took a few seconds for the woman to turn from a human being into a blazing animated stick-figure. The jaw dropped open, the skull beneath the skin becoming prominent. Like a bag of frail bones the body seemed to collapse in on itself, the organs within steaming as the liquid was boiled off in the flames. The scent of roasting meat filled the house to mingle with the other horrendous smells.

Only Mary witnessed the woman's demise, for the others were battling for their lives still, and Sue had already moved on to her next target, which was the other coldheart attacking Cindy.

The man had Cindy by the throat and was squeezing. Cindy did her best to fight him off, repeatedly attempting to knee him in the groin, but he managed to turn his hip to block her.

Sue fired again, her bullet striking the man in the back of the head. The bullet wasn't powerful enough to break free of the cranium, but it did manage to push enough at the inner part of the skull at the man's forehead for Cindy to actually see a small bump appear, as if from nowhere.

The face took on a look of complete consternation, as if the last thought the coldheart had was that there was something wrong with his brain. Then his eyes rolled up into his head and he went slack. Cindy felt the grip on her neck loosen and she shoved him aside, only to fall to the smoking carpet gasping and wheezing.

Mary jumped up and went to help her friend, as Sue continued eliminating the people attacking her group.

The entire living room was burning now, only the center of the room relatively still safe from the inferno. Smoke caused everyone to begin choking, and it was getting difficult to breathe. If the battle wasn't over soon, both offense and defense of the battle would find themselves inundated with smoke.

Jimmy's eyes were clouded from the acrid smoke and he blinked them multiple times to try and clear his vision.

It was a mistake.

The second he took his focus off his two attackers, the two coldhearts came at him, heedless of their own safety, while at his feet, the other man with crushed testicles did his best to trip Jimmy and take him down.

Jimmy was able to peer right through the hole he'd made with his shotgun in the man before him, the effect making the man's torso seem as if it was a fireplace with a fire burning warmly within. Whatever the guy was on, Jimmy wished he could take a hit of it at that exact moment. The killer barely seemed phased by the hole in his torso, and even as Jimmy watched, something wet and slimy dropped out of the hole to fall onto the carpet. It looked like a large slug, though a dark brown. A spleen or kidney perhaps, or maybe it was the guy's liver, for all Jimmy knew. Biology had never been his strong suit in high school.

He wanted to tell the guy, "Hey, pal, you dropped something," but the words stayed within him, for there was no more time for witty remarks. This shit had gotten far too serious for his liking, and he knew death was just a knife swipe away.

The man barreled into Jimmy, and he tried to shove the man away, only his left hand ended up sliding through the hole in the guy's torso, while his right hand grabbed the coldheart's wrist to keep from being carved up by the thin dagger he held. The man's mouth was wide open, yellow and cracked teeth only inches from Jimmy's face, his gaping maw of a nose-hole blowing air into Jimmy's eyes.

A flashback to fighting zombies came to Jimmy, as the man tried to bite him.

Then Jimmy's leg was yanked to the side and it was all he could do not to fall; the man at his feet was pulling harder.

Jimmy barely registered the death of the woman who had been attacking him as well. In his peripheral, he saw her go down with a bullet to the head, the crowbar she was holding falling to the floor beside her. He didn't know who had shot her and at the moment didn't care, all he knew was his own little microcosm of a world, where one man with no middle was trying to bite him, and another was attempting to drag him to the floor. His back was hot, real hot, as he was pushed towards the wall, which was now entirely consumed by flames with the exception of the small area where he was forced into it.

Jimmy's left hand was under the man's neck, desperately trying to keep the yellow and black teeth from his face. His other hand was totally useless, his arms stuck in the guy's torso up to the elbow. Jimmy's hand could be seen wiggling from out of the man's back, as if it was some bizarre magic trick.

The angle Jimmy was at made it difficult to keep his attacker at bay, and the massive wound the coldheart had suffered seemed to still be doing nothing to slow him down. Jimmy could only turn his face to the side as the yellow teeth drew ever closer.

"Gonna eat cha," the coldheart slurred.

"With what?" Jimmy screamed. "You got no fucking stomach!"

The man just gurgled in response, his tongue coming out to try and lick Jimmy's cheek. The tip did just that, flicking over the stubble on Jimmy's chin. The feeling to Jimmy was as if someone had taken a really slimy snail and placed it on his face.

"Gonna eat cha," the man slobbered again, teeth coming in to take that ill-fated bite out of Jimmy's face.

Jimmy closed his eyes, bracing himself for the coming pain.

Chapter 4

Pain didn't come to Jimmy. Instead, there was a sickening sound resembling a meat cleaver being slammed into a leg of lamb.

Jimmy opened his eyes to see the coldheart's face still before him, only now the man had something new added to his forehead. Direct center of his head, was four inches of Henry's panga. The blow had been so powerful that the blade sank halfway into the man's skull, so that the protruding part of the blade almost touched the gaping hole where the nose was supposed to be.

Amazingly, the coldheart's eyes were still moving, as if even a blade slicing his brain in half wasn't enough to put him down for the final count.

"Eat cha, gonna," the man slurred, his speech pattern affected by the blade in his skull.

"Not today, asshole," Jimmy hissed and shoved the man away from him while sliding his arm free of the torso, as simultaneously, Henry slowly slid the blade free of the parted cranium. It was the only way to get it free, for once a blade cleaved into bone, it would become stuck, so the trick was to slide it out, not simply yank it back the way it had entered.

"Gonna…gonna…" the man gargled, before dropping to the floor, dead. With the panga removed, whatever was being held in place to allow the man a few more seconds of life was gone.

As the coldheart fell away, Jimmy slid his hand down the guy's wrist and snatched the thin dagger from the loosening grip, and in one fluid motion, brought it down so that it pierced the skull of the prone coldheart grabbing his leg at his feet. The blade slid to the hilt into the man's head and the coldheart had a flash of realization that his crushed balls were the least of his problems now. But it was the briefest of flashes, for almost instantly the hands re-leased their hold on Jimmy's leg and the body slumped on the floor.

"Come on, let's get the hell out of here!" Henry yelled over the conflagration consuming the room. Jimmy didn't fully understand what Henry meant. Behind Henry, Jimmy saw another body on the floor, which belonged to the attacker that Henry had dealt with alone, after taking out the first man by crushing his testicles.

"Jimmy, snap the hell out of it; we gotta go!" Henry yelled. He didn't wait for a response, but turned to see Sue still at the stairs. "Sue, get upstairs and toss our shit out a window, then find your way outside; we'll meet you out front!"

"Right," she replied and ran up the stairs.

Mary had Cindy in her arms, practically carrying the blonde woman. "She's in rough shape, Henry," Mary said, coughing from the smoke. They all were, and speech was almost impossible. Jimmy joined them, and the four companions stood in the center of the room, as the fire raged out of control around them. Both Mary and Cindy's hair was shortened a few inches, thanks to the searing heat when they got too close to the flames.

Henry pointed to the shattered picture window, where the flaming object had originally come through. It was ringed on all sides by fire, only a thin hole in the center untouched. Briefly, he thought it resembled a ring of fire at a circus for an animal act. "That way, out the window!" he yelled.

At the rear of the room, the ceiling gave way, raining down flaming debris. The home was old, having been built back in the early 1900's, and the insulation within its walls was nothing more than newspaper; paper which had dried and cured so that it now became the perfect tool for kindling. The flames raced through the walls as if it was on a super highway, going to every corner of the two-story house, until nothing remained untouched.

The furniture was old as well, and almost all of it was not flame retardant. For a destructive force such as fire, there had never been a more perfect house for it to consume.

Three bodies of the now very-dead coldhearts were consumed instantly when the ceiling fell in. Flesh quickly was roasted, filthy clothing burst into flames, and eyes burst from sockets from the heat building within the skulls, which were devoid of hair thanks to the ravenous flames. Later, when the fire had finally consumed all it could, nothing would be left but ashes.

There was no time to lose. Only seconds remained before the entire room would be unlivable. Jimmy bent over and retrieved his shotgun from the floor, ignoring the heat the weapon had absorbed from the fire, and seeing Cindy's M16 close by, he scooped it up as well. Henry's Glock was back in its holster on his belt, and Mary had picked up her revolver, shoving it into the back of her pants for the moment, as there was no time to play with its holster.

Jimmy had a hard time holding the weapons, the heat of the metal almost too much to bear, but he persevered, knowing the firearms could be the difference between life and death. Knives were retrieved as well, taken up from where they had fallen.

With their backs practically on fire, the feeling reminiscent of standing next to a giant oven, they lunged through the window and out into the darkness.

Henry was first to go, and after clearing away as much melting glass from the lower part of the frame as he could given his limited time, he lunged out into the night. The window was set only a few feet off the ground, so the fall was thankfully short, and unless one of the group was careless and turned an ankle, no harm would come to any of the companions from the fall.

Henry was followed by Cindy, who was helped by Mary and Jimmy, each diving through the center of the flaming square. The blow Cindy had taken to the abdomen was still slowing her down, and she wheezed with the exertion of moving. Mary came next and then Jimmy, who tossed the weapons out first, then followed, falling heavily onto the ground when he landed. But he rolled a few times, taking up the impact, so landed unharmed, if not messily. His sleeve had caught fire as he lunged through the window, but it was extinguished as he rolled on the ground. It happened so fast no one even noticed it had occurred.

The combustion within the living room had doubled thanks to Henry removing more glass from the window and allowing the airflow to flow more smoothly, and with more oxygen fueling it, the flames erupted, a back draft scenario coming to pass. It was as if some magic hand had been hovering over a switch, waiting for the companions to escape before setting off an explosion.

The fire roared out of the open window, knocking everyone onto their ass, the fiery hand receding as fast as it had appeared. Trapped natural gas still in the pipes in the kitchen was set off, the flammable vapor more than enough to fuel the flames even more.

The upper floor was burning as well, the entire house becoming consumed almost instantly.

Henry pulled himself to his feet, shaking his head to clear it. There was a ringing in his ears and tiny pinpoints of light flickered across his vision.

He looked around at the others.

Mary was saying something to him but he couldn't understand her. Behind her, the flames grew ever higher, turning the night into day.

Henry shook his head again and closed his eyes for the count of three. When he opened them, the flickering lights were gone and though his ears still ringed, he could now make out what Mary was saying.

"What?" he yelled over the ringing, still wanting her to repeat what she said yet again.

"I said, where's Sue?" Mary shouted. "She's not here!"

It took a few moments for what Mary said to sink in, but when it did, Henry's heartbeat tripled in speed, the panic he felt rising to overwhelm him. Quickly looking left and right, then all around the street, he could see that Mary was correct.

Sue was nowhere in sight.

An explosion from the back of the house shook the entire structure on its frame. The home was now a complete and total blazing inferno, one where nothing human could even have a chance to survive for even a split-second before being incinerated.

Chapter 5

"Sue!" Henry yelled, his eyes darting all around him. "Sue, where are you!"

Jimmy joined Henry, while Mary stayed with Cindy.

"Maybe she's out back," Jimmy suggested.

"She has to be," Henry muttered and began running around the burning house. For if she wasn't…

Well, it was too much to contemplate.

First, Henry had lost his wife Emily when the dead began to walk. He had a tough time of it when she'd been taken from him, and when he found her turned, had personally killed her with a frying pan. He'd grieved far longer than he should have, but he'd loved her terribly. Months later, after dealing with the threat of constant death, he came across another soul who he made a connection with. It had been at a shopping mall outside of Boston. He'd become close to a woman named Gwen. In one night they had made love and Henry had finally believed that he could feel again, that he could love again.

But then the malicious leader of the enclave, a bastard called Barry, who had dealt with the food shortage of his people by cannibalizing any outlanders they came across, had thrown Gwen off the roof of the shopping mall, and in doing so, had ended Henry's chance of finding happiness.

After that, Henry had figured he wasn't destined to have anyone ever again, but then Sue had come into his life. They'd only been friends at the beginning, but as time passed, he began to have feelings for her, and she reciprocated those same feelings.

Now, though he still missed his late wife, and thought of her fondly, he had learned to embrace the here and now, and Sue was with him in the now.

So to lose her, after finding her in all the chaos that the world had become…

It was too much to take.

As he ran around the side of the house, he could feel the heat pushing against him, the house now a raging inferno.

"Henry, slow down," Jimmy called. "If there're any more assholes around we're easy taking."

Henry barely heard Jimmy as he dashed into the backyard. His eyes took it all in instantly. A swing set to the left, a tiny shed at the back of the small yard. Six-foot picket fences lined the north and south sides, while all the way in the rear, only a line of overgrown hedges bordered the yard from the neighbor's. Other homes he could see stood dark and dead, their windows devoid of light.

"Sue, where are you!" Henry called again. He turned and peered up at the house through his fingers to protect his night vision as best he could. The entire rear of the home was burning strongly, a mini inferno sucking into it anything that would burn. Flames licked out of the second-story windows, pushing back the night until the yard seemed to be bathed in an earthly glow with origins from Hell itself. Shadows danced across objects as the fire roiled and bounced, casting its pallid glow onto everything.

Half a dozen corpses lay at the edge of the yard. Henry creased his eyes to see them better, and when the light grew brighter from the flickering flames, he could make out that the bodies weren't fresh.

Seeing corpses lying everywhere the group went was a common occurrence for the past few weeks. That was when the walking dead had collapsed for no apparent reason. Henry and the rest of the group had been in a tight jam just before it had happened. A sentient zombie who had named himself Lazarus had taken all the companions hostage, and would have killed them if not for some unknown stroke of fortune that had killed all the zombies.

But one of the group had not escaped alive. Raven, with her long ebony black hair and fingernails manicured into daggers, had been killed by Lazarus before the collapsing. She'd been murdered, and Henry had been able to do nothing but watch, helpless to stop it. He still had nightmares about it sometimes.

Raven had been one of their group, and to lose her was like losing a piece of himself. The companions had been through so many adventures together since the dead first began to walk, and had come across danger countless times, but somehow, Henry had always managed to get them all away alive; usually by coming up with some half-baked plan he would pull out of his ass.

But this time there had been no plan made, and Lazarus had proved to be a formidable enemy. Henry knew deep in his heart that if Lazarus and the zombies hadn't collapsed, it would have been the end for all the companions.

And now, as he stood in the backyard, Jimmy by his side, he realized he was going to lose yet another one of their family.

As if sensing Henry's thoughts, Jimmy said, "Maybe she didn't make it out of the house." He spoke low, not wanting to be the bearer of the devastating news, but knowing someone needed to say it.

"No, I won't believe that, Jimmy. She's got to be around here somewhere." He pointed to the far side of the house, the opposite of where he and Jimmy had approached from the front. "You go that way and I'll keep searching around here."

"But, Henry…" Jimmy began.

Henry stopped him cold with a glare that would have killed if he'd had the power. " Damn it, man. I said go search the other side of the house."

With a sigh, Jimmy nodded and jogged off do to as his friend bid.

Henry turned and let his eyes rove over the yard again, taking it all in, in what he hoped was a new set of eyes.

There were desiccated bodies in the corner, a shed and swing set in the center, a large pile of bagged leaves ten feet from the house that had been raked together and shoved into black Hefty bags years ago, and was now nothing but a wet, soggy mess that was barely more than a foot thick thanks to decomposition.

The firelight caught something metal and reflective. If Henry hadn't been looking exactly at the pile of leaves at that exact moment, he never would have spotted it. Desperate for anything that might help him find Sue, he ran to the object and immediately recognized it as Sue's .22.

Thanks to a large oak tree near the house, that part of the yard was mostly still in shadow, despite the burning home, which was why at first he didn't see the black bags easily. But as he moved closer, he saw that in the direct center of the bags of flattened leaves, looking like she had been lying in the middle of a super-soft bed and had sunk into it, was Sue.

"Sue!" he screamed, then, "Jimmy, I found her!" Henry clomped into the leaf bags, slipping and sliding as he moved. It was like trying to walk in sludge, the pressure of each step causing the decomposed leaves to squirt out of the ripped bags and break down even more. The strong odor of wet earth and mossy decay filled his sinuses, so powerful it overwhelmed the odor of the burning house.

It was pure luck he didn't fall flat on his butt as he moved through the super-slick trash bags. He fell more than knelt down beside her.

Jimmy came running around the side of the house, having heard Henry call out.

"Where?" was all he said as he stopped beside Henry at the edge of the trash bags. That was when he glanced down and saw Sue lying there, still. His breath hitched in his chest when he saw she wasn't moving. "Is she?" he asked hesitantly.

"I don't know. I hope not," Henry replied and knelt down closer beside Sue. His knee pressed into a bag filled with wet leaves. Immediately, the moisture inside the bag seeped through small holes in the plastic and soaked into the material of his BDUs.

She didn't seem to be hurt; no blood was seen anywhere on her body or under her. One arm was off to her side, the other was close to her body. Henry reached down and picked up the outstretched hand. He touched her wrist gently, trying to feel for a pulse.

"Well?" Jimmy asked impatiently.

Henry shook his head, but not because he thought she was dead. "Can't tell. Shit, Jimmy, they make it look so easy in the movies." He let go of her wrist and leaned down to her face, his mouth less than an inch from hers. "Sue, honey? Please be alive," he said and then leaned even closer. He felt the slightest waft of warm breath from her nose and knew she was alive.

Sighing with relief, he kissed her, his tongue gently probing the inside of her mouth. At first she didn't respond, but after a few quick heartbeats her eyes popped open and she wrapped her arms around his neck. She pressed her mouth to his passionately, her tongue reciprocating his actions.

Jimmy stood quietly, watching the two lovers kiss. After a full thirty seconds went by and they still hadn't disengaged, he shuffled his feet and cleared his throat. "Ah, hello, people, is this really the time for this?"

Henry pulled back and gazed down into Sue's eyes. "I thought I'd lost you." He leaned back and helped her sit up, then with

Jimmy helping as well, the pair extricated themselves from the pile of trash bags.

"I rushed as much as possible, but the fire was growing so fast that by the time I gathered all our gear together, I didn't have time to get out other than by jumping out a second floor window." She looked around her frantically. "The gear; I threw it out before me."

"I got it," Jimmy said. "It must have rolled over by this tree." He came walking back with backpacks, duffle bags, and a small munitions bag hanging from his arms. "Looks like it's all here, too."

She stood taller. "Good. I risked my life for all that stuff."

"You must have landed hard enough to get knocked out," Henry suggested. "Those bags of old leaves don't have as much cushioning as they did way back when someone bagged them."

Sue glanced behind her at the flattened bags. "Maybe so, but they saved my life. No doubt I would have broken an ankle or worse if I'd jumped to the ground without anything to break my fall."

Henry hugged her again, giving her a quick kiss on the cheek, then went to Jimmy and took the pack belonging to him, and Sue's, too. Jimmy held the rest of the gear, resembling a bell boy that had been given far too much luggage to carry.

"Well, you're okay and that's what matters," Henry grinned. "Come on, let's get back to Mary and Cindy and get out of here. This fire is gonna attract anyone in a one-mile perimeter. One fight tonight is enough for us I think." He began walking back to the front of the house, Sue right beside him.

Jimmy watched them go, then began to walk as well. "I better get a good tip for this," he muttered under his breath, as he followed close behind.

Chapter 6

The second Jimmy rounded the burning house, giving it as wide a berth as possible so as not to get burned, he knew something was wrong with his friends.

The others had moved into the street, wanting to get farther away from the house and the caustic smoke and heat it gave off. Even standing in the middle of the street, it was still as bright as day, thanks to the inferno consuming the home.

He carried their gear as far as the sidewalk. The grass lining the pavement was over three feet high and falling over onto itself. The neighborhood had once been a high-end, middle class one, with trees lining the streets, and grass on the sidewalks. Now it resembled a war zone, after years of neglect.

A few skeletal bodies were strewn about the area, destroyed zombies that had been left to rot where they'd fallen months, if not years, ago. Neighboring homes were also in disrepair, with kudzu growing out of the foundations and weeds in the gutters; some of them so thick they began to drape over the house like ivy. Most had shattered windows, and many others were missing moldings and other burnable parts, taken by salvagers looking for fuel to burn.

Though Jimmy could see something was wrong, he didn't know exactly what was happening, but as he moved closer, Mary and Sue separated slightly, and he saw Cindy lying on the ground. "Cindy!" he yelled and sprinted to her side, practically shoving Mary from his path.

Mary frowned slightly when she was pushed, but only for a second, understanding Jimmy was only concerned for Cindy. The two had been lovers since almost the second they'd met, and over the years, Cindy had helped mold Jimmy into the man he now was. No more was he the wise-cracking teenager that Mary had first met years ago. Sure, he was still sarcastic, and always had something smart-aleck to say, but he had also grown into a warrior, who was fiercely loyal to his friends.

"Cindy, what's wrong, baby? Are you hurt?" That was when he looked down at her stomach, his eyes then going lower to her crotch. Her camo pants were bloody. "Oh God, you're bleeding. You're fucking bleeding!" His voice went up a notch, the panic evident to all. He looked up at Sue and Mary. "Has she been stabbed?"

Henry, though concerned for Cindy, was keeping watch, his eyes roving the street on all sides. He knew they should be moving, but he didn't want to move Cindy unless it was okay to do so. He was hoping the matter would resolve itself, but if another few minutes didn't make that happen, then he would step in and give orders; they needed to evacuate the area, and fast, before more looters, coldhearts, or cannies arrived to see what had started the fire.

That made him think of their previous attackers, who had made threats of eating the companions, while others just wanted to kill. That particular enemy had never really defined itself as to what it was, and perhaps the fact they'd mostly all been high on something was the reason.

It was true that the walking dead may have been gone, the threat from them no longer an issue, but there were still far too many dangers around to make a person's lifespan shorter than they would prefer.

The world was still in turmoil. There was almost no electrical power, except where some small towns had managed to cobble together a working grid from either solar or scavenged gas or diesel fuel. There were food shortages everywhere, and basic human necessities were in short supply, with killers around every turn, seeking to take what wasn't theirs for themselves. The planet was still a dangerous place, and it would take years, if not never, before any kind of order was restored, where trade routes could be opened between enclaves and even one day a working government.

"It must be the baby. She's having a miscarriage," Sue volunteered, going to Jimmy to try and calm him.

"A fucking miscarriage?" Jimmy repeated, though he didn't seem to understand what he'd heard. "We need to stop it. She's bleeding for Christ's sake!"

"It must have been that blow she took to her stomach," Mary offered, helping Cindy to sit up. She'd remembered seeing it happen, the powerful blow connecting directly at Cindy's abdomen.

Cindy was woozy and looked like she was going to faint, but she put on a false smile. "I'm...I'm okay, guys, really. Just a little lightheaded is all."

The fire was loud, the cracking of timber a constant sound, but then, as if a switch had been turned on, the sounds of engines could be heard through the roar of the fire.

Henry was the first to detect it. "Shit, I knew our luck was gonna run out. We got incoming, people, we need to move. Jimmy, give me a hand with your girl. We'll have to carry her, 'cause we can't stay here any longer." Henry knelt down on the opposite side of Jimmy, Cindy between them.

"I'm fine, really, I think I can walk," Cindy protested.

Henry ignored her. "No time to discuss it, honey, we need to move you right now." His eyes locked with Jimmy's. "On three, we pick her up."

Henry counted, and on three she was lifted between them. But no sooner did they do this than Henry took her from Jimmy completely. "Shit, she weighs almost nothing. I got her alone.

Jimmy, get the gear. Sue, you help him. Mary, you stay with me and watch our backs."

"Will she be okay?" Jimmy asked, his voice tight with tension.

Sue patted Jimmy's arm. "She should be. It happens sometimes for women who get pregnant for the first time. It's normal, though I know it can be hard on the mother…and father too, I imagine."

"We can talk about this some more later when we're someplace safe," Henry snapped. "Right now we need to move. We get caught out in the open, and those engines belong to hostiles, and the rest of our problems aren't gonna matter too much when we're dead."

"Good point," Jimmy agreed and glanced at Cindy.

Cindy smiled uneasily from Henry's arms. "I'll be all right, lover," she said. "I just got the wind knocked out of me when that guy hit me." She said this more for Jimmy's benefit than her own. If trouble was coming their way, she wanted Jimmy focused on the danger, not worrying about her.

Jimmy gathered the gear, Sue taking two packs as well, to lighten his load, and with Jimmy and her following slightly behind the others, Henry led them over to the far sidewalk and into the overgrown yard that was the opposite house from the inferno.

The shrubbery of the adjacent home was wild from neglect—years of neglect actually. The group made it to the backyard, Henry placing Cindy down on the tall grass, just as the first headlights from the approaching vehicles played across the weed-choked street.

Mary stood by Henry, her .38 in her hand. She glanced to her left to see the skeleton of a long dead dog, the bones still intact, the carcass nothing but dried skin and parched bones, the leash and collar still attached to the neck. The leash was tied to a tree, as if the owner had put the dog out to get some fresh air and urinate, and would later return to take the animal back into the house.

No doubt the animal had probably starved to death, tied to that tree, and its owners had either never returned, or had become the walking dead, to wander off in search of human flesh.

That made Mary think of how different the world had changed in only a few years. The world she was born into had disappeared to become one where zombies were commonplace, where basically in the wink of an eye, something that had once been the work of fiction, the stuff movies were made of, had become a reality.

But now it had changed once more.

The status quo where the dead stayed dead was now the norm, as it should have been all along, like it was years ago, before the world had turned upside down. At least now the world had finally righted itself.

The sound of car doors slamming shut pulled Mary from her reverie. People yelling floated on the wind, and from somewhere else came a tearful scream, the voice filled with pain and sorrow.

"Someone doesn't sound like they're enjoying themselves," Jimmy whispered to Henry, though the group was far enough away not to be overheard if they talked normally.

From over the roof of the house they hid behind, the flickering light from the burning house they'd vacated could be seen clearly.

More yelling could be heard, followed by a vehicle backfiring. Another pain-filled sob floated on the wind, definitely female by the tone.

Deep inside Henry, he was already wrestling with a decision. There was a woman in need of help. He knew in the world as it was today, to simply go out and try to help everyone was foolish. Nowadays, you protected yourself and the ones you loved; no one else mattered. It may have been cold but it was a guarantee of staying alive. Good Samaritans got wasted daily in a world ruled by the gun, where only the strong survived.

Henry had adapted to this world as well, and over time had become hard. Though not a stone-cold murderer, he would gladly kill an opponent if it would eliminate the threat once and for all.

But still…

What if it had been Sue who had been captured by some brigands, taken prisoner, and forced to do horrible acts to stay alive? Wouldn't he want someone to help her? To rescue her?

It only took one look at Sue's face in the pale light of the night to make his decision. Each time the mystery woman called out in pain or fear, he watched Sue wince in empathy.

"You guys stay here," Henry said and began walking towards the burning house.

"Whoa there, old man," Jimmy said quickly. "Just where the fuck do you think you're going?"

"I want to see who's out there." He began walking again, as if that was all that needed to be said on the matter, but Jimmy wasn't finished.

"Who cares who's out there?"

"Look, Jimmy, I just want to see what's there. Maybe we can take them and their vehicles. I don't know about you, but I'm sick of walking everywhere." He wasn't going to comment on helping the woman, there was no need.

"Then I'm coming with you," Jimmy protested.

"Me too," Mary added. "Sue can watch Cindy."

"No," Henry snapped. "You all stay here and wait. I'll do the recce on my own."

"But…" Mary began but Henry silenced her with a wave of his hand, raising and lowering it like he was chopping the air.

"I said no, damn it. If I'm seen, I don't want anyone else in trouble." Henry's tone was harsh, but then he said in a gentler voice, "I can move faster alone, and if there's trouble I can lead them away from you."

Mary nodded, responding to the more tactile approach. Jimmy looked like he was going to protest but Mary took his arm, and when he glanced at her, she shook her head. "Just be careful," she told Henry.

"Of course." Henry spun around and began jogging towards the fire, his body low to the ground so he could use the darkness for concealment. He slid between the overgrown shrubs and the house, wanting to get as close as possible to the disturbance without being seen.

He rounded the home, having to push the wild-growing shrubbery out of his way, and when he was looking out onto the street, he took in the tableaux before him.

There were four vehicles: two jeeps and two cars. M60s were mounted to the crossbars of the jeeps, and a Gatling gun had been welded to the roof of one of the cars, rebar welded to the base of the weapon and frame of the vehicle for support. There were around fourteen to sixteen people in total from a quick count, all hard-looking, their faces set in perpetual scowls. From where Henry was positioned, he spotted three women, their visages looking more masculine than most of the men; not that the men looked feminine. All were clearly cold-hearted bastards, who would cut a person's heart out if they were so inclined—only after these bastards cut out a heart, they would then eat it.

That the new arrivals were cannibals there was no doubt in Henry's mind.

Strapped to the grille of the first jeep, which was the first vehicle in line, was the remnants of a decapitated corpse. Nothing but skin and bones, the body resembled a large rag doll. A man was standing by the driver's door of the jeep. He was tall and muscular with long dark hair, and a face that looked as if it had been cut with an axe from a tree trunk. Henry could see the necklace he wore around his neck. It was made of human ears, more than two dozen, all dried and preserved so they would last.

Another man, a few inches shorter, stood near the one with ear jewelry. He resembled a falcon, with a shaved head and a long aquiline nose, and beady eyes that never stopped darting back and forth, as if searching for prey. This one had an adornment of his own; a necklace of severed fingers hung around his neck, more than one still with rings on the digits.

Cannies had arrived to see if there was something for their cooking pots.

When the dead began to walk, food production slowed and then ceased completely, while the other moving parts that made up civilization failed as well. Cities were the worst hit. Having all their food trucked in daily, or flown in, with no one growing food and shipping it, there was nothing to eat.

The masses fought for what scraps they could, killing one another over a can of peas or bag of rice, but when the resources finally dwindled to nothing, there were only a few choices to make.

One was to choose cannibalism; to eat man as if he was an animal.

The slang name that quickly became used throughout a ravaged America was 'long pig.'

Only the most desperate and degenerate turned to this practice. But once they embraced the culture, they jumped in feet first. When you were a cannie, suddenly food was plentiful again, and if you didn't mind eating your fellow man, you quickly found your belly full rather than empty.

Henry detested cannies with all his heart. In many ways, he hated them more than he had the walking dead. At least the dead had been mindless monsters, who only followed their basic instincts to feed. But cannies were human beings who had made the conscience decision to eat their fellow man.

Henry's hands curled into tight fists, the knuckles turning white; he wanted nothing more than to pull his Glock and shoot the bastards where they stood.

But there were too many to take on for no reason other than hatred.

No; if the cannies didn't know he and the others were nearby, all the better for everyone.

Especially if Cindy was hurt.

The entire group of cannies had exited their vehicles and began walking around the perimeter of the burning house. Sparks floated on the wind to land on the roofs of the neighboring homes but as of yet, no new fires had sprouted up. That could change of course. With the homes being abandoned, even the smallest spark could become a raging inferno in a matter of minutes.

The cannies were well armed. Henry spotted an amalgam of ordinance, from a mini-Uzi, to a Russian Kalashnikov to a Mouser, as well as the usual assortment of revolvers and guns in calibers of .45, 9mm and .38s. A few of the guns he didn't recognize, but then he had never been into guns the way some people were. What he knew now was only because he'd been forced to learn about firearms and ammunition, as well as plastic explosives and TNT, to survive. In the world he existed in, weapons of death were as commonplace as cell phones and iPods once were.

A woman cried out from the back of the second jeep, the prisoner sitting up and raising her tied hands. A cannie spun around and slapped the girl, hissing at her to be quiet. She fell back onto the backseat and didn't get up.

So there was the source of the pleading he'd heard. Henry rested his hand on his Glock, still holstered. It would take a fraction of a second for him to draw it if needed, so he didn't pull it free yet. Better to have his hands free in case he needed them.

From his vantage point he studied the men and women, trying to pinpoint any weakness. So far he saw none. The group looked like survivors, people who would not make mistakes, especially ones that might get them killed.

One of the cannies, wearing a black leather vest, carrying a sawed-off shotgun, with a wicked-looking hunting knife strapped to his leg, was looking down at the ground, as if he'd spotted something of worth.

Henry tried to see what the man was studying, but from where he was crouched in the bushes, he couldn't tell what was so interesting, and he didn't dare move from his location.

The cannie began walking away from the others, his head low to the ground, like a bloodhound. As the man crossed the street and stepped onto the adjacent sidewalk from the burning home, Henry raised himself up slightly so he could try and see the sidewalk.

His eyes went wide when he realized what the man had seen and was even now following like a crimson trail of breadcrumbs.

It was blood.

Cindy's blood.

In the companions' haste to get off the street, none of them had seen the small droplets of blood coming from Cindy's pants, the dark fluid dripping down her inner leg, to then roll onto her boot before striking the ground.

Now that Henry could see the trail of droplets, it seemed like it was the most obvious thing in the world for someone to spot. The flames of the burning house reflected off the drops like they were made of liquid glass, the trail so clear a blind man could follow it.

The cannie was most definitely not blind.

Henry watched the man move closer to his location, the cannie's gaze pointed down as he followed the trail. Henry prepared to draw his Glock but then quickly changed his mind. The gunshot would alert the other cannies he was there. No, it would be better to do this one silent. Though a bullet from a distance would be a safer bet, if he could take out the cannie quickly with his panga, he could then high-tail it back to the others, and they could all disappear deeper into the neighborhood before the cannies realized one of their number was missing.

Pulling the panga slowly from its oiled sheathe, he kept the razor-honed blade hidden in the bushes, so that the firelight wouldn't reflect off the polished metal.

So far the night had been a murderous one, with eight people killed by the companions' hands. Not that Henry felt an ounce of guilt for any of the killings. It was killed or be killed, and in the battle just passed, the group had come out on top.

Gripping the hilt of the panga more tightly, Henry raised the blade for the killing blow.

The cannie was already dead; he just didn't know it yet.

Only a few more steps and it would be over, Henry just wanted the man to come deeper into the side of the yard, so that his murder wouldn't be observed by his friends.

The man took another few steps, his attention focused on the blood trail. Once the trail went onto the tall grass, the blood wasn't as easy to spot, and the man had to look even closer.

When he was only a few feet away from Henry, the panga was raised even higher. Henry took a slight step forward so that he could bring his full weight down with the blow. He knew he couldn't sever the man's head off the body with one blow, it was impossible, for that was the stuff of movies, where the hero swiped off a head with one single swing. What with muscle, tendons and spinal cord all making even the sharpest blade hesitate as it passed through, it would take at last two swings given the size and heft of the sixteen-inch panga.

But as Henry prepared for the downward swing and shifted his weight, his foot pressed hard on a small twig beneath his heel, the soft sound of it breaking carrying before him. Though insignificant given the amount of the noise the inferno and other cannies were making, the snap still seemed as loud as a gunshot to the two men. The cannie's head snapped up, his eyes widening when he saw Henry standing in the bushes only a few feet away.

With the discovery of the man before him, the man was already opening his mouth to let out a yell to warn the others in his group, while simultaneously, Henry lunged from out of his hiding place, the panga already coming down for a killing blow.

But even though Henry knew he would kill his prey, he also knew the yell of warning would not be squelched. "Shit," he muttered as he braced for the jolt of metal meeting skull.

Chapter 7

The cannie raised his right hand, the arm coming up before his face, as if his arm alone could stop the inevitable impact of the sixteen-inch panga from cleaving his skull.

Henry was committed to the action of attack, though it was already too late to silence him. The man let out a yell loud enough to draw attention, to warn his friends there were people in the area.

The panga had been sharpened to a razor's edge, Henry spending any and all time he had on honing the weapon. He'd had it since the world first collapsed, when the dead rose and walked the earth. The simple blade had saved his and his companions' lives countless times, and though the panga could be replaced with another, the feel of this particular one's hilt in his hand, the weight of the blade, perfectly balanced—or was it just that Henry was so attuned to it that the weapon became an extension of his arm?—that when he used it to kill, he was like a painter with his brush, or a sculpture with his hammer and chisel as he worked away at a stone block to create art.

The blade cut cleanly through the cannie's wrist, the bone barely slowing the downward blow. The severed hand went flying, spinning through the air as if in slow motion. Henry watched it spin off into the shrubs out of the corner of his eye, while he simultaneously focused on seeing the panga bite into the man's forehead, to then cleave the skull almost in half. The blade stopped at the nose, the mouth hanging open, the tongue sticking out. Both eyes looked inward, as if the poor bastard was trying to concentrate his gaze on the steel blade jutting out from between his eyes.

There was no blood at first, not so much as a drop, but then the arm with the missing hand became a fountain of crimson, each pump of the dying man's terrified heart shooting the blood outwards like a small fire hose.

Henry was sprayed directly in the face; he turned and spit blood from his mouth, blinking to clear his eyes. The blood was hot on his skin, but it cooled quickly in the night air.

Returning shouts from the cannies filled the warm night. Henry looked out to the street to see a group of four had peeled off from the others, and with weapons drawn, were running directly at Henry, who was standing out in the open due to his attack.

There was nothing he could do now but get back to the others.

The man before him was dead, the eyes glazed over, the legs still twitching slightly as nerve endings fired for the last time. The odor of urine and feces filled the air, strong enough to override the smell of the burning house. The man had voided his bowels in death.

Placing his right combat boot on the still chest, Henry yanked as hard as he could to pull the panga free of the split skull. At first it wouldn't move, but then it began to slide out, and with a squelching sound popped free.

Blood spurted fitfully from the jagged wound in the head but it was pitiful. Most of the man's blood had already been exhausted thanks to the severed hand.

The body was prone on the grass where it had slumped heavily, but Henry barely noticed. He was already spinning on his heels and running away, knowing he needed to join the others and warn them what was coming their way.

As he ran, he debated if he should peel off in a different direction and try to lead the cannies away from the companions, but he quickly pushed that idea out of his head. The cannies were too close to the others for the bastards not to stumble onto his friends, and if so, his people might not be ready for it, and with Cindy hurt, there would be no time to get her to cover.

So he stuck with his first instinct, which was to warn Jimmy and the others they were about to be discovered.

While he ran, he shook the panga clean of detritus still clinging to the blade. Blood and bits of brain matter clung to the weapon and wouldn't come off even with a vigorous shaking. He needed to take a moment and wipe it clean, but there was no time, and he'd be damned if he would sheath it in the condition it was in, where the blood and gore would foul the inner sheathe. So he clung to it, and pulled his Glock as well. Knowing the time for a knife fight was over.

The cannies were only seconds behind him, their voices so close that risking a glance over his shoulder was a waste of time.

Rounding the corner of the home and charging into the back-yard, he was greeted by the gaping gun muzzles of the others, who had heard the shouts and were prepared.

"We got incoming people, get hard. No mercy," Henry spit as he joined the others. He almost fell on his ass as he tried to turn quickly while stopping on the grass; he quickly recovered, joining the line of armed men and women he called his family.

Even Cindy was ready, though she was on her knees on the ground. The M16 was a little unsteady in her hands, but still, all she had to do was aim it in the right direction, and given what was about to happen, would probably hit someone.

Sue's eyes went wide when she saw Henry's condition, think-ing he was hurt. His face was covered in blood, his eyes two white orbs peering out of the cooling crimson, his shirt also heavily doused. She opened her mouth to inquire but Henry shook his head, cutting her off.

"It's not mine," was all he said and Sue nodded, knowing what he meant.

The cannies made no attempt at stealth, and rounded the home as if they were on the tail of a rabbit in the woods.

But the instant the four men and one woman entered the back-yard, raising their weapons at the sight of the five companions before them, it was already too late for them.

"Looks like you found me," Henry said flatly to the cannies, and as if on silent cue, the group simultaneously began shooting cannies down in cold blood like they were an execution squad shooting prisoners sentenced to death by firing squad.

The cannies managed to get off a few shots amongst them, but every bullet went wide from the shock of the attack. The only bullet to come even close missed Henry's head by more than a foot.

The cannies did a dance of death as they were riddled with bullets. Ribcages exploded outward, bits of bone from shattered clavicles and femurs becoming projectiles themselves as they cut up the insides of the bodies even further. One hapless fellow was shot in the chest, the bullet ricocheting off his ribcage, where it shattered the tip of his humerus, to then exit out his left shoulder, clipping his spine on its way out and paralyzing him instantly. If he'd lived longer, he would have been in for a lot of suffering before death finally took him, but no sooner did the first bullet leave his body, then a second struck him in the center of the face, killing him instantly.

Others received headshots too, their brains exploding out the back of their skulls, eyes popping from sockets from the internal pressure. It was a massacre, the five cannies quickly cut down in a matter of seconds.

When the last gun fell silent, the night became filled with yells and shouts, the other cannies alerted to the gunfight.

"Come on," Henry said quickly, leading the others back out to the street. "We've got one chance at this. We need to hit them hard, now, before they know what's coming." He glanced at Cindy. "Can you fight?"

She nodded. "Yeah, I can fight."

"Good, 'cause we're gonna need every hand on this." Henry looked at Jimmy. "You still got that grenade?"

"Yeah. It's our last one, too." Jimmy fished in a pocket and pulled out the small orb, then tossed it to Henry, who caught it easily. The orb was immediately smeared with blood from his gore-coated hand. He smiled as he held it up to his face. "This is gonna make all the difference." He waved the others to follow. "Okay, let's do this. Jimmy, Sue, and I will take out anyone on our right, Mary and Cindy; you take targets on the left. We good?"

Everyone nodded. Jimmy went to Cindy and the couple kissed. His eyes asked if she was okay

She nodded, giving him a grin. "I'm sore, but I'll live."

Sue joined Henry and they set off. When they passed the corpses, Henry paused for a fraction of second to wipe the panga clean on one of the bodies. He planned on coming back for the fallen ordinance the cannies had dropped. That is if he was still alive in a few minutes.

A full-on attack like the companions were about to do was a tricky thing. Though they would still have a slight advantage of surprise if they moved fast, there were far too many variables to know the full outcome of their actions.

He had to trust in the skill of himself and his people to hit the enemy hard and fast, taking the enemy out before they could become unified and counterattack.

There were only nine or ten cannies left if he'd counted right upon first seeing them arrive, so the odds weren't as bad as when Henry had first spotted them. Henry had killed one with his panga, and then the other companions along with him had taken down five more.

But nine or ten was still almost two-to one odds, and when it was a fight for their lives, he would have preferred better odds than those. But fate handed out what it would, and bitching about it wouldn't change it. All he could do was roll the dice and see what came up. Of course, if he was able to switch out the dice for a pair of loaded ones, that was fine by him.

The second Henry peered around the house, he saw that the cannies were on high alert. They had heard the gunshots only moments ago and were about ready to head out in search of their friends.

Henry glanced over his shoulders at the others, their eyes easy to see in the gloom, thanks to the inferno of the home across the street. Each one nodded when he made eye contact, signifying they were ready when he was. The cannies were gathering into two groups, their weapons ready for battle, and Henry knew it would only be seconds before the companions were discovered.

His first plan was to throw the grenade out into the street, so that it would roll under one of the vehicles, but as he watched the two groups setting off to find their missing friends—the first group coming directly at the companions' location—another idea came to him. "New plan," he whispered loudly over his shoulder to the others. "Just follow my lead."

Jimmy looked at Cindy, confusion clearly written on his face. "New plan? He never told us what the fuck the old plan was gonna be."

"Good," Henry snapped, overhearing Jimmy. "Then you don't need to remember something new. Just shut up and start firing when it's time."

"How will we know when that is?" Mary asked.

Henry only smiled coyly. "Oh don't worry, honey, you'll know." And without a second of hesitation, he walked out of the shrubs into clear view of the approaching group of cannies, his Glock lowered at his side and a friendly smile plastered on his face.

Chapter 8

When the dead began to walk across the Earth, the outbreak first began in a small Midwestern town in the United States. A local reservoir had become contaminated with a bacterium that once drunk, killed the host and raised it from the dead. Later, the same bacterium was absorbed by the clouds, through simple evaporation of the lake water into the air. These clouds floated across the sky, the atmosphere really, from continent to continent, until nowhere was safe from the deadly rains.

Later still, the virus mutated, and a single bite from one of the reanimated dead was enough to infect a victim with the disease.

Russia was not exempt from all of this.

Within a few weeks of the first deadly rainfall, the U.S.S.R. had been almost completely destroyed. Almost every Russian city and industrial complex was wiped out, the few survivors of the un-dead seeking shelter on the snowy plains far from the cities.

Over time, while fighting the animated dead, remnants of KGB forces attempted to attain power, but the Red Army fought back, wanting the reigns of control for themselves. A bitter civil war had entailed with the undead mixed in the middle, and in the end, no one had won.

Well, one faction did win...in a sense.

The walking dead were able to grow their ranks.

Every armament factory and missile base had been destroyed as well, whether the men and women stationed there had died to infighting or the undead infiltrating the base, was unknown. One simple example of the latter was when a wounded soldier had returned from patrol, after being attacked and bitten. Taken to the infirmary, he would soon have died to then reanimate, before attacking his fellow soldiers, who would in turn continue the cycle.

Off to the far East of Russia in the province known as Chukotka, at the farthest reaches of the Kamchatka Peninsula, where winter still had its firm grip on the land, was a small village by the name of Alyatki. Here, life was hard, but the walking dead had not been much of an issue due to the cold, and so the small fishing village had managed to eek out a fitful living. There were over one hundred men, women and children in the small town, all with frail bodies and gaunt eyes. Life was difficult on the snowy plains, but the villagers had learned how to survive on a meager diet of dried fish and turnips, as well as other root vegetables, or the rare mammal hunted and killed by one of the hunting parties. Usually the men would have to battle the wolves for their supper, the vicious animals always following just out of sight, waiting for a chance to pounce, to take what was theirs.

If the hunting party wasn't careful, the wolves would ignore the carcass of the kill and go right for one of the men, usually a straggler who was slower than the rest of the party. Always looking for signs of weakness, the wolves would attack en mass, and the hunter would quickly find that the tables were turned and that 'he' had become the main course.

The men of the village had tried to save these hapless men, wanting to pull them from the wolves' jaws, but more often than not, only another of the hunters' number would end up falling to the wolves. So it was and always would be: only the strong survived.

When the walking dead had collapsed weeks ago, the village had not even been aware of it, as the dead were so few in reaching the isolated enclave.

Life had continued as it always did, the struggle to survive another day a continuous one.

About forty miles from the sea were the ramshackle hovels that made up the villagers homes, with smoke coming out of the roofs, as people moved about on their daily errands.

One of the children, a rather slow child to be honest, with a nose that was always running and a lazy eye that seemed to always make the boy look as if he was looking for something to the west, stood stock still and gazed up at the soldiers on horseback that were surrounding him.

With each breath the horses took, steam billowed from their mouths, making them look like dragons to the dullard of a boy. Behind the horses was a line of a dozen mules carrying supplies for the soldiers, the animals so overloaded they looked as if they would collapse at any moment from the weight of their burdens. As well as food, the mules also carried a supply of firearms and ammunition.

The boy studied the soldiers, not knowing what to make of them. Since the boy could remember, he had never seen soldiers in his short life, so he had no idea who the men were or what they represented.

The small child put on his best smile for the men, happy to see strangers. His entire life he had mostly only seen the faces from the men and women of the village, strangers a rarity, so to see new faces was something of a treat.

He was already imagining the fun he would have when he returned to the village with the strangers. No doubt the travelers would be welcomed with open arms, and there would be much celebrating.

There would be dancing too, he hoped. He liked to dance. He would jump around, waving his hands every which way, while swinging his head from side to side. His mother and father would always clap with the music, and they would cheer him on to dance even harder, jump even higher, swing his arms even faster. Oh, it would be so much fun he could hardly wait.

The man at the point of the soldiers climbed down off his horse and walked the few steps so that he was towering over the boy, his polished black combat boots crunching in the snow and ice. A little over six feet tall, with broad shoulders, a pot belly, and chubby cheeks, the man didn't look like he had suffered a day in his life. He had 'meat on his bones' as the saying went. But beneath the layer of fat was another layer of muscle. Many men had underestimated the soldier, thinking he was soft and fat.

His name was Major Ishmael Varakov of the Russian Armed Forces, or what was left of it. He was the leader of the fifty-five men in his convoy, their task to cross the frozen Bering Strait into America, to then scout the land to see if it was ripe for the taking.

His task had never been attempted before, but with Mother Russia a skeleton of its former self, there were no other options. Cargo planes were something rarer than a kind Russian woman, and any sort of armed vehicle would never be able to cross the ice due to its weight.

It had to be done like it would have a hundred years ago, which in a way, wasn't too far from where the world was now. The walking dead had seen to the collapse of civilization, and it would be more than a decade if ever, that the world might dig itself out of the anarchy it now succumbed to and return to something resembling the societies of old.

Major Varakov recalled the orders he'd received from General Dmitri Ivanov before setting off with his men.

"Comrade Major, you and the 'volunteers' I have assembled as your army have been entrusted with a great task," General Ivanov had explained in Russian, the two men sitting in the general's office, each with an empty glass that had been filled with Vodka before them. The word 'volunteers' was said in a way that Varakov knew the men had been conscripted into service. Most if not all were either rapists or looters, or worse, killers, all taken from the gulag. No doubt they had been promised freedom from prison if they followed Varakov — or death if they refused. "Now that the dead have been vanquished," the general continued, "it is time for Mother Russia to take its rightful place as the rulers of this planet. The first step is to conquer the West, and when that is done, we can then move our people there, and once we are embedded there, have a strong base to venture out even further."

"Yes, sir, I will do my best to see this come to pass," Varakov had said, the vodka warming his insides. He would have preferred to question the general, ask him if it wouldn't be prudent to get Russia back on its feet before undertaking such a monumental task, that there were hardly enough men and women to rule Russia, let alone another entire country, but with Ivanov being one of the last generals left alive, he knew it wasn't his place.

His place was to obey his commanding officer.

Besides, if he was allowed to set off with a contingent of soldiers, it would be an opportunity to kill and pillage. Varakov was a cruel man, and the world in the state it was in now suited him just fine.

"I am sure you will, Comrade Major," Ivanov had said. "As you make your way across our war-torn country, feel free to take what you need from what is left of our citizens. For if you do not accomplish your mission, all is lost." Then his eyes hardened, the face void of what little emotion the general showed on a good day. "If you do not fulfill your mission, do not return." His eyes were cold, the statement clear.

Varakov had smiled widely, his stature one of confidence. "I will return, Comrade General, and I will accomplish my mission."

The boy gazed up at Varakov, his eyes wide and trusting. He didn't show even an ounce of fear at the man before him. Naïve to the point of idiocy, strangers had yet to equate danger to him, thanks to the isolated location of the village.

"Is the village of Alyatki near here, boy?"

The boy nodded. "Yes, master, I am from there." He bowed low in respect, the way his mother and father had taught him when meeting people of power. And seeing the large handgun the soldier wore on his right hip, a gun larger than anything anyone in the village had, and a long sword as tall as himself, the boy knew the man was someone to give respect to. He couldn't wait to return to the village with the man and the others right behind him. He would get to tell everyone in there how it was he who had found the strangers, and brought them back to show everyone.

They would be so proud of him, and would clap him on the back and sing his praises.

Varakov nodded. "See how the boy bows to his betters?" he said to the men closest to him. "It's good to see the elders in the village teach their young respect." He looked at the child of around ten years of age before him. "Boy, tell me; if we go there, will the loyal villagers of Alyatki supply us with food and water, perhaps a warm bed for the night? Will they give us all we need for our long trip across the Strait?"

The boy blinked at the questions, puzzled, not fully under-standing. He knew the village didn't *give* things away. They couldn't, for they had so little for themselves. "Give you, Master? I...I don't think so, as we are a poor people. But I know if you want to trade, the leaders would be open to it." He paused and added, "But we welcome strangers when they come. We will even have a party to celebrate your arrival."

Varakov swiveled in his saddle so that he was looking at the man directly to his left; his second-in-command. "Did you hear what the boy said, Comrade Streltsy? This proud child says his people are poor, that they will not give us anything, but are happy to trade with us." A malevolent smirk creased his lips, but he kept his face turned away from the boy, so the child didn't see.

Sergeant Streltsy returned his leader's smile with an evil grin of his own, one not so hard to read. "We are lucky they are so generous to us."

But the boy had caught a glimpse of some of Varakov's tight smile, and it chilled him to the bone. Even a dull boy like him could feel that something wasn't right, that something was different about the man from when the boy first met him. Slowly, he began to shuffle backwards, his homemade shoes pushing the snow to the side as he moved an inch at a time.

"Where are you going, boy?" Varakov demanded. "I did not give you permission to leave yet." Though there was no anger in the voice, and the face was neutral, still the boy felt his terror growing.

He was so frightened that he began to urinate, the warm liquid dripping down his leg and soaking into his home-spun made pants. Almost instantly the warmness turned cold, as the icy temperature froze the urine to his leg. The puddle at his feet took slightly longer to freeze, but not by much.

"He doesn't seem to want to listen to you, Comrade Major," a fat soldier called Rhzhdestvensky added with a chuckle, some of the men in hearing distance also adding to the laughter.

"Yes, Rhzhdestvensky, you appear to be correct. The boy does not seem to want to obey me." Varakov shifted in his saddle so that he locked eyes with the boy, who had stopped moving backwards. "I believe he must be taught some manners after all."

Revnik, a thin soldier with a face like a rat, added, "There is one sure cure for a boy with bad manners, Comrade Major, is there not?"

Varakov grunted a reply and reached into his jacket and pulled out a shiny 9mm Makarov PM. It was a compact and handy automatic pistol with a double action trigger. All the men had been outfitted with one before setting out, along with an assortment of Kalashnikov rifles, Stechkins, and a few Walther PPKs.

The boy froze in abject terror at the sight of the gun. Some of the men in his village had firearms, but they were old, and had been repaired so many times it was a wonder they still worked. The guns were mostly used for hunting, as there had never been any form of incursion from human enemies. The walking dead had been easy to kill, usually with spears and long blades, or even a simple wooden club. Slow and lethargic from the cold, they had been easy to take down.

The boy dropped to his knees, his legs too weak to hold him in his terror. A few other soldiers withdrew their guns as well, laughing at the sight of the frightened child, with a puddle of freezing urine surrounding him.

The boy began to shake uncontrollably. Varakov moved his horse closer, so that he was right above him, a tall shadow covering the boy and blocking out the sun.

The child gazed up at the giant looming over him, and though dimwitted and petrified, something inside him knew he needed to move, to fight past his terror and run. He needed to return to the village, to warn his family that these particular strangers were not friendly, that they would only bring pain and death to his people.

With an act of bravery even the boy didn't know he possessed, he jumped to his feet, spun around, and began to run back the way he'd come, his loping gait allowing him to not slip and fall in the snow. His feet crunched the ice and snow heavily, and all he could hear was his own heart beating within his chest.

"Look, Comrade Major," Streltsy said to Varakov, "it appears your little bird is flying away."

"Stop, boy. I command it," Varakov demanded, his voice sharp like a gunshot.

"The boy does not listen, Comrade Major. He ignores you," Streltsy commented.

In response to his second-in-command's statement, Varakov leveled his weapon at the fleeing child, and without preamble, fired three times.

The first bullet struck the boy in the leg, a little above the knee. It was a glancing wound and it didn't stop the boy from running, though the pant leg quickly became saturated with blood. The second bullet was slightly more on target, and it hit the right clavicle. But the bullet ricocheted off without doing too much damage, and though the boy stumbled forward, he did not fall. Deep inside, the child knew if he fell he would never get up again.

Wet tears slid down his cheeks as he sobbed for his mother. His cries of terror floated across the tundra, though the sounds of pain did nothing to affect the hard features of the soldiers.

The third shot was right on target, despite the shifting boy's body. Striking him directly in the back, an exit wound the size of a fist suddenly sprouted from the boy's chest. Ribs cracked and shattered, lungs were pulverized, becoming nothing but ribbons of tattered tissue. The boy's gait faltered as he was pushed forward by the force of the impact, and bright arterial blood shot out of his mouth to coat the pristine-white snow crimson.

The boy's cries for his mother, for help, ceased immediately, and he stumbled and fell face first into the snow. He had been running so fast he actually slid two feet over the ice and snow before coming to a halt.

But he wasn't dead yet, and though mortally wounded, he began crawling on hands and knees, his blood soaking into the ice to leave a red trail behind him. Steam floated up from his body, the hot blood quickly cooling as it left his small frame. A mewling floated on the wind from the dying boy as he continued to crawl away.

"I grow bored. It is time to end this." Varakov took aim one more time, sighting down the barrel of the gun to line up the boy's head in his sights. When he was satisfied with the target, he fired one last time. The report of the weapon cracked across the tundra, seeming rather unimpressive given the state of what was happening; the ballet of life and death.

Varakov had planned on shooting the boy in the back of the head and ending the little tableaux, but at the last moment, the target moved his head, shifting slightly to the side so that his profile faced Varakov. The bullet crashed into the right cheek, breaking free the lower jaw and pulverizing flesh. The jaw hung fastidiously to the tiny face however, the right side not letting go.

Teeth shattered and broken, the lower jaw swung back and forth under where the boy's chin had been; a blood-soaked pendulum, tick-tocking in rhythm with his movements.

"You missed, Comrade Major," Revnik said from behind Varakov, the humor in his voice infectious to the others.

"So I did, Revnik. Would you be so kind as to finish the job I have woefully bungled?"

"It would be my pleasure, Comrade Major." Revnik kicked his horse in the side and the animal galloped across the plain, halting when the boy was only a few feet away. Somehow, the boy was still alive, his legs kicking in the snow like a cat with a broken spine. The mewling was still there as well, though it had lowered in pitch.

Revnik didn't bother to dismount his horse, but leveled his gun at the back of the boy's head and fired one time.

Pink brain matter painted the snow, and finally the legs went still, only the faintest twitch remaining. The child shit himself as well, though already having emptied his bladder earlier, nothing more remained.

Revnik smiled proudly at the slaughter of the innocent child. He sat taller in his saddle and spun his horse around to return to the others. "See, Comrade Major, it was not very hard at all to—" His words were cut short when his face exploded, the back of his head all but disintegrating from the force of the two bullets that struck him unexpectedly. Almost simultaneously, the first round had hit a little left of his nose, the second one, a little below the right eye. His body flipped backwards off his horse and he dropped down only inches from the boy he'd just murdered. The horse whinnied and galloped a few feet away, not understanding where its master had gone, and well-trained enough not to be spooked by gunshots or the smell of spilled blood.

Varakov moved a few feet away from the men he was in charge of and spun his horse around to face them. His gun was still in his hands, though it was not pointed at anyone in particular, however his posture said that could change at any moment. "Would anyone else like to critique my marksmanship?" he asked matter-of-factly, not even a hint of a threat in his tone. Not that he needed to of course. Brutally clear as to his true intent, the cooling corpse of Revnik made his point far better than simple words ever could.

Two heartbeats later, when no one replied to his query, Varakov nodded in approval. "Good then." He pointed to Rhzhdestvensky with the barrel of his gun, but the motion was unthreatening. "Go and take anything of value from Revnik and divvy it up amongst the other men, then gather his horse."

"Yes, Comrade Major, right away." Rhzhdestvensky galloped past his leader and was soon doing what he was ordered, while the other men watched silently.

It took only minutes for the body to be stripped of anything of importance. Even the dead man's boots were taken, as good boots were hard to come by. His weapons and ammunition were quickly distributed amongst the other conscripted soldiers.

Major Varakov gave the order to move out, and once more the large group of soldiers—now minus one—began to move across the snowy plain.

When they reached the two bodies, Streltsy couldn't help but toss a jibe at his commander, knowing his joke would not be considered an insult. Unlike most of the men in the column, Streltsy had known Varakov for years, and was also a true soldier, not a conscript, the two long-time friends. "But the boy still has no manners, Comrade Major, you have not taught him a thing," he said with a grin as they galloped past the two bodies.

"No, Comrade Streltsy, I have taught him something—and Revnik as well." Varakov waited a heartbeat before finishing. "I have taught them that death finds us all eventually."

"Yes, Comrade Major, I suppose it does at that." Streltsy shifted in the saddle to get more comfortable. "Where to next, Comrade? Do we make the crossing now?"

"No, my friend, not yet. We still do not have enough supplies for our long trip across the Strait. Next we will go to the boy's village of Alyatki and hopefully, his elders will have more manners than he did."

"And if they don't?"

Varakov chuckled deep in his throat, the sound more like the growl of a wild animal. "Then we shall do our best to teach them the same lesson as the boy and Revnik." He shifted in the saddle and raised his voice for the others to hear. "And if that is the case, there will be spoils for all: women to take, food to eat, and wine to drink!"

The other men yelled their enthusiasm, hoping beyond hope that this was the case, and knowing in the hearts that no matter what, that would probably be the conclusion Varakov would make, no matter what the villages did or said.

Major Ishmael Varakov kneed his stallion to gallop faster, smiling widely as he rode on point. His men were happy, anticipating the pillaging and raping to come. This was good. It was fortunate he was able to give pleasure to others in such a harsh and unforgiving world. And in that pleasure would grow loyalty from his men, where he did not have to threaten them, for they would obey him knowing the rich rewards doing so would grant them.

The column marched on, leaving the two bodies behind, and it wasn't long before the strong winds began to cover the corpses with snow.

But as the last man in line disappeared over the far rise, the first of the four-legged scavengers had appeared from hidden places nearby, their mouths already salivating in preparation of rending the still-warm flesh from the bones.

Chapter 9

Henry plastered the largest smile he'd ever managed to create onto his face, as he stepped out of the overgrown shrubs and faced the five cannies. He made sure to hold his Glock high in the air with his right hand, so he didn't appear a threat to the three men and two women.

His left hand was slightly hidden by his side from the way he stood, and the palm faced away from the cannies so that they only saw the back of his hand, the grenade hidden in his grip. The pin had been pulled before he stepped out, and only his hand around the lever, keeping it pressed to the grenade, prevented it from exploding and making Henry a wet smear on the side of the house he stood askance of.

He strolled into the open like he was simply going for a walk in Modern-day America, a peaceful man who just wanted to go for a jaunt to work off the roast he'd eaten for dinner. "Don't shoot, fellas, I surrender," he said calmly.

The cannies leveled their weapons at him, but seeing a helpless prisoner surrendering, they held their fire. Henry gambled they would do this, for they might have simply shot first and asked questions later. Lucky for him, it was the former they chose this night.

"Easy, guys, I'm surrendering, no need to shoot." Though not possible, Henry actually managed to smile even wider.

"We heard shots, and some of our group hasn't come back. You know anything about that, asshole?" one of the male cannies asked, by the look of it either the leader or someone who took charge when the leader wasn't around.

Henry shrugged casually, acting as if he didn't have a worry in the world. Of course, inside his mind, he was shitting his pants.

He didn't have a death wish and coming out with his gun raised in surrender before these coldhearts was about the stupidest thing he could ever have imagined doing. But the only other option was a straight-out firefight, and that wouldn't guarantee his people coming out on top. "Don't know. I heard shooting and got scared, then I saw you guys and I figured I'd surrender so I don't get shot in whatever's going on around here."

"This fucker's lyin'," another male cannie said, a whip-thin man in his early twenties. "Let's kill him and toss him in the jeep, then go find the others."

"Yeah," another cannie added, one of the women this time. "I bet he'll cook up nice."

"I call dibs on his cock," the other woman said, licking her lips.

Despite himself, Henry swallowed the knot that popped up in his throat. This bitch gave the term 'man-eater' a whole new meaning.

"Guys, guys, no need to fight over me. I'll go quietly. I don't want any trouble."

The lead cannie smiled evilly. "Asshole, do you know who we are and what we'll do to you?"

Henry shook his head, his face blank. "No, I have no idea. I assume you'll give me food and shelter." He gestured to the women cannie who wanted to eat his dick. "Well, not her, I assume she wants to sleep with me, after what she just said."

The lead cannie blinked in astonishment. Was this guy serious? Here he was, standing with his people with guns aimed at Henry threateningly, with severed human ears and fingers for necklaces, and this idiot acted like he'd never heard of a cannibal before. Had this guy been living under a rock for the past few years? The man decided something wasn't right, so he slapped the cannie beside him and ordered, "Go get his gun and then tie his ass up. We'll figure out what to do with him later after we find the others."

The cannie broke off from the pack and moved towards Henry, who smiled happily, looking like the friendliest person on the planet. "Sounds good to me, guys," he said as he placed his right hand out slowly, the Glock in his hand spun around so he could hand the weapon to the cannie, holding the pistol by the barrel so the man could take the gun by its grip. "But before you tie me up there's something you might want to see." Then, as casually as if he was simply picking his nose, Henry tossed the grenade at them, while simultaneously grabbing the cannie before him around the throat and spinning the man around so the guy was facing his fellow cannies.

A woman caught the grenade, too stupid to figure out what it was, so taken off guard by Henry's placid demeanor. But when she saw what it was, she prepared to throw it far away, the others already turning to run as well.

But it was too late.

Her arm was behind her head in mid-throw when the grenade went off, blowing off her hand and turning the entire right side of her body into a sloppy-red jelly. The left half was thrown ten feet into the street; she was dead long before she landed.

The other woman had managed to turn away to run when the grenade went off, but she didn't get far. She was thrown forward from the force of the explosion, to then soar through the air before coming down hard on her own gun. The weapon impaled her through the heart, killing her instantly.

The lead cannie was able to get far enough away not to be killed, though he took a face full of shrapnel anyway. Blinded, he crawled around on the ground, screaming for help.

At the exact instant the grenade went off, Henry held the cannie who was going to tie him up securely, using the man as a human shield; he yanked the guy's right arm behind the cannie's back and pushed upwards, immobilizing the man for a few seconds. When the grenade exploded, the poor bastard took the full brunt of it, Henry only getting a few scratches on his arms where he held the man tight, though both of them were thrown to the ground from the shockwave.

Still a little stunned from the blast himself, Henry shoved the corpse off him and tried to focus. He spun the Glock around in his hand so he was gripping it firmly, but the man he used as a shield was already dead. The cannie's eyes were nothing but red ruin from the blast, the face and upper chest a mangled hunk of bloody meat, but that wasn't what had killed him. A piece of the grenade had hit the cannie in the throat, slicing it open at the carotid artery, the man bleeding out before Henry had even shoved the limp body off him.

With the blast still ringing in his ears, Henry turned to see the others had joined him as he got back to his feet. Mary was first, followed by Jimmy, then Sue and Cindy. Mary spotted the corpse next to Henry and shot the cannie in the head. Brains exploded out of the back of the corpse's head, the body twitching in the grass with the impact. Henry didn't bother telling her the guy was already dead; it didn't matter. Then seeing the bloody, blinded lead cannie crawling away on the ground twenty feet away, the man's eyes nothing but gaping, bleeding holes, she walked over to him.

The man was whimpering in pain, his world now nothing but blackness. For the briefest of moments she considered not killing him, for a blind man would have little chance of surviving in the world, such as it was. But then she decided the hell with it; one less cannie in the world, even a blind one was always a good thing. She shot the man in the head without another thought, then scanned the street, and seeing it was empty, she returned to the others.

"Shit, old man, that was some signal," Jimmy said, seeing the carnage the grenade had wrought. Body parts were everywhere, a fine pink mist hanging in the air from the human meat that was pulverized.

"I have my moments," Henry said. "And what did I tell you about calling me 'old man'?"

Jimmy grinned. "Ah shit, Henry, you know you love it."

Henry opened his mouth to rebut when footsteps and yells came from around a nearby house two homes down from where the companions were standing.

The explosion and gunshots had attracted another five cannies, the other group that had split off upon their arrival, and Henry and the others quickly found themselves ducking for cover. The firefight Henry had hoped to avoid was happening anyway, the cannies taking up positions behind their vehicles the moment Henry and the others returned fire.

Henry watched the jeep with the M60 and the car with the Gatling gun. If someone managed to get up there and use either one, he and his friends wouldn't stand a chance. The heavy-duty rounds would slice through anything the companions used as a shield like it was paper mache.

"Watch out for those guns on the cars!" Henry called out to the others, voicing his thoughts. "We don't want to have to deal with those heavy weapons!"

No one responded, too preoccupied with firing and ducking. Jimmy was the only one not shooting, as the shotgun wasn't within range of the cannies. His shotgun was for closer brawls, and until he could move closer, he was impotent.

Cindy was beside Jimmy, the two having taken refuge behind a parked car with no rims or windows, both having been scavenged years ago. The doors were gone as well, and the interior had been gutted right down to the plastic that made up the moldings. They both hunkered down behind the rear quarter panel, as the metal panel of the old Buick, being welded to the frame, had been too hard to remove without a blowtorch to cut it off.

A cannie tried to climb into one of the jeeps to use the M60 but Mary fired at him, hitting the gun, the ricochet sending sparks that made the guy duck back down behind the vehicle.

"Nice shot," Henry told her. She was by his side, Sue next to her as well. They had taken refuge behind a massive pile of trash, over four feet tall. Every form of debris was within the mass, including the skeletal remains of long-dead humans. The mass was more than three feet thick, and Henry hoped it would be enough to stop the small arms fire the cannies were using. Of course, the M60s would be another thing altogether, and that was something he didn't want to think about happening.

Another cannie made a try for the Gatling gun, and he actually managed to grip the weapon and spin it around so it was aimed at Henry and the others hiding behind the refuse.

"Get down!" Henry yelled, shoving Sue and Mary to the ground, expecting the barrage of bullets that was sure to arrive at any second. But before the man could get off his first shot, Cindy stood up and fired her M16, three 5.56mm rounds hitting the man in the chest. His ribcage was pulverized from the impacts, his heart a second later. He fell backwards off the car and didn't move when he landed, his body already nothing more than a sack of pulverized meat.

A female cannie with dark red hair cropped short screamed in anger at the sight of the man being killed. Henry, upon realizing he wasn't about to be shot to pieces, popped his head up to see the cannie screaming.

She must have been the woman of the recently deceased man; there was no other reason for such a show of emotion. She fired erratically at the companions, the other two male cannies doing the same. Behind them, the inferno of the house continued to burn, but it was a fraction of the fury it once was. There was barely anything left of the house but the wooden skeleton.

He wanted to use the burning home in some way that would help to take out the cannies, but nothing came to mind.

For the next five minutes the two groups returned fire, ducked for cover, and repeated. But Henry and his team had the disadvantage of having to keep their enemies from using the heavy weapons, and each time a cannie made a play for one of the M60s, precious ammunition had to be wasted to keep them at bay.

When another five minutes passed and the only thing that had changed was that the companions now had less ammunition than before, he knew something would have to change or the stalemate would never end—or it would end horribly for the companions when one of the cannies finally managed to use an M60 or the Gatling gun. There might have only been a few cannies left, but they were in perfect defensive positions.

Then the stalemate was broken when Cindy scored a hit on the last car, a three-round burst hitting the vehicle right around the location of the gas tank.

One of the men had been hiding behind it, and he was blown to the side from the force of the explosion. He landed hard, more than half his body on fire. He flopped around on the ground screaming, and didn't stop until one of the other cannies, a man with a Mohawk, fired two shots into the twisting body to put his dying friend out of his misery.

Henry saw this and used the chance of mercy to shoot Mohawk as well, but the man ducked down and the two bullets missed entirely.

The other cannie, a man with a Bobcat Trailer baseball cap and scruffy beard, tried for an M60 again, but a few well-placed gunshots from Henry made the man lunge for cover, swearing a string of curses. From the sound of it, Henry had at least clipped the guy once or twice, though how bad the wounds were was anyone's guess.

After that things grew rather silent. Another twenty minutes passed with only sporadic gunfire from both sides. The remaining cannies realized the same thing Henry had. It was a stalemate.

Jimmy duck-walked from the old Buick, always keeping low, until he was beside Henry. "Shit, old man, this isn't ever gonna end if we don't do something. Whoever these guys are that are left, they aren't stupid."

"Yeah, I was thinking the same thing," Henry replied, as he peered over the refuse, keeping low, his eyes studying the burning house. It was still aflame but now there were spots where the fire was all but out. The neighboring homes weren't burning, evidently the sparks not enough to ignite secondary fires. "We need a way to flank them without them knowing."

Mary fired off a round when she saw Baseball Cap poke his head up, then shook her head upon hearing Henry's statement. "No way to. Where they're positioned on the street, there'd be no way to come at them without them seeing."

Henry didn't respond, as he was still caught up in thought. A plan was forming, but he was still working it out.

Jimmy frowned upon seeing Henry's countenance. "Oh shit, I know that look. You're thinking of a plan, aren't you? Does it involve one of us risking our lives in some fucked-up way?"

Henry stopped thinking and looked Jimmy in the eyes. "To answer your first question: Yes, I am as a matter of fact, but don't worry. As for your second: No, I'll do this one myself. All I need you to do is be ready when I put it into action."

"Of course," Mary added. "Just tell us what you need."

Henry nodded. "Okay, I'll tell you guys and then Jimmy, you fill Cindy and Sue in."

Cindy heard her name mentioned and she glanced at the others, seeing everyone huddled close to Henry. "Well, it's about time, Henry," she said, knowing if the group was huddled like that, then Henry was filling them in on an idea.

Henry looked over Mary's head at Cindy, and called, "You people know me way too well for my liking. You know that?"

Jimmy snickered. "That's what happens when you spend as much time with the same people as we have. Shit, Henry, since we joined up, we've all done practically everything together, including bathroom breaks and bathing."

Henry grimaced. "Yeah, tell me about it. I've seen your skinny white ass far more than anyone my age should have to."

"I know, right?" Mary added. "Hell, Jimmy, I've seen you naked almost as much as Cindy has, and I'm only your friend; she's your girlfriend!"

Jimmy looked hurt. "Hey, I'll have you know that Cindy thinks my ass is nice. She says it's perfect for my body type."

Cindy let out a bark of laughter. "Yeah, but he forgot to mention I said he's built like a stick."

"I'm not built like a stick, I'm just lean," he remarked proudly. "Okay, enough of this shit. What is this, 'pick on Jimmy day'? I'd think we have more important problems at the moment than how skinny my ass is."

But then a staccato of gunfire came from the cannies, a distraction so that one of them could try and make a break to flank the companions, while another went for the Gatling gun, changing the mood dramatically back to the issues at hand.

Cindy and Sue sent both cannies scurrying back for cover with a few well-placed rounds.

"Yeah, Jimmy's right," Henry said, sobered by the recent attack. "Okay, here's what I'm gonna do. Now, the back of the house we were in before it was set ablaze has a pool, right?"

"Sure, but the water is about the foulest, scummiest shit I ever saw. Hell, I wouldn't even call it water unless you made me."

Henry smiled. "Exactly."

Chapter 10

Movement against the white tundra on the horizon caused Major Ishmael Varakov to pause his horse, the other fifty-three soldiers doing the same.

He reached for his Kalashnikov, knowing a 7.62 mm round was right for the job.

Bringing the weapon up to his chin, he sighted the target and fired. The crack of the gun seemed unimpressive out in the open, but the results of that report were just as devastating.

"Rhzhdestvensky, take Liev with you and begin field dressing that bear, and when we reach you, you better be done; you can add the meat to the supplies and continue on with us, or else you can catch up if you can. But if so, I want every scrap of meat brought with you."

"Yes, Comrade Major," Rhzhdestvensky said, and with Liev, a tall, thin man, by his side, the two galloped across the icy plain to the bear Varakov had killed. The bear was large, and to carry the meat on their two horses would be difficult, so Rhzhdestvensky knew his only option was to work fast so as not to fall behind, so that the pack mules could suffer the extra burden of the weight. Varakov often gave his men challenges such as this. It was his way to weed out the weak of his army.

"We will eat well tonight, my brothers," Varakov said loudly. "Fresh bear meat for every man!"

There was a chorus of cheers.

"And soon we will be at that boy's village, where there will be even more fun," Varakov added, but only the closest men to him heard his words.

Varakov set off again, setting the pace for the others. It took a full half hour to reach the killed bear, and by the time his stallion's front hooves touched the blood-red snow, the spilt blood from the field dressed animal, Rhzhdestvensky and Liev had finished their tasks, if only just.

"Good, good, I am glad you are finished." Varakov eyed the bear pelt greedily, seeing it was relatively intact. It would make a wonderful rug or coat when it was cured. "Do not forget that." He pointed to the pelt.

Rhzhdestvensky nodded, and the two men began gathering the meat for the pack mules to carry. He had taken extra care on the pelt when dressing the bear, and had hoped to win his leader's favor, but he should have known Varakov would not have shown any form of formal gratitude. Still, the fact he wanted the pelt added to the supplies told Rhzhdestvensky his commander was pleased.

Varakov began moving again, the line of soldiers right behind him.

It took another half hour before the first ramshackle house signifying the outskirts of the village came into view. The structures were so low to the ground they were almost invisible, but with the high winds that battered the open plains, it was a necessity to keep them intact.

Night was falling, and with it, the temperature would begin to drop well below freezing. Varakov was pleased they had reached the village; it would be good to have a roof over his head tonight, as well as for his men. He could already feel the bite of the cold when he pulled his scarf down off his mouth to spit.

His breath plumed before him in a wide fog cloud, and his extremities tingled slightly, telling him he needed to find warmth.

Though the army had been outfitted with supplies before leaving, and the bear meat would add to their food, the convoy was still woefully under-supplied for the journey they were undertaking. More food and water would be needed to carry them the long miles across the Bering Strait, where there would be nothing to scavenge for sustenance other than the ice itself.

Alyatki would serve nicely as a way station for himself and his men.

Sitting proudly and fearlessly upon his horse, Varakov led his small army into the village. His posture dared someone to take a shot at him.

But as he entered the small circle that made up what would be considered a town square, no one came out to greet him. Frowning deeply, he pulled out his pistol and fired a shot into the air, then waited for what he expected would be confusion from the residents when they appeared.

A full minute passed before he slid off his horse and took another look around. The place remained deserted; not so much as the sound of a mangy dog could be heard.

"Start searching for the villagers," he ordered. "They have to be here somewhere."

Streltsy strode up beside Varakov. "They have run away, Comrade Major. Somehow they were alerted to our coming."

"Yes, Streltsy, I agree with you. Perhaps there was a scout out who saw us coming and notified the others."

The men fanned out, charging into the small squat structures with swords and knives in hand, searching for the villagers. The sound of their ransacking the place floated on the wind.

Varakov and Streltsy stood in the center of the enclave, waiting for news.

It didn't take long.

Doing his best to fight his captors, an old man was dragged out of a hut located at the outskirts of the village. Held tightly by two burly Russian soldiers, he could do little but squirm in their grasp. Dragged kicking and screaming, he was thrown at the feet of Varakov and his second-in-command.

"And who is this old fellow?" Varakov asked softly.

"We found him in one of the huts, sir, hiding," one of the soldiers said.

"Good job, Private Petroff," Varakov told the soldier standing on the right. "And you too, Temerovna," he told the second soldier. "You may go back to the hunt. I think myself and Streltsy can handle this man."

"Yes, Comrade Major, at once," Petroff said, he and Temerovna moving off.

"So, old man, it seems your little village is not as deserted as I first thought."

The old man said nothing as he lay on the ground. Slowly, he sat up, but he didn't stand. He looked to be in his eighties, with a thick white beard to match the hair on his head. His eyes were a dark blue, and they bespoke wisdom of someone so elderly. The man had seen so much in his long life. He had also seen men like Varakov come and go, and so wasn't intimidated in the least. He gazed up at the Russian Major defiantly.

Varakov returned the old man's gaze with a cold stare of his own. He saw the defiance there and it angered him. With the back of his right gloved hand, he slapped the old man, the elder falling back to the icy ground. "You do not seem afraid of me, old man. It is a mistake you will soon come to regret." He knelt down so he was almost at eye level with the prone man. "I will give you one, and only one, chance to tell me where the rest of your people are. Tell me this willingly and I will kill you fast, but I warn you now, do not tell me what I wish to know and I 'will' get it out of you in the most excruciating way imaginable. It is up to you. Either way I will get the information I need, the only thing is whether you suffer greatly before I do."

"Devil, go to Hell!" the old man rasped, spitting blood from a split lip suffered from where Varakov had struck him. "I tell you nothing!"

Major Ishmael Varakov nodded calmly, as if he knew this would be the old man's response. He glanced at Streltsy. "Have him brought to one of the huts and prepared for interrogation."

"Yes, Comrade Major." Streltsy picked up the old man and handed him off to two other soldiers who were hovering nearby on Varakov's orders. "Comrade Major, do you want me to get…"

"Of course, I do," Varakov cut his second-in-command off. "And tell him to make sure his blades are sharp, too."

That was half a day ago.

Almost a full twelve hours.

The old man had stuck to his guns and had not talked; at least at the beginning. But no man could take unrelenting torture forever; no man could mentally not break when the pain was never-ending, where even to close his eyes was something virtually impossible to do, because his eyelids had been sliced off hours ago.

The pathetic, mewling and naked thing on the bed barely resembled a human being now. It couldn't hear its own pitiful sounds however, as both eardrums had been punctured hours ago with a sharp blade. It also hadn't heard its own words when, with the pain unbearable, had given away the hiding place of its people.

Beneath the double-wide hut used to store the village's communal food, a deep dark pit had been dug. Used as a fruit cellar, it also served well to hide the villagers if a need ever arose.

Packed side by side, so close they could barely move, they had huddled in the darkness while the soldiers tore apart the food stores, taking what they wanted.

When the soldiers had left, they believed themselves safe, but hours later the fruit cellar door had been pulled sharply off its hinges and the cold faces of men had stared down at them.

After a few of the villagers had been killed, the soldiers shooting indiscriminately into the cellar, the rest had followed orders when told to evacuate the pit.

The entire village had been lined up in rows of twos, the men separated from the women and children. Some cried when they were separated from their mates, but a punch to the face or a rifle barrel to the gut quickly silenced them.

The men were led to the edge of the village, more than forty of them, of all sizes and shapes. The youngest was seventeen, the oldest over seventy.

Once more they were lined up, and when the last one was in place, ten soldiers opened up with automatic rifles, shooting the villages down in cold blood.

A few tried to run for it only to be shot in the back. The soldiers quickly moved about the fallen bodies, shooting anyone in the head they thought might not be dead, but only pretending.

With the slaughter complete, the soldiers returned to the wailing women and children. Now the fun could truly begin.

The old man knew none of this, for he was lost in his own private hell of pain.

Blind from the removal of his eyes, and being deaf, too, he only had his suffering to inform he wasn't dead yet.

He never heard the screams of the women as they were raped, or of the children either.

He never saw his own daughter in the same room as himself, three men taking her at once, while others waited in line for their turn.

He didn't see a soldier sodomize his own frail wife, and when the man was finished, slice her throat from ear to ear. Her blood splattered the soldier's boots; he kicked her away, cursing loudly at her for fouling his footwear.

The old man hadn't seen his grandson, barely ten years of age, forced over a barrel while a burly man with a beard had his way with the child, and when satiated, had snapped the boy's neck like it was a twig. The soft crack of the neck was barely audible, and even if the old man hadn't been deaf it would have been difficult to hear over the din of rape and murder filling the entire village.

The pillaging, murder and rape went on long through the night, Varakov letting his men get their fill so they would be satisfied for the long journey to America.

The village cattle, hens and a few goats, were all slaughtered and cooked up, the fresh meat adding to the bear Varakov had killed earlier in the day.

Varakov stood inside the hut the old man was in, the pitiful creature rolling slowly from side to side, its hands secured to the edge of the bed.

The Russian Major glanced over to the corner of the hut, where his torturer was busy cleaning knives and other instruments of pain. Once the old man had talked, the torturer's task was finished and so the man began to clean and pack up his gear.

"Well done, Ivan. I have to admit, this time I did not think you were going to get the information I sought. This old man is made of sterner stuff than I would have imagined."

Ivan merely shrugged. "Perhaps, Comrade Major, but I have not met a man or woman yet who can suffer my skills for too long."

The old man moved his head back and forth. He could tell people were in the room with him by the vibration of their feet on the worn wooden floorboards. He tried to move his secured hands and feet but none would work. His fingernails were long gone, only weeping sores where they had been torn off. Wooden spikes had been forced into the soles of his feet, and both feet had swollen to double their original size. The tender insides of his elbows and behind his knees were nothing but burned flesh from the heat of candles, and his genitals were just a bloody mess of gore and scorched meat.

Still, he had refused to talk, despite the utter agony he'd been subjected to.

Before he had lost his eyes he had almost broken and talked, however. The torturer had brought in one of the soldiers, a thin man with a girlish face. The soldier was a homosexual, but despite this, as he was also a ruthless killer, Varakov had allowed the man to be part of his army. Varakov, though merciless, was a rather enlightened killer himself. Gays did not bother him. What a man or woman did when they wanted to get off was entirely their business, as far as he was concerned.

The old man had lain in the bed, helpless, as the soldier had undressed and climbed onto him.

Though filled with revulsion when the gay soldier took his flaccid penis into his mouth and began working like a two-dollar whore at a cat house, the old man couldn't fight his own body and though he wanted it to stop, he found himself becoming aroused.

It only grew worse when the soldier stopped sucking him, slathered his now hard penis with grease, and then climbed on and began fucking him.

The old man cried tears of shame as he watched the male soldier bounce on top of him, the man stroking his own penis as he rode the prisoner like he was a bull at a rodeo.

When the soldier climaxed, he clenched his internal muscles, and the old man, though over eighty, found himself climaxing as well. The soldier slid off him and began to get dressed, and with a wave to the torturer, left the hut.

Though filled with remorse and anger for letting his own body betray him, the old man could only watch in horror when the torturer walked over to him, leaned over, and took his spent penis in a strong left hand, and with a sharpened blade the right hand, surgically cut off his member right before his eyes.

The old man began to scream as blood shot forth, and though horrified, deep down he knew he would die of blood loss and the soldiers would never get the information they wanted, but then the torture used a hot steel blade, the tip so hot it glowed red. His spurting half a penis was quickly cauterized, the odor of burned blood filling the hut.

The old man had passed out after that, but his time being unconscious was cut short with a bucket of ice cold water.

And so the suffering commenced again, with all his teeth being pulled out one at a time with a pair of metal pliers, then getting his eyes gouged out one at a time. His last two visions were of a rusty spoon coming at each eyeball, the lower lip of the spoon going out of sight as it dug into the bottom of each eye to then pop them out of their sockets.

When his nipples had been burned off it had barely felt like a pair of bee stings, such was the agony the rest of his body was feeling. He was in so much pain he didn't even know when he'd talked, betraying everyone he loved.

Major Varakov gazed down at the raw wound that was the old man and he sighed. "It is time to send this poor peasant to the afterlife, Ivan. We have gotten all we need from him."

"It is true, Comrade Major. I shall do it at once."

"No," Varakov said. "Don't get up. Finish what you are doing. I will be the one to finish this poor fool off." He walked over to the side of the bed so he was standing over the old man, who turned his head, as if sensing someone was there. Varakov didn't know if the old man truly knew what was going on. "You could have saved yourself a lot of needless suffering, you old fool, but you made your choice." He sighed regretfully. "I suppose it is not all bad. Ivan needed to hone his skills and wield his blades. We do not want his tools becoming rusty from lack of use."

Ivan chuckled at his leader's words as he wiped the blood from a blade and slid it back into the cloth holder he stored his tools in. The holder had once been used by a chef to hold his knives, but now it served Ivan equally well with his craft.

Varakov leaned over the old man, and without further preamble, slit the pitiful creature's throat from ear to ear, before quickly stepping backwards so as not to get his clothes soiled with spurting blood, which geysered from the neck wound to spray across the bed and floor. The major was actually quite impressed with the volume and amount of the blood spurting. He would have figured the old man would have had very little blood left after Ivan had finished with him.

The blood flow only lasted a few seconds, then the wound began to sputter meekly. Varakov could have sworn he saw the old man smile, but with a mouth lacking teeth, it was difficult to discern. The victim's bowels had emptied long ago during torture, soaking into the bed and making the entire hut stink of urine and feces. The miasma of a charnel house floated in the air.

A soldier drunkenly barged into the hut, saluting when Varakov glanced his way. Varakov could see that the man must have found the sour beer the villagers no doubt had stored somewhere. If this man was drunk, then the rest of his army was probably drunk as well.

"Well, don't just stand there, fool," Varakov snapped. "Speak."

"Comrade Major, I have come to report the status of found supplies." He stopped talking, and just stood there, swaying from side to side, as if he was dancing to some slow ballad only he could hear.

Varakov spun on his heels and crossed the few feet separating him from the private. The bloodied blade was still in his hand, and Varakov placed it under the soldier's nose. "So help me, Private, if you do not speak right now and tell me what you came here for, I will cut off your nose and feed it to the pitiful farm animals this village has left."

The soldier swallowed deeply, and suddenly didn't appear as drunk as before. Clarity now shined in his eyes.

"Comrade Major, forgive me, please. I report that all the animals have been killed and are even now cooking over an open fire. There was not much in the hut used to store food. A few goats, one cow, and a few chickens. Mostly all there is to eat is cabbage and turnip soup."

Varakov nodded. "It will have to be enough then. What about the villagers? Are they all dead yet?"

"Yes, Comrade Major, all the men have been killed; the rest are still being used for sport."

Varakov nodded. "I see." He glanced at Ivan, who was just finishing up packing his tools. "The men like to fuck, Ivan. If you do as well, I suggest you go and find something before the men go through the rest still alive."

Ivan stood up, shrugging his pack over his shoulder. "Thank you, Comrade Major, I will do just that." He exited the hut after a brisk salute.

Varakov grunted in response and dismissed the private. Alone in the small hut, he paused and looked down at the mess that was the old man. "It did not have to be this way, old man, it could have been so much easier on you." He shrugged with a sigh. "But in the end, I suppose dead is dead, yes?" As he exited the hut, he took a brief moment to knock the lit oil lamp on a small table onto the floor. The oil splashed everywhere, and in seconds a fire was burning strongly. It wouldn't take much longer for the entire hut to be consumed.

Stepping out into the night, he pulled his coat tighter against his body, the cold seeping into any crevice in his outfit it could find. Fires burned everywhere, and with the exception of some huts on the far side of the village that were left untouched for the men to use as barracks, the rest of the village was in flames. Screams of pain and suffering filled the night, as the soldiers fucked, raped and killed the surviving villagers.

It was good to be out in the fresh air, and Varakov sniffed, detecting the odor of the cooking meat. His stomach rumbled and he decided to go get something to eat.

Streltsy came up to him and saluted. "Comrade Major, the village is completely ours. There was zero resistance. One of the huts has been allocated for you to use, of course."

"Good, Streltsy, well done." He grinned hungrily. "Has what I want been put there yet?"

Streltsy nodded. "Yes, Comrade Major, I had it put there myself. It's waiting for you now."

"Good, as soon as I eat I will want to have some fun. Make sure the men are ready in the morning. At first light, we head to America. We cross where the Strait is narrowest, perhaps ninety kilometers wide if that. Any man not awake and on his horse when we set off will be shot on sight."

"Yes, Comrade Major. It will be done." Streltsy saluted and ran off on some errand.

Varakov strolled through the carnage, nodding here and there at a soldier. Female villagers of all ages called out to him for help, as they were spread-eagle on the ground, some mass of hulking flesh on top of them, pumping away while others waited for their turn. Their cries for mercy fell on deaf ears.

Varakov ate quickly, relishing the savory meat. The goat was charred on the outside but was blood-red on the inside; cooked just the way he liked it.

With his hunger satiated, he went to the collection of huts on the outskirts of the village. It was not hard to find the one designated for him, for there was one with a large V painted in blood on the door.

Entering the hovel, it was what he expected. Nothing but a small bed, table and chair, and surprisingly, a small bookcase filled with old books.

But what he was most interested in was what was tied to the bed, arms and legs each secured to one of the four small posts.

She looked to be around nine or ten years of age, with deep green eyes and dark black hair.

Though her body was young, there was still the hint of the woman she would one day be; under her shirt, were the hint of small bumps where one day perfect breasts would form, and her waist was curved just right to give her an hourglass figure. Her skin was smooth and the color of porcelain.

She was naked from the waist down, the juncture between her legs still void of hair due to her age.

The girl was gagged so she could not do more than let out muffled screams.

Licking his lips in anticipation, Varakov began to strip, laying his clothing on the one chair in the room.

"Well, hello there, my little flower," he smiled. "You and I are going to have some fun." Then the smile vanished. "Do exactly what I want and this will go smoothly for you, but do not give yourself to me and I warn you now and only once; things will not go smoothly for you at all."

He sat on the bed and his hands began to go where they wanted, caressing, pinching, squeezing the tender flesh. The girl began to shiver in fear, her whimpers held back by her gag.

Yes, she would suffice for the night.

But in the morning he would have to have a talk with Streltsy.

Though the girl would do, normally, he preferred them younger.

Chapter 11

The remaining cannies were working together as a team; some firing while others were reloading. They had also begun making their way to even better positions, hoping one of their group could get to an M60 or the Gatling gun. If they managed this and didn't get shot before they began firing, the fight would be over instantly.

The M60 would take apart the cars and rubble the companions were hiding behind like the things were made of wet paper. There would be no way the defenders could stand up to the onslaught of the high-caliber meat-shredders.

Then the wind had shifted, the smoke from both the house fire and the burning vehicle blowing away from the firefight. The car fire had mostly burned out, though it still smoked heavily.

Mary ducked down as bullets ricocheted off the fender of the car she was crouched behind. "God, you'd think we could take out the last of these guys easily."

"They seem to be smarter than the other ones, too," Cindy said, dropping down behind the car after firing a three-round burst. She popped the depleted magazine out, took another from her ruck-sack, and slid it into the rifle. "Getting low on ammo, too. I have one more clip left after this, then I'm out."

"I wish they were closer," Jimmy added. "Then I could take a few shots at them with this." He gripped his 12-gauge tightly, wanting the chance to use it. Though he'd never needed anything but his shotgun before, he was glad he had the .45 pistol as well. He checked his wristwatch to see the time. "Henry should be ready soon."

"I just hope his plan works," Sue said. "He's taking a lot of chances, you know."

Mary smirked at Sue's words. "Sue, please believe me when I tell you, compared to some of the crazy ideas Henry's come up with over the years, this one's pretty tame."

Sue's rebuttal was lost when more gunfire could be heard near the cannies, and within the noise, the unmistakable sound of Henry's Glock could be heard.

"That's our cue," Jimmy said, getting to his feet and sliding over the front of the abandoned car he'd been crouched behind with the girls. "It's show time, guys. Do or die." Only Sue remained behind, as she was far from ready for a pitched battle like the one they were in. Mary and Cindy stood up, and together followed Jimmy across the street, their guns blazing.

Five minutes ago.

Henry worked his way directly behind where his friends were hunkered down, backtracking. He jogged onto the second street over, then began making his way back towards the burning house. It wasn't hard keeping it in view, as it was the only light source in the area.

As he jogged through yards and driveways, he expected to be jumped at any moment. Though the walking dead were finally gone—something he still had no clue how it had happened, not that he was complaining—after years of dealing with animated corpses, to just drop his guard still didn't seem right.

Besides, there were far more enemies in the world than just the walking dead. He knew this all too well, and also realized that the gunfire and flames from the house could attract even more troublemakers than just the cannies.

It took almost ten minutes to work his way around, having to give the area of the burning house a wide berth.

It wouldn't do to be seen before he was ready to enact his plan.

When he was halfway there, he was stopped in a yard by four mangy dogs a few feet before him. The animals seemed as surprised to see Henry as he was to see them.

They looked like they were starving, with ribs pushing out through their fur, the skin tight on their bones. They were an amalgam of breeds: a Doberman, a poodle, a pit bull and a Collie.

They were the odd couple of dog packs if there ever was one.

But the most relevant thing about them was that the two largest dogs were slavering and foaming at the mouth, the others also panting heavily with tongues hanging out of their mouths, but no foam yet.

The first two dogs were rabid.

The two that were foaming at the mouth would be dead in days, the poodle following shortly after, as it was showing later signs of the disease.

That didn't matter to Henry, for the dogs were still very much alive right now, and blocking his path. If he even received a scratch from one of them, he would only have a few days at most to find a rabies vaccine. If he wasn't able to procure it, then he would end up dying like the pack.

Henry raised his Glock on instinct, already preparing to shoot the largest dog, the Doberman, when he paused before squeezing the trigger. If he fired, then the cannies would hear the shot and know someone else was nearby, and that would end his little plan of subterfuge.

Slowly holstering his Glock, he slid his panga out of its sheathe, the sixteen inches of razor-honed steel catching the firelight of the distant, burning house. He was taking a terrible risk by not using his Glock, but the alternate was his plan wouldn't work and that would cause serious issues for his team.

"Okay, boys and girls," he said softly, the panga held out before him. "We can do this the easy way or the hard way."

The Doberman leaped forward, its powerful legs launching it into the air, directly at Henry's throat, foam flying from its mouth.

"The hard way it is," he muttered under his breath, ducking low and sidestepping to the side, while slashing the panga heavily across the dog's stomach.

The tip of the blade slid in easily, cutting through muscle and tissue and into the stomach, creating a ten inch wide gash that had the dog's insides spilling out onto the ground. The dog landed heavily, sailing past Henry, to fall hard onto the overgrown grass.

"Ooh, that's gotta hurt," he said cockily. The truth was that he wasn't even a little bit intimidated by the dog pack. In the past few years, Henry had battled everything from giant zombies to slavers, to wild dogs so blood-thirsty and numerous that it was a miracle he'd survived at all.

But here there were just four, flea-bitten hounds—them being rabid not too much of an issue—that looked like if they missed one more meal they'd be ready for the grave, despite the disease eating them from the inside out.

He was confident he could deal with the threat and come out healthy on the other side of the fight.

The Doberman was flopping around on the ground, mewling softly. Henry went to it and beheaded the animal, or came close. He swung the machete like an assassin would cleave off a victim's head for his king. The head almost came off in one blow, but some tenacious bit of muscle and spinal column wouldn't let go. The head twisted from side to side as the dog's legs kicked a staccato on the ground, the nervous system firing down, only slower than usual.

Henry didn't care. The animal was dead, even if it wasn't aware of it yet. The poodle came at him, nipping at his heels and yapping up a storm. Grimacing in annoyance, Henry kicked it like it was a four-legged football. Yipping as it soared through the air, the annoying dog landed in a neighbor's backyard, the yelping coming to an abrupt halt. No more sound could be heard from that particular canine, nor would there ever.

The collie and pit bull attacked at the same time, each one coming at Henry from a different side. Henry had to swipe down low with the panga to protect his lower legs. The dogs were fast as they darted around him.

Henry gritted his teeth in frustration, realizing perhaps he was being foolish by not using his Glock. The Doberman had been brash, simply charging in, but these last two were more cunning. He wanted desperately to use the gun and end the battle quickly, but he knew it would be a choice he would regret. He was so close to the burning home he could hear the sporadic gunfire from the continuing gunfight. If he fired the weapon, discovery wasn't a possibility, it would be a fact.

The collie nipped at his right heel, Henry just managing to jump back, but the pit bull was waiting and snapped at him as well. Teeth found his right pant leg. Henry yanked his leg free, the material ripping in the dog's mouth. He knew if the pit bull got a limb in its mouth, the powerful jaws could snap his bones like they were twigs. Of course, that wouldn't matter as once he was bitten he was pretty much a dead man.

He needed to wrap this up; the others would be waiting for him to enact his plan.

Deciding it was time to go on the attack, he kicked out at the pit bull, hissing loudly to scare it. The dog's head went low to the ground and backed away a foot. It respected the man before it, for he had already killed one of its pack and kicked the other one so far away the pit bull couldn't smell the poodle anymore. Though rabid, there was something within the animal that still retained the canine cunning that allowed it to hunt and survive.

The moment the pit bull retreated slightly, Henry spun on his heels and jumped at the collie, who had been watching warily. The dog didn't expect this, for whenever the pack attacked their prey, the prey would always fight but in a defensive posture.

Henry swung the panga wide, the sixteen inches, plus the length of his arm, just enough to reach the collie's snout.

The blade slid through the animal's nose easily, a stream of hot blood shooting out of the wound. The dog yelped loudly and jumped backwards, but Henry wasn't finished with it. Jumping forwards, he swung the panga the opposite way, simply reversing his swing while spinning the hilt in his hand. This time the blade sliced across the dog's eyes, slicing the orbs in two, and leaving the animal blind.

The dog went wild, yelping and whining, the sound causing a chill to go down Henry's spine, as it was so human-like.

The dog began running in circles, blood shooting from its muzzle, and the pit bull, smelling blood and sensing weakness in one of its pack mates, decided there was no more reason to keep attacking the man before it, for the prey seemed to deal death with each passing minute.

As the pit bull turned on its pack mate, and ran after the collie, it quickly took the animal down, sinking its powerful jaws into the collie's neck.

Henry was ignored completely. He winced slightly when he heard the loud yelp and the louder snap of neck bones; the collie went limp. The pit bull never let up, its teeth still clamped to the dead dog's neck, wanting to make sure of a good kill. Though hardened to sights of death, Henry felt pity for the dead dogs, and though these particular ones had tried to kill him, he knew they weren't evil, just doing their best to fill their empty stomachs.

Which the pit bull began to do, using its claws to rake open the collie's stomach and begin feasting. Still, such was the cycle of life and death. In the world he now lived, only the strong survived, the weak becoming food for the strong. Though it had always been like that in a way, now the ways were much more pronounced, more savage in their exaction.

Henry didn't have time to admire his handiwork in setting up the pit bull's kill, or ponder the betrayal of one dog to the other. He needed to keep moving.

The pit bull's eyes followed Henry as he began moving away, the snout covered with warm blood as it chewed on an inner organ.

Henry only paused long enough to wipe the panga clean on a fistful of grass, then on his pant leg to finish the job. His right leg felt the night air now, thanks to the torn material, but better he need new pants than a new leg.

Glancing over his shoulder, he could just make out the form of the pit bull as it feasted. Shaking his head, he muttered, "Never a dull moment," and began to jog towards the house fire again.

Minutes later when he arrived at the backyard of the burning home, he ran right to the in-ground swimming pool, staring at it.

The water was foul and gave off a rank odor. Scum floated on its surface, and multiple years' worth of dead leaves filled the deep end. The flames of the burning house reflected on its dark surface like a black mirror.

There was no time to waste. His eyes searched the yard and he quickly found what he needed. An old cloth tarp. It had once been white but now it was almost completely black after years of exposure to the weather. He wrapped it around his shoulders, using a torn piece on the edge to tie it around his head so it draped over him like a cloak. Placing his Glock and panga on the ground at the side of the pool with steps leading into it, he walked into the water. It was cold, and he began to shake with chills immediately after his thighs were even with the water's surface.

Holding his breath, he slid under the surface, only staying down long enough to make sure he was as wet as he could possibly get.

As he moved around a little, he stirred up some of the pool's contents, and as he turned and began climbing back up the steps, he felt something rub his leg.

Visions of sewer alligators or swamp monsters flooded his mind, but he quickly shook them off as foolish.

Still, he quickened his pace as he climbed out of the pool. But something was pulling at his leg, and he had to sort of pull himself out of the water, using the metal railing that lined the steps.

When he was all the way out, he turned and looked down. Attached to his pant leg by a crooked skeletal finger, was the desiccated corpse of a human body.

Bile rose in his throat at the thought that he had basically just bathed in the same water the corpse had been occupying. But he forced it down. The cadaver was nothing more than a skeleton with bits of flesh still attached. The organs were long gone, though the skull still had little pieces of matted scalp filled with thin hair; black if he was correct. He forced down the thoughts that the body had decomposed in the pool, and that even now, bits of the body were on Henry, in the wrinkles of his clothes, in his hair, his face.

He may have fought and killed dozens of zombies in his life, but there were some things that grossed out even him, though there was no rational reason why.

The air temperature was higher near the burning home and though soaked, he wasn't too cold, despite the chilled water.

Picking up the Glock and panga, he checked the clip on the pistol, making sure it was a full one, then pulled the panga from its sheathe.

Water ran down the handle from his wet arm to drip across the blade. One single droplet beaded on the honed tip, the firelight becoming caught in it, the tiny orb of moisture reflecting the light in all directions. Then other droplets struck the initial bead and began to drip off the blade. Henry began jogging directly at the house, his eyes searching for an opening. There were many actually, the outer walls of the house having fallen in, and half of one side of the second floor as well.

Taking a deep breath like he was going underwater, he charged into the flames, using his right arm to cover his face. Though the smoke had died down, within the waning inferno it was thicker. He knew he didn't need to get far, just cross the foundation of the house until he was on the far side.

Careful not to fall, he immediately felt the heat around him, the hairs on his face exposed to the heat waves curling up like dying bees. He reached the living room first, and had to be careful not to trip. Scorched bodies and debris, the corpses either smoldering or still ablaze, littered the floors throughout the house. Henry pushed onward, his head low, his chest already pounding from lack of air. He realized it was almost no different than if he was under water. The temperature was too hot to even attempt to breathe. If he tried, he would end up inhaling smoke and fire, asphyxiating in seconds.

His pulse pounded in his ears as he climbed over a couch that was nothing more than springs and charred wood. Then he was at the edge of the living room, almost right where the entire scenario had begun minutes ago. Or was that hours? Or days?

There was no stopping, no way to recce what waited for him once he was free of the flames. If he didn't move fast, it would be his funeral pyre, for he was getting tired from lack of oxygen. Though only two minutes had passed, holding his breath for two full minutes while climbing and moving was a monumental feat, something he never would have been capable of doing years ago, before the dead began to walk. But Henry was so much more than

he once was—he was no ordinary man any longer. Henry Watson was a warrior for the new world, one where the mantra was *adapt or die*, and by fucking God, he had adapted.

Jumping out of the picture window for the second time that night, he landed on the grass before the house, his mouth already open and sucking in air. He grew light-headed for a second as his body became oxygenated, the sudden rush better than any drug could provide.

But even while this euphoria filled him, he was already moving across the charred lawn, his Glock before him, panga leveled for any closer enemies he came upon.

He didn't know that the tarp covering him had caught fire, the upper half of his right shoulder and back burning strongly. As he came out of the flames and jumped down to the grass, running towards the enemy at full speed, he looked like a demon from Hell had found a portal to this world through the fiery tendrils of the inferno.

Blinking to clear his eyes, he searched for his first target—and found it a heartbeat later.

It was the female cannie.

Redhead was hiding behind the third car, the other car nothing but a smoldering wreck. She either heard him or that sixth sense that's always discussed, alerted her to someone behind her, but either way she turned to see Henry coming at her, his upper half nothing but flames, his face hidden within the burning tarp.

She began to turn around, her gun already coming up to shoot the apparition charging at her, but she was too slow. Whether it was because she didn't recognize the figure coming at her as a human foe, or she was simply a little too slow on the draw in reacting, was irrelevant.

The fast lived to fight another day, and the slow died.

And today, Redhead was the latter.

Henry fired from the hip, sending a three shot pattern directly at her face, his reflexes going for the head shot from so many years of battling the walking dead.

His aim was dead on, and the woman's face was turned into Swiss cheese in the blink of an eye. The skull stayed intact, however, though the back of her head was basically disintegrated. She was thrown backwards against the car, to then slump down to the ground in a heap of flopping limbs. Blood squirted out of the holes in her face, her gun flying from her hands.

One down.

Henry swiveled at the hip, sighting the second cannie in his crosshairs, the one with the Mohawk. The man was facing Henry, the commotion giving him warning of trouble from behind. Henry began to squeeze the trigger, but he had a feeling in his gut he was going to be too slow on the draw this time. Now it was his turn to suffer the consequences of not being fast enough.

Mohawk laughed loudly in triumph, realizing he had the upper hand, but as he put pressure on the trigger of his gun, his head suddenly exploded in the most gruesome way possible, brains and bone fragments splattering the ground like heavy rain, a loud report of a firearm following immediately after.

Henry didn't have time to ponder how he was still alive, but when he looked past the jeep the cannie had been hiding behind, he spotted Jimmy running towards him. Finally, Jimmy had used his shotgun, after racing across the street just in time to save Henry's ass.

Henry turned to face the last cannie still standing, but found Baseball cap already dying in a pool of blood in the street. Mary and Cindy had been ready for Henry's attack, and while Henry had been dealing with Mohawk, the women had done their part by taking Baseball cap down.

The cannie had been riddled with bullets, but he was still alive. He was a tough one, no doubt about it. He got to his knees, his gun coming up, but Henry reached him and kicked the weapon free of his hand. Weak from being shot, the grip was loose, and the gun went flying.

"We had you fuckers cold," Baseball cap hissed, bloody spittle dribbling out of the sides of his mouth. His breathing was labored. He had a punctured lung, among other mortal wounds. He had been shot in the upper chest and shoulder, both women missing the head shots they'd been going for, but the cannie wasn't in the position to criticize their marksmanship. "How the hell did you get the drop on us?"

Henry stood over the man while shrugging off the tarp. It fluttered to the street, still burning. Henry gripped the hilt of the panga tighter. "Cause we're better at killing than you are, you cannie piece of shit." Seeing the man up close, he could see Baseball cap's teeth were filed into points, something many cannies did to recognize one another. Seeing that, Henry's blood began to boil. That special place inside him that detested cannies so completely grew even larger. To him, they were even worse than the walking dead. Once more he reasoned that at least the dead had preyed on people because that was how they'd been created, some strange instinct unknown to him.

But cannies chose to eat the flesh of people, to slaughter their fellow humans. Food might have been scarce, but there was still sustenance around. There was no reason to do what they did. Cannies chose the easiest way, not wanting to have to work for their supper.

"Will you...will you eat me? Will you eat my woman and my friends?" Baseball cap wheezed, his body swaying from side to side, as if he was drunk. Blood poured from his wounds, dark-violet bubbles coming from his mouth. Amazingly, his baseball cap was still perched squarely on his head, if not slightly askew.

Henry spit, a foul taste appearing in his mouth at the thought of it. "No, we aren't going to eat you. You might be a degenerate, but the rest of us are still trying to hold on to what small piece of humanity we have."

The cannie began to laugh.

Jimmy, Mary, and Sue came up beside Henry, but not too close to intrude. They saw there was something going on there. Henry and the cannie were locked in a battle of wills, both men looking at one another and nothing else. Of course, Henry had seen his friends coming up in his peripheral vision and knew they were watching his back for any signs of danger.

"What's so funny?" Henry demanded.

"You are," the dying man replied. "You think you're so superior to me, 'cause you don't want to eat long pig. You'll kill me but you won't eat me." He managed a feeble shrug. "Seems like a fucking waste of good meat to me."

Henry took a step forward and sliced the panga across Baseball cap's throat. The blade slid in deep, slicing through the man's voice box and jugular.

His hands flew to his neck, where he tried to staunch the blood, but all it did was squirt around his fingers. He didn't fall over, but continued to kneel. His hands finally dropped to his thighs, his butt slumping back slightly onto his heels. He was perfectly balanced so that though dead, his body wouldn't fall over. His head dropped so that his chin touched his chest, his visage hidden by the brim of the baseball cap.

Mary walked up to Henry and touched his arm. "Why did you do that? He would have been dead in another minute on his own."

Henry didn't look at her, only shrugged. "A minute longer of that asshole sucking air was too long for me." He began walking to the vehicles. "You guys start checking the jeeps out; we can use one or two of them. I'll see if anything in the car is worth taking." He walked a few feet and then stopped at the passenger side door of the car, then turned to see the others hadn't moved. "Come on, people. Let's get a move on, times a wastin'." He began reaching for the door handle of the car to pull it open, his guard down slightly, confident the threat was over for the moment.

There was that saying about the fast living and the slow dying?

Well, this time, Henry wasn't going to have the same outcome as before. As he opened the passenger door, he barely registered the gleaming blade coming straight for his throat, the figure that had been crouched down in the back seat of the car lunging directly for him.

Chapter 12

The fires could be seen from all directions across the snowy plain, although there was no one there to see it, unless you counted the wolves that had already begun investigating, their noses detecting the scent of fresh meat and spilled blood. They would eat well this day when the fires finally died, and they crept low into the village to see the carnage first hand. In the frigid temperature, the human meat would keep for a long time, allowing the wolves to feast for weeks, if not months. Their powerful jaws and razor-sharp teeth were no match for the meat once it froze.

Miles away, their tracks easy to see in the snow, Varakov led his men away from the destroyed village of Alyatki. He smiled as he swayed gently in his saddle. It had been a good day yesterday. He had eaten well, satiated his sexual urges, and fulfilled his murderous ones, too. So had all his men, though some had been more aggressive than others, some seeming to want to kill and torture more than fuck, spending far more time than necessary making their victims suffer, before finally using them for sex.

But it was good they did this, Varakov thought. Like men going off to war, wanting to have one last fling before departing, so too did his army need to vent. And there was no doubt in his mind he and his men were going to war.

Once they reached America, who knew what the Soviet army would find. It had been assumed that America would be in worse condition than Russia was in now, simply due to the fact that the men who had made the decision to invade couldn't imagine anyone on the planet being as strong and resilient as the population of Mother Russia.

But Major Ishmael Varakov knew this assumption might be false, and that America was probably doing fine, and that he and his men were walking directly into the mouth of death, with barely a wave to say hello before doing so.

But if all ideas were correct, it would be simple to take a portion of Alaska and set up a temporary base, then he would send two messengers back to notify his superiors, and even more Soviet troops would travel to America.

Off to the south, on a low rise, the morning sky as their backdrop, were the shapes of at least four wolves. They sat silently on their haunches, watching the traveling army.

"I wonder how they survive out here," Streltsy wondered, speaking to no one in particular as he watched the wolves.

It was Varakov who answered his second-in-command. "They eat the weak."

"Ah," Streltsy replied, considering the reply, then added, "But, Comrade Major, what if there are no weak?"

Varakov considered this, his eyes watching the wolves as well. " There is always the weak, my friend. But if there wasn't, I suspect they would eat each other, much like humans would do if they had to live in such a harsh place."

"If that happens to us," Petroff jokingly said from behind Streltsy, "I call first dibs on eating Rhzhdestvensky!"

The fat man frowned deeply, not liking where the conversation was going. Hoping to turn it around, Rhzhdestvensky snapped, "Or we could eat you, Comrade Petroff. I would think that despite the meat being thin and stringy, I propose there is still more than enough for all of us to have a few bites!" He paused, as if he was telling a joke and ready for the punch line, then added, "At least till we get to your manhood. Then there hardly will be enough to feed a hummingbird!"

The men in hearing distance began to roar in laughter, Varakov letting them have a good laugh to keep up morale. But when he glimpsed Petroff's face and saw that the man didn't like the tables being turned on himself so quickly, Varakov watched Petroff warily, and wasn't at all surprised when he saw the soldier's hand reach into his coat for a gun.

"It's all in good fun, Petroff," Varakov said loudly to override the laughter, while fast-drawing his Makarov and aiming it at him. "Hardly a reason to die this day, not when there is so much more to look forward to once we reach the Americas."

"You would kill me, Comrade Major?" Petroff asked.

"No, not outright," Varakov replied. "I would shoot you in the leg and leave you without a horse. It wouldn't be long before the wolves found you."

Petroff's hand instantly stopped moving, and Varakov saw in the man's eyes a hesitation, as if the soldier wondered if he could pull his weapon in time to kill Varakov before his commander could shoot, but the look was quickly gone, an afterthought.

Ever-so-slowly, Petroff slid his hand out of his coat. "I agree it was all a joke, Comrade Major. I was caught up in the heat of the moment; that is all."

Varakov nodded, though the Makarov did not waver from being aimed at Petroff. "See that it does not happen again, or next time there might not be a chance to change your decision."

"Of course, Comrade Major. Thank you."

"Go to the back of the line and check on the pack animals, make sure they are all right," Varakov ordered. "The mules are carrying more supplies from what we took from the village. I do not want it lost if a mule wanders off if its tow line breaks."

Petroff saluted and galloped off to the rear of the army. He glared at Rhzhdestvensky as he passed the fat man, but was only greeted with a sly grin.

Petroff raged deep inside himself. He had been made a fool in front of everyone, before men who only respected strength. Rhzhdestvensky would get what was coming to him for his remarks, then Petroff would see who laughed at whom.

Varakov watched the soldiers gallop to the rear of the line, then called out to the rest of the men, "There will be no talk of cannibalism—ever. Another man even jokes about it and he will be shot in the leg and left naked in the snow for the wolves to feed on. Is that clear?"

There were only a few grumblings of ascent so Varakov yelled louder, "I said: is that understood?"

This time there were responses of "Yes, Comrade Major." "Got it, Comrade Major," and so on.

Varakov had slowed his mount slightly so he could see the faces of more of the men as they passed him. Now he galloped back to the front, joining Streltsy.

"I thought we were going to be another man short there for a second, Comrade Major."

"Yes, as did I," Varakov said. "The men think it is a joke, but what they speak of is sacrilege to all of us. There is no crime as heinous as that one."

Streltsy didn't reply, understanding Varakov's meaning. In Russia, when times had grown too tough for many to take, many of its citizens had succumbed to one of the worst crimes a human could do. They had reverted to cannibalism. Of course, it was crushed any time it was discovered, but with the Russian government in the same state as the United States, it was difficult to stop it everywhere it appeared, as there was no police force or army to seek it out.

Varakov shifted in his saddle to look behind him one last time before getting comfortable. They would ride for another two hours before he planned to make camp for rest and a meal. First, he watched his men as they moved across the plain, then over their heads, at the horizon, where he could see the thin cones of smoke that was all that remained of the dead village from his vantage point. The men rode in silence for a time, each one contemplating his place in the world.

A little before sunset, a harsh wind began to blow, the strong gusts cutting into each man and finding any weakness in their clothing. One man's toes became frostbite, the big toe and the one beside it turning black.

The army had not stopped while the man was attended to. The soldier designated as their doctor had seen to the amputation, using nothing more than a razor blade and a wad of bandages as the two men sat in the snow. The toes had simply been tossed aside to land where they fell. Then, bandaged and with his boot back on his foot, the soldier and the doctor had set off quickly, knowing they needed to move fast to catch up.

Once the men were gone, the wolves had appeared as if from thin air. One, a large brute of an animal, at least a quarter the size of the others of the pack, which was why it was the alpha of the group, devoured the leftover toes in one bite, swallowing them whole along with a mouthful of snow. The others only watched, wishing it was they who had eaten the appetizer.

When the morsel was gone, the alpha began moving again, the rest of the pack, a dozen strong, following directly behind. The wolves didn't need their tracking skills to follow the army, all they required were a pair of eyes, as the snow showed two score the amount of horse and mule prints, along with the dung the horse and mules left every so often. The pack knew if they waited patiently for long enough, sooner or later more food would find its way into their bellies.

So it always would be when dealing with the animal known as man.

Chapter 13

Henry never saw the girl coming at him with the blade, too preoccupied with searching the vehicles and moving on. He should have been, and only the universe and whatever deity lived within it, watching over everyone, knew why he had dropped his guard.

Henry had been in enough fights, enough life-threatening situations, to know that to drop his guard for even a moment before being well away from a dangerous area was asking for a ticket on the last train west.

But though a strong man in character, with a will that defied most others, in this one particular situation, his awareness lapsed in taking in his surroundings.

The girl had been beaten, and was covered in blood from head to toe. She looked to be around nineteen years old, but with her face a mask of congealed blood, her dark hair a mass of tangles, it would have been hard for anyone to figure out her age, and that was if she'd just been simply sitting there, letting someone examine her.

But that was most certainly not the case here. The girl didn't simply 'lunge' out of the car; her actions were more like the attack of a wild animal.

Henry had been looking away, his eyes studying the M60 on the jeep closest to his position, when he opened the car door. His gaze was already moving to face forward, but the girl was in motion before Henry had even pulled the door open a hairline from its locked position.

The instant the door popped open—the mechanism adjusted so the door could not be opened from the inside—the girl attacked, seeing her chance to escape, and not knowing or caring who was giving her an opportunity to flee.

Unknown to Henry, the girl had been captured weeks ago, and the only reason she hadn't been put into the 'pot' so to speak, was because the cannies had been having fun with her. Sometimes at night, at the cannies' camp, she'd been forced to have sex with the men in the group, usually more than once, one after the other. One night one of the female cannies had come to her, bearing a long dildo more than a foot in length. Though the men had been difficult to take inside her, the girl had to admit it was when the woman raped her with the dildo that had been the worst of all.

She'd been told often since her capture that she better perform, because when the group became bored with her, she would then change from sex slave to food. She had fucked for her life, and as days passed, she'd started to wonder if it was all worth it, that perhaps she should just accept her fate, stop submitting, and though they would beat her and take her anyway, in the end they would kill her and the living nightmare would be over.

Her name was Kathy, but since her capture, she'd been made to answer to the name 'slut' or 'whore' when she was told to. Though most of her spark of spirit had been crushed, or more accurately it had been 'fucked' out of her, deep down there was still the slightest little flicker.

So when the gunfight began and the cannies became focused on the shooters, that tiny flicker had begun to grow. It hadn't been hard for her to slip out of her restraints, and then find a knife in the front seat of the car. The cannies had assumed she'd been cowed more than a week ago and in truth, they'd been correct, but human beings can surprise one another sometimes, and this was one of those times.

Henry could only stare in surprise for that brief instant the hellcat shot out of the open door, the blade thrust outwards in front of her, the tip aimed straight for Henry's throat.

It was more luck than skill that saved Henry's life.

As Henry opened the car door, he stumbled slightly on the rough ground, which caused him to shift a few inches to the left. So when the girl thrust forward with the blade, instead of it puncturing his Adam's apple and continuing deeper into his neck, it barely grazed Henry's skin. The tip left a thin slice in his skin only, the blade then cutting empty air.

Henry didn't think when the attack began, only reacted, and as the blade slid across the side of his throat, he reached out, grabbed the arm holding the weapon, bent it so the knife was turned on its attacker, and slid the blade home into the girl's chest—all of this happening in less than a heartbeat.

The girl's eyes went wide in shock as the blade slid past her ribs and into her heart. She was dead before the blade was fully within her.

Sagging to the ground, Henry let her fall.

The others ran up to Henry, seeing the attack but too far away to help.

"Shit, she's just a kid," Jimmy said, arriving first, followed by Cindy, who was slower, but moving well enough given her condition.

Mary and Sue were right behind them.

"Maybe, but she was a kid who just tried to kill me," Henry replied. "If I'd been a second slower she would have accomplished it, too."

Sue knelt down behind the girl, brushing hair from her face to get a better look. "Why did you do that? Henry wouldn't have hurt you. You could have been safe with us," Sue whispered, reaching out to gently close the girl's eyes. When Sue stood up, sadness crossing her features over the waste of human life, Henry snapped her from the morose thoughts brimming within her.

"Okay, what's done is done," he said. "I wish I hadn't had to kill her but it happened. Let's get back to searching these cars so we can get moving." He glanced over his shoulder at the burning house, the flames at about half the vicious power they once had. Everything flammable had been consumed, and in a few hours the rest of the blaze would die out. It was a miracle no other fires had sprung up, despite the wind beginning to grow stronger.

The companions quickly began going through the vehicles, and it was decided they would keep the two jeeps, and damage the engine on the remaining car so that no one else could use it. Jimmy did this by simply pulling the spark plug wires. He then walked a few feet and tossed them into a pile of trash that had been there since the dead first began to walk after the deadly rains came down in the area. It seemed like a lifetime ago when it had all begun, and in a way it was.

Henry removed the firing pin from the Gatling gun, leaving the weapon mounted on the car. Without the pin, it was useless to anyone passing by, unless they had a replacement pin, wanted to try and salvage the weapon for parts, or were going to melt the gun down for its component metal.

Sue went around to the fallen cannies and gathered their fallen weapons, holding them in her arms like they were kindling for a campfire. The guns and blades could be used for trade as they traveled.

It was as she was picking up a gun from a fallen cannie that a blood-covered hand suddenly snapped up and grabbed her by the throat, making her drop everything she was carrying. The second hand immediately followed the first, both squeezing her neck like it was clamped inside a hydraulic vise.

Almost instantly her air was cut off and she began to turn blue.

Worst of all, with the way she was on the ground, hovering over the man with her back to Henry and the others, none of her friends could see that she was in mortal danger.

She tried to punch him but he ignored her blows, his face a mask of blood. She didn't understand how the hell he was still alive. In the blink of an eye she flashed back to a second ago, as she'd leaned down to pick up the man's fallen weapon.

Had she failed to see the slightest hint of movement on the supposedly dead man's eyelids? Had she even looked? No, probably not, as the cannie sure as hell appeared dead. Cindy had shot him three times with her M16 and his chest resembled hamburger more than anything once human. Even if he was alive now, he wouldn't remain that way for much longer.

But somehow, life still pulsed within the damaged body, and now that life wanted to take hers with it before expiring.

Pinpricks of light flashed before Sue's eyes as her body screamed for oxygen. She had only seconds before she would pass out, which would be the gateway to her death.

She had been with Henry and the others for over a year now, and in that time, she'd killed people with her .22, something she never would have believed possible before the dead began to walk. She'd seen Henry and the others kill countless times, and always because they were defending themselves.

Sometimes, when Henry and Sue had a chance to get away from the others, when they were in a safe place for the night, the two would talk softly, their faces no more than an inch from one another. They would lay in the gloom of whatever structure they were calling home for the night, and talk about the past, the present, and even the future.

But they wouldn't always talk. When they knew they were safe, and if one of the group was on watch for the night to prevent any unexpected visitors, on those few occasions when it was safe to do so, they would make love.

Both were in their forties, and when a middle-aged couple made love it was usually much different than a pair in their twenties, more tender, more about love and not just lust. Though Sue had never been married, Henry had been, and because of this he knew how to please a woman—that is, Emily had never complained. One thing that had always gone well in his marriage to his late wife was that she had never left the bed wanting. No vibrating toys ever were turned on when he rolled over to sleep after one of their sexual bouts.

It hadn't taken long for Sue to fall deeply in love with Henry Watson. He was a kind, caring man, who showed mercy when it was warranted, but at the same time, if needed, he could be cold and merciless, and when it came to the group, he was like a mother bird watching over its chicks. No one would escape his wrath if they messed with his people.

When he killed, it was for a reason, never just because he could. With no police or other agents of law, the only rules men lived by was their own moral code.

Unless someone came upon one of the small towns that had set up to prevent the walking dead from infiltrating it. Usually, these enclaves had tall walls no zombie could climb, and guards would walk the fortifications looking for possible signs of trouble. Of course, now the dead were gone, but those same walls remained. Where the dead were once the main threat, now the threat came from other humans, who saw something they wanted and were willing to kill to take it.

Looters, slavers, cannies, brigands and biker gangs still roamed across the once great United States.

All this flashed through Sue's beleaguered mind in the breadth of a second, and in the back of her mind, she wondered if this was her life flashing before her eyes before she got on the last train west.

She felt herself slipping away, her vision going dark. Her eyes drooped.

Drooped some more…

Then they suddenly snapped open, her will to live too strong to simply let her slip into oblivion without a fight.

Frantically, her eyes darted around her, taking it all in. There on the ground, a foot from her, was the pile of weapons she'd been carrying. Most had fallen out of reach when she'd dropped them, but there, closer than the rest of the guns and blades, was a hunting knife.

Her left hand stretched outward, and at first it barely went in the right direction, but she forced her arm to do as she commanded and the hand moved closer to the hilt. It was the hardest thing she'd ever done. The air was gone from her lungs, and only her heartbeat pulsed inside her head. She was in a void, where nothing but that beating heart pulsed.

The man's grip loosened slightly on her throat, but there was still more than enough pressure to strangle her; he was finally dying, but not soon enough for her liking. Though eventually he would succumb to his wounds, it would be too late for Sue, for she was only seconds from passing on to what waited in the next plane of existence—if there even was anything there.

Her fingers caressed the hilt and she began to flex them, trying to pull the blade closer, but still she couldn't manage this simple task.

She was about to go down, there was no more time!

It was either do it now or there wouldn't be a never!

Drawing up any reserve of strength she had deep within her, she willed her fingers to grab the hilt.

They obeyed!

She didn't hesitate, knowing there was no time. With the hilt firmly gripped in her fist, she brought it up and down onto the man's face. The tip of the eight-inch blade sliced into the cannie's right eye, splitting the eye in two before going even deeper.

Two inches into the eye, the blade slowed and screeched to a halt.

The edges of the knife were too wide to fit in the eye socket, so she couldn't penetrate the man's brain!

Her only hope was dashed before it could come to fruition.

But she wasn't finished yet. With her last ounce of energy, she swung her other hand around and joined it to the hand holding the knife, and with all her body weight pushing against the man's locked arms, she managed to get the knife past the obstruction that was holding it back.

With a grating noise reminiscent of fingernails on a chalkboard, only it sounded for less than a millisecond, the blade was forced free to continue deep into the brain.

The man's hands tightened around her neck for a moment, the move enough to cause Sue to cringe in pain. Her mouth dropped open as she tried to suck in breath that wasn't there, but no sooner did the pressure arrive then it passed. Like a light switch being flicked, the man's hands went limp, before dropping to the ground, releasing Sue's neck.

She slumped over the body as if she was hugging it, ignoring the blood and gore soaking into her shirt.

She sucked in air, wincing at the pain it caused from her bruised windpipe, coughing from the discomfort. Later, she knew there would be black and blue welts where the cannie's hands had left their mark. Sue gently rubbed her neck, feeling the tender flesh beneath her fingers. She had been so close to death she didn't want to think on it for too long.

Henry, oblivious to the life and death struggle that had occurred only yards away, glanced over to see her hunched over a dead cannie and called out, "Sue, you all right over there?"

Forcing air into her bruised throat, she raised a hand and wiggled it, signifying she was fine.

"Then get a move on, we need to hit the road before more trouble comes. This place is like Grand Central. We've been lucky so far, but that's not gonna last forever."

She wiggled the hand once more, the gesture enough to make Henry ignore her and continue on his task of siphoning fuel from the remaining car to use in one of the jeeps.

Coughing a few more times, she closed her eyes and slowly breathed. Already, the discomfort was lessening, though she knew it would be painful to breathe for at least a day or two.

With one last glance at the cannie before her, she left the knife in his eye socket, not wanting to try and remove it, knowing it was in there pretty damn good.

Gathering up the fallen weapons again, she carried them back to the jeeps, knowing that down the road, when she and Henry were alone once more, he would see the bruises on her neck and would want an explanation.

But that was for the future.

As she walked back to join the others, she held herself taller, for though the companions had always been there to watch her back and keep her safe, this one time she'd had no one to rely on but herself.

And the fact that she was still alive, still strong, meant that though she now had people who loved her, and she loved them in turn, in the end, she knew she could trust herself to do what had to be done, and that she could rely on herself to come out strong on the other side.

In ways even Sue didn't understand, the trauma she'd experienced made her like a phoenix rising from the ashes.

Only minutes ago she had still been Sue Anders, a middle-aged woman who was mostly beholden to the people she traveled with, despite making strides of independence.

But now, she had finally broken free of the boundaries she'd been placed into since the first day the dead began to walk. Sue now knew she could be there for her friends, and if the time came, do whatever needed to be done.

Unknown to Sue, it would be this epiphany that would perhaps save the companions from certain doom one day, her newfound confidence giving her the strength to prevail, no matter what the cost.

Chapter 14

Just before night had fully fallen, the harsh wind had become a maelstrom, threatening to blow the entire army right off the face of the frozen plains.

Major Varakov had commanded the men to take shelter, and when none was available, they used their knives to hack frozen blocks from the snow, then made crude igloos to weather out the storm. The structures had to be large enough for the horses as well, or else the animals would freeze to death by morning.

As the wind howled outside, each man sat huddled together, seven or eight to an igloo. The smell was challenging to say the least, with the odor of the horses' bodies and their feces permeating the air within the igloos, along with the ripe scent of the men. Not that the men noticed, for in many instances, the men smelled far worse than the horses ever could. But at least with so many bodies huddled together, man and beast, the air within the igloo was above freezing.

The igloo that had been made first was the structure only for Varakov and Streltsy to share alone with their horses. Their igloo was smaller than the rest, but still took almost as much time to create. The wind had been so biting that Varakov had helped to build his own igloo, instead of sitting back and allowing his men to do it for him. Streltsy had also helped, eager to be out of the cold and wind as soon as possible.

The two men sat across from one another, eating rations of cold meat taken from the village a day ago. Behind them, the horses stood silently, a brief snort or a whinny coming from them every now and then.

"What do you think we will find in America?" Streltsy asked while chewing extra-hard on a chunk of gristle. When thirsty, he simply shoved his hand into the ground and picked up a fistful of ice, then ate it.

Varakov shrugged, the gesture mostly lost within the folds of his clothes. Only his jacket had been removed, so he had something to sit on other than ice. "There is no way to know, my friend. The United States had to deal with the dead as much as we did, so there is no telling how many living people remain, or if there are any at all."

Streltsy nodded. "Would it be a good thing or a bad one if there were no people?"

Varakov considered the question, not replying as he chewed on a chunk of cold meat. Finally, he spit out a small piece of bone and said, "I think it would be a bad one. If we make it there and find nothing but the fallen dead, there will be no one for us to conquer. We need men and women, and children too, as a work force, so we can begin rebuilding, then, once we have something going, we can take the resources created and send them back to Russia, for our homeland to use and become stronger."

"Do you think there is still any kind of an American army, Comrade Major?"

Varakov shook his head emphatically. "Doubtful, very doubtful." Then he smiled. "Even if there is one, how large could it possibly be? Besides, one Russian is worth any three Americans. No, Comrade Streltsy, whatever we find, it will be a boon for Russia. The 'bear' will rise again, you mark my word."

"The Americans are well known for not taking invaders lightly, Comrade Major. We may find ourselves in a pitched battle from the moment we reach any sort of civilization."

Varakov began to laugh. "If we come across any resistance, we will squash it before it can even raise a gun to us. You will see, we will be victorious, and when we return to our homeland, we will be showered with praises."

"I hope you are correct, Major, for if not…" He hesitated, only the wind outside filling the tiny igloo. "If not, we will be far from home with no chance of reinforcements, in a strange land with people who want us dead all around us."

"Bah, I relish the challenge. Anyone who does not give us the respect we deserve will feed the worms in the ground."

Streltsy didn't reply, satisfied that the conversation had run its course.

The two ate in silence for the remainder of the night, while outside, the wind continued to howl.

The next morning, with the sun just cresting the horizon, the Red Army was on the move once more. It was cold again, but with each passing minute the temperature was rising, and though it wouldn't get above freezing, at least it wouldn't be a day where the thermometer hovered in the 'teens.

Resembling jagged teeth, high cliffs loomed over the packed, gray-green ice that made up the Bering Strait. No life was visible for miles.

A thick mist hovered over the frozen sea, making breathing difficult. Filled with moisture, it was like trying to suck in pea soup with each breath the men took. As they rode, the horses breathing could be heard even over the crunch of hooves over the snow, the steady rhythm almost hypnotic in its pattern.

Somewhere far in the distance, across the frozen sea, was a place called Alaska, a wild land even before the dead had begun to walk. An area mostly untouched by man, where nature ran wild and free.

Major Varakov had read a book about Alaska after he'd been assigned his mission. He'd found the pictures of the far land beautiful; the majestic glaciers, the sea lion and other exotic creatures he'd never seen before in the Soviet Union.

Only a few years ago, half a million people had been spread out over six hundred thousand square miles of rugged land, but how many remained in Alaska now was anyone's guess. The first number could be close to the same, or there could only be a few thousand still left alive—or maybe even far less than that. For all he knew, only a few hundred people might remain after the living dead had gotten through with the population.

It didn't really matter to Varakov which number it was. He had to remind himself this wasn't an invasion so much as it was a simple incursion. If the enemy numbers were too great, he would return to Russia with his report, and the general could decide whether to invade or not. If he returned to Russia without completing his mission, well, his fate would be his fate. As a loyal soldier, he could do nothing but obey.

But despite his loyalty to Mother Russia, he was no fool, and as each hour passed, he wondered if he would indeed return empty-handed, with nothing to expect but punishment for his failure.

Perhaps if the numbers in Alaska were few, Varakov wondered if he might simply take over the area for himself. He could set himself up as a king in this new land, and when he and his men did not return, the Russian Heads of State would assume he didn't survive. No doubt they would cancel their plans to invade, assuming the Americans would be waiting for the attack.

Only Varakov knew of his plans, not even Streltsy was aware of his aspirations. When the time came, Varakov would let his second-in-command in on his ideas; if it was possible to enact them of course.

Varakov turned his horse so he was facing his men, who looked on with curious eyes. "Men, we have reached the beginning of the end of our journey." He pointed out to the frozen sea. "We travel that way, to America. Once there, we will crush the American dogs under our heels and take what we want. Their women, their wealth, all of it will be ours for the taking. Are you with me?"

A chorus of yells and hoots followed, the men eager for more looting and plunder. It had been days since the sacking of the small village and already their lust for violence and sex was at an all time high. Even the cold did little to dampen their bloodlust.

"Excellent, men, excellent," Varakov smiled, proud of his men and that it was he who led them. "We will rest here for an hour within the shelter of the high rocks surrounding the sea. Once the horses have been fed and watered, and you men have eaten, we will set off for America."

More yells filled the air, the men eager to continue on the last leg of their journey.

"Rest well, my comrades," Varakov said, his tone unforgiving. "For soon we will reach the land of the free, and the home of the many dead."

Chapter 15

The two jeeps drove slowly away from the fading house fire, the companions packed into each one.

Wearing fresh clothes, his old BDUs left on the side of the road, Henry was driving the lead vehicle with Mary by his side, the second one having Jimmy as the driver, and Sue and Cindy sitting askance of him. Henry's boots were strapped to the roll bar behind him, spread wide open so the wind would go into them, and it would dry them out after the dunking he'd taken in the filthy pool water. In the warm air the boots would be dry in no time

The idea of this seating arrangement was so that if trouble occurred, there would be someone who could handle the M60s mounted on the jeeps' roll bars.

Cindy had taken a few minutes while the others prepared, to go and clean up, especially wanting to change her pants away from the others at the back of the second jeep in line.

"Can I help you?" Jimmy had asked, the concern for his woman apparent on his face.

Cindy had shaken her head, a slight smile on her face. "No, I'm fine, and I want to do this alone."

"But…" Jimmy had begun, his love for Cindy overruling his common sense. There were times when a woman needed to be alone, and no matter how much protesting the man did it would not end well for the man.

Henry had heard the brief exchange and walked over to Jimmy, clapping the younger man on the shoulder. "She'll be fine. And Mary or Sue can help if she really needs it." He lowered his voice so only Jimmy could hear. "She needs to be alone I think, Jimmy; just let her be."

Jimmy looked at Cindy, who was waiting quietly, as she didn't want Jimmy following her, and after a few moments of reflection, one where Jimmy gazed at Henry, who only nodded and smiled that it was good he let her alone, he sighed and nodded. "Okay, babe, but if you need me just shout."

Now she sat quietly beside Jimmy, Sue on her right, the wind blowing her hair back, as the windshield of the jeep had been folded down. Jimmy reached out a hand and placed it on her thigh. She looked at him, smiled, and placed her own hand over his. The two locked fingers. Nothing was said, nor did it have to be. Cindy was already healing, her strong sense of will and her adapting to the harsh life she lived helping her get over something that a modern woman would have taken weeks or even months to overcome.

Sue saw this in her peripheral as she gazed out her side of the vehicle. She only smiled to herself, glad Cindy was on the mend. Many, many years ago Sue had experienced a similar occurrence. She had been right out of high school and her sweetheart of two years had finally convinced her that it was okay if they went all the way together. She had loved him dearly, and had also decided it was time, though her boyfriend assumed it was all his convincing. Men could be so stupid sometimes. As if they 'ever' had a choice when the woman decided it was time for sex.

A month later she'd been late on her period, and from there it hadn't taken long to figure out what had happened. She'd decided to keep the baby, and after a long talk with her boyfriend, he'd agreed as well.

So it was quite a shock when two weeks after deciding to keep the child, she'd woken in the middle of the night with her inner thighs wet with blood. Crying, she'd washed the sheets that night, while praying her parents didn't wake up if she made too much noise, for they hadn't been told yet, and now there would be no reason to.

The next day she'd broken the news to her boyfriend, who though sympathetic to her pain, still couldn't hide the relief he was obviously feeling.

That had given her a valuable lesson in the way men thought, but looking at Jimmy, and the way he treated Cindy, and the way Henry treated her, Sue knew that not all men were made alike.

Jimmy had been pretty torn up about the entire situation as well. It had been his child after all, but he'd been so busy worrying about Cindy, he'd had no time to grieve for his lost child. Each time the thoughts would rise within him, he pushed them back down again, not wanting to deal with them.

Henry steered the jeep onto Route 88. Though he had no destination in mind, he figured the highway would still get them all there faster—wherever that may be. He wasn't in a rush to leave Nevada. At the moment, it was hot but not oppressive, and though there were no more weather updates, from the look of the clear-blue sky he was confident the weather would hold out.

The highway stretched on for miles, and Henry leaned back in his seat and let the warm wind wash over him. It was mid-morning, the day still ahead. The first attack at the house had occurred just before dawn, and later, the cannies had arrived shortly after. The entire battle with both groups had taken a few hours, and once the companions had set off in their newly-acquired jeeps, the sun still hadn't touched the crown of the sky.

Prone bodies could be seen lining the road, more than a few on the road itself. Henry drove by them slowly, still expecting one or two to rise at his approach.

"Still feels weird, huh, Henry?" Mary said by his side, as she too, studied the corpses.

"Yes, it does," was his single reply.

"I keep expecting them to…" she began but was cut off.

"Yeah, I know; me too."

A few buzzards and ravens were feeding on the tattered remains of most of the bodies. After weeks of lying in the hot sun, the flesh, what was left of it, had changed to the consistency of beef jerky.

As the two jeeps rolled past, one buzzard raised its head and let out a loud screech, warning the humans to back off, that the food was for itself and its brethren.

Jimmy swerved his jeep so that it was rolling directly at the buzzard and the body. The right front tire rolled over the skull, crushing the head to dust. The buzzard flew off, only to return a second later when the vehicle had passed. It cawed some more, annoyed that its meal had been disturbed, but then seeing the inside of the skull now exposed, though most of it flattened by the jeep's tires, it soon forgot about the two vehicles and continued feeding.

"Why did you do that?" Sue asked.

"Because that's our Jimmy," Cindy replied, as if that said it all, and in a way it did. Though having matured over the years, changing from the irresponsible teenager he had once been, Jimmy still retained the wise-ass personality he'd always had. At one time, Henry and Jimmy had enjoyed more of a father-son dynamic, but after years of fighting together, each man relying on the other countless times for their lives, the two now had become more like partners, where a mutual respect had bonded the two forever. Still, Jimmy could never resist a quick jibe if given the opportunity and loved razzing Henry every chance he got.

Henry hadn't seen the trailing jeep swerve, or if he did, he would have figured Jimmy was just avoiding a corpse in the road. As the two vehicles continued onward, the air grew slightly cooler. There was a mountain range to the west and it was helping to keep the cooler air from escaping what appeared to be a slight incline to the land.

For the next ten miles the highway was empty, only a few bodies and abandoned cars to dot the long road snaking through the desert. As the sun rose higher, the temperature increased, until it felt like a heat lamp was hovering over each of the group.

Far ahead, the highway cut between the center of the raised land, so that the landscape resembled a valley or gulley. While they drove, Mary became bored, and with no music to listen to, she began to search the jeep more thoroughly. After going through the center console, she turned to the glove box. Pulling out an old registration, a parking ticket, and some Kleenex, which she shoved in a pocket for future use, she took out what appeared to be a map.

Henry had his windshield pulled back upright from earlier, as the wind hitting him in the face had quickly become annoying.

With the paper edges flapping from the wild wind stream, Mary studied the map. "Henry, you need to look at this."

Henry didn't shift his head, only used his eyes to take in peripherally what she was reading. "Why? It's a map, so?"

"No, Henry, it's what's 'on' the map." She turned it slightly so he could get a better look.

Turning his head, but using his peripheral to keep one eye on the road, he saw what she meant. Someone had used a black magic marker to circle a place in the middle of the desert. Beside the circle were the words 'Government facility—underground. Area 51?' On the side of the map along the margin, there were numbers and words scrawled as well, all of it looking like nonsense to Henry.

"You don't think that's…"

"That it's real?" Mary finished for him. "I don't know, but then it if isn't, why bother stashing the map inside the glove box? One of the cannies must have found out the location from someone they captured and they were planning on going there. In fact, there were four cars when they arrived and a lot of gear in each one. They might have been on their way when they were detoured by us."

Henry considered her rationalizing. In the back of both jeeps were now a generous pile of supplies, not to mention an assortment of weapons stripped from the fallen dead.

The first thing the companions did was toss away all the dried meat they'd found within the supplies, fearing what its origins were, but they kept the assorted fluids, such as water, wine and a case of Snapple. There were also sleeping bags, extra clothing, and assorted sundries. The cannies had been on a long trip, and if they'd had ignored the house fire, no doubt they would have still been on their way.

Henry nodded, having to agree with her logic. "Well, we know these government installations really do exist, and Area 51 was one that was at least well known to be real. Then there was the redoubt in that Colorado lake we got taken prisoner in. You remember the name of the town there? What was it called? It began with a C I think."

"Crescent Falls," Mary said while giving herself a hug to fight off the chill running down her spine, despite the heat of the day. "Don't talk about that place. I still have nightmares of what happened to me there."

"Yeah, tell me about it. That place was a horror show. We were lucky to get out of there alive."

"Some of us didn't," Mary said softly.

"You mean Jack, I take it."

She nodded and replied softly, "Of course."

Jack had been a boy of around thirteen years of age. They'd found him on their travels in Colorado. The kid had been a wise-ass, and Jimmy and Jack had quickly become adversaries, though it was more like sibling rivalry. Mary had said it was because Jimmy had seen too much of himself in the child.

Jack had been killed by a security guard in the underwater complex, gunned down mercilessly.

"He was a good kid," Henry said.

Mary folded the map after studying it for a few more seconds. "We should try for the complex; it might have everything we need to stay for a while."

"Sure, but it could also still be manned. We might end up driving right into a hornet's nest. In case you don't remember, we've never had much luck with the military."

"You're talking about Miller now, I assume," she said.

Henry nodded curtly. "Who else? That guy was certifiable."

Colonel Miller had been assumed to be the last ranking commander in the U.S. Army still alive, who had set up base at Fort Knox with the few soldiers still under his command. He'd ruthlessly conscripted civilians in the surrounding area as a slave work force, to hopefully build a new America strong enough to destroy the walking dead. The companions had become tangled in the madman's plans and had been lucky to escape alive.

Mary considered Henry's statement, agreeing. "Well, we could always do a recce of the place, see if there's any activity. If it looks occupied by soldiers, we keep going. But if it isn't, there could be lots of stuff we could use. And with the base being in the middle of nowhere, it's unlikely anyone else is there."

"That's true, but still, if there's any sort of military presence occupying…" Henry repeated trailing off.

"Then we turn around and get out of there. But it's worth a look, isn't it?" She smiled at him. "We have to go somewhere, so why not there?"

"Okay, I see your point, but before we make any decisions, we need to ask the others what they think. We all have to be on board before doing something like this."

She rubbed Henry's arm affectionately. She looked at him with admiration, the two closer than most fathers and daughters ever were. "I wouldn't have it any other way," she replied, satisfied the others would agree with her point of view.

The two jeeps were approaching a split in the mountains, the air temperature dropping even more. Within the split, the sun barely reached the ground, thanks to the towering sides of the ravine on both sides. Unless the sun was at its zenith, the highway would always be bathed in shade. Water runoff also cascaded across the pavement from the north, some underground spring or melt water from higher up the land wetting the ground constantly.

But none of this was what caused Henry to slam on the brakes suddenly, Jimmy almost rear-ending him, before also seeing why the lead jeep had stopped so quickly.

Dead center of the highway, where the water was heaviest, the entire area was covered with corpses.

From a quick glimpse, there had to be more than a thousand bodies, all packed tightly together. The air overhead was a billowing mass of black clouds; at first it looked like fog, but soon the clouds were revealed to be thousands upon thousands of blowflies, all feeding on the decaying corpses.

Fat rats of all shapes and sizes hopped from corpse to corpse, picking the choicest morsels. Though the eyes, tongues, and cheeks of the bodies had long been picked clean by scavengers, most of the corpses were still intact, intestines still moist, and what internal organs remained still relatively squishy.

More than a quarter mile of road was covered, the corpses going all the way to the end of the ravine.

Buzzards and ravens also feasted; a smorgasbord of food that seemed to go on forever for them. The sounds of arguing birds, and sometimes the screech of a disgruntled rat, echoed off the ravine walls, and more than one fart or belch from a bloated corpse sounded, the symphony of decay never ceasing.

The wind shifted and all the companions had to hold their breath or risk gagging. The miasma of rotting meat left out in the exposed air for so long was overwhelming, and it was only their strong constitutions from dealing with zombies for years that prevented each of them from vomiting onto the warm pavement, though not by much.

Dead center of the long sea of bodies, not far from the beginning of the muck, a single car sat silently—a Fiat of all things. It was obvious the car hadn't been there when the zombies had collapsed, but had belonged to a traveler who'd attempted to drive through the corpses. The car was skewed to the right, its driver's-side facing the companions. The car had made it all of fifty feet before becoming bogged down in the muck of bodies and bones. The tire wells were clogged with drying gore, and it was a safe bet the driver and anyone else inside the vehicle was long gone, having no choice but to set out on foot after traipsing through the muck and ooze of hundreds of rotting bodies, leaving the Fiat behind.

The Fiat's once blue paint job was covered on all sides with dried gore, the splatter resembling a mad painter's bid to copy Rorschach, who was always a wonderful analogy to use when describing the blood and gore patterns the human body could create.

Henry put the jeep into Park and slid out of the driver's seat, then pulled his boots off the roll bar and slid them on. Sure enough, they were completely dry. Then he walked to the first corpse sprawled on the road, and with his boot only inches from it, he waved away the blowflies that tried to settle on his face.

The fetid reek struck him in the face like a giant fist, threatening to overpower his senses. Breathing through his mouth and covering his lower face with his arm to try and staunch the rank odor, and trying not to think about the microscopic bits that must be in the air, that were being sucked into his lungs, he gazed out across the sea of gore.

"Shit," he muttered under his breath, while the others looked on, waiting for what to do next.

Chapter 16

Major Ishmael Varakov kneed his horse, urging the animal to go faster. Less than a quarter mile away, the snow-tipped sea cliffs of Alaska could be seen through the fog.

Gulls could be seen soaring high overhead, their cries echoing off the ice.

Varakov turned slightly in his saddle for the hundredth time that day to look behind him. His neck hurt from doing this every few minutes, and he'd been doing it for hours. He couldn't help it. Ever since he'd lost more of his men to thin ice, he'd found himself constantly checking back to ensure his remaining men were still with him.

There were only forty-four soldiers left, along with Streltsy and himself, the rest having been taken by the ice, their horses with them.

The surviving men all wore ashen faces, each expecting the ice to swallow them whole at a moment's notice. Death waited for every man with each step of their horses. Eyes were riveted to the ice, attentions focused on the jagged contours, gazes seeking the softer outlines that might expose thin ice.

Varakov could still hear the cries of the drowning horses as they were pulled into the icy water.

At first it had been mostly silent on the solid ice flow, only the scrapes of hooves on the ice and the howling wind to listen to. But then, with a sound of a rifle shot, the ice parted, and two horses and men went down. A moment later, more men were sucked into the cold embrace of the frozen sea.

The men barely had time for a shout of alarm before the water covered their heads. Their clothes soaked through in an instant, hindering movement, and along with their heavy weapons, the men were quickly pulled under as if a lead weight were attached to each man's foot.

The horses were another matter.

Plunging into the frigid sea, their tough hides gave them longer to attempt an escape. But their body weight wouldn't allow it. Each time a horse managed to get its hooves onto the ice, the piece would break off, to then plunge the terrified animal back into the swirling water.

The screams were the worst. Varakov had never heard horses scream like he did that day. Almost human they sounded, the panic and terror prevalent with each decibel of noise produced. The mules were almost lost as well, and it had been quick thinking by one of the trailing men to hack the tether secured to each mule. One mule went down with the horses, the supplies it carried also taken. The animal never surfaced again, simply dropped through the ice and was gone forever. Not so much as sound of alarm was raised by the creature.

Luckily, the rest of the pack mules remained safe—at least for now.

It was over in less than a minute, the last horse succumbing to the cold water and sinking down into the dark depths. He saw the eyes of the last animal before it went under, the pure terror something he would never forget. The horse knew it was about to die, and it sure as hell didn't want to.

Varakov had galloped as close as he could without risk of falling in himself. His eyes had frantically searched for a sign of his men but there'd been none. He wondered if any of the men had succeeded in overcoming the weight of their sodden clothes and managed to swim back to the surface, only to find it blocked by a sheet of ice. Having lost sight of the opening they'd fallen through, they would have banged on the underside of the ice desperately, despite knowing there was no hope.

When their oxygen had finally run out, they would have had no choice but to open their mouths and suck in the freezing sea. He hoped it had been fast for them at least, that they did not suffer. To him, it would seem a terrible way to die, to see salvation before you but unable to break through to the other side.

He had once heard that drowning was a relatively easy way to die, if one way was truly accepted as better than the next.

Varakov would choose none of the above, if he was given an option. An analogy Varakov often thought of was: Though the way to the inn might be harder than usual, filled with rainstorms and mud-filled roads, once you arrived at the inn, your destination was before you, and the long road to get there was irrelevant.

Streltsy saw his commander turning in his saddle to check on the men, and the two made eye contact. Nodding slightly, the simple gesture Streltsy made spoke volumes between the two soldiers. It said that the remaining men were all there—for now anyway.

Varakov returned the gesture and turned in his saddle to face forward. He rubbed his neck again, trying to work out the kink that had appeared. It didn't matter, for even if he was able to erase the annoying pain, it would only return anew each time he spun around in his saddle to check over his army like a mother hen.

Until he and his men were off the treacherous ice, he would be on edge. When they finally reached Alaska, their journey would be over, and they would be safe. He could only pray when that time came, the number of his army would be the same as it was now.

His eyes focused on the sea cliffs once more. They were closer than the last time he looked. They would be there shortly.

Soon, America would taste the might of the Russian Army, and though small in number now, once his mission was complete and he'd reported back, more men would be sent, to quickly crush the weak Americans under the heel of Mother Russia.

Chapter 17

Footsteps sounded behind Henry as he gazed out at the sea of rotting corpses. The only reason he wasn't gagging fully on the odor was that the wind was blowing in the opposite direction.

On some parts of the road, the flies were so thick he couldn't see through the clouds to the other side.

"Must have been a horde that collapsed when whatever happened killed them," Henry said to whoever was behind him.

"Do we really have to drive through *that*?" Sue asked, the repulsion she felt clear on her face. She moved so close to Henry he could feel her pressing against him.

Henry looked to both sides of the ravine the road cut through. "I don't see another feasible way around. We could try circling around the mountains but we might end up going for hours only to find the way impassable."

"Plus, this is the best way to Area 51," Mary added, then quickly filled Jimmy, Sue, and Cindy in on the map.

"So that's where we're going now?" Jimmy asked.

Henry shrugged. "Seems as good a place as any to go, don't you think?"

"Sure, as long as there aren't any jarheads there," Jimmy added. "In case you've forgotten, soldiers and us don't get along too well."

Mary nodded. "Henry and I were talking about that earlier." She then quickly told the others of their conversation, about the chances of the military base being deserted or not.

Henry glanced over at Cindy, who was staring out across the bodies. "How're you feeling?"

Cindy looked down at her boots, then at Henry. "I'm okay. There's still a little blood, but not much more than if I was on my period."

"A tampon appears to be doing the trick," Sue offered.

Henry only nodded slightly, glad she was okay. In the old world, such information wouldn't have been taken without someone frowning, not wanting to hear the gory details, but those days were gone. At least they were for the small group of people that were closer than most families ever could hope to be. Henry was pleased to hear everything that was happening, for even something small left out could cause one of them to be in peril down the road.

"Jimmy, can I talk to you for a second over here? Just the two of us," Henry asked, already moving back to the jeeps, expecting Jimmy to follow him, which the younger man did. The others stayed at the edge of the corpses, talking softly about their next move, the military base, and the reason the zombies had all collapsed at once.

"Yeah?" Jimmy asked.

"We've been so busy just trying to stay alive, I haven't had the chance to tell you how sorry I am for Cindy's miscarriage…and yours too I suppose."

Jimmy looked straight at Henry, at first keeping his emotions bottled up, but when he saw the genuine concern in Henry's eyes, he suddenly let it all out.

"I was gonna be a dad, Henry. Me, Jimmy Cooper; local screw-up. I'd just gotten used to the idea and now it's gone, pulled away like it was never there."

Henry placed an arm around him, and Jimmy seemed to deflate in Henry's embrace.

"I know, son, and I'm so sorry this happened."

Tears welled in Jimmy's eyes as he thought about a future that would never be. "I mean, shit, old man, having a kid in this world was fucking crazy enough, but I was ready for it. I would have made damn sure that kid was okay, you know?"

"Sure, Jimmy, I know you would have. We all would have raised that child like it was all of ours."

"I know, right? That kid would have had a shitload of parents." He'd slumped slightly but now he stood up, his emotions in check once more. Stepping away from Henry, he grinned widely while wiping his eyes with the back of his hand.

Henry could tell the smile was forced but he didn't let on.

"But I guess it wasn't meant to be. Besides, it's probably for the best. This world is too fucked up to have kids in any way."

"Sure it is, Jimmy. I agree with you; whatever you say."

The two talked a little more, as Jimmy worked his way through a few various emotions. Sadness, denial, anger, all came and went like the wind.

"You guys done clucking over there like a couple of hens?" Mary called, growing impatient to move on. "These flies are driving us all crazy!" She accentuated her last statement by waving her hand around her face to swat away some troublesome flies, as did the others.

"Sure, Mary, we were just finishing up," Henry called, as he and Jimmy turned around to begin walking back to join the others.

As they walked, Jimmy stopped one more time and said in a winsome tone, "You know, Henry, it would have been fucking awesome to be a father."

"Yeah, Jimmy," Henry replied with a smile, "it sure would have."

Minutes later, they were all gathered around the lead jeep, wanting to get far away from the corpses to avoid the annoying insects. A few rats had become curious as well and sat on hind legs at the edge of the bodies, watching the humans intently. One with a gray streak on its head seemed more curious than the others, its gaze asking the question: "You guys coming in here, too? Feel free. We've got an appetite for as many of you humans that want to feed us."

Jimmy picked up a rock from the side of the road and threw it at the group of rats, screaming, "Fuck off, you little bastards!"

His aim was good and he connected with a rat to the left of the one with the gray streak. The rat screeched in pain and fell over, wounded. The moment this happened the other rats pounced on their fallen brother, tearing it apart and running off with the morsels.

The entire time, Gray Streak never moved, only watched the humans defiantly.

Jimmy picked up another rock and prepared to throw it, but held off at the last second as he watched Gray Streak. Then he pretended like he was throwing the rock, only he held it in his fist.

Gray Streak remained immobile, not so much as flinching.

Jimmy tossed the rock aside, not bothering to throw it any more. His eyes never left the rat. "Shit, man, you're one tough son-of-a-bitch, aren't you?"

The rat glared at the man for another ten seconds, then spun around and ran off into the sea of corpses, lost within moments.

"Jimmy, will you stop messing around over there and join us, please," Henry called. "We need to decide the best way to do this. We need a plan."

"Oh please, old man, not this time we don't. All we need to do is step on the gas and drive right through that gunk. It'll be like four-wheeling in the mud."

"That sure isn't mud," Sue added.

"No, but it's close enough," he replied.

"So you think all we have to do is just drive through that stuff and we'll be okay?" Mary asked, her arms crossed over her chest.

"I sure as hell do. Henry may love his plans, I know, but this time there's no need for one."

Mary pointed to the Fiat in the center of the corpses. "That guy tried it and failed miserably."

"Yeah, but he used a regular car, and a Fiat of all things; we have jeeps, four-wheel drive jeeps," Jimmy said.

"You know, guys," Cindy butted in, "I hate to admit it but this time my knucklehead of a boyfriend might be right. The jeeps should be able to handle it."

Mary turned to Henry, who had been considering all their options. Sue and Cindy joined her, everyone now looking to Henry for his response.

"Well, Henry, we all think for once Jimmy's on the right track. Let's just go through there full throttle. The jeeps can handle it."

Henry looked at the faces of the women, then past them to see Jimmy's smug countenance as well. Finally, he threw up his hands in surrender. "Fine with me. If you all want to go charging through that muck without a plan then I'm not going to stop you. Just don't blame me when we get stuck and have to walk our way out of there."

"Oh he of little faith," Jimmy said, walking over to Henry, a victorious look now plainly plastered on his face. "You'll see; it'll be a piece of cake. Why, all this time we've wasted talking about it, we could've been through it and on our way again."

Five minutes later, they were ready to go. Henry had suggested they wear masks to protect themselves from the flies, and sunglasses if any were available.

Sue wore a pair, as did Cindy, the sunglasses found in compartments of the jeeps.

The seating assignments had changed as well. Sue now sat with Henry in jeep one, while Jimmy drove jeep two, with Mary and Cindy as his co-pilots.

"We need to keep moving once we get in there," Henry called. "And we need to get up some speed, too, or else the wheels'll get bogged down in gunk."

"Just go already, old man!" Jimmy yelled over the engines. "We're wasting daylight."

Henry frowned, the gesture hidden behind his cloth mask. Sue had taken a few shirts and cut them up to use. The group now looked like bandits ready to rob a bank.

Shifting in his seat to get comfortable, Henry gazed out over the uneven surface of the rotting bodies.

Water runoff from a hidden source continually trickled into the bodies, thus keeping them moist. Add the high mountains on both sides and the entire area was mostly cast in shade all day. So instead of desiccated and dry cadavers left out in the sun for weeks, this section of road had become a Petri dish of rotting meat, filled with millions of maggots.

Henry pressed in the clutch with his left foot, shifted the transmission into first gear, and began easing the jeep forward, picking up speed with every second. If he went too fast he would end up losing control, sliding in the muck and gore as if he was on a sheet of ice. But if he went too slow, he would get bogged down in the goop, the tire wells becoming clogged with rotting body parts.

"Hold on tight!" Henry yelled to Sue, who was gripping the overhead support bar so tight her knuckles had become white. Both wore seat belts, not wanting to risk falling out of the jeep, despite wanting to be able to make a fast getaway if trouble arose.

Then the front tires touched the first of the bodies, the squishing, squelching sound enough to make even a hardened psychopath cringe slightly. The instant the rear wheels entered the muck, Henry felt his steering go from great to terrible. Gobbets of flesh and bits of brain matter sprayed out behind the jeep as the tires churned the slop up even more than nature was doing.

The clouds of flies parted slightly as the jeep entered the quagmire, and rats and crows scampered and flew off, most screeching and cawing at their meal being disturbed.

"Henry, look out!" Sue screamed, and he didn't need to ask to know what she was yelling about.

He was heading directly for the Fiat, and he had little to no steering.

"Turn it! Turn the jeep!" Sue shrilled.

"What the hell do you think I'm trying to do!" he shouted in return, all the while turning the wheel this way and that.

The steering was sluggish—driving through the remains of a thousand human beings would do that to a suspension system, and Henry doubted the designers of the jeep had planned on adding four-wheeling through people as a selling point.

Crows careened out of the sky, diving bombing the jeep, wanting to chase the annoyance away so they could get back to feeding.

Henry ignored the birds, his attention solely focused on keeping the jeep from becoming stuck. Flies were everywhere, a layer already coating the vehicle anywhere gore had stuck to it.

He missed the Fiat by an inch, the rear tires spraying the abandoned car in gore, then he was past it and heading for the end of the corpses.

The tires slipped and spun, trying to gain traction, and more than once there was a loud knocking sound as a piece of bone got caught within the tire wells. Henry was just waiting to hear a loud pop from a bone shard puncturing a tire.

The tires couldn't gain purchase, and he expected to become bogged down in corpses at any moment.

But it didn't happen; the jeep kept moving forward. Then he was driving over the last body and onto clear pavement.

The jeep skidded to a halt, the entire chassis dripping gore on all sides. The radiator steamed from the flesh and blood stuck to it and the odor of cooking meat permeated the air. The vehicle looked like it had been dipped in a bucket of decaying blood.

Henry and Sue had bits of splatter on them as well, thanks to the spray from the front tires. Henry used the mask over his face to wipe his forehead clean, before cleaning the sunglasses he'd worn as well. "That was harder than I thought it would be," he said while wiping his face.

"I thought you were going to hit that other car." Sue was spitting into the cloth and wiping at her cheeks, using the side mirror to see herself.

There was a loud whoop from what could only be Jimmy, and then the sound of an engine floated on the wind, overriding the noise of the buzzing flies.

"I think Jimmy's going to give it a try," Henry said. Jumping out of the jeep, he walked to the edge of the corpses. He couldn't see well with the flies endlessly buzzing in the air, but he could just make out the other jeep as Jimmy began his run over the sea of rotting bodies.

Jimmy did the same thing as Henry, and like a re-run of the same trip, Jimmy's jeep began to skew to the side, heading directly for the abandoned Fiat.

Only Jimmy wasn't as quick with the steering, his reflexes not as good as Henry's, and as the cloud of flies parted to allow the jeep to pass, Henry got a clear view of the accident in the distance.

There was the sound of rending metal, and the screech of bumpers locking, then there was silence.

Once more, the flies coalesced near the ground, feeding and mating and having a good time.

Henry could only watch from a distance, waiting to see if anyone was hurt.

He was about to tell Sue to stay behind, and was going to begin trudging through the slop to check on the second jeep, when he heard a voice yell angrily, "Shit!" Followed by, "Henry, the fucking jeep hit the Fiat. We're stuck!"

"Is everyone okay? Anyone hurt?" Henry called, cupping his mouth to prevent any flies from zooming between his lips.

"No, we're all fine, but these fucking flies are gonna eat us alive! Come get us out of here!"

Sighing heavily, Henry went back to his jeep, Sue waiting in the passenger seat.

"I heard," she said. "What do we do now?"

"You stay here and wait for me to return with the others," Henry said as he dug through the small area behind the front seats. He pulled out a tire iron and a small toolbox. He didn't know what he needed to help Jimmy but these were about as good as it got.

"Fine, but what are you going to do?"

Henry shook his head as he shoved the gear into a small duffel bag and threw it over his shoulder, making sure his hands were free. "I'm going to do what I always do." He began walking.

"And what's that exactly?" she called.

"Simple. Get Jimmy out of another jam because he was too cocky for his own good."

Sue chuckled softly, but kept it muffled so Henry couldn't hear. "Well, be careful. I don't need you falling in that stuff. God knows how many diseases you'd catch."

"Tell me about it," he muttered as he placed his first foot into the muck, his boot sinking deep into the intestines of what might have once been an old woman. Dark brown goo squirted out around his heels and he hoped to God his boots were water tight.

The thoughts of the remains of people getting into his footwear, where it would then squish around between his toes, was simply too much to bear. Even Henry had his limits when it came to gore.

Taking each step at a time, careful not to fall, he slowly made his way to the second jeep, his feet squelching each time he took a step, the suction causing him to move slower than he wanted to.

It was easy to find Jimmy and the others, despite the thick clouds of flies blocking his vision.

All he had to do was follow the sound of cursing, as Jimmy swore to every God mankind had invented since its existence first began.

Chapter 18

When I was a young man,
My mother said to me,
Grow up strong, grow up brave,
But take any dark secrets to the grave.

The singing floated over the rocks to Major Ishmael Varakov and his men, who were standing silently in an open area. The land was still frozen, but here and there were the signs of greenery, evidence that Spring came to even this harsh landscape eventually.

Varakov was the only soldier who understood English, and his skill was monetary at best. He had learned English years ago when he'd been a child in school, but had found he'd had very little use for it upon graduating. Other than the errant tourist he might come across in the city, he almost never used his learned skill.

Still, he was able to make out bits and pieces of the song, but not enough to actually understand what was being sung. From the lyrical way the man spoke the words, it was obvious he was singing however.

Movement near the rocks had Varakov and the rest of his men perk up in alertness, but it was only the scout Karamatsov, who had been ordered to go ahead, sent forward alone, to see what lay beyond the boulders.

"Comrade Major, there is a lone man laying lines below an ice stream. He is old, I could kill him easily. I would have but I wanted to report back first."

Varakov nodded, pleased with his scout. "And it is well you did. He is the first American we have seen since arriving here. I wish to lay my eyes on him myself." He waved his men onward. "Follow me, men. Let us see our first brave American."

The American they spoke about, a trapper by the name of Michael Thompson, was fifty-two years old and lived in a small village three miles inland. His wife had been killed three years ago, taken by surprise by a group of walking dead. This was before most people fully understood the dangers of the dead, and his wife, seeing that two of the zombies were her friends, had thought she could reason with them. To her mortal mistake, she'd found out there was no reasoning with the dead.

Michael and his late wife never had children, the explanation for this never explained between them. Perhaps his wife had been barren, or maybe he had been shooting blanks, either way, no matter how many times they had tried when they were younger, it wasn't meant to be.

Each morning, if the wind wasn't too unbearable so it felt like his skin was being flayed from his bones with each gust, and the temperature was survivable, he would venture out and lay traps by the streams, hoping to catch one of the beavers that lived there. The water was saved from freezing due to an underground thermal that kept the water warm enough that even in the worst of winters, ice would not form throughout the stream.

As he knelt in the snow and set his traps, Michael sang to himself, his own voice helping to fight off the loneliness and isolation he felt when out on his forays alone. It were times like this that he wished the most that he had a son to help him, along with keeping him company.

By his side was a battered Remington M-700 sporting rifle, the leather strap connected to it allowing him to carry it over his shoulder. But when he was laying traps, he found that the weapon would get in his way, so he would place it by his side instead. Still, he was always alert for wolves, which were an ever constant threat.

One time, after having a particularly fruitful day, and catching three beavers, he had cleaned the catch and set off back to the village. When he was less than halfway home, the wolves had appeared. Five of them, all mean-looking brutes that would have been happy to settle for Michael as their prey if they could not get at the beavers he carried.

Michael had managed to shoot one of the wolves, and the other four had quickly pounced on their wounded brother. No honor among the hungry, he assumed.

He had taken off running, hoping the wolves' appetites would be satiated by the dead one, but before he had made the halfway mark home, they had returned. Blood covered their muzzles from where they'd fed, but the look in their eyes told him their bellies were far from full.

They'd quickly split up, surrounding him, and this time they'd kept moving. He'd wasted three shots before one of the wolves snuck up on him from behind, taking him down to the snow.

Using the rifle as a bludgeon, he'd swung it around, the stock connecting with the wolf's muzzle. The animal had yelped and fallen away. But during the brief skirmish the other wolves had come closer, and Michael knew he needed to act fast or he was done for.

Unslinging the beaver carcasses from his shoulder, he'd taken each one and threw it as hard as he could, each one spinning away to land in the opposite direction of the way he wanted to go.

The wolves had quickly ignored him, chasing after the dead beavers like dogs fetching sticks. He'd taken off running and hadn't stopped until reaching the village.

That had been a sad day for him. The entire day had been wasted, and he'd retuned home with nothing to show for it.

Well, he'd still had one thing, he'd figured. He'd still been breathing, not dead and torn apart on the frozen tundra.

So there was that. But it was a bitter pill to swallow when he went hungry that night other than a few scraps left over from a previous meal.

He stopped singing and cursed under his breath, as he tried to untie a stubborn knot in the trapping lines. He was about to remove his gloves so he could get at the knot easier, when he detected movement out of the corner of his eye. Sliding off the goggles he wore to protect his eyes from the wind, he let go of the lines and stood up.

Silhouetted against the skyline, on a slight incline to the land, was an imposing figure on a large horse, a stallion if Michael was correct. In the figure's hands was a rifle, the polished metal reflecting the sun. Michael was pretty confident the figure was man, and by the way he sat on the horse, he sure as hell looked like a soldier.

This seemed odd as there was no United States military, and even if there was, they sure as shit wouldn't be riding horses.

A second later, another man on horseback joined the first, followed by a third, then more, until there were too many to count. Each figure held a shining firearm in its hands. So many men in one place, all mounted, with what looked like new firearms, well, they could take over an entire state without even trying. Michael wondered if this was some new baron coming to call, to let the people in the area know he was now in charge. No doubt the baron would be expecting some form of tribute.

Being far away from any of the large cities, such as Anchorage, no one had bothered to attempt such a thing before, but Michael had heard rumors about such as this. Slowly, he picked up his Remington, leveling it at the armed men.

He had little enough for himself, and he'd be damned if he would give even that to some damn fool baron who thought his shit didn't stink.

Standing tall, he waited for the men to approach, as they had begun to move down the incline just as Michael stood up.

As they moved closer, he wondered if he'd been wrong, and perhaps these men were only traders. He spotted the pack mules at the end of the convoy, and considered that maybe this second assumption was correct.

But when the first of the men became close enough for Michael to make out their clothing, his eyes went wide in recognition. The men wore Russian uniforms, the heavy coats also of Russian manufacture.

Michael felt his knees go weak, but he held fast and leveled his Remington at the men. His mind was working overtime as he tried to figure out what to do. He was one man against dozens, and all with better firearms than he had. These men were from another country; how had they gotten to Alaska was one question he sure as hell wanted answered. Others were: Were there more of them? Was this an invasion? Or were the Russians sending help to a beleaguered America? Maybe with the dead gone, countries were out helping one another, that the dead had ended up bringing world peace to a warring planet.

Major Varakov stopped his horse a dozen feet from the man before him, studying the trapper with curious eyes.

No one said a thing, and with the exception of the snorting horses, and a belch or cough here and there, not a sound could be heard in the open plains in the heart of Alaska.

Varakov wasn't impressed with what he saw before him. The man looked poor, his clothing old and worn. The rifle he held was also old, as if it had been fixed a dozen times or more, each time something on it malfunctioned.

The man appeared to be nothing more than a peasant, no different from the people he'd left behind on the Russian side of the Strait.

"Who the hell are you people? You coming to help or hurt us?" Michael asked, finally cutting through the silence. He aimed the Remington menacingly, despite being woefully outnumbered.

"What did he say, Comrade Major?" Streltsy asked. "Should I kill the dog now before he tries something? He looks like he might try to shoot at us, stupid an act as it would be."

"No, Comrade Streltsy," Varakov said with a wave of his hand. "I speak some English, though I am not too good. I think he wants to know who we are. That is all." He turned back to face Michael and said in broken English, "Good day to you, sir. My name is Major Ishmael Varakov. I greet you from Russia. I come to you in pieces." He meant to say the word 'peace', but as it was stated, his English was more than a little rusty. The fact he managed that much clarity would have made his teacher proud.

"You don't make much sense there, stranger, but I reckon you said you're all from Russia. That's a long way from here. What're you doing here in America?"

"Yes, America," Varakov repeated, as that was all he understood Michael say. The rest made no sense to him.

One of the soldiers behind Varakov snickered loudly, followed by another one or two.

Angry, Varakov turned in his saddle to face his men. With scarves and masks covering their faces to keep them warm, he had no way of seeing who it was who had first chuckled. "If I find out who it was who laughed, they can tell me what they find so funny while I slit their belly open and leave them for the scavengers to find."

The men immediately went silent, all eyes looking down, most deciding there was something interesting in the manes of their horses.

Michael was growing impatient. His toes were freezing inside his old boots and he was worried he would get frostbite. He wanted to finish up and get home, and these men were holding him up. So with impatience in his tone, he said, "Just who the fuck are you guys? What do you want of me? You need directions? Are you trading shit? What?"

Varakov decided to try again. "Greetings, sir. Could you tell me where is the beach? I am on vacation here."

"Beach? Vacation? Are you fucking serious?" Michael was really getting angry now. Was this some kind of a joke? Were these men simply playing with him? None of this made any sense at all. Perhaps another man would have handled the situation better, for Michael had never been considered 'good with people.' Even on one of his good days. But today he was in an ornery mood and he had no time for fools. He gripped the Remington tighter, the barrel now raised and pointing directly at the men on horseback, though his finger was not near the trigger, which was the only reason why one of the soldiers hadn't shot him: with or without Varakov's order.

Major Varakov was also growing annoyed also. He'd thought his English was acceptable for what he needed it for, but was finding out that he was terribly unequipped for the task at hand. He could tell the trapper was also becoming angry, and the man was growing more agitated with each second.

Varakov decided to try one more time. "I wish to use the toilet. I like Italian food."

"Food? You want my food?" Michael asked in shock. He knew it; these men wanted to rob him.

Rhzhdestvensky rode up beside Varakov and stopped his horse when it was beside his leader. "Comrade Major, this fool is threatening us with his gun. Let me kill him before he tries something stupid. He does not seem to understand he is helpless."

Varakov opened his mouth to respond, to tell Rhzhdestvensky to get back behind him, when Michael raised the rifle to his shoulder, while yelling, "That's fucking it. I've had enough of you assholes. You're not getting shit outta me!" Then he fired at Varakov, the man he figured was the leader of the group.

Rhzhdestvensky saw what was about to happen and kneed his horse in the sides, the animal surging forward as its rider pulled a handgun from within his coat.

But Michael's rifle barked first, and if not for Rhzhdestvensky surging forward, it would have been Varakov who was shot. The 7mm bullet struck Rhzhdestvensky high in the right shoulder, the force of the impact sending the fat man flying off his saddle to land heavily in the snow.

Michael grinned at his success and turned to shoot the next closest man. If he'd taken even a second to consider his actions, he would have realized how absolutely ridiculous he was being. Forty soldiers, all armed to the teeth, stood before him. What did he think he was going to do before he was gunned down? But adrenaline and fear had taken over his mind, and all he could see now was the color red from anger.

The other Russian soldiers leveled their weapons, about to riddle the trapper with bullets, when Varakov began to gallop forward at the man, yelling out an order to his men. "Nyet! Do not shoot! The dog is mine alone to kill!" He pulled his long sword from its sheath on his side, his horse galloping at a full run.

The galloping of hooves distracted Michael from his next shot, and he turned slightly to see Varakov coming straight at him.

Frantically trying to swing the rifle around, he wasn't good under pressure, and his finger couldn't seem to find the trigger.

Varakov was on the trapper a moment later, just as Michael fired the rifle. The bullet missed Varakov's head by less than inch, and the Russian Major felt the round buzz by his head, as if an angry bee was near his left ear. All this happened in the single pulse of a heartbeat, perhaps even less. Varakov raised the long sword high, bringing it down directly onto the trapper's head.

Only Michael's instincts were not totally gone, and he raised the Remington to block the downward blow of the glittering sword.

But the rifle was no match for the quality-honed steel, and the sword cut through the stock of the weapon a few inches behind the trigger guard, taking with it three of the five fingers from that hand, before slicing into Michael's right shoulder and becoming wedged in the collarbone.

Michael shoved himself off the sword and fell back onto the snow, the pieces of the Remington scattered around him. His face a mask of pain, he got to his knees, while doing his best to staunch the flow of blood from his missing fingers, his shoulder wound pumping his life's blood with each beat of his heart.

There was no way he could hope to stop both wounds at the same time, and each one would be fatal if not attended to. After a few seconds, he realized his fate was sealed and he stopped trying.

Varakov had galloped back around and was now before his men once more. Streltsy handed his leader a cloth and Varakov wiped his sword clean before re-sheathing it.

Michael was coughing up blood, his shoulder wound spurting in rhythm to his heartbeat. He peered up at Varakov and his men. "You bastards got me, that's for sure, but at least I'm dying a free man! Fuck you all!" He spat onto the ground before the soldiers, the crimson spittle staining the churned-up snow dark red.

Varakov had had enough of this. Pulling his sidearm, he shot Michael in the face. The bullet made a small hole just to the left of the trapper's nose, though the exit wound was much, much larger.

Big enough to put a man's fist through, the back of Michael's skull exploded outwards, brains and bone matter coating the snow vermillion and pink.

For a few seconds, Michael remained kneeling, as if he was contemplating his death, but then the body slumped over, slid onto its side, and lay still. Blood still pumped from the first two wounds, but it was fitful at best.

"This is only the first American to die by us," Varakov said to his men. "If they will not bow to us, they will all die!" He gestured to Rhzhdestvensky, who was standing by his horse. "Your wound, how is it?"

"I will live, Comrade Major," Rhzhdestvensky said. "The bullet went right through."

"That is too bad," Liev joked. "If we had to leave your fat carcass for the wolves, they would have enough to eat for a fortnight!"

The other men laughed, enjoying the joke.

Rhzhdestvensky didn't find the quip as amusing and he flashed the *fuck off* sign with his hands at Liev, who only laughed louder.

With help from two other men, Rhzhdestvensky climbed back onto his horse, a thick piece of cloth under his jacket to help stop the blood from his wound. When Varakov called for a rest later, that would be when his wound would be looked at.

"Enough, it is time to move on," Major Ishmael Varakov said, getting his men under control. He gestured to the cooling corpse lying in the snow. "If all Americans are as soft as this fool, we will own this land in no time. He must have come from a nearby village. It is there we will find what next we seek." He waved his right arm forward in the direction he wanted to go, and with Streltsy on point, the army began to move again. Varakov stayed to the side, making eye contact with each man as they passed by him, letting each one know he saw them personally, that they were all in it together.

When the last pack mule had passed by, Varakov also turned to follow.

As he rode past Michael's blood-soaked corpse, the knots in the trapper's ropes still lying close by the stream, he paused and said in English, "Thank you for your help, sir. Have a nice day."

He kneed his horse and galloped after his men, so he could lead his invading army deeper into Alaska.

Chapter 19

With the odor of rotting meat permeating the area, Henry began the long trek to Jimmy's jeep. Careful not to slip in the rotting quagmire, it was a constant balancing act not to tumble face-first into a decomposing spleen or a bubbling abdomen.

"Don't fall, Henry!" Sue called.

He didn't need to be told twice, and he simply waved his hand overhead, signifying he'd heard her.

Now that he was walking through the sea of corpses, he got a better appreciation of the sheer size of it. The horde had been massive, and wherever they had ended up would have been bad news for anyone unfortunate enough to be waiting. But then the zombies had died; just like that. Like a switch had been flicked, turning them off.

Once more he pondered it all, wondering how the hell the dead had ceased being animated.

He was again thankful for the face mask, and only wished he'd had glasses or goggles as well. The flies were ferocious, resting on him to feed on his sweat. It was like being inside a giant bee hive, the buzzing never stopping. Rats hissed at his feet as he passed them, angry at being disturbed. Dozens of buzzards were feasting as well, and they screeched at Henry, fearing he wanted their meal for himself.

"Just passing through, fellas. Don't mind me," he said through the mask, his voice muffled. The carrion-eaters screeched some more and then went back to their feast.

Louder hissing at his feet caused him to look down. A dozen rats of varying sizes were surrounding him, their posture telling Henry they were considering if they should attack the new meat walking through their midst.

A quick swipe of the panga, decapitating the closest rats, changed the minds of the others instantly, the gesture clear: Keep feeding on the dead and leave the living the fuck alone. Bounding away, they quickly disappeared amongst the carcasses.

"That you, Henry?" Jimmy called when the older man grew closer to the jeep and Fiat.

"Who the hell else is it gonna be?" Henry growled through his mask. He shook his boots, trying to get the maggots that had attached themselves to him to let go.

"No shit, old man, but still, just checking. Wouldn't want to have some cannie walk right up and blow me away before I knew it wasn't you." He waved at his face to dislodge the flies. "Case you haven't noticed; it's a fucking fly fest around here."

With arms out for balance, Henry finally reached the jeep. Mary and Cindy, along with Jimmy, their faces covered like Henry's, all watched him approach. He quickly inspected the damage. The jeep had locked bumpers with the Fiat, and with traction so terrible, the two vehicles were melded together.

"Shit, this doesn't look too good," Henry said.

"Ya think?" Jimmy quipped from the driver's seat.

"Someone hand me a crowbar," Henry said as he sloshed around in some dead guy's intestines. Each time he moved, a squelching sound could be heard.

"Here, Henry," Mary said, reaching around behind her and pulling out a tire iron. "This is the best we can do."

"It'll have to do then." He looked over at Jimmy. "You, this is your fault, so come over here and help me get this apart."

Jimmy's face blanched. "Oh no, I'm not getting out of the jeep and walking around in that nasty shit. You do it. You're already in it."

Henry's eyes went hard. He was in no mood for Jimmy's shenanigans. "Jimmy, this is the last time I'm going to ask you. Get out of the jeep and come over here and help me or so help me…"

"So help you what? Come on, Henry, don't play the tough guy with me. I know you too well. Look, old man, you're already covered in that gunk, so it might as well as be you who gets us unstuck. Then I can drive us all out of here and no one else gets covered in shit but you."

"Last chance, Jimmy," Henry said, his voice muffled by the mask, which was perhaps why Jimmy wasn't taking the older man as seriously as he should have. Facial gestures go a long way when giving someone an ultimatum, and when only a muffled voice was giving that warning, too much could be lost in translation.

"Maybe you should go out and help him, Jimmy," Cindy suggested.

"Yeah, don't be such a wuss," Mary added.

"Wuss?" Jimmy replied. "I don't see you volunteering to help him, Mary."

Before Mary could respond, there was another squelching sound, then the flies parted as something soared through the air to hit Jimmy square on the chest.

The younger man glanced down to see something black, brown and smelly slowly sliding into his lap like toy slime a child had thrown against a wall, the squishy green blob then slowly moving downward.

He was shocked. Henry had thrown a piece of some zombie's internal organ at him.

Jimmy opened his mouth to say something but then another, nastier piece of a body part hit him on the shoulder, where it stuck there. Looking to see what it was, it sort of resembled a liver or perhaps a kidney. Maggots squirmed in the meat, the organ riddled with tiny holes.

"Next one gets you in the face, Jimmy," Henry warned. "Now get out here and help me or so help me I'm going to pull you out of there and throw you into the deepest part of this crap. I'm out here so you can be, too. Have one of the girls get into the driver's seat."

"Well, he did ask nicely at first, Jimmy," Mary said, stifling the laugh on her lips.

"Son-of-a-bitch. I can't believe you just did that," Jimmy said in amazement, before slowly climbing out of the driver's seat. His footing was slippery and he had to hold onto the side of the jeep or risk going down. But with one hand on the jeep, he bent over and scooped up something long and stringy, then before Henry could warn him not to do it, Jimmy threw it at Henry like it was a custard pie and they were two clowns doing a bit together at a show. The stringy substance hit the older man on the right thigh, where it then slid off to splash in the goop.

"There old man, how do you like it?"

"I don't, but now you're out here in it with me, so stop screwing around and come help me over here. If you don't, both of the girls are going to have to walk through this stuff. Do you want that? You want Cindy to have to trudge through all this?"

"I can carry her," Jimmy said defensively, not wanting to capitulate.

"Oh really. You gonna carry Mary, too?"

Jimmy shrugged as he joined Henry at the intersecting bumpers. "Hell no, she can walk."

"Thanks a lot, Jimmy. I love you, too," Mary spat, crossing her arms angrily.

"Hey, sorry, Mar', but I've only got two hands." Jimmy lowered his mask for a second and flashed her one of his patented smirks, but the look in Mary's eyes told him he was glad she didn't have a rotting body part to throw also.

Henry shoved Jimmy slightly to get his attention. "Focus, Jimmy. Here, you pull while I use the tire iron to see if I can separate this mess you got the jeep into." He began working at the connecting bumpers. "Damn it, Jimmy, you wedged them together good, too."

"Hey, it wasn't my fault." He almost fell and it was only Henry beside him to stabilize him that allowed the younger man to remain upright. The goop was so slick, and with loose bones floating within it, that the footing was completely treacherous. Only by having one hand on something, such as the jeep, the Fiat or each other, enabled the two men to keep from toppling over.

"Hold me up," Jimmy snapped.

"I can't hold you up if I'm trying to get the cars separated," Henry rebutted.

Jimmy's left foot went out from under him and he reached out to grab Henry, who had two hands on the tire iron and so wasn't able to keep from falling as Jimmy went down, pulling Henry along with him. The two men fell onto their butts, the slop spraying out all around them.

"Oh my God," Mary gasped, finding the entire situation hilarious. She leaned into Cindy and said. "You can almost hear the Three Stooges theme song while watching them, can't you?"

"It's not funny, Mary," Cindy said at first, but as she watched the two men floundering, she couldn't stop the smirk creasing her lips from appearing. She was glad to be wearing a mask covering the lower half of her face. "Well, maybe it's a little funny."

Meanwhile, the two men were doing their best to get up, but like the slickest ice ever was underfoot, all they did was fall back down to splash around in it. In seconds, they were completely covered from head to toe in a sloppy mess of fetid blood and guts.

"Well," Mary added, trying to be positive. "At least they've managed to keep it out of their mou…"

"Fuck!" Jimmy spit. "I got some of this shit in my mouth!"

"Whoops, I guess I spoke too soon," Mary said, and Cindy had to stifle a laugh.

"Goddamn it!" Henry yelled. "Jimmy, will you hold still for a second so we can sort this shit out!"

"You hold still, old man, I want to get out of this shit!"

"Then give me a chance to get up and then I'll help you." Slowly, Henry got to his feet, using the jeep as leverage to prevent him from falling again.

Jimmy didn't reply, instead he began to vomit, the idea of having the stuff in his mouth from where it had soaked through his mask too much to bear. Turning his head to the side, he yanked the mask down and projectile vomited right onto Henry's boots.

Henry looked down at his feet, his eyes wide in awe. "Seriously, Jimmy? Did you really just do that?"

"I'm so sorry, Henry. It's just that I can't…" he vomited again, this time missing Henry and spraying the wheel of the jeep.

Henry sighed. "Well, it can't be worse than the rest of this crap all over me, I guess." He looked down for the tire iron, found it, and picked it up, taking a moment to shake off the blood and guts. But it wasn't really blood, not anymore at least. After weeks of being soaked in water runoff and mixing with decomposing body parts, it was more of an amalgam of everything, all mixed together to make the most awful-smelling, pungent odor he'd ever had the misfortune to experience. He'd thought zombies had smelled terrible, but compared to the mess he was standing in, a walking zombie was downright the scent of a summer breeze.

Deciding it was time to ignore Jimmy, or he would never separate the two vehicles, Henry began working at the two bumpers again. Luckily, it didn't take long to get them separated, and with a wrenching sound of metal, the jeep popped free and rolled a foot before stopping.

"There, that wasn't too hard," Henry said, then looked down at Jimmy, who was still sitting on his ass nearby. "No thanks to you."

"I'm sorry, all right? How many times can I say it already? I'm fucking sorry."

Cindy had slid behind the steering wheel and she started the jeep, but the second she stepped on the gas pedal, all the tires did were spin.

"Hold on a second, Cindy," Henry said, seeing the problem. "You'll need a push to get moving again." Reaching down, he picked up Jimmy, the younger man almost taking Henry down once more. Only Henry's iron grip on Jimmy's arm prevented them from doing a retake, and when Jimmy was eye level with Henry, who had pulled his mask down, he said softly so that only Jimmy could hear. "Enough, already. Man the hell up and cut it out. It's not funny. Sue's waiting for us and if something happens to her while we're screwing around here I'll never forgive you." He glared at Jimmy. "You hear me?"

"Yeah, Henry, I hear you. Lighten up. Let's do this thing." Jimmy didn't smile, completely serious now. He realized he'd crossed a line somehow, though for the life of him he didn't understand how. It wasn't his fault the damn jeep had swerved like that. It was just bad luck.

Henry didn't reply, but instead shoved Jimmy to the rear of the jeep, then followed. "We need to push so Cindy can get some traction. Go over there and I'll push from here," he told Jimmy, who only nodded. "Okay, Cindy, give it some gas, but not too hard," he instructed. "And make sure the front wheels are turned so you don't drive back into the other car."

"Got it," Cindy said and did as she was told; she slowly stepped on the gas. Goop, bones, and gore sprayed out from behind the jeep, a lot of splatter hitting the two men. But neither cared anymore, as they were both covered from head to toe. Flies also landed on them in even larger numbers, feeding on the goop covering the two filthy men.

Blinking flies from his eyes, Henry put his back into it, as did Jimmy, and after only a few fitful seconds the jeep began to move.

"Don't stop, Cindy, Jimmy and I will catch up on foot. You stop and we'll have to push you again."

"Okay, Henry, we'll wait with Sue for you to get back." Then she was driving away, the jeep swerving back and forth.

Jimmy pointed at the retreating jeep. "See Henry? It's slippery as hell. Cindy's having a tough time of it, too."

"Jimmy, I really don't care anymore, okay? Let's just get out of this mess so we can change clothes and wash up."

"I know but..."

"What did I just say? I don't care."

"Yeah, I know but if you'll just let me expl..."

"No, goddamn it. Jimmy, will you just leave it alone already?" He was trudging through the muck, using the tire tracks of the jeep as a trail, the tires having managed to shove a lot of goop to the sides of the twin rows, though it was already flowing back over the tracks, the sludge the consistency of mud. Moving faster than Jimmy, he quickly outdistanced the younger man.

"But, Henry."

"So help me, Jimmy, if you don't shut the hell up I'm going to shoot you. I swear on Emily's grave I'll do it."

Jimmy sighed and stopped walking for a second, the goop flowing back in around his boots. A rat came up and sniffed at his leg and Jimmy kicked it away, sending it sprawling. It jumped back up, shook itself as clean as possible given the situation, hissed once, and then sprung away.

Jimmy stared at Henry's retreating back, wondering how things could have gotten so fucked up, so fast, then with his head hanging low, he followed Henry out of the sea of corpses. One thing he'd noticed; the longer he'd been covered in the muck, the less it was affecting his olfactory senses. It was true; a person could get used to anything given enough time.

When Henry finally reached the edge of the corpse sea, and he stepped out onto the solid asphalt of the highway, Sue ran over to him, but quickly halted when she saw what he looked like. Mary and Cindy had filled her in quickly about what happened, but she still wasn't prepared for the sight of Henry covered in gore from head to foot.

"Oh my God, are you all right?" she asked in amazement.

Henry shook his head yes, while gobbets of flesh sloughed off him to splatter onto the road. "Yeah, I'll live. I just need a shower and some new clothes." He waved his hand before him to chase away the blowflies, which were relentless.

Jimmy stepped out of the goop next, and he kept walking past Henry until he was on the side of the road, where the girls had set up a half-ass decontamination station with what supplies they had. Both jeeps looked like extra vehicles in a splatter movie, the sides dripping gore by the handfuls.

"Oh, okay then," Sue replied, not knowing what to say. "Just come over here; we've been setting something up for you two."

Henry nodded and did as she asked, Sue keeping well clear of him. When they were halfway there, Henry stopped in the road to look back at the sea of corpses. The flies had descended once more so that visibility into the interior was almost nothing. The rats and buzzards, and a lot of crows, too many to count, had also descended again, glad to have their meal to themselves once more. Henry turned his gaze on Sue, his hair covered in a gooey mess. "Sue, do me a favor, will you?"

"Of course, Henry, whatever you need."

"The next time we come upon a situation like this; remind me to have us take the long way around."

Chapter 20

After Jimmy and Henry washed briefly using nothing but a few bottles of water, and changed clothes, the two jeeps set off once more, their soiled clothes left where they'd dropped them on the side of the road. The mood of both men was subdued, neither pleased with getting covered with rotting body parts.

And though pants, shirts, and underwear had been changed, other gear such as combat boots, holsters for weapons and sheathes for knives were still soiled and needed to be addressed.

So when Henry spotted a weathered sign for a golf course, he turned off the main road, Jimmy following right behind him.

"Why are we going here?" Sue asked. "I thought we were going to Area 51."

Henry nodded in agreement. "We will, but golf courses have ponds, so hopefully Jimmy and I can get a more complete wash than what he had earlier. Of course, with no one maintaining the course, and the heat, there might not be any water there anymore."

She wrinkled her nose. "That sounds like a great idea if it's possible. I didn't want to say anything, but you do still stink pretty badly."

"Yeah, I know, and hopefully this'll correct that issue." He shook his head like an annoyed father. "Damn Jimmy. He's always getting into messes. From the first day he picked me up in an old Delta 88 on a road outside of my hometown after everything began, he's been getting me into trouble."

"True, but he's saved your life often enough too, hasn't he?"

Henry sighed. "Yeah, I suppose he has. It's just…"

"I know, Henry, you don't have to say it. But he's family now, isn't he?"

"Of course he is; all of you are."

Sue reached across the seat and took Henry's right hand in hers. "Right. And family sticks together, even when they can be a pain in the butt."

Henry didn't reply, as he was pulling the jeep over instead on the side of a skinny road. It led to a gradual rise up to a mansion-like home that was the country club for the golf course. The bottom floor of the structure had a floor filled with large glass windows, all shattered now, the large square frames signifying the bottom level had been for the golf store, pro shop, and maybe even some form of restaurant located at the back and out of sight.

"I thought we were going all the way to the top?" Jimmy called, his jeep parked behind Henry's, the engine still idling. "Why're we stopping here?"

Henry turned off his motor and climbed out of the jeep, as did the others. "No reason. I doubt there's anything there after all this time anyway." He pointed to a small pond off to the side, the water level almost nonexistent. It was really more of a large puddle than a pond.

"That's where I'm going. I need a real bath, you too, Jimmy, and we both need to wash our boots and gear."

"A bath? But it's not Saturday night?" Jimmy replied. "Ouch!" he yelled when Cindy smacked him on the back of the head.

"Go and wash up, Jimmy, you still smell terrible," Cindy ordered. Then she whispered, "If you ever want me to kiss you again, or do anything else for that matter; go wash up some more."

"All right, fine, sheesh, you make it sound like I've been rolling around in garbage."

"Garbage would have been preferred, Jimmy," Mary added as she walked over to join the others.

Henry didn't waste time, and after grabbing some spare clothing to use as towels and rags, and some gun oil to clean his Glock and polish his panga, he grabbed Jimmy by the arm and hauled the younger man behind him, the two moving down the incline to the waiting water.

When the two were at the edge of the water, Henry gently shoved Jimmy forward, the younger man falling head first into the pond. "You go first and tell me how deep it is, will you?" Henry asked, with more than a little mirth in his tone. True, he was being mean, but it was a playful kind of mean. He still had some pent-up aggression towards Jimmy and he needed to vent somehow. This seemed rather harmless.

Jimmy splashed down head first in the water, and came up sputtering, his hair plastered to his face. "It's not too deep," he said as he blew water from his nose. Then, like a playful five-year-old, he splashed Henry a few times, and before the older man could do anything, he jumped back in, splashing around and having a fun time of it.

Henry couldn't help but laugh at this. He should have known better than to try and beat Jimmy at being silly. After setting his Glock and panga down at the edge of the pool, he jumped in as well, clothes and all. Jimmy had splashed him pretty well so there was no point of stripping first. Besides, neither man had been able to clean as well as they'd wanted to, and the clothing they wore wasn't as fresh as when they'd first been put on. But it was a warm day in Nevada and he knew the clothes would dry fast once he and Jimmy were out of the water.

Mary crossed her arms under her full breasts as she watched the two men playing like children. "Look at them, horsing around like it's swim time at the local watering hole."

"Ah, leave them alone," Cindy said with a grin. "It's good if they can relax for a bit. Henry's always so tense; if Jimmy gets him to let his guard down, it'll be good for Henry."

"So what do we do then? Just wait like good little women?" Mary asked.

"Hell no. I want to check out that clubhouse. You in?"

"Sure."

Sue had been standing nearby, listening to the conversation but not interrupting. Now she leaned in and added, "You two go and investigate. I'll stay here and keep watch on the boys and our stuff."

"Okay, just hit the horn if any trouble appears," Mary said.

"As it often does," Cindy tossed out as the two women began walking further up the hill.

The sounds of Henry and Jimmy splashing quickly faded away as the two women walked together.

"I bet this place was something else before, well, you know," Cindy said, wanting to break the silence.

"Yeah, I know what you mean," Mary replied.

The golf course had been a vision of luxury at one time, where the middle-class golfer would have had to save up for a bit to do eighteen holes, and that was only if someone who was already a member was sponsoring them for the day.

But that luxury was now only a memory. The grass, once perfectly manicured and maintained daily with water, was now nothing but denuded ground, and where clumps still held on to life, the grass was an ugly, burnt yellow.

Trees lined both sides of the small road, but now the trees were bent and broken, some overgrown. The pavement was filled with cracks, weeds thrusting forth from the ground to ever widen the openings. As the two women reached the end of the road where it opened onto a large parking lot, the clubhouse looked no better.

It hadn't looked too bad from a distance, with the exception of the first floor shattered windows, but now that they were closer, they could see there was fire damage. Bodies lay everywhere. Thankfully, they were nothing but desiccated husks, the moisture long sucked out of them by the Nevada sun.

The facade of the clubhouse was riddled with bullet holes, signifying a gunfight had occurred sometime in the past. Both women spotted the holes and looked at one another.

"Think they're fresh?"

"Only one way to find out," Cindy replied, then unslung her M16 from where it had been hanging over her shoulder, always within easy reach if signs of trouble appeared.

Mary already held her .38 in her right hand, the weapon poised to fire at the first sign of danger.

Walking side by side, but further apart so as not to make an easy target, the two women moved forward, their eyes constantly searching for anything amiss.

A sign for the Pro shop creaked in the wind, and an old soda can clinked as it rolled across the empty lot. These were common sounds the women were used to in a desolate world where only a small fraction of the population still existed.

Cindy motioned they should go around the left side, and together they began moving faster, wanting to come up on anyone who was waiting for them quickly, and hopefully take them by surprise.

Mary watched Cindy as the woman moved ahead of her, and Mary was pleased to see her friend seemed to be looking better. Mary had never been with anyone to the point a potential child had become part of the equation, and she'd never had a miscarriage, so though she felt empathy for Cindy, deep down she knew there was no true way to know what Cindy was feeling about it all. But she could be supportive and a friend, and there to talk if Cindy ever needed it.

Reaching the back of the clubhouse, the fire damage was a sight to behold. The entire rear of the building was nothing but a framework of scorched beams, with blackened rubble covering the ground.

"Wow, some real shit went down here in the past," Cindy said as she took in the damage.

"It's funny; you'd never know it was this bad from the front."

Cindy nodded at Mary's statement. "Should we go inside? We can use the front entrance."

Mary shook her head. "I don't think we should. The fire's probably weakened the rest of the building, too. For all we know, once we step inside, a strong wind will have the place coming down on top of our heads." She shrugged. "Besides, I doubt the boys feel the need to go golfing anytime soon, do you?"

Cindy laughed. "I know, right? I can just see those two out there now. Hell, it might be worth the risk to get some clubs just to see that."

Mary smiled as well, imagining Henry and Jimmy on the course. Jimmy would never take the game seriously and Mary knew Henry well enough to know the older man would. The result would be nothing but Henry yelling at Jimmy to get serious for a full eighteen holes.

Some of the rubble stirred and began to shift. Both Mary and Cindy swiveled at the hip, their weapons lining up on the potential danger. But it was nothing but a stray cat, a dead mouse stuffed in its jaws. The cat saw the two humans and its tail fluffed up, its head going low. It would have hissed a warning if not for its mouth being full.

The two women locked gazes with the cat for a full twenty seconds, then the animal turned tail and ran off deeper into the building.

"Guess he thought we wanted his lunch," Cindy said.

"Let's walk around the rest of the building." Mary began moving again, Cindy following.

When they were on the far side of the clubhouse they found abandoned vehicles. Doors hung open, trunks and hoods as well. The cars were all luxury models, or had been before being exposed to the weather for years. A family of possums had made its home in a Lincoln Town car, and as they passed a green Jaguar, a rattlesnake made itself known, the snake using the shade from the car to take a noonday nap.

"I don't think we want to check out these cars, either," Cindy said while eyeing the snake warily.

"Amen, sister."

They continued walking, wanting to finish their recce and return to the others. On the far side of the clubhouse there was mostly dense shrubbery, the years of neglect allowing the foliage to grow twenty feet tall in some places.

Mary spotted the large vehicle within the clump of shrubbery first. It was almost hidden from view, but when the wind blew the bushes, they shifted enough to allow the faded, dirty white paint to show through.

Together, the two women ran over and quickly began pulling branches clear to get a better look.

When most of the rear of the vehicle was gone, they took a step back and took another look.

The cracked and faded face of a smiling baby gleamed back at them. The baby's mouth had one tooth in it, making the child the cutest thing ever. There was a painted twinkle in the right eye, and even after all the years of the sun baking the paint, weathering the image, the baby still made any woman who loved children smile.

But not this time, however. When Mary glanced over at her friend, she saw Cindy was staring at the visage, her mouth hanging open, tears forming in her eyes. She didn't move, the M16 slack in her grip, the painted face hypnotizing her in grief. Slowly, she knelt down on the ground, the M16 slipping from limp fingers.

With her hands covering her face, Cindy began to cry.

Though Cindy believed she'd dealt with the miscarriage and put it behind her, in reality she'd really been forcing it all down. There had been no time to truly mourn her lost child, to grieve for her loss. Since it had happened, she'd been on the run, one crisis after another taking up her time. Though she'd talked a little with Sue and Mary, she still hadn't really let out the terrible guilt she felt.

But like sometimes can happen, the trigger to a breakdown can come from the simplest of things, and at the oddest times.

Mary took a quick look around, making sure the area was still devoid of human life, and satisfied it was, she went to Cindy and knelt down by her friend's side, placing an arm around her.

Cindy accepted the embrace but continued to cry.

Mary said nothing; knowing there were times when the best thing a person could do was just be silent.

As Cindy sobbed into Mary's shoulder, Mary stared at the smiling, angelic face of what might have been.

Chapter 21

Just over an hour later, with Henry and Jimmy clean, the five companions stood around the back of the truck trailer, the entire trailer and cab shoved deep into the shrubbery, all the tires flat, signifying it had been sitting there for years. Someone had been trying to hide it, and if not for the brush thinning over time, the trailer might have remained hidden forever. A thick padlock secured the double doors from opening.

Close by, the two jeeps sat alone, their engines cooling in the warm air. Luckily, the warm desert wind was blowing away from the companions, the jeeps on the far side of the group, so the odor of rotting meat from the still-covered vehicles wasn't hitting them. It was a welcome respite.

Cindy stood beside Jimmy, looking like her old self again. Mary glanced at her and Cindy noticed; much the way a person knows they're being looked at as if by a sixth sense. She nodded and smiled to Mary, who responded in kind.

What had occurred between them would stay that way, and Mary felt good knowing she had been there at Cindy's time of need.

Henry and Jimmy looked a million times better, both men having a good bath in the pond. Henry had then taken some time to clean his weapons, stripping his Glock and then reassembling it with a generous portion of gun oil. The hardest part was getting the panga's sheathe clean without saturating it with water. But the sheathe had been given a coating of oil as well, and Henry was satisfied his favorite weapon, his baby, would be all right once the sheathe sat out in the hot sun for a few hours to dry. For now, the naked panga hung from his belt by a piece of rope tied to the hilt.

"You gonna shoot the lock off, Henry?" Jimmy asked as they gathered around the trailer.

"Suppose so, unless you got that tire iron handy."

Jimmy shook his head. "That thing was covered in shit. I left it where it got dropped."

Henry grunted. "That's what I figured, so yeah, I'm gonna shoot the lock off. Everyone stand back, we don't need a ricochet hitting someone."

"Now that would be embarrassing," Mary said as she stepped back with the others. "All the firefights we've been through and to get taken out by one of our own bullets."

"I could use my shotgun," Jimmy suggested, hefting it to waist level.

Henry shook his head quickly, wanting to stop the younger man before he shot without waiting for a reply. "No, Jimmy, that's overkill. Besides, though it's pretty obvious what's inside there, if it's something else, we don't want to damage it. Just let me do it, all right? I think I can handle it without your help."

Jimmy lowered the shotgun and waved Henry onward with a free hand. "Fine, old man, but wear your glasses so you don't miss."

"I don't wear glasses, damn it. And I'm not that old. You just wait until you hit forty, then you'll see."

"You're a lot older than forty," Jimmy snickered.

"Will you two please stop bickering and get on with it?" Sue asked politely. "I'm curious to see what's inside the trailer."

"Closer to fifty by my count," Jimmy added, enjoying himself immensely.

Henry glared at Jimmy, but didn't respond. He didn't know why Jimmy could always get him so riled up. He knew the younger man only did it to get a rise out of him, so why did he always take the bait?

Seeing everyone was a good distance away, he took a few steps back himself to prevent a ricochet from hitting him as well, and standing at a slight angle to the lock, he lined up the barrel of the Glock and squeezed the trigger.

The bullet slammed into the center of the padlock, leaving a clean hole the size of a dime in its wake, before penetrating the thin shell of the left-side double door.

As he was holstering his pistol, Jimmy was starting forward to open the doors, eager to see what was inside the trailer.

"Careful, Jimmy, the lock's probably hot," Henry warned but Jimmy had already grabbed the lock to then jump back, the lock too hot to touch just yet, a fresh curse escaping his lips.

"See, I told you. It's from the friction of the bullet passing through it. Just give it a minute and it'll be fine."

Jimmy frowned, then used the edge of his shirt to yank open the lock. With its internal mechanism shattered, the padlock popped open easily. "Or I can do this," he said snarkily and tossed the lock to the ground.

"Or you could do that," Henry repeated with a grin.

Jimmy tugged on the twin doors, trying to open them, but they wouldn't budge.

This time it was Cindy who showed him what he was doing wrong. "Jimmy, love, you need to twist that bar there upwards."

He made an annoyed face and did as she said. "I know that, I was just checking out something."

"Sure you were," Mary said with a grin.

Jimmy tried to pivot the slide bar but he was having a difficult go at it.

Finally, Henry stepped in to help, and with a gentle shove, said, "Here watch me do it," and worked the bar open. With a quick look that the others were ready with weapons in hand and aimed at the trailer doors, he tugged on the right-side door and jumped backwards as it flew open, as did Jimmy.

"I had it, old man," Jimmy snapped.

"Focus, Jimmy, not now," Henry hissed. There was no telling what was inside the trailer, and though highly doubtful there was anything dangerous within due to it being locked, careless people often ended up dead.

Everyone was ready for an attack, for a horde of zombies to come pouring out, but those days were over. There was nothing inside the trailer but stacks of boxes.

"Looks clear," Henry said and walked back to the doors, reached inside, and worked the closure on the other door, opening that one as well.

Light spilled deeper into the trailer, illuminating even more stacks of boxes.

"Just boxes by the looks of it," Jimmy said.

"True," Henry replied and climbed up into the trailer, then sat down, grunting slightly as he pulled his legs up and stood up. He was in the best shape of his life, but he was still a few years shy of fifty, and every now and then he felt it. "But it's what's in those boxes that matters, and if my guess is right, I know what's in them, too." He walked over to the first stack of boxes and ripped open the top, tossing the cardboard aside. Reaching into the box, he pulled out a small jar that fit nicely in his palm. Tossing it to Jimmy, he took out a few more.

Jimmy read the label and stared at the smiling face of the baby on the side of the jar. "Baby food? Seriously?"

"Sure, why not?" Henry asked. "It's got lots of vitamins, and as long as the caps aren't popped, the food within should be fine." He opened the jar of strained peas he was holding and poured the contents into his mouth. "See? Delicious." He smiled, his teeth now bright green."

"Yeah, and the best part it looks the same going in as it does going out." Jimmy cracked his own jar of strained carrots open and drank down the contents.

Henry began taking the boxes and carrying them to the edge of the trailer. He gestured to the others. "Here, carry these over to the first jeep, then to the second one, too. I want to load as much as we can, then when we can't fit any more boxes, start opening them and shoving the jars anywhere they'll fit."

For the next twenty minutes, no one spoke, concentrating on the task at hand. Only a quarter of the boxes were able to fit inside the jeeps, and that included putting the loose jars anywhere there was room. Henry even slid a few into his pockets and had the group do the same. No one complained, knowing the jars of baby food could mean the difference between life and death if food grew scarce.

"Okay, Henry," Sue said when they were all brimming with jars of food on their persons. "That's all we can hold."

"Uh-huh, we're not finished yet. Okay, everyone take some more of these and eat all you can. Before we leave here we should all be stuffed to the point we'll explode." He placed a few more boxes at the edge of the trailer and then jumped down as everyone began opening jars and eating their fill.

"Jesus, the beets taste terrible," Jimmy said, wincing as he swallowed the food. The inside of his mouth and inner lips were already stained red.

"You think those are bad, try the green beans," Mary added through a mouthful of just that.

"I just did, and you're right," Jimmy agreed. He looked at Henry. "Can I have some more of the peaches or maybe the pureed pears? Those weren't too bad."

Henry frowned. "Jimmy, I can't believe I have to tell you to actually eat your vegetables right now. Those veggies have a hell of a lot more vitamins than the fruit does. So eat up, you're a grow-ing boy."

"Not his mouth," Mary joked. "That's as big as it's going to get."

"Ha, ha, you're so funny, Mary," Jimmy pretend-laughed. "You should take that show on the road."

She stuck a green tongue out at him and he did the same, though his was bright red from the beets.

After that it grew quiet, each of the companions concentrating on filling their stomachs. Fingers were used to clean the sides of jars when the contents wouldn't come out.

It was late afternoon and Henry decided they might as well laager down where they were, rather than roll out and have to make camp in an unknown place later on when it became too dark to travel.

He ran it by the others, who all agreed it was a sound idea.

They made camp right by the trailer, with one of the group standing watch by roving around the parking lot surrounding the clubhouse. But with only one road in and nothing around for miles but an empty golf course, and no walking dead to worry about, the general consensus was that any surprises would come from the road.

Mary volunteered to stand first watch, and both Jimmy and Cindy, and Henry and Sue, paired off like always, with the younger couple going for a walk, Jimmy saying they planned on being a few hours. They'd taken a blanket with them, so Henry was pretty sure the couple would find a secluded spot within earshot, and would enjoy some alone time to reaffirm their devotion to one another. What they did with that time at the moment, Henry wondered, given that Cindy just had a miscarriage, he doubted if the couple would be fooling around anytime soon.

Henry picked the inside of the trailer as the perfect place to have some private time with Sue. After stacking a few boxes of baby food near the open doors, he spread out a blanket on the floor of the trailer, then tossed a few bags full of gear at the top of the blanket to use as pillows. There was still plenty of light to illuminate the interior and he went back to the exit and called over to Sue, who had been waiting near one of the jeeps.

"All set, you can come over now."

She walked over as he asked, Henry admiring the gentle sway of her hips, the way her full breasts shifted beneath her shirt. Around the same age, the pair were great friends, which is how their relationship had been when he'd first met her. Only later did they become lovers. There had been a time when Henry thought he would never love another woman, and he often thought how lucky he'd been to find Sue.

In many ways she looked a lot like Cindy, and in the old world, if the two had been out together, no doubt people would have assumed they were mother and daughter. About five-seven with an hourglass figure, and long blonde hair, Sue wasn't model-skinny. More voluptuous in many ways, she had never seen herself as a sex object and so was as grounded a person as far as looks went as someone could get.

Henry thought she was stunning, and had told her so many times. He loved the way she'd blush from the compliment. He helped her onto the trailer edge, pulling her up easily. But he used too much force and she flew into his arms.

"Whoa, slow down there, lover-boy. We'll get to it in a minute."

"I hope so," he replied. "Come see what I set up for us."

She walked around the boxes set up for privacy and smiled when she saw the makeshift bed. "Wow, Henry, you sure know how to spoil a girl, don't you."

He shrugged. "Hey, I made do with what I had to work with."

She leaned in and kissed him softly. "And you did a marvelous job. It's not the Ritz, but it'll work in a pinch." She moved past him and sat down, then laid her head on one of the gear bags. She stretched like a cat, her back arcing seductively, her breasts pushing outwards against her shirt. Henry smiled as he watched her. She didn't even know what she was doing, such was her innocence. All she thought she was doing was stretching; completely unaware it was ridiculously provocative.

"Come here," she said with a knowing smile.

He didn't need to be told twice.

In a heartbeat he was lying beside her, the two lovers staring into one another's eyes. For a few moments there was an awkward silence, as if the two had forgotten what to do. Such happened when too much time passed between their lovemaking. But like riding a bike, it took neither of them too long to get into the groove again.

Henry reached out and his right hand brushed a stray hair from her forehead, his callused fingers then caressing her cheek tenderly. He felt her shudder with the raw tension filling her and he smiled. Leaning inward to him, she picked up on his movement and did the same, their lips touching softly.

The kiss was gentle, caring, and when he pulled back from her, Henry saw her eyes were filled with sexual tension. He leaned in again and they kissed once more, her tongue sliding between his lips to caress his teeth. He opened his mouth to accept her advance, and the kiss became more passionate. Her hand slowly snaked down his chest, across his stomach, pulling his shirt out of his pants. Resting her hand on his warm skin, she caressed the curling tendrils of hair at his waist, only inches from his growing manhood.

"Looks like someone's awake done there," she said and nuzzled his neck. "Does little Henry want to come out and play?"

"You know I hate it when you call it that," he said, kissing her neck and sucking on an earlobe. "We're not teenagers, you know."

"And I'm glad of that. Teenagers don't know how to do it well. They just slam away at each other. No finesse. Now, when you get our age; we know how to take our time, really enjoy it."

He grinned. "I won't argue with you there." He began removing her shirt as she fiddled with his belt, wanting to take off his pants.

It wasn't often they were able to get completely naked. Normally, the best they could hope for was with pants down at their ankles, while they got a quickie in somewhere in the woods, usually with Sue standing up against a tree for support. It was a truly rare thing for them to feel safe enough to get nude, and so fully appreciate each other's bodies.

In a familiarity they both knew well, they quickly finished undressing, helping one another whenever possible.

Sue laid back on the blanket, naked, her hair flowing around her face. Henry had never thought she'd looked more beautiful than just then. Lying down beside her, they kissed once more, his hands roaming freely over her body as she too, took hold of his manhood and began slowly stroking him. His mouth soon moved down her body, and he began sucking on each nipple, feeling them harden beneath his tongue.

As his oral ministration continued, he used a free hand to slide it down her taut form, over her fluttering stomach, until stopping between her parted thighs. Quickly finding the tiny bud of flesh nestled there amongst the blonde matt of hair, he rolled it between his thumb and finger, eliciting a low moan of pleasure from her. Her continued rubbing, her breathing coming in short gasps, her eyes closed, her back arched. It didn't take long before she let out a higher-pitched moan and shuddered, her legs twitching as she basked in the afterglow of her orgasm.

Henry removed his hand from the juncture of her thighs but still continued to caress her breasts.

Suddenly she sat up, pushing him down to lay flat. "Now it's your turn," she breathed and knelt over his manhood. But then she stopped and peeked out of the falling hair draped over her face and said, "I wouldn't be doing this if you hadn't had that bath, you know."

"Don't I know it. I'm thanking God right now that the pond was there, believe me."

Then he gasped as she took him inside her mouth, Sue's head bobbing up and down in a slow, easy motion. She was good, and Henry had been amazed the first time she had tasted him, had sucked him until he'd reached a mind-blowing orgasm.

And she'd only gotten better since the first time they'd been together, as she now knew what he liked, and 'really' liked.

It didn't take long before he felt himself explode, Sue never removing her mouth from him, taking all of him, swallowing hard while continuing her bobbing motion.

When he became too sensitive to take it any longer, he squeezed her arm and she stopped, then crawled back up to him until she was lying by his side. She leaned in for a kiss but he balked, knowing what she'd just been doing and she laughed, but still forced a kiss on his cheek.

"That was nice," he said. "Thank you."

"You're very welcome, Mr. Watson, but I hope that's not all for the night. We don't get much time like this; we should make the most of it." She nuzzled his neck, her tongue flicking out and tasting him. She tried to give him a hickey and he stopped her, which made her laugh, and soon he was too. They lay together in the warm air, naked, sweating, their bodies intertwined, one of his hands cupping her ass, while his other hand caressed a breast, his fingers pinching the nipple playfully.

"Ouch, not too hard," she snapped, slapping his hand playfully.

He grinned and dialed back the pressure.

Fifteen minutes later, she sat up abruptly and Henry was about to jump up as well, assuming she'd heard something outside and they were in danger. But all she did was swing a leg over his chest until she was sitting on his stomach.

She grinned evilly at him, and he was about to ask what she was up to, when she slid her body closer so that her inner thighs were around his face. Knowing what she wanted, as it was painfully clear, he opened his mouth and began ministrations as she fully slid down on top of him.

Sue was soon bucking her hips and squeezing his face between her thighs to the point he was beginning to feel claustrophobic, despite the sexual arousal he felt simultaneously. He couldn't breathe, and each time he exhaled, his breath slapped him in the face, hot and stifling. For a few brief seconds it was actually pretty uncomfortable, like being smothered by a blanket. But still, he trudged onward like a good soldier, and in a few moments, Sue stopped squeezing his head and began shuddering. Then she slowly slid down his body so that she lying on top of him.

Her crotch was even with his waist and she slid a hand under her body and grabbed his rock-hard member.

"Well, well, looks like you're ready to go again. Not bad for an old man."

"I have my moments," he said proudly. "And be thankful for it 'cause it's not like I can pop down to the local drugstore for some Viagra."

She didn't reply, but instead grasped him and quickly guided him into her body. He gasped as the warmth seemed to fill him from head to toe, and for a few brief instances, his entire being was focused solely on his crotch.

Tightening herself around him, Sue began rocking up and down, the motion slowing building with each progression. Henry's hips rose to meet her, so that he penetrated deeper and deeper with each thrust. Gripping her by the arms, he pulled her to him, and they kissed passionately. She moved even faster, and he too, began thrusting upwards harder, until their bodies were slapping together loudly, flesh meeting flesh, raw passion unfiltered, until they were nothing but two animals feeding the naked lust for one another.

When she brought him to a raging orgasm, he would have sworn his entire body was going to explode from the release. Bursting inside her, even after he'd climaxed he managed to stay hard long enough for her to reach her peak and orgasm yet again.

Finally, with both of them feeling fulfilled, she rolled off him and they lay together in each other's arms.

Henry drifted off to sleep briefly, but never one to sleep heavily, knowing it was an easy way to get killed, he awoke soon after and dressed again, making sure his weapons were in place. If danger did arrive, the critical time it took to get dressed could mean the difference between life and death.

He looked down to see Sue had already dressed earlier when he'd been dozing and was still sleeping. Kneeling down on the makeshift bed, he kissed her forehead and whispered, "I love you," to her sleeping face.

Then he laid back down and was soon asleep again. But no sooner had he stretched out again, rolling over onto his side, then Sue's lips creased into a smile. She had been awake when Henry had stirred, but seeing he was only dressing, she'd closed her eyes and mimicked sleep.

Sue was glad she had, for Henry had told her something she had always known, but the man had been afraid to say, but now, when he thought he was unobserved, he'd actually said the words.

She reached out and wrapped her arm around him, her face going up against his back. He grunted in his sleep but didn't move.

Hugging the man she loved, Sue drifted back off to sleep.

Chapter 22

The sky was a clear blue, the sun rising more than an hour ago. Henry was startled awake by Jimmy banging on the side of the trailer.

"Come on, old man, get up! We got company coming!"

"Huh, what's going on?" Sue asked, opening her eyes

Henry had already jumped to his feet to move to leave the trailer. "I don't know. I'll see. You stay here until someone comes and gets you."

Sue stood up, fixing her clothes she wore. "Nothing doing. I'm not some little woman who needs to hide behind my man. I'm coming, too."

"Fair enough," he said and then was out the door and dropping down to the ground. The instant he left the trailer he caught the rough growl of multiple engines. Motorcycle engines if he was correct.

The others were near the jeeps and Henry joined them, Sue close behind Henry.

"What's going on?" he asked when Jimmy turned to face him.

"What's going on is we got about forty to fifty bikers coming right for us and there's no time to make a run for it."

"Well, how the hell did they get on top of us so fast?" Henry snapped.

Jimmy raised his hands in surrender. "They must have been here before because one second I was out front, just hanging out and keeping watch, and the next second there was a shitload of bikers riding up here."

The engines were louder now and there were only seconds before the vehicles would be on top of them.

"Maybe they won't come around back," Sue said hopefully. "Or we could hide until they leave."

Henry glanced at her as he hopped up onto the first jeep, swinging the M60 around and aiming it at the front of the parking lot, where he figured the bikers would appear first. Jimmy was doing the same in the second jeep.

"Wouldn't you do a full recce of this place before settling down for the day? We did. And once they see these jeeps they'll know their owners have to be close by." Henry made sure the M60 was primed and ready for action, Jimmy nodding that his was also war-ready.

"Oh, I didn't think of that," she replied. The rumble of the engines was growing louder by the second.

"Well, I did, and so did Jimmy and everyone else," Henry said and gestured for Sue to join him. "Now, come over here and get behind the jeep. Maybe we can talk our way out of this mess before it gets hairy." He patted the M60. "This time we have some negotiators to make sure our point of view is considered."

Then there was no time for talk as the bikers arrived, roaring onto the parking lot, more than half of them circling around the clubhouse to do a recce.

The noise was deafening, many of the engines having little to no mufflers. Birds flew shrieking from nearby trees, startled by the bedlam, and the very air seemed to tremble with the power of the motors.

The second the bikers spotted the two jeeps, and Henry and Jimmy armed with M60s on top, the riders slammed to a halt and weapons were pulled, while one of the men spun around to drive back to the others in front to notify them they weren't alone. With hands off throttles, the bikes only idled, but the noise was still too great for casual conversation.

"Oh shit, this doesn't look too good!" Jimmy yelled over the engines as he took in the biker gang.

Henry had to agree with him on that assumption. He counted around twenty men and women, all on a wide range of motorcycles. Though Harley-Davidson was the predominant choice, there was a smattering of Indians, Triumphs and Nortons, and even a handful of Gold Wings; one man drove what looked like a World War 2 motorcycle, painted a dull green, complete with a side-car combination. The rider looked old, well into his sixties, and when he smiled he only had a few teeth left. He wore an old Army helmet with a chrome spike embedded in the center; a pair of Aviator sunglasses covered his eyes.

The entire gang looked mean, like they would rip out a man's throat for looking at them wrong. All wore denim and leather jackets with a large skull either painted or embroidered on the material. The eye sockets of the skull, a deep black, had blood dripping from them, and a long-stemmed rose was clenched in the skull's teeth. Their pants were mostly denim as well, and the entire outfit looked about as filthy as a person could get. Their clothes looked like they had been dipped in vomit and shit, swirled around for a while, and then were re-donned. The hairstyles of most of the gang, be it man or woman, was either long hair down to their shoulders, or buzz cut so that they were almost bald. Most of the men had thick beards, but a few were clean-shaven. The gang was a multi-color of races, from black, to white, to Mexican and Asian.

From where they sat on the bikes, the odor of the gang wafted to the companions, who winced at the foul smell. The walking dead had given off a better aroma.

Every man and woman had pulled out a sidearm or some other weapon at the sight of the companions, and with engines idling at a dull roar, they sat on their bikes and waited for the command to fire.

A second later, more bikes came around the side of the building, adding to the cacophony of living sound, around fifteen or so by Henry's quick count. They also pulled up beside the others, mimicking the first group's actions.

"Just stay calm, guys," Henry told Jimmy and the women. "No one shoot until I do." He swiveled the M60 slowly from side to side. "Maybe we can get out of this without bloodshed for a change."

Jimmy snickered. "Yeah, fat chance of that ever happening."

"Well, there's a first time for everything, isn't there? Stop being so pessimistic."

One rider drove through the gang, weaving around each individual cycle until he was directly at the tip of the phalanx. Completely exposed if Henry wanted to shoot him, the man flaunted the fact that if anyone did, or tried to, the rest of his gang would rain hell on the two jeeps like there was no tomorrow.

Turning off his ignition, he slid off his bike, while a woman who had been riding 'bitch' remained seated. The bike was a powerful Harley Davidson Electra Glide, fully chromed from front to back, with saddle bags on everything from the handlebars, to over the rear tires, to the back end. The woman could remain seated, move around, even stretch out, and the machine would barely be nudged on its kickstand.

The man raised his arm and then brought it down like he was chopping wood, and all the engines were turned off as one. After the continuous blast of noise, the silence was almost as deafening as the revving engines.

"Who the fuck are you people?" the biker leader asked, his tone making it sound more like a command to answer than a question. "And give me one good reason why I don't fucking kill you right now." He was tall, a few inches over six feet, with dark black hair that hung to his shoulders. His skin was a dark tan, but not black or Mexican dark. Henry would have guessed the man was either full or part Indian. He had a scar on his right cheek that went from his mouth to just below his eye, which made him always look like that eye was squinting. He appeared to be in his late thirties or early forties. A cigarette hung from between his lips, smoking away. His chin was hidden by a goatee, and long sideburns rounded out his face.

He withdrew the cigarette and walked ten paces in front of his people, blowing smoke out of the corner of his mouth. His dark hair blew softly in the wind and Henry had to admit he had to give the guy credit for having courage. The man was either incredibly confident he wasn't going to get shot, or he was incredibly stupid at not seeing the danger he was in.

The M60s could mow down the gang in seconds, and though some of the bikers might get a few shots off, the devastation would be brutal for the enemy's side of the fight. Still, Henry didn't want to chance a battle if he didn't have to. At least he was negotiating from a position of power for a change.

"Shit, that guy has some big ones," Jimmy said out of the corner of his mouth.

"Quiet," Henry snapped.

"I said…" the biker leader asked again but Henry cut him off.

"I heard you the first time, and I could ask the same thing of you."

"Sure you could, but I ain't sayin' shit till you tell me who you are and what the fuck you're doing here." He flicked the still-lit cigarette away from him, the butt rolling across the parking lot.

"You should step on those when you're done with them," Henry stated. "That's a good way to start a fire. No Fire Departments around anymore, you know."

"Oh, so you're with the fucking Forest Service, is that it? You go around with those big guns preventing forest fires?"

"No, not exactly," Henry replied with a grin.

A few bikers behind the leader grew agitated and talk began. These members wanted to shoot the strangers and take their stuff, in that order. They didn't understand what all the talk was for.

The gang leader turned around and looked at the faces of the men and women he knew were causing discourse. "Any of you fuckers got a problem with how I'm dealing with this shit, fucking tell me to my face. Don't whisper behind my back like a bunch of old women. You get me?"

Most of the gang lowered their eyes, not making eye contact. Satisfied his men were cowed for the moment, he turned back to Henry and the others.

"Like I was saying, man, you better tell me what the fuck you're doing here or this shit is gonna get ugly."

"Yes it will, but I promise you it'll be your people who get the worst of it."

"How the fuck do I know if those meat-grinders even work? Shit, man, for all I know they're just there for show."

"You need proof, is that it?" Henry asked.

"Sure as fuck do, man."

"Okay, don't anyone shoot, see where the barrel's pointing?" Henry swiveled the M60 upwards to the sky and let off a quick burst. The M60 echoed across the parking lot, the sound telling everyone the guns worked fine, the empty shell casings tinkling as they fell around Henry's feet.

"Shit, man, I guess those fuckers do work. But it still don't change shit." The biker leader took a step closer. "I asked you a question and I still don't have an answer."

Henry swiveled the smoking barrel of the M60 around so it was once more aimed at the biker leader, then he smiled widely.

"Okay, don't take this as a sign of weakness, but for the sake of ending this peacefully, I'm willing to go first." He quickly went through the roster of his group, showing everyone to the bikers, more than one of the gang whistling like wolves when the women were introduced.

The gang leader turned and glared at his people, silencing them immediately.

Henry didn't know why, but despite the bravado, he liked the guy standing before him. He couldn't put his finger on it, but the man didn't seem to be a total scumbag, despite his outward appearance.

"And we're not doing anything here that matters. We just picked this spot at random to make camp for the night. If you'll let us go peacefully, we'll leave now and we can be done with one another."

The gang leader nodded when Henry finished, then said, "Okay, man, your story holds water in my book, but you can't just fucking leave."

"Why the fuck not?" Jimmy interjected.

"Because we want your women, that's why fucking not."

"Is this guy serious, Henry?" Jimmy asked, his grip growing tighter on the handles of the M60. The ammunition belts gleamed in the sunlight, ready to be instantly fed into the weapons.

"You can't have our women, and we'll kill every damn one of you to make sure that doesn't happen," Henry said flatly, deciding he didn't like the gang leader as much as he first thought. So much for first impressions.

"You might think so but I bet you we get to you before you get us," the leader replied, then with a wave of his hands his men behind him left their bikes and began to spread out more, so that Jimmy and Henry didn't have grouped targets anymore.

Henry saw this and yelled, "Don't anyone move or this is gonna get bloody real fast!" His warning was ignored.

Henry aimed the M60 over the bikers' heads and fired a quick burst, sending the gang scattering even more.

A few rounds began to return fire but the biker leader never moved a muscle, and after a few seconds, he got his men to hold their fire. Henry had thought that the talking part was over and was relieved the leader had regained control of his men. A lesser man would never have been able to stop his people from attacking, and Henry had to admit the guy ran a tight ship.

Knowing that, Henry came up with an idea, and though he didn't know if it would work, he gave it a try anyway.

"How about instead of you taking our women by force and a lot of people getting killed on both sides, my people and I join your gang instead?" His suggestion was greeted by laughs from a lot of the gang.

"Come on, Vincent, let's kill these assholes and be done with it!" a man called behind the leader.

Vincent turned and locked eyes with the man who'd spoken up, the man actually taking a step backwards from the powerful force of the gaze. Then he turned his eyes back onto Henry. "What the fuck do you know about being in a biker gang, man? We're the Skullfuckers and we've been surviving all across Nevada since the dead began walking around like they owned this country. Now they're gone and we're taking back what's ours." He sneered with disdain. "You don't just join our chapter by asking, man. You need to prove yourself first."

"Okay, Vincent, what do I have to do?" Henry asked, using the man's name now that he knew it. "Let me guess, I have to fight you or some macho shit like that. Am I right?"

Vincent smiled. "Sort of right, man. You need to fight to the death with one of my brothers, my champion. You win that fight and as the leader of your people, I'll let you all become Prospects."

"Okay, sounds fair. But what if I lose?"

"Then you die and we kill the other guy"—he pointed to Jimmy—"and then we pull a train on each of your women before they join my chapter as mamas."

"What's a mama?" Cindy called out.

Vincent kicked a pebble with his boot. "We got two types in our chapter for women, sweetcheeks. We got old ladies and mamas. Old ladies means you're with one guy, and no one else can touch you but that guy. Mamas are property of the entire chapter, and anyone can fuck you any time, whenever they want to. You can't say no, not ever."

"Hey, Henry, you're not really serious about this shit, are you?" Jimmy asked.

Henry looked at Jimmy in the next jeep. "Yes, I am," he said in a soft tone so his voice wouldn't carry. "I can take Vincent, or I think I can." He lowered his voice even more. "Look over to the left and right, at the people there. They have grenades, Jimmy. We can't shoot everyone before some of those fly at us. We don't win if we're dead. Maybe this is a chance to get us out of this predicament and then later, we can sneak off when no one's looking."

Sue reached up and touched Henry's arm. "But what about if he kills you? What then?"

"Then I'm dead and the rest of you can pretend you're okay with what he said and make a break for it whenever possible." He looked at each of them, making eye contact briefly. "Look, people, we're in a shitty situation and there are no good options, but there are still options nonetheless."

"Well, what the fuck's your answer?" Vincent called. "My men are itching for a fight. Whether it be a brawl or a gunfight, it's all the same to them."

"If I agree to this, you give your word if I win that my people and I can join you and no one else will be harmed?"

Vincent looked offended. "You calling me a fucking liar, man? No one does that." He turned to his gang and yelled, "You hear that shit, guys? Fucker doesn't think I'll keep my word."

More than two dozen of the gang began yelling taunts at Henry, angry their leader's integrity was being questioned.

Vincent turned back to Henry and walked closer, so that he was less than ten feet away. If a firefight broke out, Vincent would be the first to die.

"I'm the President of my charter, man, and my word is my bond. No one gets where I am without being two things. A hardcore motherfucker and someone whose word is gold." He crossed his arms over his powerful chest. "If I give my word on something, that shit happens. I swear it on my life. You don't believe me, then blow me the fuck away now and let's end this shit. Tell ya the truth, man, this is all getting old. And I need to take a piss. We'd been riding for hours before we decided to chill here. So either let's start shootin' or let's shake hands and have us a brawl."

Henry gave Jimmy a look that said he'd made up his mind, and before anyone could stop him, Henry jumped off the jeep and crossed the short distance separating himself from Vincent.

Now was the time for betrayal, and Henry tensed, waiting to see if Vincent was true to his word or a liar. All the lives of the companions were riding on that one single thing.

Henry reached Vincent and looked up at the scarred face a few inches above his, then he held out his right hand for the biker leader to shake. "Okay, I agree to your terms. So, when do we fight?"

Vincent turned and waved to his people. "We've come to terms. Everyone lower your pieces! It's all good. Looks like we've got some potential Prospects." He pointed to the man who'd wanted to start shooting earlier. "Wolf, set up camp, we're gonna be here for at least a day while we sort all this shit out."

Wolf began yelling at members, and more than half mounted their bikes and drove them off to the side, each one backing in and lining them up in neat rows.

Two large cargo vans, used for transporting food, tools, weapons, and doubling as carriers if a motorcycle broke down on the rode and couldn't be fixed, or if a member couldn't ride from an injury, were parked at the far end of the lot.

Meanwhile, mamas and old ladies both began unpacking supplies from overstuffed saddle bags tied to the sides and backs of the bikes. When one of the members found the trailer of baby food, he let out a yell for others to join him. Within minutes, half the remaining boxes of food were offloaded and sitting in the parking lot, a lot of members already scarfing the food down greedily.

The tension was passed, at least as far as the bikers were concerned, and no one paid Jimmy or the other companions the slightest bit of attention, with the exception of the men eyeing Sue, Mary and Cindy in the hopes of screwing them later.

Eventually, Jimmy left the M60 he'd been manning, though he didn't go too far from the jeeps at any given time. Outnumbered more than four to one, the M60s were the only equalizers any of the companions had.

Beer was unpacked by the bikers, and Henry was handed one, and though it was warm, it tasted like the sweetest nectar to him.

As he and Vincent talked, he found it odd that soon he would be fighting the man to the death, and so he couldn't help but bring the subject up once more, wanting to know more about how it would go, the rules, weapons used, and any other relevant facts.

Vincent laughed when Henry inquired, and after telling a few other brothers, they all began laughing. Henry frowned, knowing the joke was at his expense. The rest of the companions were close by, all within eyesight. Each would continually look to Henry and then each other, waiting for a sign that things were going bad. But true to Vincent's word, once the gang knew a truce had been made, they now looked at the companions as allies, if not actual friends.

The companions were ignored by most of the members, as well, and Sue and Mary found it odd as some of the members and their old ladies began screwing right there where they'd made camp, nothing but a blanket spread out on the dead grass at the side of the clubhouse parking lot. Many of the women were in what appeared to be gang bangs, where they were taking a member with both mouth and other orifices simultaneously.

"It's like Woodstock around here," Sue told Mary as the two women stood off to the side, amazed at the total lack of inhibitions.

Henry had gotten tired of everyone laughing at a joke he didn't know so he forced Vincent to let him in on what was so damned funny.

"What's so fucking funny, Henry, is that you think you're fighting me, but if you think back, I never said it was me you'd be fighting. I said you'd fight the chapter's 'champion'."

"Oh, okay, then who's that?" he asked, figuring if Vincent was the President and ran the outfit, then the champion couldn't be too much harder to beat.

Laughing so hard he had beer dripping from his nose, Vincent turned, looked around for a moment, then pointed to someone at the far end of the lot where they'd made camp. "He's over there."

He pointed at a man who looked to be around five feet tall, his head seen through the other members who were all standing around.

Jimmy had sidled up beside Henry and had overheard the conversation, and he also saw the man Vincent was pointing to. "He doesn't look too tough," Jimmy said.

Vincent cupped his hands to his mouth and yelled, "Hey, Foulmouth, get over here and meet the guy you're fighting later!"

"Why do you call him that?" Jimmy asked.

"Because he suffers from Halitosis and ulcerous gingivitis, man, that's why. Worst case I've ever seen, now and before the world went to shit. The dude's mouth is a fucking mess." Vincent grinned knowingly. "And he's bi, that is he likes to fuck both chicks and dudes, so before he kills someone he makes sure to give them a long kiss goodbye. Tongue and all, man. It's fucking nasty."

Henry watched as the head of the man he thought was standing, but who had only been kneeling, slowly rose almost three more feet, until he was towering over the other members of the gang. Turning, the man-mountain began walking towards Vincent, Henry, and Jimmy.

By the time the giant reached the three men, both Henry and Jimmy were staring upwards at the mountain of flesh and muscle before them. The guy was huge, weighing at least two hundred and eighty pounds, and though a lot of it was fat, there was also hard muscle rolling around beneath the blubber. He was a mix of black and white, so his skin gave him more of a perpetual tan look. His hair was long, hanging well past his shoulders, and it was died bone white; he had a beard cut so close to his face that it was hard to tell what color it was, but brown or black would be someone's first guess.

The eyes, though not dull, did not sparkle with high intelligence, and it was obvious that though a powerful man physically, he didn't have the will or skill to be the president of the chapter. He was the weapon Vincent used to rule, however.

Foulmouth smiled widely with an open mouth, and the instant he did, an odor of raw sewage wafted from his parted lips, making everyone in the area gag. It might have been Henry's imagination, but he thought he saw a fly buzz too close to that gaping maw and seize up in mid-flight, dead instantly.

"Close your fucking mouth, man, before you kill us all," Vincent barked; obviously this was an issue he'd addressed in the past.

Foulmouth did as he was told.

"Okay, you can go now," the President of the chapter ordered.

Foulmouth nodded and walked away, like a small child being told to go to his room, not saying a word.

Jimmy cast a long glance at Henry, his eyes still wide in amazement at the sheer size of Henry's opponent, knowing that if Henry lost, Jimmy would be next to die before the girls were absorbed into the charter. "Shit, old man, we're both so fucking dead it hurts."

Chapter 23

"I mean it, Henry," Jimmy said. "You know the saying 'we need a bigger boat?' well, we don't just need a bigger boat, we need a bigger everything that matters! What the fuck were you thinking? That guy's gonna kill you—and then they're gonna kill me, too! Shit, at least we had a chance of taking some of the bastards with us, but now…"

"Thanks for the support, Jimmy, makes me feel a whole lot better," Henry stated as the women joined them in the midst of the camp. Vincent had left Henry alone for a while, the biker leader going off with his old lady for some fun. "How you guys doing? Anyone messing with you?" he asked the girls, his eyes mostly focused on Mary.

"A few have tried making passes at us," Mary explained, "but nothing we can't handle."

Cindy agreed. "I had to stick my hunting knife in some creep's stomach to get him to back off, and Mary had to do the same with her .38, and one of the biker chicks made a play for Sue, of all things, but we can handle ourselves."

Henry smiled, knowing the capabilities of the women he traveled with. "I have no doubt."

"Look, Henry," Jimmy continued, "we need to get in our jeeps and just blast our way outta here. Take our chances. It's a hell of a lot better than staying around here."

"Jimmy, look over to your right. See that guy with the Mohawk? Then turn to your left; the guy with the red scarf around his neck?"

Jimmy tried to be nonchalant about it but Henry told him not to bother. "They don't care if we know they're watching us. They've been with us since Vincent first accepted my challenge."

He gestured to two other bikers standing five feet away, both cradling SMG's in their arms. "Those guys are on us, too. We even try and move to the jeeps and we're gonna get an ass full of lead for our trouble."

"Well," Cindy interjected, changing the subject. "If anyone wants to know; I found out what pulling a train means."

"What? Tell us?" Jimmy asked, curious.

Cindy wasn't smiling, and she made eye contact with Sue and Mary as well before responding. "It means were basically raped by the entire gang one at a time, or maybe all at once. They force us down and one at a time, men or women, can screw us however they want, in any hole they want."

Jimmy raised a fist, his face scrunching up in anger. "What? No fucking way is that gonna happen to my Cindy. I'll kill them all first?"

"Thanks for the offer, Jimmy," Cindy said, "but you forget this is 'after' they've killed you to make sure you can't do exactly what you just said."

Henry went over to Sue, who had been standing silently while the others talked. He wrapped an arm around her and she moved in close, hugging him tightly.

"You haven't said anything yet," he stated. "How you doing?"

All around them, the bikers yelled and laughed, some fighting with one another. In one corner of the camp was a small orgy, and in another, a tent had been erected where Vincent and his old lady had retired to.

The odor of cooking meat filled the air. Another time, another place, the camp would have resembled a biker rally, where groups from all over the country gathered to race, blow off steam, and catch up with old friends.

But with every man and woman armed to the teeth, it was very clear the days of old were over.

Sue pulled away from Henry slightly and she looked up into his eyes. "I've been better. I keep trying to get the image of that monster of a man you'll be fighting out of my mind. I heard some people talking. He's never lost a fight—ever." She sighed heavily, and it turned into a small sob but she forced it away. "I wish we could go back to last night, just you and me inside that trailer."

He brushed hair from her face and kissed her gently, and despite being surrounded on all sides by an army of killers, for one brief moment, it was just her and him.

"Yeah, me too, but the past is gone. We only have today."

"But…but what will you do?" she asked, referring to the upcoming fight.

Henry's face grew hard, his eyes creasing slightly. "It's simple. I don't know how, but I'm gonna kill him."

The rest of the day the companions were left alone—with the exception of their escort, that is. Henry and Jimmy had made a casual play to reach the jeeps, but were quickly blocked by some of the bikers. Smiling like they were old friends at the men, the two warriors had turned and moved away, like it was no big deal.

"See, Jimmy, I told you they won't let us near the jeeps."

"Well, we tried at least," Jimmy replied. He fingered his 12-gauge hanging by a lanyard over his shoulder. "At least they let us keep our weapons, which I find stupid on their part."

Henry shook his head, his hand going down to touch the holster of his Glock for reassurance it was still there. "No, Vincent knows exactly what he's doing. He wants to let us know without saying a word that he's not scared of us. In fact, he's so not intimidated that he let us keep our stuff."

"Yeah, but we could take out a shitload of their people before they got us all," Jimmy commented.

"Sure, but you're forgetting one thing, Jimmy."

"Yeah, what's that?"

"These people don't fear death, and in fact they revel in it. That's why they're stronger than ever now that the dead are gone. Even before the world collapsed, people like this were outside the fringe of civilization. I bet their lives haven't even changed that much since the dead started walking around. Hell, I bet their lives have actually been 'easier' since it all happened. After all, no more police to hassle them, no more towns where they get forced out." He sighed. "No way, Jimmy. These people were made perfectly for the world we now live in. Maybe even better than us and the girls." He glanced over to the jeeps, which so far had been untouched. "At least Vincent's as good as his word. No one's gone near the jeeps at all. If I win the fight, we get to keep all our equipment, which means we have a better chance of escaping later."

"You really think you can take that guy?"

Henry shrugged. "I've fought bigger. You remember that giant, eight-foot deader I had to fight in that arena?"

"Yeah, Henry, but that thing was dead, it didn't think like a man. That guy, what's his name, Foulmouth. He might not be the brightest guy in the world, but he still thinks like a human, and the guy obviously knows how to fight."

Henry ground his teeth as he considered Jimmy's words. Would he have committed to the challenge if he'd known he had to fight Foulmouth? He didn't truly know.

Jimmy was still waiting for an answer, and when none was provided, he nudged Henry in the arm. "Well, old man, what're you gonna do?"

Henry was pulled out of his thoughts and he turned and faced Jimmy, his eyes cold. "Like I told Sue, somehow, some way, I'm going to beat him."

* * *

The sun was just beginning to set when Vincent had all the companions gathered together in the parking lot behind the clubhouse. Off to the side, the trailer sat empty, the entire supply of baby food either eaten or destroyed by the Skullfuckers.

Small splotches of assorted colors covered the lot in many areas, the remnants of the smashed baby food jars.

The Skullfuckers liked to destroy things, and they didn't think too far ahead on where their next meal would be coming from. All that wasted food could have fed the chapter for an entire week.

Vincent sat on a makeshift throne cobbled together from wood taken from the clubhouse, his old lady standing on his right. Before the throne, head-sized rocks had been taken from the golf course and set up to make a circle roughly twenty feet in diameter.

Henry had seen the activity earlier.

They'd been making a half-ass arena for the upcoming fight.

Without warning, Henry was shoved hard from behind, so that he nearly flew into the circle. He landed hard, but he rolled with it, coming up in a crouch, on one knee. Standing up, he wiped his pants off where gravel had become embedded.

"Henry!" Sue called out, frightened when he was thrown from her.

"I'm fine, Sue, stay back, all of you."

"That's good advice," Vincent said from his throne. He stood up, his hands going into the air to quiet down the chapter, who were all gathered around the circle, smoking, drinking and doing whatever the hell they felt like.

"My brothers, and all the old ladies and mamas, we're here tonight to see some blood spilled. One motherfucker is gonna die in this circle, and I think we all know who it's gonna be!"

The gang roared with bloodlust, yelling and spitting in their passion to see blood spilt.

Vincent let them shout for a full minute before raising his hands for silence. "But let's be fair here, brothers. The challenge has been cast and we'll do it the way it's been written down in the bylines of our chapter. We, The Skullfuckers out of Las Vegas, Nevada, accept this man, Henry Watson, and the rest of his people as fucking Prospects if he wins the fight tonight!" A few people hooted and booed but most applauded. Accepting new blood was a necessary practice; the charter needed to keep their numbers up. Every now and then a skirmish with cannies, or slavers or some baron's forces would shrink their numbers down, and only accepting Prospects built the gang back up to a decent fighting force.

Vincent pointed to Henry. "Lose the piece and pig sticker, man. You're not fighting with those."

Henry knew it wasn't a request and he waved Jimmy to come over; he handed the younger man his weapons.

"Good luck, Henry, we're counting on you," Jimmy said, then stepped back out of the ring.

Foulmouth appeared from the far side of the circle; he stepped over the circular line of rocks to cheers and applause. His chest was bare, his white hair tied back in a ponytail. In one hand he held a long drive-chain from a motorcycle, and in his left was a ten-inch Nazi bayonet with a white bone handle, the tip hooked like an eagle's beak, the edge sharpened to perfection on only one side. "I'm gonna gut ya good, ya little bitch, then I'm gonna fuck the shit out of your woman." He smiled, showing off his rotting teeth and gums. His voice sounded like gravel being ground together, and it bellowed across the circle as if it was hooked up to a speaker system. "When it's my turn when we do a train on her, I'm gonna make sure to be the first one to fuck her in the ass!"

The other bikers laughed at this, cheering their champion on.

Henry couldn't help but glance at Sue, who had her hands to her mouth in terror, imagining what would happen to her if Henry lost. And seeing the giant of a man Henry had to battle up close, though terrified for Henry, a part of her was also frightened for her own survival.

Mary and Cindy had the same look of terror, knowing all they could do was pray Henry somehow came out on top.

Meanwhile, Jimmy was taken from the women, to be brought to the top of the circle, to stand beside Vincent's throne. The throne was set high off the ground by three feet, so though sitting, the President of the chapter was even with Jimmy when Vincent looked at him.

Jimmy opened his mouth to say something to Vincent, but before he could illicit so much as a syllable, he was forced to kneel on the ground, and a knife was placed at his throat, his shotgun, .45, and hunting knife stripped away.

"The second you lose, Watson, the kid dies, then we have some fun with your women."

More hoots and cheers were chanted as the bikers got excited for the orgy to come.

Mary, Cindy, and Sue moved close together as they were corralled by ten bikers, who quickly stripped them of any weapons.

When Henry saw this an eyebrow went up in curiosity, and Vincent commented on the unasked question.

"That's just to make sure no one gets any ideas, man," Vincent explained. "We've had chicks either shoot at anyone they can hit before killing themselves or they just commit suicide like fucking cowards so they don't get caught up in a train. Not that it mattered much. A lot of the brothers don't care if there's an extra hole in a chick's head, not if the body's still warm. Am I right, bros?"

More catcalls and laughter filled the air.

"Shit, we got us a few sick fucks who would actually fucking prefer it!"

More yells and screams, the gang knowing what Vincent said was true.

Henry walked a few feet closer to Vincent, now only able to see by the bonfires burning in the parking lot. With their numbers, the bikers could take on any gang of cannies or scavengers stupid enough to mess with them, so they did nothing to hide their camp.

Off to the side, Foulmouth swung the chain back and forth, getting ready for his fifteen minutes of fame with the chapter. He wasn't the most popular person in the gang, but when he killed a potential Prospect and got the chapter more women legally, like in this particular case, according to the bylines, he was always welcomed to party with the chapter President and Vice President for a night.

Sometimes, when Vincent was really, really drunk and horny, and his old lady was passed out from partying too hard, he would even let Foulmouth give him a blow job. It didn't happen too often, but Foulmouth always looked forward to it when it occurred.

"You act like the result of this fight is already fixed," Henry said. "But you're forgetting your promise if I win."

All the bikers laughed, and Vincent smiled widely. "My word is fucking gold, man. You somehow be the first one to beat Foulmouth, and you're in the chapter, all of you." He gestured to Jimmy. "But the second Foulmouth takes you out, your man here's a dead man. We don't want him trying anything crazy to save his woman, or anyone else for that matter." He locked eyes with Jimmy. "Sorry, little bro, it's nothing personal, but business is business."

Jimmy blinked at that and said, "Oh, no, Vincent, I totally understand. I wouldn't want my living to become an issue for you."

"Glad to see you understand."

"Oh, and Vincent?" Jimmy called.

"Yeah, man?"

"You can go fuck yourself."

Vincent only smiled, then pointed to Foulmouth. "Okay, man, it's time."

"Wait a second!" Henry yelled. "You took my knife and gun, and fatso here's got a blade and a chain. Don't I get the same?"

Vincent frowned deeply, and began to look as if he was deep in thought. "Oh shit, man, you mean no one gave you any?"

"No, you know that," Henry said, crossing his arms.

"Well then, man, I guess it's hard-fucking-luck for you, fucker."

"What?" Jimmy yelled. "But that's not fair!"

"Life's not fair, asshole," Vincent replied with a sinister grin. Then he raised his right fist and snapped it downward. "Let the fight begin!"

Chapter 24

The instant Vincent started the fight, Foulmouth charged Henry like a locomotive, the drive-chain swinging over his head so fast it was a blur.

Henry was expecting it, and as the giant of a man came at him, Henry pivoted on his right foot and dashed to the aside, the chain missing his head by inches.

Foulmouth couldn't stop, however, his inertia so large that he needed distance and time to pull his body back under control, and by the time he did, Henry was on the opposite side of the circle once more.

All around the circle, the chanting and catcalls continued, most yelling for blood to be spilt—Henry's blood.

Only Jimmy and the women cheered for Henry, doing their best to show him moral support.

Henry watched Foulmouth's eyes, but not just those. A good fighter wouldn't let his eyes give him away, and if the massive biker had won all his fights, he had to be a good fighter. So Henry also studied Foulmouth's entire body, looking for a sign of the next attack.

He didn't have to wait long.

No sooner had Henry reached the far side of the circle, then Foulmouth was coming at him again.

But this time Henry was more prepared, and as his enemy pulled his arm back to swing the drive-chain and begin running forwards, Henry did the same thing, dashing straight at Foulmouth.

Before Foulmouth could bring his arm around to slash Henry with the chain, Henry was there, within the blow, so that the chain came down on empty air. At the same time, Henry parried the hand holding the bayonet, while jabbing a fist straight into the biker's groin.

But just as Henry expected, Foulmouth was a damn good fighter, and he shifted a hip to block Henry from hitting his privates, the hip taking up most of the force from the blow.

As the two men separated, Henry running to the far end of the circle, the drive-chain caught him a glancing blow in the center of his shoulders, causing him to stumble. But he made it to the far side a moment later and stood up and faced his enemy. A hand went around to his back, fingers touching the torn shirt and the wound beneath. His fingertips came back wet with blood, but not too much. As wounds go it was about as bad as scraping his back on something by accident.

"First blood goes to Foulmouth!" Vincent screamed, one hand holding a beer. While Henry was fighting for his life, the bikers were having a party.

Foulmouth didn't come charging in this time, but held back, moving sideways, Henry doing the same.

When Henry made eye contact with the large man he saw a hint of concern where there had been none, and at least there was now a mutual respect between the fighters.

Then Foulmouth came at Henry again, moving faster than his bulk should allow. This time he weaved the drive-chain in a figure eight before him, while the other hand prepared the bayonet by holding it point up, ready for a gutting blow.

Henry's mind was working on overtime, as he weighed the pros and cons of his enemy. The man was big, too big to grapple with, so he couldn't take him down by getting too close.

No, he needed to strike like a Cobra and then back off, for if Foulmouth locked his hands on Henry, it was possible there would be no breaking free.

Henry needed to slow the man down a bit, so he couldn't keep charging across the circle like a rampaging bull. That was when his eyes dropped down to Foulmouth's legs, and more specifically, the man's knees.

The knee joint was one of the most delicate parts of the human body, the delicate musculature vulnerable to attack, and the sheer size of a man didn't matter when it came to the knee joints.

In the movies, when the hero knocked the bad guy through a window with a punch to the jaw, he then took his time strolling out onto the street to finish the job, which usually gave the bad guy time to gather himself.

Not so in real life; after that first blow was thrown, the second punch was already being considered, and it would come a moment later, thus giving the bad guy no time to gather himself. It was that vital half-second of thinking ahead, letting reflexes take over to carry the person through what he was doing first, 'and' what he'd be doing in a moment, that was the difference between winning and losing.

Foulmouth was on him a moment later, and Henry dropped down to the ground, feinting right at the same time. The drive-chain swished over his head, missing him by a full twelve inches.

He hit the ground arms first, and used them like levers, so that he pushed up off the ground and swung his right foot around and kicked at the bayonet, blocking the thrust aimed at him. Then still on the ground, Henry spun around so that Foulmouth was directly in front of him, and as the chain rose high to come crashing down on his head, Henry snap-kicked out with his right boot, the sole connecting solidly with Foulmouth's left kneecap.

The fragile joint collapsed under the force of the kick. The bottom of the femur was splintered, cartilage rupturing and displacing the patella, which was a tiny, crucial bone directly in the center of the knee.

The result was instantaneous.

Foulmouth stumbled away, a high-pitched scream coming from his mouth, the chain coming down on empty air. He toppled to the ground and grabbed his shattered knee, his shrieks only going louder in pitch.

Henry was about to charge at the fallen man and end it fast when he was grabbed from outside the circle by a couple of bikers, who booed and jeered at him, angry their champion had been taken down. Held fast, Henry couldn't break free of the men holding him.

The sound of an SMG erupted, cutting through the din, the reports of the rounds making the men let Henry go.

"I see another man touch one of the fighters and they're fucking dead!" Vincent warned, waving the SMG in the bikers' vicinity, which was enough to make them step away from the circle.

With the chance of attacking unhindered stopped, Henry was hesitant to take a run at Foulmouth, now that the man had been given a chance to recover. So he moved as far away from Foulmouth as possible and took in the situation. He felt emboldened now. The blow to the biker's knee had felt good, felt right. Like crushing an egg, the knee had given under his boot sole. That should slow the behemoth down, if not outright stop him in his tracks.

Maybe now Henry had a chance of coming out of this thing alive.

But it was far from over, and Foulmouth began moving again, though he was still whimpering like a wounded animal.

But that was when animals were at their most threatening, when cornered and wounded. Even with his shattered knee, if Foulmouth got his hands on Henry, he could snap Henry's neck in an instant.

Henry glanced down at Foulmouth's knee to see it wasn't doing too well. The knee looked like it would come completely apart at any moment, the way the lower leg was sort of hanging there under the material of the man's pants.

He prayed the biker wouldn't get fully up, that he was down for good. Deciding it was time to see how he was, Henry moved a little closer and called, "Hey, Foulmouth, what say when this fight's over, you and me go for a walk and talk all this out, huh?"

Foulmouth stopped whimpering and turned to glare at Henry, then gave up trying to stand and dragged himself into the center of the circle.

Sitting upright, he waved Henry to come to him, his face a mask of anger and pain.

Henry glanced over at Vincent who shook his head, that no, the fight wasn't over.

"Someone has to die, Watson, not just get hurt. You need to finish the fucker off if you think you can."

"He can do it," Jimmy said to Vincent. "That asshole's down for the count."

"We'll see," Vincent said with a smile. He had to admit he didn't expect the fight to go the way it had. His champion was down, but not out, and though the fight was far from over, it didn't look too good for Foulmouth.

Henry was circling Foulmouth, making sure to stay about nine feet away so that he couldn't be hit with the swinging drive-chain.

All around the circle, the bikers were going wild, angry that their hero had been taken down by such a smaller man.

"Kill him, Henry! Do it for me! Please!" Sue screamed, wanting to see Foulmouth dead like nothing she'd ever experienced in her life. The alternative was too much to bear. Henry and Jimmy killed, then herself and the other women used as sex slaves. Henry had to win, and if he needed to kill the disgusting biker, then so be it. Beside her, Mary and Cindy yelled similar words of encouragement.

Henry kept circling the wounded man, who spit curses at Henry repeatedly and tried to keep an eye on his attacker while lashing out with the drive-chain. It would whistle through the air to slap the ground, to then be pulled back for another try.

"Wow, those are some swears there. I guess there's another reason why they call you Foulmouth, eh?" Henry joked, wanting to get the man to lose his temper and drop his guard. Wounded, and somewhat helpless, and all of it happening before his fellow bikers, the humiliation the man felt must have been incredible.

Henry reached around and touched his shoulder, the blood coming back sticky and tacky. The wound had stopped bleeding already, which was a relief.

Turning painfully, Foulmouth lashed out again with the chain, the tip missing Henry by almost a foot.

"Hah, you missed me," Henry laughed. "Not so tough now, are you, you ugly bastard." He grinned widely. "Even if you kill me now, I doubt you'll be dancing on that knee anytime soon; more like forever actually." He paused then added, "Shit, you'll probably never stand again without crutches, and so much for riding a motorcycle."

"You come over here where I can grab you and we'll see who's gonna be dancing later, you little fucker," Foulmouth hissed, spittle flying from his lips.

"Let's get this fucking show moving, guys, or you're both dead and that's that!" Vincent yelled, the threat apparent. There would be no dragging it out. The bikers wanted action, not talk. If Henry didn't finish the fight, he would be shot anyway.

Henry had an idea and began putting it into motion. He began running around the stricken man, moving faster with each revolution.

Swiveling painfully around, Foulmouth did his best to keep up with Henry's position, knowing the man was up to something.

Suddenly, the bikers stopped yelling, cheering and booing, as if they sensed the penultimate chapter of the battle was about to come down. Only Henry's boots crunching in the gravel of the parking lot could be heard.

Henry needed to take out the chain hand first, and he watched Foulmouth as he raced around the fallen man. His goal was to tire the brute out, who if he hadn't already, would soon go into shock from the destroyed knee.

Round and round Henry went, making Foulmouth dizzy from having to constantly keep turning with his foe. Henry watched the arm with the chain closely, then moved in closer, knowing Foulmouth saw it, too. But Henry had done it in such a way that Foulmouth wouldn't know that Henry had done it on purpose, that it wasn't a lapse in judgment.

Thinking he had his foe unawares, Foulmouth pushed up with the hand holding the bayonet to raise his body, as the one holding the chain came up and around like the chain was a whip.

Henry was ready for it, and the instant he saw the movement of Foulmouth pushing up off the ground, he swiveled on his heels and came at Foulmouth full on.

The wounded man was committed to his actions, and though slower now from his shattered knee, he couldn't stop in time.

Like before, Henry was too quick for the larger man, and as the chain came up and down, Henry had already darted to the right, the chain only slapping the ground harmlessly.

Pivoting on his right foot, Henry kicked out again, the toe of his boot connecting with Foulmouth's wrist.

The radius and ulna were both shattered under the pressure of the blow and the hand opened, the chain flying off and away.

Henry jumped backwards out of the way instantly, and still almost didn't make it, as the knife hand came slashing around to gut him. The blade missed him by less than an inch. But an inch or a foot, a miss was a miss.

Foulmouth dropped limply to the ground as the pain of his fractured wrist filled him from head to toe. His eyes went glassy and he screamed angrily.

"Guess you won't be playing the piano anytime soon either," Henry joked as he continued to circle around the man, knowing he needed to take out the knife hand before the fight could be finished for good. "Gripping the throttle on a bike is probably out, too."

"Fuck you, you prick!" was the reply, Henry laughing loudly.

But it wasn't how he truly felt. It was all a show. Only a fool talks and chats while in a fight for his life. But he needed to get Foulmouth as riled up as possible, and cracking jokes like Jimmy would do seemed the best course of action. But all the while he talked, his mind was focused on the task at hand, so that he barely heard his own words.

Henry knew Foulmouth was still as dangerous as ever. He'd learned a long time ago not to take anything for granted. Henry had been in similar situations and he'd come up on top, thanks to the training he'd received from other men who knew how to fight. But a lot of what Henry now knew about fighting was from his own experiences and grace under pressure. One time, trapped in a cannie's grip, his arms useless at his sides, he'd used his bare teeth to rip out the cannie's throat when in a fight for his life. Until the enemy was dead, the battle was never over.

Henry knew the large man before him only had one option left, and when it finally came, it was actually pathetic in its predictability.

Foulmouth threw the bayonet at Henry, who was circling around at a walking pace. So badly injured that the giant had no balance to think of, the knife didn't even come close to Henry, and sailed past his head by more than two feet. It landed on the far edge of the circle, the blade glinting in the firelight.

He was so focused on the fight, Henry hadn't realized it had become full dark, with only the bonfires and torches to light the area. The moon was high in the sky tonight, which gave the parking lot a pallid glow along with the firelight.

Foulmouth's eyes reflected the nearby firelight, as he propped himself up with his one good hand. Sweat poured off his face and chest, dripping onto the ground in pools.

The bikers began low murmurs, which soon became louder.

Henry stopped moving and faced Foulmouth from a distance of about five feet. "So, asshole, you still think you're going to kill me and screw my woman?"

"I still have one good hand, you piece of shit. Let me get hold of you and we'll see who walks away tonight."

Henry took two steps closer, so he was barely out of reach of Foulmouth.

"You think so, huh?"

Foulmouth wasn't too alert now, thanks to all the damage he'd suffered, and Henry could see it wasn't an act. The man's reflexes were almost nonexistent. Turning away, he walked over to the edge of the circle and picked up the knife, ignoring the drive-chain.

Walking back to Foulmouth, he picked up his pace and began running, and when he was eight feet from the fallen man, he threw the knife as hard as he could.

It wasn't a throwing blade, not that Henry cared. He needed a distraction for what would come next.

Seeing the blade coming at him, Foulmouth raised his good hand and covered his face. The knife hit his arm harmlessly, the hilt ending up striking him before bouncing off.

But the result had been what Henry wanted.

As soon as the knife rebounded off Foulmouth's arm, the giant was already lowering his arm to look at Henry, who was still coming.

Before Foulmouth could react, Henry kicked the large biker under the jaw like Foulmouth's head was the ball in a game of kickball. The head snapped back with terrible force, the body following with it, smacking the ground hard, Foulmouth was dazed for a few seconds. His jaw was shattered, and loose teeth filled his mouth like pebbles.

But he wasn't dead yet.

Henry had run a few feet past Foulmouth after delivering the kick, and he swiveled on his heels and came back, looking down at Foulmouth. He didn't wait for the man to do or say anything, nor did he offer any amusing quips. The moment for that was over, now there was only death.

Raising his right foot high in the air, Henry brought it directly down on Foulmouth's nose with all his weight behind the blow, the heel of his boot taking up most of the impact.

The nose shattered immediately, and blood squirted out from beneath the crushing boot. The gristle, cartilage, and bone at the base of the nose were shattered first, and it was all pushed deep behind the eyes until finally reaching the brain and killing him.

Henry jumped backwards as the large body began to thrash around on the ground. The damage to the biker's central nervous system was total, and his good hand and leg convulsed for a full minute before finally going still. Foulmouth's breath rasped in his throat for a few more seconds, his face covered in blood. Then finally even that stopped.

Henry waited to make sure the man wasn't going to get back up, then almost casually, he sent one last kick directly behind the left ear. There was a loud crack and the head snapped to the side, the eyes popping back open after closing on their own accord. Only now those eyes saw nothing.

The entire circle was still, no one believing Henry had actually won the fight.

Sure enough, it was Jimmy who broke the silence. "Yeah, fucking A, man. See, Vincent, I told you Henry would kick that guy's ass!" He let out a loud whoop and shoved the man who had a knife on him away. The biker was too shocked to do anything and he didn't fight Jimmy.

Henry turned and walked across the circle until he was standing before Vincent. The biker leader had his chin in his hand, his elbow propped on the hand rest, supporting his head as if deep in thought.

Locking gazes with Vincent, Henry simply said, "Well?"

Vincent said nothing, the bikers all waiting for their President to speak. Finally, Vincent stood up and walked up to Henry, the two men facing one another eye to eye. Vincent was a little taller than Henry, who had to look up slightly.

Then Vincent moved fast, too fast for Henry to counter after his ordeal. But the President wasn't going for a weapon, or an attack; instead he wrapped Henry in a tight bear hug. "Son-of-a-fucking-bitch, man, I never thought you could take Foulmouth in a fight. Shit, no one ever has." He let Henry go, turned to face the rest of his chapter, and yelled, "This man won fair and square. He's one of us now, brothers, he and his people are now full-fledged prospects, and his women are their old ladies so hands fucking off. No funny shit or you answer to me." There were a few cheers, and others also yelled congratulations. Vincent pointed to five men, then gestured to Foulmouth's corpse. "You guys take care of him.

Later, we'll give him a warrior's funeral." The men nodded and moved off to deal with the corpse.

"So what now?" Henry asked.

"Now?" Vincent repeated. "Now?" he said again. "Why, my newfound bro, we fucking party!" Yelling the last part, all the men and women around him began cheering and somewhere nearby a battery-powered CD or cassette player was turned on. Minutes later, more alcohol was flowing, more pot was being smoked, and the party was back in full swing.

Vincent patted Henry on the back one more time, which caused him to wince in pain, then the President was moving off to party.

Jimmy was the first to join Henry, and the women were there a few seconds later.

Sue jumped into Henry's arms, kissing him passionately. "I knew you could do it!" she cried as she kept kissing him.

"Yeah, Henry, that was something else," Jimmy said. "Great job."

"Next time 'you' fight the giant in a life and death battle, okay, Jimmy? I think I'm too old for this shit."

Mary and Cindy were next, hugging Henry and congratulating him. When everyone had said their peace, Sue took Henry away to get him cleaned up. The others following close by.

They were allowed to the jeeps, their escorts now gone, and Sue took out a First Aid kit and began cleaning Henry's back wound after he removed his shirt.

"It's not too bad," she said. "Barely broke the skin. As long as you keep it clean it will heal without a problem."

"Good to know," he said. "I got off lucky with that guy."

"No shit," Jimmy said. "I have to tell you, I was sweating bullets there for a while."

"You and me both," he said and slapped Jimmy on the leg where he was standing nearby.

Vincent came out of the crowd and joined them. He had a beer in each hand and both were for him. His old lady was right behind him and she looked on silently. Henry watched her and bet she knew everything that went on inside the chapter. He could tell she was a person who knew that listening was better than talking most of the time.

"Henry, my man, how's it hanging," Vincent asked. "You hurt bad?" He glanced at Henry's wound. "Looks like Foulmouth got a piece of you after all."

"I'll live," Henry replied. "When can we get our weapons back now that we're part of the gang?"

"Not gang, man, chapter. We're called a chapter."

"Okay sure, chapter then. Our weapons?"

"After Foulmouth's send-off I'll get you your shit back."

Henry nodded, then winced as Sue cleaned an area of the wound that was a little deeper.

Vincent stood silently, watching Henry, and finally Henry asked, "Was there something else, Vincent?"

The President seemed to snap out of a fugue state and he nodded. "Huh? Oh sure, man, yeah, that was why I came over here. So, here's the deal, like I said, you guys are part of the chapter now. No one will fuck with you like you're outsiders, but something was brought to my attention that you need to know right fucking now."

Henry hoped there wasn't going to be some kind of a catch. But if he thought they were about to be taken as prisoners again, he was very wrong, and the next words out of Vincent's mouth was something he hadn't even considered.

"See, every chick has to be either an old lady or a mama. You get that right?"

Henry nodded. "Yes, you explained all that to us earlier."

"Right, man, right. So Jimmy there and that hot blonde chick are together, right?"

"You bet we are," Jimmy said, his fist raised for a fight.

"Calm the fuck down, man, no problem here. Like I said, she's your old lady and no one can touch her but you."

"Okay, good," Jimmy replied.

Vincent pointed to Sue with a beer in his hand. "And she's your old lady, right, Henry?"

Henry nodded, not needing to speak.

"Cool, man, cool. She's a nice piece of ass, too, for her age."

"Thank you. I think?" Sue said as she continued working on Henry's wound.

"Sure, babe, not a problem." Vincent then pointed to Mary. "But her. What's her name? Mary? She's not with anyone, which means she's not an old lady. That makes her a mama."

"Okay, so?" Mary said, speaking up as it was she who was now the topic of the conversation.

"Well, babe, a mama is the property of the entire chapter. Anyone can fuck you whenever they want, and you can't do shit about it. You say no and there's gonna be trouble." He glared at Henry. "Real fucking trouble. You get me, man?"

Jimmy was the first to object. "Now wait a goddamn second, no one touches Mary without her permission."

Henry spoke up before Vincent could reply, knowing this wasn't an issue that could be won. The chapter had rules and Mary, by not having a man, had fallen into a different category for women than Sue and Cindy. No amount of arguing would change that.

"Okay, Vincent, we understand what you told us. And you're President, so what you say goes."

"Cool, man, cool. Glad you're on board. I'd hate to have some bad shit go down after you went through the trouble of killing my best man and all—especially now that you're all one of us." He gestured to the jeeps. "Later, we're gonna have to find you guys some hogs to ride. Foulmouth doesn't need his now that he's dead, so two more and you're all set." He looked at Henry and Jimmy. "You know how to ride, right?"

"Of course we do," Jimmy snapped.

"Cool, man, 'cause we don't teach prospects how to ride. Kind of part of the fucking job and all that shit." He turned and began walking away. "Peace, brothers, see you at the funeral in an hour."

The second Vincent walked away and was out of sight, everyone began talking at once. Finally, Henry hissed for them to be quiet.

"I'm not going to be the local whore, Henry," Mary said angrily. "I'll kill the first person who lays a hand on me, too. I'd rather die than be one of those mamas."

"I know that, Mary. We're just going to have to keep you out of sight until we can make a run for it."

"And when's that gonna be?" Cindy asked, nervous for her friend.

Henry shook his head in frustration. It was one problem after another. "Shit, guys, I thought we might've been able to lay low here for a few days before trying anything. I mean, we're part of them now, we're safe. But this thing with Mary changes everything."

"Damn straight it does," Mary snapped.

"I know, I know. Okay, we'll leave just before dawn tomorrow. That way we can get our weapons back and rest for a few hours."

"Okay," Jimmy said, "but what about right now? What do we do now?"

Henry stood up, Sue patting him on the arm and whispering she was done cleaning his wound. As he slid back into his shirt, he looked at each of them before saying, "Now, I'm going to go use the bathroom, wherever it might be. It feels like I've been holding it forever."

Chapter 25

Major Ishmael Varakov was pleased with the invasion into Alaska so far. But his one frustration was that Alaska didn't seem too different from Russia.

So far, the three villages he'd come across were about as poor as the ones in Russia.

Opposition had been next to nothing, as well.

When Major Varakov rode into an enclave, his army behind him, the villagers had been cooperative, and even when he demanded everything of value, whether it be food, young daughters or treasure, little defiance had occurred.

The villagers knew they were outnumbered and outgunned, and knew fighting would be useless.

Petroff had three of his toes amputated from frostbite after his horse fell into a pool of water, soaking the man to the bone. Varakov hadn't wanted to wait for the man to dry off, so Petroff had ended up managing as best he could.

Despite the temperature, his clothes eventually dried around a fire, but his boots were another matter and it wasn't long before blackness had come to his left foot, followed by swelling.

But the man was Russian and so had used his own knife to remove the offending digits. There was very little blood.

Later that night, when another fire had been built, Petroff was finally able to dry off his boots and socks, but the damage had been done.

Unknown to Petroff, Varakov had used the Private as an example to the rest of the men. He wanted it known that he would afford no weaknesses in his men.

Two of the villages that he'd found and destroyed, raping and pillaging and setting fire to all he didn't want, were smaller than some of the enclaves back in Russia.

One village really couldn't even have been called a true village, for there'd been a total of ten people scattered among four hovels. Two of the men had tried to kill their wives when Varakov and his men had appeared out of the fog that day, but they had done a terrible job of it. Perhaps, though knowing they were doing a kindness to their loved ones, they were still not able to complete the act out of love.

One woman had been knifed in the chest by her mate, but the blade missed hitting anything vital, though the wound bled profusely, and another woman was bleeding to death from a throat wound but was still alive when Varakov's men found her. While the women bled out on the ice, the Russian soldiers had raped them repeatedly, and even when both finally expired, the men kept going, for as long as a body was still warm, it was considered fair game.

The men of the small village were slaughtered in true Soviet fashion, and then the rest of the hovels had been searched.

Major Varakov had decided to make camp in that village and he'd even made sure to keep one of the villagers alive a little longer for some personal enjoyment and information of the area.

The boy was no more than seventeen, with a scrawny frame and long shaggy hair. Stripped of his clothing, his naked body was tied to a skinning rack found in one of the huts. The skin was pink from exposure, and the boy's teeth chattered incessantly from the cold. Only a few feet away, lying in the churned-up snow, the boy's parents lay dead, the mother sodomized before his eyes before they slit her throat. His father now had half a head, the brains having spilled out to soak into the snow, thanks to the bullet that had gone through it. Both the father's arms had been broken before the killing, the Russians having some sport with their prey.

The boy had a young sister as well, of not more than six years of age. With flame-red hair and an ivory complexion, she was beautiful for her age, and when she reached adulthood, she would be stunning in her beauty. The boy had no idea what had become of her.

The boy was numb with grief and terror for his own safety. In one fell swoop, his entire life had been destroyed. His family killed, himself soon following no doubt.

Varakov needed information, and after the miserable results of dealing with the old trapper days before, he'd been practicing his English some more, making sure he had the correct phrases.

"Where is your army located?" Varakov asked. "We look for fighting men to kill."

He didn't respond, only stared at Varakov with tear-soaked eyes that saw nothing, the boy locked in a fugue state.

Varakov slapped the prisoner hard on the face, the hand leaving a bright red mark. The boy was alive; the Major knew that. Breath seeped from the cracked lips each time air was exhaled, to then mist in the cold air.

The slap did little to snap the boy out of his delirium, so Varakov leaned closer, placed his right thumb onto the right eye, and pressed hard until his thumb slid into the warmness of the eye, puncturing it like it was a soft-boiled egg. Pinkish-white goo slid out around his thumb, resembling the egg yolk of that metaphorical egg, dripping down the boy's right cheek like tears.

The boy immediately began screaming in pain, his hands curling into fists at his sides. The fingernails on each hand were raw and bloody from where they'd been torn off one at a time.

The pain was so intense he lost control of his bodily functions, and shit and piss slid down the insides of his thighs to splash onto the ice and snow, where it steamed for a few seconds before freezing.

Varakov, disgusted at this, stepped backwards while cursing in Russian, so as to not get splashed. He shook his right hand rapidly to shake off the eyeball gunk clinging to it.

A few soldiers standing nearby, watching the interrogation, laughed at this, and Varakov spun around and flashed them with such a strong warning gaze that all the men realized they needed to be somewhere else, anywhere that wasn't near Varakov.

Streltsy moved up to the boy, a carving knife in his hand. "Let me cut off is genitals, Comrade Major. That will get him to talk."

"No," Varakov snapped, the tone of command prevalent in the order. "I will do this."

"Yes, Comrade Major, forgive my impulsiveness," Streltsy stepped back a few feet to give his leader room.

Major Varakov looked at his second-in-command and merely nodded, accepting the apology.

In the next hut, the door wide open to allow them to be seen, a group of soldiers were gathered around a cooking pot filled with vegetables and melting snow. When it was cooked, a hearty soup would be ready. In the corner of the hut, the firelight showing the actions by the flickering flames, a village woman of around forty years of age was being brutally raped repeatedly by three soldiers. At the moment, the woman was being taken from behind, while another soldier had his member thrust deep into her mouth, choking her. A knife was at her throat, making sure she wasn't stupid enough to try and bite him. With tears filling her eyes, and sobs of pain that were muffled from the male organ shoved down her throat, all she could do was lay there and be used until the men grew tired of her, and though it would not be seen as a kindness by the men, to her, when they finally killed her, it would be the sweetest mercy of all.

Major Varakov stepped closer to the boy so that their faces were only inches apart; he was careful not to place his boots in the stained snow beneath the prisoner. The odor of shit had faded as soon as it was frozen. "Where are the military complexes? Where are the fighting men?"

The boy shook his head. "I don't know nothin' about no complexes, I swear. Please, don't hurt me any more. I'm beggin' you."

Varakov ignored the boy's protests, understanding some of it, though also getting that his prisoner wasn't telling him what he needed to hear.

"We wish to meet with your generals, to accept their surrender." He felt good about that sentence, having had to mull over it for a bit before speaking it. With each phrase he used, he was remembering more of the English he'd learned so many years ago.

The boy stared at Varakov with his one good eye, no sign of understanding forming there. He didn't get what these men wanted. They had ridden into the village and began slaughtering his family and friends without cause. His sister was gone, probably dead, and he knew he wasn't long for this world as well.

The sounds of debauchery filled the tiny village, the soldiers having fun with whoever was still left alive.

Already the boy's extremities were turning blue, and soon would become black. He wasn't shivering as bad as before, and though he didn't know it, he was about to slip into hypothermia. He barely felt the cold on his exposed skin, and though his body was racked with pain, all he wanted to do was sleep.

"I don't know what you're talkin' about, mister. What do ya want me to say?" He began to sob.

Varakov turned to face Streltsy. "I will try one more time. Maybe this boy is deaf like that old man." In the last village they'd come to, they had come across an old man. Varakov had asked the man repeatedly for help, only to receive nothing but a blank gaze.

When his temper was fit to explode, that was when he'd figured out that the old man was deaf as a stone. So aggravated at the time he'd wasted, Varakov had shown mercy by merely shooting the old buzzard in the head, instead of letting his men torture the old man for a while. But now he was failing miserably again, and this time with a child of all things.

The boy looked from Varakov to Streltsy, not understanding the Russian the men spoke. He hoped whatever they were saying was something good, that perhaps they might still set him free and let him live.

His fingers and toes were numb, and when he tried to wiggle them he couldn't tell if he actually was. The urine and feces that had run down his inner thighs was now frozen solid, and when he moved slightly, the stained ice would crack and flake off his cold flesh.

If the boy only knew what the men wanted, he would have gladly given them any information they requested. If his parents had not already been murdered and lay dead by his feet, he would have gladly betrayed them now, if only to stop the pain.

"We wish to find the great city, where generals are. We wish to rule you. We want to know where food and clothing is located." Those sentences took all Varakov had to create with his limited knowledge of English. He was proud of it, too, and when he looked at Streltsy for confirmation of his prowess, his second only looked on with a blank stare. Of course, Streltsy didn't understand a word of English and so Varakov's words were gibberish to him. For all Streltsy knew, Varakov was spouting nonsocial sentences.

But Major Varakov knew he had done a good job this time, and when he looked at the boy's remaining eye, he saw a spark of recognition swimming within the single brown orb.

"Ya want to find a big city?" the boy asked.

"Da?" Varakov queried, reverting to his native tongue.

"Yes?" the boy asked again, not understanding.

Major Varakov nodded for the boy to proceed.

"Well, mister, I ain't never been there. It's over fifty miles away, southeast, but the biggest city nearby is called Anchorage. I reckon that's where ya want to go for any of the stuff you're lookin' for." He stopped talking when Varakov waved a hand for the boy to be quiet.

The Major scrunched up his face in concentration and said, "I am on vacation and do not know English well. I learned in school. Please speak slowly." He smiled at that one. Those sentences were taken right from his school learning; he remembered using it often while practicing.

"You want me to talk slower? Okay, mister, I can do that." He repeated what he said, finishing with, "Anchorage is huge and it has a lot of dead people walking around there, but I reckon they're as dead as the ones we got 'round here—or used to."

"Ank Ridge?" Varakov repeated and pointed southeast of his position. "That way? Generals? Food?"

"Sure, mister, sure. You got it. Please don't kill me. I told ya what ya wanted to know."

Varakov wasn't listening; instead he was considering his next move. He reached out and patted the boy on the head, almost like a proud father would after his son had done something to please him. Then he turned to Streltsy. "Have the men gathered in two hours so we can inform them of our next move. At dawn we go to this Ank Ridge, where if there is any opposition, it will be there."

"Right away, Comrade Major. It will be done," Streltsy replied and as Varakov began walking away, he added, "What about the boy?"

Varakov didn't turn around, only waved a hand over his shoulder, as if he was dismissing an annoying lackey. "Kill him; there is nothing more we need from him."

"No! No! No!" the boy screamed as Streltsy pulled a knife from within his coat and walked casually up to the boy. "I told ya what ya wanted to know. I told ya!"

The knife was sliced across the boy's throat as if Streltsy was merely slaughtering a goat for supper. He felt neither sadness nor pleasure in the act. It was simply something that needed to be done. He made sure to step to the side as he cut, in order to avoid the hot spray of blood.

Staining the churned-up snow red five feet from the boy, the spray quickly became a sputter, and then nothing but a slow gurgle, the hot liquid cooling fast in the frigid air.

Major Varakov retired to a hut to rest, relishing the warmth from the small fire he'd ordered made for him earlier. Tossing his jacket to the side, next he washed his face in the bowl of melted snow left out for him by one of his aides. The hut was Spartan; three chairs, a table, and a bed in the corner.

When he was clean and feeling refreshed, he sat at the table and picked from the bowl of cooked vegetables on the table, then drank from the pitcher of wine his aides had left. Outside, the sounds of the pillaging and raping continued, but it would soon become quieter as his men ran out of victims. Then, they would gather for a briefing, and with the night still ahead, they would drink and sing and be merry. For to be alive was reason enough to be happy. Being Russian was a hard life, where the weak were quickly either killed outright or used as playthings for the more powerful.

And that was before the dead began to walk. Now, with the Russian government a shadow of its former self, and anarchy reigning in the streets, it truly was a place for only the strong to survive.

Finishing his meal, he undid his pants and went into the corner of the room and urinated into the bowl there. He assumed the bowl was there for this purpose, a makeshift chamber pot, and even if it wasn't, he didn't care.

Wiping his mouth on the back of his sleeve, he left his pants unbuckled, and turning to face the bed, he smiled cheerfully as he walked over to it.

"Now to have some much-earned fun."

Gagged and hogtied, a rope connecting the feet to the hands and neck, so that there was no chance of escape, and to even try to stretch the legs could mean strangulation, a beautiful girl of no more than six years of age lay whimpering softly.

She had flame-red hair and skin the color of ivory.

The following morning, Major Varakov and his Russian army left the small village behind as they set off towards Anchorage.

Behind them, the huts burned brightly in the pre-dawn, causing shadows to flicker everywhere. Bodies were strewn across the small village like ragdolls dropped by some giant child who had finished playing for the day. The snow was soaked in blood, the fires warming the air enough to begin to thaw the red ice.

Hours later, when the fires had dwindled to smoldering embers, the wolves came out of hiding. Creeping through the village, they sniffed the blood floating in the air, and without hesitation, began to feed on the murdered villagers.

One wolf, an alpha male, who was only second to the leader, and in time would make his play for that, strode into one of the smoldering huts, careful not to step on anything hot and burn a paw. Let the others fight over what lay in the small paths between the huts; this wolf knew that to venture off a little would sometimes yield food he didn't have to battle others of the pack for.

The hut had been sparse in furnishings even before the fire, and now, there was barely anything recognizable.

Not finding anything to eat, the wolf was about to turn around and search somewhere else when it detected the odor of cooked flesh overriding the other scents filtering throughout the village.

Padding over to what was once a bed, it sniffed the ashes, and after a moment of hesitation, began pawing at the charred pieces until finding something appetizing.

Opening its jaws wide, it leaned down and clamped its jaws tightly on a small object that was scorched black and still a little hot from the fire, but not too hot that the wolf couldn't hold it in its mouth—as long as its tongue was shifted a little to the side.

Happy with its treasure, it spun around and ran out of the hut, wanting to be back in the open air once more.

Somehow not entirely consumed in the flames, a few stray strands of hair were still stuck to the object. They waved peacefully in the breeze as the wolf padded away, showing just a glimpse of the beauty that once was.

The few tendrils of hair were flame-red.

Chapter 26

As it turned out, Henry and the others ended up making a hasty retreat from the bikers before the morning had even arrived.

The incident that caused them to leave even earlier than when Henry had wanted was simple in its explanation, and when Henry looked back on it, he should have expected it to happen.

It was well past midnight on the same day the group had become Prospects, and the party was still going in full swing. The bikers partied every chance they got, and Vincent had explained that the bikers' lifestyle hadn't truly changed much over the past years, even after the dead began to walk.

The companions had retreated to their jeeps, setting up their own small camp on the far side of the vehicles.

Bikers were everywhere, and if Henry had thought to make a run for it then, he knew it would have been foolish. Even if he'd thought to shoot the bilkers with the M60s and then try and escape, there were simply far too many variables for him to want to risk it.

His plans were to wait a day or two, and when the time came that Vincent and his chapter let their guard down, figuring Henry and his people had accepted their new life as Prospects, only then would there be a break for freedom and the open road.

But Henry didn't take into account what it meant for Mary to be classified as a 'mama' instead of an 'old lady.' He thought by keeping her out of sight that it would prevent any issues, but he underestimated the lust the bikers had for new women in the gang.

After the battle with Foulmouth, the companions had stayed together, away from the rest of the chapter. Henry had ventured into the midst of the wild party only to find Vincent and gather his weapons, and those of his friends. Then he'd withdrawn back to the jeeps.

More than a dozen motorcycles were parked around the jeeps, though a respectable distance away. The set-up was clear. The jeeps weren't going anywhere without Vincent's approval unless Henry wanted to ram through the parked bikes, which to a biker gang would be suicide for the driver foolish enough to try it.

"I need to go to the bathroom," Mary said from where she sat, her back pressed against a jeep tire.

Henry was next to her, his eyes closed, and despite the crashing din of the party, he was trying to get some sleep. The wound on his back from the fight had been cleaned and dressed, and if he didn't move too fast, it barely pained him. Jimmy was sitting in the passenger seat of the other jeep with Cindy, the two talking privately. But Jimmy was also standing guard over his friends. Sue was sleeping in the other jeep, stretched out on both seats.

It was agreed that though they had been welcomed into the chapter, it would be foolhardy not to sleep with one eye open.

"Hold it until those assholes go to sleep, then you can go," Henry told Mary, his eyes never opening.

"I have been holding it, Henry, for hours now, and if I don't go soon, I'm going to go right here in my pants."

"Then go over there a few feet away and go already," Henry said, his eyes still closed.

"What? Don't be ridiculous. I'm not going right here. There's a good place over by the trailer. I can go over there. It's not too far away but it's not too close to the bikers, either."

Henry considered her suggestion and decided it should be fine. The trailer was around thirty feet away, and the bikers were on the far side of the parking lot, where the clubhouse was nothing but charred wood. That was also where the large bonfire raged, the fuel for it taken from the clubhouse wreckage.

He cracked his right eye and looked at her, seeing her features clearly even in the darkness thanks to the overhead moonlight filtering down through the clouds. "Okay, that sounds safe enough. But have Cindy go with you, just to be on the safe side."

"I don't need Cindy to go with me. This isn't high school. I can go to the bathroom by myself." She stood up, wiping the back of her pants with her hands.

"I know that, Mary, but you heard what Vincent said. You're free game for those guys. They see you and one of them is going to try something. I know it and so do you. We need to keep you out of sight till we make our escape."

She sighed. "I can take care of myself, Henry."

Now he opened his eyes, wanting to get a good look at her as she stood before him, her arms crossed before her. But he didn't need to look up to know what her face would look like. Her jaw clenched, her eyes set tight. Lips just a thin line.

"I know you can, honey, but these guys aren't for messing around with if we don't have to. Please, just take Cindy with you to watch your back while you…you know…"

She considered his request, and more because it was a request and not an order, she finally nodded that it was fine if Cindy came. Then figuring he couldn't see her nodding, she said, "Okay, Cindy can come."

"Thank you." He closed his eyes again to sleep.

Mary walked over to the second jeep, and quickly filled Cindy in on what Henry and she had discussed.

"Sure, Mary, no problem. In fact, I could go, too, so it's not a waste of me coming along." Cindy began sliding out of the jeep.

"Yeah, and you girls can check your makeup in the mirror or whatever you do when you go to the bathroom together," Jimmy joked, his smile from ear to ear.

"Shut up, Jimmy," Mary snapped, hating it whenever he made a joke at her expense.

"Ignore him," Cindy said, and slid fully out of the jeep, then she and Mary headed off.

Mary made sure to keep her head down, the two women doing their best to avoid any wandering bikers, who were everywhere.

Minutes later, in the bushes near the trailer, Mary was crouched down with her pants at her ankles, peeing, while Cindy waited for her to finish. As Mary knelt down, her bladder being difficult now that she was ready, she listened to the din of the partying bikers. Men and women yelled and cheered, and once in a while someone fired a gun into the air, or for all Mary knew, at one another.

She forced herself to relax and block out the sounds around her, and once she had, her bladder finally released and she peed. With the pressure relieved, she let out a small sigh of happiness, that anyone who has been holding it for too long knows well.

When she was truly done, she finished up with the small tasks women do compared to men when they pee, and then pulled up her pants and secured the belt.

Stepping out of the bushes, Cindy smiled, nodded, and went into the bushes to repeat the process.

Mary leaned against the rear of the trailer, while she waited for her friend to finish, so they could return to the jeeps and the relative safety of being surrounded by friends. It was as she waited that she glanced down at her boots, and she frowned when she saw she'd gotten some urine on them. Annoyed at this, she knelt down and pulled out a piece of tissue from a pocket, wanting to wipe the wetness away.

It only took her a few seconds, but when she stood up, she found herself surrounded by two bikers, both with black beards and scraggly hair. One man was rather obese, with a stomach that hung over the waistband of his denim pants. The other was more on the skinny side, though the arms were still muscled. 'Wiry' would be the best descriptive term for the man.

"Well, well, Mick, look who we have here. It's that babe that belongs with the newbies," the fat biker said to his buddy.

"It sure is, Holland," the skinny one replied. "She must be out lookin' for some dick, and lucky for her, she found us."

Cursing her bad luck, Mary slowly raised her left hand, palm outwards, before her, as her right went to her side, the hand grasping the hilt of the knife she had there. "Now, fellas, I don't want any trouble. Just had to pee."

Holland laughed, his multiple chins jiggling as he did so. "Shit, honey, if I'd known that, you could have peed all over me." He rubbed his chest and belly sexily. "I'm into that kinda shit."

By the trailer, they were mostly wreathed in shadow, and if she could act quickly, she could kill both men before any of the other bikers knew what had occurred, then all she had to do was drag the bodies into the bushes to hide them.

After that, well, she wasn't thinking that far in advance. One step at a time, the first being survive the encounter with the two men, who wanted to rape her, and could do so with the full blessing of the rest of the biker gang.

Mary was weighing her options on how fast she could stab one of the men and then the other before the second man retaliated. She figured she'd go for the skinny one first, as he'd be quicker in a fight, then with him down, she could deal with the fat one.

But all the plans in the world couldn't take into account the unexpected, such as the two men being through talking and wanting to have some fun.

Reaching out and grabbing her before she could even get her knife out of its sheathe, Holland was much faster than she ever could have imagined, his thick arms snapping out like a Cobra's to grab her tightly, while Mick moved in and wrapped her hair in one hand, pulling her head back and making her grimace.

Mick licked her cheek, his tongue rough like a cat's. "Mmmm, tastes sweet." He yanked her face down a little more and whispered into her ear. "You're anyone's bitch, baby, and it looks like me and Holland get first crack at you." He reached around with his free hand and squeezed her left breast roughly through her shirt. "You like anal, bitch? 'Cause that's my favorite."

Mary didn't respond; there was nothing to say. She knew any pleading she made would only excite the two men further.

Before she could try to pull her knife again, she was slammed against the back of the trailer, causing her to wince in pain. A second later, rough hands were pulling at her pants, yanking them down to her ankles, while she remained pinned.

Holland held her fast while Mick dropped his pants and stood before her, his throbbing member only inches from the juncture of her thighs. A small drop of moisture coated the head of his penis, telling her how excited he truly was.

The setup was as followed. Holland was on her right, his two beefy arms holding her left arm pinned to the trailer, and Mick used his left arm to pin her right arm, so she was basically trapped and unable to squirm free.

Not about to take the rape without a fight, she brought up her right knee, hoping to crush Mick's testicles and end his passion right there, but the biker was ready for it and he turned his hip to take the brunt of the blow.

Mary received a hard slap in the face for her trouble, the blow stunning her.

"Try anything like that again, slut, and I'll make sure you can't walk for a week," Mick hissed into her face. "You're a fucking mama now. Act like one."

He leaned in once more, the tip of his manhood touching her stomach. He tried to kiss her and she turned her head. He didn't push it, and instead started to suck on her neck, while his hips began to gyrate as he dry humped her.

Then, he slowly lowered his body a little so he could line himself up and plunge into her warmness.

Mary was doing her best not to cry, knowing she needed to remain strong, but she also knew she was only seconds from being penetrated by the disgusting creature before her. He smelled terrible; vomit, excrement, and stale beer, all rolled into one foul odor.

Holland chuckled beside Mick, his free hand squeezing her breasts, pinching her nipples so hard she knew she'd be sore in the morning, her shirt now torn open to expose her chest to the warm night air. The bra she'd worn was on the ground, ripped free of her so hard the material had left friction burns on her shoulders.

Mary tried to snap forward with her head, her mouth opening to sink her teeth into Mick's throat and tear his jugular out like a wild animal, but the biker was quicker and he moved his throat away from her reach, then a backhand to the face told her that he wouldn't be taken down so easily. He said nothing, only smiled as he licked his lips in anticipation of what was coming.

Mick was just about to slide himself home, after taking a moment to line himself up just right. He moved his head just a little closer, so that his face was inches from Mary's face, his eyes ready for her to try an attack again. He wanted to be looking into her eyes when he penetrated her, to see the look of either pain or pleasure that would appear. He didn't care which one he saw; either one would turn him on.

Knowing what was about to happen was inevitable, Mary locked gazes with Mick, her jaw set taut, her eyes cold. Even as she waited to feel him slip inside her, she was already imagining herself finding the man later and killing him as he slept.

Mick's penis was right at her opening now, the tip even slightly inside her, but just barely. It was just so he knew he could now slam himself into her and would find no obstructions.

His hips went back a little more as he prepared to push his entire body forward to thrust himself deep inside her. Mary braced for the feeling she knew was coming, her entire body shaking in revulsion, furious she was helpless to stop it all.

Mick's face was alight with pleasure, Mary's eyes never looking away.

And then, just as he was about to thrust forward, Mary saw the eyes of the biker open wider, way wider than she ever would have expected. His mouth flapped open and closed, as if he was trying to speak; a trickle of blood dripped from one corner to slide down his chin and drip onto the juncture of Mary's breasts.

That was when she looked down, past his nose, which seemed fine, past his mouth and chin, which other than the trickle of blood there, were also fine.

But then her gaze dropped lower still, to the man's throat to be exact, directly where his Adam's apple was.

Only now there was a new protuberance there: the shiny, bloody tip of a knife.

Mary could only stare as she saw the knife tip begin to twist, the blade opening the wound even more. Then the blade was retracted and blood squirted from the wound, missing Mary's face by inches, and splattering the side of the trailer.

Mick was already dead on his feet; he just didn't know he needed to lie down to finish the job.

What happened next pretty much happened simultaneously, Mary lost in a whirlwind of blood, death and violence.

As Mick's throat squirted blood, he let go of Mary, his hands going to his throat to try and staunch the blood. Then another face appeared to the side of Mick's, Mary seeing Cindy standing behind the dying biker.

Holland, seeing blood shooting from his partner's neck, let go of Mary in surprise, and upon Mary realizing that Cindy had come to her aide, she took the chance to act as well.

Mary simply turned to the side, her left shoulder still pressed up against the trailer, and brought up her right knee as hard as she could. An instant later, she felt the satisfying impact of her knee crushing Holland's testicles. She might have been mistaken, but she could have sworn she actually heard the man's testes 'pop' from the blow.

The air whooshed out of Holland's lungs as his family jewels were pulped into a pink paste, and he knelt over, wobbling on his feet. Then he couldn't take the pain and went to his knees, his hands cradling his destroyed genitals. The fat biker wouldn't be fathering any kids anytime soon—or probably ever.

With the fat biker temporarily disabled, Mary slid down the trailer with her back still pressed to the metal, then one of the tires. When she was crouched as low as possible, she reached to her pants, which were around her ankles, and found her knife, the blade still in its sheathe and attached to her belt.

Her fingers found the hilt in less than a heartbeat, and she slid the blade free of its home and jumped back up, ignoring her dropped pants, all before Holland could so much as suck in another pained breath into his laboring lungs.

In one fluid motion, honed from years of fighting for her life, she slid the knife into the fat biker's chest.

The blade slid through the layers of fat, then past the first and second ribs easily, and continued deeper until impaling his heart. Mary felt the slight resistance as the blade punctured the heart, and as Holland reached out and grabbed her around the throat, she twisted the blade hard and ripped her arm to the side, slicing the fat man's beating organ in half.

"Suck on that, fatso," Mary hissed as the light went out in the biker's eyes and he dropped heavily to the ground, landing on top of Mick, who had already slumped to the earth a second before.

The entire altercation, from when Mary had been grabbed and the two men were slaughtered, had taken less than two minutes, and both women knew though the danger was over for the moment, it would only make things worse in the long run.

Cindy moved close to Mary. "Are you all right? Oh God, Mary, I was only gone for a few minutes, I had no idea what was happening. I'm so sorry."

"Save it, Cindy, you have nothing to apologize for. You saved me and then some. Another two seconds and…" She trailed off, not wanting to contemplate what would have happened.

Cindy glanced down at the corpses at her feet, then kicked Holland in the side. "Fucking bastards," she spit.

Mary pulled her pants up and tucked her shirt tails into her shirt to keep it closed as best she could. The buttons had been ripped off and only this kept her shirt from hanging open. Both women took a second to wipe their blades clean on the back of the fat biker's shirt, then they re-sheathed them, knowing what they needed to do next.

"We need to hide the bodies," Mary said, Cindy nodding in agreement.

Mary knelt down and tried to shift Holland's massive bulk but she barely managed to move the body an inch. "Give me a hand, this guy weighs a ton."

"Okay, sure." Cindy joined Mary but even with both of them trying, they simply weren't strong enough to move the dead weight of the deceased biker. And if they couldn't move Holland, they couldn't move Mick, who was trapped under his fat and very-dead friend.

"Shit, this isn't going to work," Cindy said and stood up, breathing heavily. She pointed to Mary's left cheek. "You got some blood, you know," and she wiggled her finger in a circle.

"Thanks," Mary replied and used the sleeve of her shirt to wipe the blood away. She didn't ask if it was all gone, for it didn't really matter. There were more pressing concerns that they needed to deal with, such as hiding the two corpses. If it was discovered that Mary and Cindy had just killed two of the Skullfuckers, well, Mary didn't think the future for the companions would be too bright.

"What are we gonna do?" Cindy asked, her eyes darting out into the large parking lot. Luckily, they were still alone, the rest of the gang partying at the far end of the lot. But if Holland and Mick had appeared as if from nowhere, no doubt at any moment more bikers could wander over.

Mary scanned the area, seeing nothing but shrubbery. "Here, let's cut some branches and cover the bodies with them."

"That's not gonna work for long," Cindy rebutted. "The second these two assholes are found, we're all dead meat."

Mary fumed as she looked at Cindy. "You have a better idea, girlfriend?"

Cindy tried to come up with another option but nothing came to mind. Seconds passed and then she shrugged. "Nope, I got nothin'. Your idea sounds fine."

"Good, let's get to work."

They pulled their knives again and began cutting branches, and a few minutes later there was now a pile of cut shrubs and branches at the back of the trailer. Both women took a few steps back and admired their work, Mary nodding in satisfaction. "It won't pass when it's daylight but it should be good till then."

"Yeah, unless someone thinks this is kindling and wants to take some for the bonfire over there."

"One thing at a time, Cindy. Come on, let's tell the others. Who knows how long we have."

Checking one more time that no one was watching them, the two women fast-walked back to the jeeps to report to Henry, Jimmy, and Sue.

Chapter 27

"You did what!" Henry yelled and then quickly lowered his voice, not wanting to be overheard by any bikers that might be close by.

Cindy had just finished telling the story, while Sue saw to Mary, giving the younger woman a new shirt and consoling her.

"Well, shit, Henry, it's not like there was another option," Cindy snapped in reply. "What was I supposed to do; let the assholes rape her?"

"No. No, of course not. I never meant to say…" Henry trailed off; knowing this line of talk was a waste of time. The companions were now on a clock, one that when time ran out, would mean the deaths of Henry and Jimmy, and the women would probably end up in servitude in what came down to basically being sex slaves for the biker gang. "Never mind. Looks like we're going tonight. Shit, it would have been nice if I could have gotten at least a 'few' hours of sleep before we had to start running for our lives again."

Mary joined Henry and Cindy, Jimmy standing nearby and listening quietly, Sue also standing silent.

"Gee, Henry," Mary said, annoyance clear in her tone, "the next time two guys try to rape me, I'll try and make sure it's more convenient for you."

"That's not what I meant, Mary, and you know it." Henry waved a hand before him, dismissing the subject altogether. "Look, thank God you're all right; that's what matters. Now we need to get out of here."

Jimmy moved closer, speaking up. "So, what now? We're gonna run their blockade of bikes and make like a bat out of Hell?"

"Yeah, pretty much." Henry pointed to Sue. "Gather all our stuff, would you, and get it all stowed. I want to be out of here in ten minutes or less. Who knows how long before those bodies are found."

Sue nodded and got to work.

"You know," Cindy added, "we did hide them pretty well. They should stay hidden until morning at least."

Henry shook his head. "Not good enough. All it takes is one guy going to take a piss or wanting to see if there's any more baby food, and we're sunk. No, honey, we need to go now, while the element of surprise is with us. Vincent would never except us to make a run for it tonight, not after I won the fight and we got accepted as—what did he call it?—Prospects I think he called us."

"We do this, and there's no turning back, you know that, right, Henry?" Jimmy said, knowing the older man did but wanting to voice what they were all thinking. "Vincent is gonna come after us. It's not gonna be easy."

Henry sighed heavily and patted Jimmy on the shoulder. "Nothing ever is, Jimmy. Nothing ever is."

It turned out that preparing to leave in ten minutes still wasn't enough time. Five minutes to the second, a yell sounded from over by the trailer, followed by another. Homemade torches taken from the bonfire began floating in the darkness as bikers made their way over to where the alarm had been sounded.

The two bodies had been found by a biker and his old lady, the couple having thought to go over to the trailer and use the inside of it to get some much needed screwing time in, and wanting some privacy.

The biker, drunk off his ass, had stumbled over the leg of Holland, which was sprawled out on the ground. The man had first believed he'd tripped over a tree branch, but when he reached back after falling to pick up the offending branch, he found that the 'branch' was covered in denim and was attached to a very dead biker, one who he'd called brother for years. Flicking open a Zippo, the light had exposed not only Holland, but the corpse of Mick as well, and the man's drunkenness had faded away instantly as adrenaline pumped through his system. Calling out for others, in moments more of the chapter were gather around by torchlight.

"Looks like it's time to go," Henry said as he jumped into the jeep and grabbed hold of the M60. Mary was driving and Sue was in the passenger seat. Jimmy manned the other M60, Cindy driving.

As soon as the words left Henry's mouth, the torches began making their way from the trailer over to the two jeeps. Guns and knives were drawn, the metal reflecting the torchlight.

"Oh, shit. Looks like the jig's up," Jimmy said and swiveled the M60 around, ready to fire on Henry's order.

"Mary," Henry called down from behind her, "I'm gonna fire a short burst over their heads as a warning. When they duck for cover, you floor it."

"Why?" Jimmy yelled. "Why don't we just shoot as many as we can now?"

"Because we don't want them any angrier than they have to be, that's why," he said.

"Shit, old man, I doubt they can get much angrier than they are now."

Henry didn't reply.

"But what about the motorcycles surrounding us?" Mary asked quickly.

"Go through 'em or over 'em, whatever you need to do, just go!"

She started up the jeep, Cindy doing the same, which made the bikers begin moving faster upon hearing the engines.

"Okay, Jimmy, get ready!" Henry yelled. He squeezed the trigger of the M60, bracing for the impact of the gun shaking on its mounting and the loud report.

Only nothing happened, not so much as a dry click. Henry looked down at the gun, wondering what the hell was wrong, and knowing he had seconds to figure it out, but unless he began disassembling the gun with a manual by his side, there was no way to know what the malfunction was. And even then it would be an iffy thing. Though he'd learned about ordinance over the years to survive, breaking down and reassembling an M60 wasn't on his résumé just yet.

"Jimmy, mine's not working, you have to do it," Henry said as he stood helpless.

"Will do," Jimmy said, licking his lips in anticipation of the mayhem to come. He squeezed the trigger, expecting what Henry had assumed would happen. But his machine gun was silent, too.

"What the fuck?" Jimmy spat. "The fucking thing isn't working!"

Vincent appeared out of the darkness, a torch held in his left hand. In his right, he held some miscellaneous metal pieces. "Looking for these?" he asked, stopping ten feet to the side of the jeeps. The bikers surrounding him all held an assortment of weapons, mostly firearms.

Henry frowned, knowing what the metal pieces belonged to instantly.

The firing pins to the M60s.

When the companions had received their weapons back after Henry won the fight with Foulmouth, he had told everyone to go through them and make sure they were okay. Henry had checked Sue's .22 for her. All the guns seemed fine, and he was confident they were in perfect working condition. But due to this, he hadn't thought to check the M60s, which when he thought about it now, had been out of his line of sight for many hours at a time.

He'd broken the cardinal rule of survival.

Never trust anyone, for any reason, no matter what.

He should have checked the M60s beforehand, and if he had, he wouldn't now be in such a very tenuous situation.

There was a brief silence hanging over the area as Henry weighed his options, only the yelling of the bikers near the trailer, as more men and women found their fallen brothers, to break the silence.

Finally, Henry said, "So what now?"

Vincent slipped the metal pieces into a pocket of his jacket and pulled a chrome Colt .45 revolver from behind his back. "Now you and the kid die, then we take your women, if any survive, for some sport, before they die to—" Vincent was finishing the word 'too' but he didn't get a chance to, as Henry, knowing there were no options but fight and run, pulled his Glock in a fast draw he'd taken years to perfect and double-tapped the trigger, sending two rounds directly at Vincent.

The bullets were lined up perfectly; one would strike the biker leader in the chest, the second one in the head, both striking almost simultaneously. In the chaos of their fallen leader being gunned down so suddenly, Henry planned on having himself and his people make their getaway.

But Henry underestimated Vincent's tenacity for survival, and as the bullets sliced the air, the President of the Skullfuckers reached out and yanked the biker standing beside him in front of him, using the man as a human shield.

A fraction of a second later, the two rounds impacted human meat, striking almost exactly where Henry wanted them to, only now he had shot a different man.

Multiple things happened simultaneously, as both sides of the fight went into action.

Henry yelled to Mary to drive, to get them the hell out of there, Jimmy hearing the same, as did Cindy. While Mary sent the jeep surging forward, sending bikers scrambling for their lives or risk being run down, Henry fired from behind his useless M60, using his Glock to make the bikers duck for cover. Jimmy did the same on the second jeep, firing with the shotgun one-handed, the recoil making him feel like he was going to break his arm, but knowing there was no choice. His other hand held onto the M60 for dear life as Cindy swerved around in a circle, following Mary.

At such close range, Jimmy took out four bikers at once, the wide pellet spray sending the men falling to the ground with an assortment of minor wounds. Nothing was life-threatening, but each wound hurt like hell and the name of the game right now was slowing the bikers down, not killing them. There were too many to kill, and all the companions knew that; now was a time to run for it, and to hell with fighting the enemy.

Sue was shooting from the passenger seat, her .22 doing no small amount of damage as the jeep swerved from side to side.

Vincent hadn't been standing idle as the companions' jeeps surged forward, scattering his people.

"Stop those fuckers!" he screamed while shooting at Henry, who was a hard target to hit as the man swayed back and forth as the jeep drove around the parking lot. "Shoot the fucking tires out!"

More bikers responded to his orders and began shooting at the jeeps, the companions having to duck down as low as they could or risk being riddled with rounds.

Mary ran straight into a tall skinny biker who hadn't moved fast enough. The man had time for one brief shout of fear before he was run down, his face appearing above the hood of the jeep for a moment, the countenance of terror locked in the headlights, before he was pulled under the vehicle. A second later, the jeep jumping a little as it ran over the obstruction, the biker rolled out from under the rear end to come to a stop as nothing but a bag of scraped meat wrapped in leather, the face having dragged across the gravel parking lot for a second, shredding the skin to a bloody pulp.

"Rocko!" Vincent shrieked, watching his man go down. He fired again at the jeep, seeing red, his fury was so complete. "I want their fucking heads on poles by morning!"

Bullets zipped past Henry's head as he returned fire at the bikers, doing his best to keep them scattered and off guard. If they managed to form a decent resistance, like a blockade of armed men, there would be no escaping it. The companions would be riddled with bullets, along with the vehicles, and that would be the end of that.

A bullet ricocheted off the barrel of the M60, Henry feeling the bullet cut through his shirtsleeve, missing his arm by a millimeter. There was now two holes in the shirt from the bullet's passing.

Jimmy let out a grunt as he was shot in the thigh, but he ignored the pain, and wincing as he fought through it, continued to use the shotgun. When it ran out of shells, he let it drop to his chest by its lanyard and pulled a .45 from its holster. After the last battle with the cannies, he'd taken another gun, the .45, pilfered from a dead cannie, to use along with his shotgun. He killed a biker just before the man got off a shot that might have hit Cindy, and once more he was glad he'd decided to start carrying a sidearm along with the shotgun. It had been Henry's idea, mostly, but Jimmy would be damned if he'd ever tell the older man that Henry had been right.

Mary had managed to make a full circle of the parking lot. She swerved around the bonfire, hitting a woman covered from head to toe in tattoos with the jeep's front fender, sending the woman flying into that same fire. Then she floored the gas pedal and made for the road that would lead to freedom.

Behind Mary, the tattooed biker screamed as her hair was incinerated in an instant. She stumbled out of the fire, her clothing making her a human torch; she shrieked and wailed in utter agony.

Vincent saw what was occurring, turned, and shot the dying woman in the chest, killing her and ending her suffering.

He sent three more bullets at the fleeing jeeps, and when his Colt clicked on an empty chamber, he roared to the heavens in frustration.

"Hold on!" Mary yelled out as she drove headlong at the line of Harley's and Indians that were blocking the only exit out of the golf course. The motorcycles were big, and it was possible there wouldn't be a way to break through the line of metal and steel.

She was only a second away from plowing into the first of the vehicles when Sue leaned over and grabbed Mary's steering wheel.

"Sue! What the hell are you doing?" Mary shrieked as the jeep swerved hard to the right, jumping over a low rise and landing on the denuded grass of the golf course.

"We don't need to try and crash into those bikes!" Sue screamed. "This isn't a movie where we need to make the largest explosion. The golf course is fine for this jeep. It's made for that kind of terrain."

There was no time for a rebuttal as the jeep landed on the grass, sinking in but still maintaining traction. Cindy, seeing the lead jeep swerve, followed without question, assuming Mary and Henry knew what they were doing.

Jimmy didn't understand what was happening, and why they weren't crashing through the bikes like they were in an action movie, as if there was one thing he liked to do, it was cause damage. So as he swerved past the parked motorcycles, he sent a few shots at a large Harley, firing as fast as he could squeeze the trigger of the .45. At first, he didn't think he'd accomplished what he'd hoped, but just as the second jeep flew past the bike blockade as Mary took a detour around them, the last bullet did its job. The other bullets had managed to hit the gas tank of one bike, allowing the gas to begin leaking out of the fresh holes, but it was the last bullet, which went wide but had struck the exhaust, that created the much-needed spark that ignited the fumes from the leaking tank.

Night turned to day in that brief moment, as the full gas tank erupted into a blazing fireball that took another five motorcycles with it, each one then erupting in consecutive blasts. The roar of the explosions was deafening, the blast wave enough to put many of the bikers on their ass.

From the main road that the golf course was on, anyone looking up to the golf course would have assumed World War 3 was happening, as the sound of explosions and gunfire filled the night.

It was rough going as Mary tried to keep the jeep aimed back to the main road that would lead to freedom. The golf course grounds were riddled with imperfections that caused the jeep to bounce and jump like the passengers were on a rollercoaster.

Henry managed to climb down from the M60. He plopped down between Sue and Mary, pleased to have the stability of sitting down again as the jeep bucked like a wild horse being broken in. He glanced over his shoulder to see Cindy and Jimmy following close behind, and past the second jeep, the flames licking at the sky as the motorcycles burned. Secondary explosions filled the night as other motorcycles caught fire

Mary had to drive far and wide to reach the main road again. There were the remains of the pond where Henry and Jimmy had bathed to circle around, then they had to double back when an old sand trap blocked their way. Jimmy had wanted to try and get through it, but Henry didn't want to take the chance.

Later, a massive tree that had fallen in a past storm blocked the only feasible way to escape. Henry used his panga and cut a swathe through a massive tangle of sagebrush, while inspecting the ground to ensure it was solid enough for the jeeps. Satisfied it would be okay, that there were no sinkholes or depressions that would stop the jeeps from passing, they continued onward.

There was a reason why the bikers hadn't thought the need to block the companions from using the golf course as a getaway. The terrain was too difficult to navigate after years of neglect.

As the two jeeps drove around the golf course, slowly making headway to their final destination of the main road, behind them somewhere they could hear the bikers en masse. Gunshots could be heard; though as to what the biker gang was shooting at was anyone's guess. The slow rumble of dozens of motorcycle engines filled the air like far away thunder, but no one was following the two jeeps—yet.

Three-quarters of an hour later, which felt longer due to the stress of danger hanging over all their heads, Mary managed to reach the main road, coming out nearly a quarter mile from the clubhouse.

She pulled onto the road and slowed to a stop, after Cindy kept beeping repeatedly that she needed to talk to them.

Henry jumped out of the jeep before it had even come to a full stop, climbing over Sue to do so. "What's the matter? We don't have time for breaks right now. We need to keep moving."

"I know that, Henry," Cindy snapped, her voice filled with concern. "But Jimmy's been shot—and Henry; he's not moving!"

Chapter 28

Jumping out of the jeep, Henry ran to Cindy and a slumped Jimmy, who was lying with eyes closed beside the M60, his arms wrapped around it in unconsciousness.

"Help me get him out of there," Henry said, the others assisting him in getting Jimmy out of the vehicle and placing him on the ground before the jeep, so that the headlights could give off their much-needed light. He was placed on his back, a rolled-up jacket used for a pillow. "Someone give me some more light, damn it," Henry snapped as he tried to see where Jimmy was hurt.

Sue appeared with a flashlight, and she held it over Jimmy's prone body.

"That's good," Henry said while studying his friend. It took only a second to discover the darker patch of material on the younger man's upper thigh. He couldn't be sure, but it didn't look so bad that the big quadricep muscle was damaged, nor a major artery severed. But it was still a bullet wound and that was never a good thing. "Someone give me a knife; the panga's too big for what I need to do."

"Here, use this," Cindy said, handing Henry what looked like a pairing knife. "I found it in the supplies that were in the jeep."

He nodded. "This'll work fine." He cut Jimmy's pant leg, slicing into the material so he had room to work, but careful to avoid the flesh beneath. Once that was done, he opened his mouth to ask for water, but before he could speak, Mary held out a canteen, knowing what he needed next.

"Thanks," he said and washed the wound. He reached around to the back side of Jimmy's thigh, not finding an exit hole. "The bullet's still in there; it needs to come out now. But first I need to tie off the leg or he'll bleed to death before I can finish."

Sue handed Henry a towel and he quickly ripped it into strips. Taking one good length of material, he tied off Jimmy's leg high as he could above the bullet hole, then he inspected the wound once more now that blood wasn't pumping out of the hole, but only seeping.

"Will he be okay?" Cindy asked, the panic in her voice apparent to all. When she'd turned around and seen Jimmy slumped against the M60, her heart had skipped a beat in terror. It was all she could do not to stop and check on him the second she discovered him unconscious, but Sue knew she couldn't until it was safe.

"I don't know yet. I sure as hell hope so," was all Henry could think to say. Now wasn't the time for coddling her; he needed to keep working.

"Wait, here. Use this on the knife, Jimmy, and your hands, too," Mary said and handed Henry a bottle of whiskey.

He took the proffered bottle and looked at her, Mary's face bathed in darkness on one side, the light from the headlights showing her other side clearly.

"Where'd this come from?"

"Found it in the stuff in the jeep, too. I've been saving it for a good time. This seems about as good as any."

Henry nodded and washed his hands with the liquid, the knife, and then poured a good amount over Jimmy's wound to help sterilize it. He took a good swig himself, as he sure as hell wasn't a surgical doctor and needed all the liquid courage he could get.

"Someone find me some Duct tape if we have it. I'm gonna need it later."

"I'll do it," Mary said and went in search of the tape, something they tried to have on hand at all times. The tape was versatile, and before the dead walked, was used for everything from repairing car fenders to wrapping up just about anything a person could think of.

"Okay, here goes nothing," Henry said and got to work.

"Just help him," Cindy said, pleading.

"That's the plan, honey." Using the pairing knife, Henry sliced the wound open a little more so he could get his fingers into the cut, then after doing it, he splashed some more whiskey onto the wound. Jimmy stirred, moaning softly but he didn't wake up. Henry was glad. Without anesthesia or a local, the pain of him digging around in Jimmy's thigh would have been unbearable.

Using two fingers, Henry slid them into the hole and began poking around. It was warm, and he fought off the revulsion he felt as he dug around inside Jimmy. He'd seen the insides of human bodies countless times since the dead walked, but this was an entirely new experience. This was his friend Henry now had his fingers in, and he tried not to let it shake him.

"I found the bullet, now all I have to do is pull it out," he said, and he tried to grasp the slippery lead slug with his blood-slick fingers. The bullet kept slipping free and he had to try again. "Do we have long nose pliers by any chance?"

"I'll check," Mary said and ran off to go through the limited amount of tools they had. She returned a minute later. "I didn't see any, sorry."

"That's okay, Mary, I guess we can't always be lucky."

Jimmy was moaning louder and Henry was getting worried the man would wake up. He looked at Mary and Cindy. "You two get over here and hold him down. I don't need him jumping around if he comes to, especially while I have my hand inside his leg."

They did as they were asked, one woman on each side holding an arm. But Jimmy wasn't moving other than some low moaning, his head shifting from side to side, as if he was lost in some wild nightmare.

He was sweating profusely, and Cindy used the back of her sleeve to softly pat his face. "Hang in there, lover, you're gonna be all right," she said while fighting off the tears welling in her eyes.

"Damn straight he will," Mary concurred

Biting his upper lip in concentration, Henry kept working at retrieving the bullet, and after the fifth try, when he thought he might have to make the opening even wider, he let out a low yell of celebration as his fingers popped out and the bullet came with them. "Got it!" He pointed to the makeshift tourniquet. "Sue, get ready to release that when I say. If it's kept on too long it could mess up his leg if it isn't getting any blood flow."

"Okay, just tell me when," she replied.

Henry barely heard her, as he was wiping his hands clean for the next part of the operation. First he poured some more whiskey on the open wound, then did his best to wipe away any excess liquid, be it whiskey or blood. Then he pulled his Glock from its holster, popped the clip out of the pistol, and took out two bullets.

"Cindy, hand me your Bowie knife," he said. "Sue, give me some light here; hold it steady."

Cindy passed Henry her knife, and a second later Henry was using the edge of the blade to pry open the bullets. When this was done, he poured the gunpowder inside each round onto Jimmy's wound, then pulled a cigarette lighter from a pocket. All the companions carried lighters, be it Zippos or disposables.

"Okay, guys, hold him tight. If he's gonna wake up, this'll do it. Sue, look away for a second, it's gonna be bright." Before anyone could respond, Henry touched the flame to the powder, then turned his head to protect his face as a bright flash lit up the night and the odor of scorched flesh filled the air. Jimmy's eyes popped open and he howled loudly, only the two women keeping him from jumping up and doing God knew what. But no sooner did he yell, his eyes as large as dinner plates, then the full force of the pain hit him and he passed out, unconscious.

"Sue, honey, give me some light over here again," Henry ordered, and Sue did as she was told. The flashlight illuminated Jimmy's wound. Henry touched the edges of it carefully. The wound was now sealed thanks to the gunpowder, though it was far from perfect. "Okay, release the tourniquet."

Sue did it and Henry crossed his fingers as he watched the wound. A small trickle of blood seeped from the center, but it was very little. Satisfied his patch job would be good enough for now, he took another rag from Sue and wrapped the leg around the wound, tying off the two ends, and then wrapping the bandage with the Duct tape Mary had found earlier to keep it secured. "Okay, that's good enough till the wound can be stitched up, and we just have to hope he hasn't lost so much blood that he won't recover. We'll have to wait and see. Let's get him back onto the jeep and get moving again."

As if on cue, the sound of motorcycle engines filled the night, and in the distance, the horizon was definitely lighter than it was a second before. It wasn't a false dawn, it was the hint of the dozens of single headlights cutting through the night as they searched for the two jeeps.

"Damn it, our time's up. Come on, people, we need to move, now!" Henry snapped.

"Where are we supposed to go?" Mary yelled.

"Head for Area 51. If we don't lose them before then, maybe there's something there we can use to stop them."

"Is that a good idea?" Mary asked.

"Hell if I know. I'm making it up as I go. Maybe we can find a building that's good enough to hole up in. Hell, Mary, I don't know. This is the first time I've had a homicidal biker gang on my ass. How 'bout you?"

It took less than a minute to get Jimmy into the back of the second jeep, and as they mounted up, Cindy called out to Henry just before they started the engines and drove off, "How did you know how to do that with Jimmy?"

Henry gave her a shrug as he slid into the passenger seat, Sue beside him. Mary joined Cindy in the second jeep. The headlights of the second jeep illuminated Henry's features clearly. "Would you believe I saw it in a movie years ago?"

"You're joking," Cindy said, her mouth open in amazement.

Henry shook his head. "Nope, I didn't even know if it would really work, or whether it was just something made up for the movie."

"Huh, go figure," Mary said, impressed.

"What can I say," Henry added. "Sometimes life imitates art and sometimes it's the other way around." He put the jeep into drive and the wheels crunched over some loose gravel covering the road as he began to pick up speed.

With a smile on her face, Cindy looked at Mary, whose face was barely discernable in the darkness.

"Don't look at me," Mary said from the passenger seat. "I never saw that particular movie."

Chapter 29

The wind whipped past Henry's face as he floored the gas pedal of the jeep, Cindy doing the same with hers, which was now in the lead, as Mary still had the map leading to the location of Area 51. They needed to get there now more than ever. If Jimmy was to survive, he would need antibiotics for his leg—if not it wouldn't be long before infection set in, followed by gangrene. The best chance was the government base having some medicine somewhere within its bowels.

From past experience, he knew there were hidden government bunkers, or redoubts, as they were also called, scattered across America. Of course, some were deserted, and others were still filled with remnants of the old military, which usually were more dangerous than any other threat in the area.

But Area 51 was a well-known government installation; one where anyone could have gone for refuge once the dead began to walk years ago. A hardened installation, most of it rumored to be underground, it would've been the perfect place to ride out the zombie apocalypse.

Behind the two jeeps, the bikers were gaining fast, and Henry was getting worried.

Just as they'd drove away after patching up Jimmy, and began driving again, the jeeps had ridden side by side so the passengers could confer, and it had quickly been decided that Mary and Cindy would take the lead. Mary had studied the map in more detail and was confident she knew where they were going. Henry, with no other ideas, had deferred.

Even over the sound of the wind in his ears, Henry heard the motorcycle engines approaching; he knew sooner rather than later that the bikers would catch them. The jeeps weren't high-speed vehicles, and against the powerful motorcycles the Skullfuckers used, there really was no contest to speak of.

But there was nothing the companions could do but keep driving.

The land on either side of the highway was sparse, nothing but sagebrush and thin shrubbery, but the ground looked uneven, like the perfect terrain for four wheeling. It was the kind of land the jeeps were made for.

Honking his horn, Henry got Cindy to pull over slightly so he could come up alongside.

"We need to get off this highway." He pointed out across the road to the open area beyond. "It's rough going out there. Those bikes behind us aren't made for hard riding, they're all city bikes and for touring. We might have a better chance if we go off-road."

"But what about going to the base?" Mary asked, the wind whipping her long hair around her face. She had to constantly brush errant strands away, only for it to happen again.

"We can circle around if we lose the bikers, but we need an advantage," he explained. "We have almost no firepower to fight them with and we're down a man as well. We need to run balls out and hope for the best; it's our best chance of coming through this with our skins intact." He paused and then added, "I didn't go to all that trouble of patching Jimmy up just to have him die by some biker's blade."

The first headlight of a motorcycle appeared in Henry's rearview mirror, a scout with a faster biker than the others probably. Henry could see little of the rider, the headlight beam hiding the figure in the glare and stopping a closer study.

"Let's do it," Cindy said. "It's better than simply staying out here on the road to wait for them to catch us."

"I agree!" Mary yelled over the wind.

In reply, Henry swerved his jeep to the right, taking the vehicle off-road. Cindy was right behind him, now taking second place.

Henry felt his stomach drop as he left the road, the shoulder lower than the rest of the ground. The jeep landed hard, almost throwing him out of the driver's seat, and he instinctively reached out and grabbed Sue, who was doing fine on her own. She smiled at him, appreciating the gesture nonetheless.

As the two jeeps began driving along the rough terrain, for a few moments the biker gang was clearly seen. Dozens of headlights lit up the night, pushing the darkness away, the dull-throated roar of their engines filling the night.

Henry glanced over his shoulder, and squinting hard, was sure he could see Vincent, riding in the midst of the pack, his chromed-out Electra Glide reflecting the light from the headlights of the other bikes behind it. Making out any more details wasn't possible due to the distance between them.

Then he spotted a scout motorcycle pull out from the center of the pack to ride point, far ahead of the others, to then drive off the road and follow the companions, the rest of the gang trailing right behind.

Henry could only hope his plan was a sound one and that the jeeps could handle the difficult terrain better than the motorcycles built for highways.

The two jeeps left a wake of dust behind them as they raced across the denuded, desert-like ground, as was most of Nevada. The jeeps bounced repeatedly until it felt like the passengers were on a rollercoaster.

Sometimes the ground was so pockmarked it felt like they were driving on the moon, the jeeps coming out of the crater-like holes to jump free of the earth, before coming down and bouncing on shocks that were already too old for the kind of abuse being forced on them.

Henry looked at Sue beside him, the woman holding on for dear life as the jeep was jolted and thrown every which way. "Look at the bright side, Sue," he said quickly. "If we're having this hard of a time, Vincent and his people should be even worse off."

Sue looked over her shoulder to see the biker gang gaining distance, and as she watched, she spotted two smaller motorcycles shoot out from the pack, taking the hillocks and imperfections that made up the ground easily.

There were two people on each bike, a man driving and a woman as the passenger. Each woman carried something in her hand, something about three feet long and the shape of a tube. Sue had no idea what the objects could be, and why the bikers would be carrying them.

Then the jeep jounced hard and Sue almost fell out of her seat. Sand and grit hit her in the face, the residue kicked up by the back tires of the lead jeep. The headlights of her jeep illuminated the vehicle in front of her, Cindy having overtaken Henry, the rear bumper shifting and moving constantly as Cindy tried to steer a straight course across the land.

Sue tried not to think how dangerous it was to be driving at the speed they were moving at, on what was basically a prairie, with no light to navigate by but the feeble headlights of the jeeps and what moonlight there was. Anything could be out there before them: an old car, a boulder, a deep crevasse—and they wouldn't know about it until it was too late to turn.

She turned in her seat to see how much of a lead they had over the bikers, and she spotted the two dirt bikes closing the gap just a little more. Once more she wondered what those odd tubes were the women were holding, but try as she might, in the gloom of the night she couldn't make out what they were. She was about to tell

Henry, thinking he should at least know what was happening, when both tubes suddenly ignited.

An instant later she realized what the objects were and screamed a warning to Henry, as she watched in horror as the twin lines of fire streaked through the sky, directly at her and Cindy's jeep.

The woman in the lead bike had fired what Sue quickly discovered was a weapon, the second rider firing a moment later. The tubes were LAW rockets of all things. Where the Skullfuckers had come across small bazookas was anyone's guess, but it was obvious Vincent was out for blood and wanted the companions dead in any way possible.

The small missiles arced out of the tubes, smoke also shooting out of the rear.

"Henry! They've got missiles!" Sue shrieked, and when Henry turned around in the driver's seat to see what Sue was talking about, his eyes went wide in surprise. "Oh, shit!" he yelled when he saw the duo contrails making a line across the night sky directly towards the two jeeps. "Where the hell did they get those?"

Both rockets were heading straight for Cindy's jeep, and though Henry beeped the horn repeatedly to get either Cindy or Mary's attention, the noise of the engines and the crunching tires as they rode roughshod over the ground, plus the wind whipping at their ears, meant that neither woman heard the warning of their impending doom.

There were only seconds to go before the rockets hit, and by the looks of it, the missiles were right on target.

Henry's mind raced with ideas and nothing came to mind.

Shouting at the top of his lungs, neither of the women would acknowledge him still. Why wouldn't they turn around to see what was happening behind them? He could see Jimmy's prone form lying in the rear of the jeep, oblivious to his coming death.

The rockets soared closer, a few precious heartbeats away.

Only seconds remained before impact.

All he could do was watch helplessly, as his three closest friends were destroyed in a blazing fireball.

Chapter 30

Before the missiles struck Cindy's jeep, an idea came to Henry in a flash, a desperate chance that might save his friends.

Acting fast, and hoping his idea would work, he slammed his boot down on the gas pedal, the jeep surging forward with a jump. Coming alongside Cindy's jeep, the blonde woman glanced at Henry, a confused look on her face. She looked even more confused when Henry suddenly sideswiped her vehicle, ramming the two jeeps together and sending Cindy swerving to the right, while Henry bounced off her jeep and went to the left.

Before Cindy could open her mouth and berate Henry for doing something so foolish, the ground between the two vehicles, where both jeeps were a moment ago, erupted in a barrage of dirt and debris, the shockwave of the LAW rocket's explosion shoving both jeeps further away from one another as everyone on board each vehicle was pelted with rocks and grit.

The second missile impacted twenty feet in front of Henry, a massive cloud of smoke and dust obscuring his path.

Driving on instinct more than anything else, Henry managed to swerve around the blast crater, barely maintaining control. He heard and felt debris as it was kicked up and thrown at the undercarriage, the exposed mechanics taking a beating.

Cindy's jeep wasn't so lucky, and as it rode over a particularly uneven spot in the land, the front right wheel came down too hard, the strut, shock absorber or a ball joint snapping clean off, causing the vehicle to list like a capsizing boat. Cindy found her steering was gone, and the jeep kept moving towards the right, no matter how much she tried to stop it.

Henry spotted the second jeep swerving and saw that it wasn't keeping up. Spinning the wheel, he spun around and began driving perpendicular to his original course, racing to reach Cindy, Mary, and Jimmy before the bikers did.

The two point dirt bikes of the Skullfuckers was well ahead of the rest of the gang, and in their excitement to catch the companions, they were a little too overeager.

Henry's jeep slid to a halt, kicking up more dust as he reached the second jeep. "What's wrong?" he yelled.

"The damn steering's shit!" Cindy replied.

"Then forget it. Get Jimmy and come onto mine, there's no time to screw around." He slapped Sue on the arm to get her attention, causing the woman to wince. She didn't say anything, knowing adrenaline was pumping through everyone, given the situation. "Help them, Sue, we're about to have company."

Sue jumped out of the jeep and ran to help the others with Jimmy, while Henry turned in his seat and watched the two dirt bikes closing the distance between them, their twin headlights slicing through the darkness. They would be arriving in seconds, the rest of the chapter more than a minute behind.

A lot can happen in a minute, Henry knew well.

Henry's jeep shifted on its suspension as Jimmy was placed in the back, some supplies pushed out of the vehicle to make room. Then Cindy and Mary jumped into the back as well. Sue was once more in the passenger seat and Henry stepped on the gas again, while yelling, "Cindy, take out those assholes on the dirt bikes!"

"Will do," Cindy replied and was handed her M16 by Mary, who had been holding it during the vehicle transfer, as Henry drove off, the tires spinning only a little in the dirt. He didn't go as fast as he could have, wanting to keep the jeep as stable as possible for Cindy.

The dirt bikes gained more distance, bumping and jouncing over the rugged terrain like the two riders were off-roading on a fun Sunday afternoon. But their over-eagerness was about to get them killed.

Cindy lined up the first dirt bike, now so close she could see the bearded black face of the driver, and the long black hair of his passenger as the woman's feral face gleamed with anticipation of the prey being trapped.

She exhaled slowly, concentrating through the iron gun sights molded to the top of the rifle, tuning out the rest of the world. She squeezed the trigger just as the jeep bounced, which would have allowed her to miss. But the bullet was fired a split-second before the jeep shifted, and a heartbeat later the first dirt bike went down, the rider taking a bullet in the upper left shoulder.

"Nice shot," Mary congratulated from behind.

Cindy shook her head, her shoulder a little sore from the kick-back of the rifle. "Not really. I was going for a head shot." She shrugged. "Force of habit."

Henry turned the jeep and was headed back to the highway, a section open where there were no guardrails or other obstructions. Or so he hoped. The shadows were heavy, and there were places where the moonlight didn't pierce. For all Henry knew, those areas had objects within them that he sure as hell didn't want to run into.

Mary noticed his new direction. "Why are we going back to the highway? I thought that wasn't a good idea?"

Henry didn't look at her, his attention focused solely on driving. "I have an idea to shake some of the bikers." As he drove back to the road, the remaining dirt bike was able to close the distance even more. Apparently seeing the first bike go down wasn't much of a deterrent to the second one.

Cindy waited for the second dirt bike to be as close as possible, even to the point that a few gunshots were fired by the old lady in the passenger seat. Cindy aimed by lining up the dirt bike's headlamp, before shifting her aim a little higher. When she finally did shoot—a three-round, semi-burst in quick succession—the second and third bullets did their job, if not the first.

The first bullet missed completely, but the second 5.56mm round struck the driver in the stomach; he took the impact with a grunt and kept on coming, thanks to the ounce of cocaine he'd sniffed just before the chase had begun. He was a large man, well over six feet tall, and he weighed around two-eighty, all of it muscle. There was a reason why the man had survived so long in an apocalyptic world. The woman on the back was equally as tough, and the two had been lovers for years.

Cindy knew trying to kill someone by hitting them in the chest wasn't a foolproof way to stop them, not like in the movies where someone was hit and dropped down for the count, or if charging at the hero would spin around and fall, never moving a muscle. The chest cavity being mostly air, a man could take a hit dead on and still have the momentum from his charge to do major damage to his shooter before he went down for good. Adrenaline was another motivator. An attacker could take a bullet to the heart but still have enough life left, running on sheer fury to kill or maim his enemy before falling dead.

But none of that mattered in this case. The third and last bullet hit the motorcycle's gas tank, just to the left of the main fork, and though the machine didn't explode at first, once the gas began to seep out and the flammable liquid touched the hot exhaust, the bike instantly became a rolling fireball, all the more impressive as it was night. The woman on the back seat was consumed in flames, as was the driver, their screams lasting for long seconds before their lungs were scorched. Both bikers died in moments, though the dirt bike still kept rolling. The tires caught fire as the gas splashed everywhere, and still the dirt bike kept rolling for-ward, sheer kinetic energy keeping it moving.

Henry watched as did the women, almost hypnotized by the rolling funeral pyre. It was like something out of a Viking movie, only instead of a boat, it was a modern dirt bike. The bodies weren't moving anymore, the flames doing the job of snuffing out both lives. Hair was gone from scalps, as were eyeballs from sockets. The clothing of both corpses, so soaked with oil and grease from years of riding in the chapter, allowed the fire to keep burning long after it should have been extinguished.

The dirt bike hit a low hillock, the uneven ground sending the bike careening to the side, where it finally fell over. Even in death, the two lovers remained embraced, the blackened corpses intertwined forever.

As the blazing dirt bike went down, gunshots emanated from the rest of the biker gang, the Skullfuckers furious that four more of their chapter had been killed, or by their point of view, murdered by Henry and his people.

Bullets kicked up little divots of dirt around the jeep, but even if one found a target, it was unlikely to do much harm. The distance was too great.

"Jesus, Henry, they sure are pissed off," Cindy said as she sat back down, placing the M16 by her side.

"Yeah, so what? It's not like they wanted to have us over for coffee before. Tell us all is forgiven and welcome us back into the fold." Henry shook his head. "I don't think so. Even if they caught us before you took out those dirt bikes, we were all dead, or a fate worse than death. Screw 'em if they can't take a joke."

The jeep jumped the shoulder of the road and was back on asphalt. Almost no weeds lined the cracks in the pavement, the hot Nevada sun killing any Kudzu or crabgrass that attempted a foothold. The roads of Nevada would be around long after mankind was gone, with the exception of some sort of state-wide cataclysm such as an earthquake coming.

Now on flat road again, Henry floored the gas pedal, the jeep surging forward. The Skullfuckers turned as a group, like migrating birds flying together, and were soon doing a beeline for the road as well. Henry knew by doing what he had planned to try and shake the gang, he was going to lose any form of a lead he might have had. But there would be no outdistancing the Skullfuckers by speed alone; the jeep wasn't made for that. He needed an edge, and he believed he had one.

Once more the wind whipped at the companions' hair as the jeep traveled down the highway. For the next ten minutes there was no action, only everyone sitting restlessly as Henry tried to keep the jeep's speed up.

It was Mary, who, sitting between Henry and Sue, while Cindy stayed in the back with Jimmy, realized she recognized landmarks they were passing, such as an abandoned car, a faded road sign, or a corpse sprawled a certain way in the road.

"Henry, why are we going back the way we came? You know what's down there."

Henry glanced at Mary, then used his rearview mirror to scan the road behind him. The Skullfuckers were still there, slowly gaining ground. In minutes, the fastest of the gang would reach the jeep. Cindy was ready, her M16 in her hands, ready to shoot any who came too close, her eyes focused on the motorcycles. A few stray gunshots sounded now and then, but they went far wide of the escaping jeep and did no damage.

"I sure do, but I don't think Vincent does," Henry replied to Mary's query.

"How so?" Sue asked, curious.

"Those bikers didn't come this way, they must have come from the other direction when they found the golf course. If they did, and they'd tried to get through what we did, their engines and tires would have been covered in gunk. They weren't though, they were all spotless."

"And?"

"Let's just see what happens, all right? Just be ready to shoot when I say so."

Coming from the direction he was driving, Henry knew the sea of corpses wasn't visible until rounding a bend in the highway, and by then it would be too late to stop for an unwary driver. Stepping on the gas pedal harder, the jeep managed a few more miles per hour, and he gripped the steering wheel with white knuckles as he prepared for what would come next. He was only minutes away from the corpses, and as he drew closer, he began to doubt his plan. A million and one things could go wrong, all of them ending with the death of his people, or worse, sex slaves for the women. But then he fought off his self-doubt, he needed to stay strong, hold his resolve. That would be the only way to see it through to the end.

Cindy realized where they were going only moments before the jeep reached the corpses, and she yelled out a "What the hell?" Just before the jeep entered the sludge of decaying bodies, puddles of slop glistening in the moonlight.

The sea of rot hadn't gotten any easier on the nose since the last time the group had passed through. If anything, it smelled ranker than before. The miasma of decaying flesh was prevalent in the air, the flies hanging even thicker over the entire sea of human slush. The entire pond was a true microcosm in miracles. The way the land on each side shaded the road from the worst of the sun, and how the ground water from the incline trickled into the bodies, keeping them saturated continuously. Maggots feasted on the cadaverous meat, to then spawn flies that added to the mix. The flies hung over the entire area like a dark cloud, shading the area from the worst of the sun during the day when the land couldn't do it.

Scavengers still feasted, their body waste dropping where it may, the feces adding to the goop, to then spawn more maggots and flies, the birds feasting on the insects as much as the carrion. The circle of life repeating itself ever more.

None of this went through Henry's mind, or the others, as the jeep hit the first body, the tires running over it and popping the bloated corpse like a balloon. Dark sludge went flying to the sides and the tires crunched into the rib cage, then the gaping skull, flattening the entire form into a dark, black-red paste.

"Hold on!" Henry shouted, the jeep starting to skid the second it entered the sludge pool. The clouds of flies shifted out of the way, and any winged carrion eaters took flight as the four legged ones ran away at the disturbance, as if a giant hand had waved at them to move. The jeep skidded to the right, and Henry tugged on the steering wheel to no avail. It was like driving on ice, and at the speed he was going, well over sixty miles an hour, there was nothing he or anyone could do but hold on and pray for the best.

The Fiat was still in the center of the sea of rot, as if waiting for its owner to return one day, the glass glistening under the stars where it wasn't covered in gore. The area around the little car was also still churned up, though the damage was slowly healing itself, as the sludge of corpses slowly melted back to fill the places it was disturbed, the goop resembling mud in its consistency.

The jeep swerved hard to the left, almost going sideways, and Henry did his best to correct the direction of the vehicle. If he was doing anything at all, he couldn't tell. The Fiat was coming up fast, and there was nothing he could do. Instinctively, he raised his right hand to the side to shield Mary and Sue from hitting the dashboard, then he braced for the coming impact, knowing the speed the jeep was going, serious harm could come to the group, even death a possibility.

His plan was about to end before it began.

On the bright side, if they all died in a car crash, there would be nothing Vincent could do to them when he caught up.

But a second before hitting the Fiat, the jeep swerved a little more to the side, and instead of hitting the stationary car head on, it was only sideswiped. Everyone inside the jeep felt the jarring impact, but then the jeep was continuing forward, past the Fiat and sliding to the edge of the corpses.

In the rear of the jeep, Jimmy remained unconscious, never knowing how close they had all come to hitting the Fiat at more than fifty miles an hour.

Cindy was almost knocked clear out of the jeep, but just before she fell out, she managed to grab hold of the useless M60, hanging on to it like it was a life preserver.

And then, like someone had snapped a picture, in the blink of an eye, the terror was over and the jeep was careening on hard pavement again, only the blood and gore-covered tires not allowing the vehicle to have full traction yet.

Henry hit the brakes, the jeep skidding for more than thirty feet before coming to a full stop, the vehicle rocking from side to side, ending up perpendicular to the yellow lines dividing the highway.

A long stretch of duo tracks led from out of the slush-sea to where the jeep came to a stop, and sludge and gore, as well as a heaping amount of maggots, clung to every part of the vehicle.

"Ugh," Henry said, disgusted. The jeep had become cleaner over the past day, the first coating of dried bits of body parts having fallen off thanks to the hot sun. But now the jeep was once more covered in gore. But there was no time to waste, the bikers only seconds away.

"Everyone ready a gun and get ready," Henry ordered as he jumped out of the jeep and pulled his Glock. "The second those bikes hit that shit there's gonna be chaos, and I want to add to their discomfort."

The women quickly figured out what Henry meant and did as ordered, each one getting out of the jeep and setting up on the far side, so that the vehicle was between them and the approaching biker gang. Not that there would be much need for cover, as they all knew too well from their own adventures in the corpse-sea what was coming.

Mary stood beside Henry, her .38 held in her hands in a two-handed Weaver grip. Her left hand was folded over her right one, her elbow bent to provide stabilization for her almost straight right arm.

Cindy briefly checked on Jimmy, seeing the man was still unconscious, though when she checked his breathing, it was slow and steady. She wasn't a doctor but he seemed to be sleeping more than knocked out. She lovingly ran fingers over his lips, then his cheek, before getting ready for what was to come. She didn't have to wait long.

The motorcycle engines reverberating off the sides of the road echoed back and forth to the point all conversation was stopped, as no one could hear anything.

Then the headlight of the first motorcycle came screeching around the bend, moving far too fast for the rider to stop upon seeing the road covered in decaying corpses.

The biker, a black man with an ink-black beard, didn't go more than five feet before his back tire slipped out from under him. The man did his best to remain upright, but like driving through a layer of Vaseline, it was virtually impossible.

Going down hard, he let go of the handlebars, instinct telling him that when crashing was imminent, the bike needed to be separated from its rider, or else risk the machine crushing the human body. If that happened, the machine always won. The instant the rider hit the muck, he began sliding through it, slop and gunk rising up and striking him in the face, thanks to his boots acting like a plow. Spitting goop and a few stray teeth—from a decayed zombie, the teeth floating in the sludge—the man began to vomit, actually relishing the taste of his own bile compared to that of the slop he'd just ingested. He didn't even come to a halt from sliding as he threw up all over his colors, splashing hot vomit across his chest and stomach.

The hapless biker barely finished heaving before a hole appeared in his forehead, a larger one blowing out large chunks of brain matter from the back of his head. The eyes rolled up, as if trying to see the new forehead hole for himself, before the body flopped back into the muck never to rise again.

More motorcycle headlights came screaming around the bend, only for the bikes to begin slipping and sliding a moment later. The companions were ready, and they began firing indiscriminately at the helpless men and women, which against the backdrop of the night, could still be seen clearly, thanks to the numerous headlamps of the Harleys', Nortons' and other bikes.

It was a slaughter, the bikers never even getting a chance to return fire.

More than a dozen men and women were down before the Skullfuckers were able to halt their progress before entering the sludge. Unfortunately, none of the slain had been Vincent.

With the sea of bodies separating the two parties, a gunfight ensued, neither party gaining the upper hand, though there were still triple the number of bikers compared to Henry and his people. But the odds were slightly better than they were only a minute ago.

"Okay, it's time to leave," Henry said, after firing a few times to keep the bikers from getting too overzealous. A few of the Skullfuckers, too doped up and angry to care about the danger, had tried to make their way through the muck on foot, only to be killed before making it halfway to the Fiat. "Staying here and shooting it out isn't an option. We don't have enough ammo for a sustained fight, and sooner or later Vincent isn't going to get his people to outflank us. We need to be gone before that happens." He got Cindy's attention. "I need you to lay down sustained covering fire while the rest of us get back into the jeep, then you hop in the back while Sue and Mary cover you. Then we're out of here."

"I can do that, Henry!" Cindy yelled, her ears ringing, as were the others, from the constant reports of gunfire. "But let me switch out mags before we go so I have a full one."

"Do it."

Cindy reached around to her back, pulled a fresh magazine from a pocket, and quickly did as she said, then feeling good that she now had a fresh, thirty-round magazine prepared, she nodded to Henry and the others she was ready.

"Go!" Henry yelled.

Cindy began firing the M16 on full auto. The maximum firing range for the M16 was around six hundred yards, and she was well within that range, so each bullet she fired that struck something did so with devastating efficiency. As the barrage of bullets hit the bikers, who were huddled behind their motorcycles for cover, not one person in the gang was brave enough to return fire, knowing it would be instant death.

The thirty-round magazine didn't last long, but it was enough for Henry to get back into the jeep and drive away, and with Cindy jumping onto the back, Mary and Sue began firing their handguns, which held off the bikers from returning fire for a few more precious seconds.

By the time the Skullfuckers realized the M16 wasn't shooting at them and it was only sidearms, Henry was racing away from the battlefield, only sporadic gunfire aimed at the jeep, but all of it going far wide of its mark.

Vincent popped up from where he'd taken cover behind his Harley, his face a mask of anger. He began firing repeatedly at the retreating jeep, but then the jeep's taillights vanished as it entered a curve in the road. Other bikers did the same, and some continued to fire even after the jeep had vanished from sight.

"What the fuck're you assholes shooting at? They're fuckin' gone!" Vincent screamed, which eventually caused the rest to cease firing. "I want those motherfuckers bad. Ya hear me? I want them bad!" Through the gloom of the night, he scanned the sea of corpses, and at the fallen motorcycles scattered everywhere, the bodies as well. He'd lost a quarter of his chapter in one fell swoop. "I need some help salvaging whatever we can from our fallen brothers' hogs: weapons, the hogs that can still ride, gas and supplies. Then we get after those fuckers and finish this shit."

"What about the brothers and old ladies who went down, Vincent. Are we gonna bury them?" This came from a small, thin biker that everyone simply called 'Rat', as he resembled one in his features; his nose slim, a weak chin, thinning hair and beady eyes.

"Fuck 'em," Vincent replied. "What's left is nothin' but meat. The brothers we knew are gone now."

No one complained, knowing how the chapter felt about life and death. The way of a road warrior was hard, and when one of them died on said road, what had been the person, the personality so to speak, had fled the body, only leaving behind a meat sack devoid of anything that mattered.

Foulmouth had been given a warrior's funeral because there had been time, but now, on the road, chasing prey, such luxuries were a waste of time.

"Well? What the fuck are ya doing just standing around? Get to work?" Vincent ordered, his harsh tone brooking no argument.

Immediately, six brothers got to work, trudging into the muck to retrieve whatever was salvageable.

Vincent looked on for a while, silent. Eventually, his gaze rose higher until he was staring out at the open road beyond the corpse-sea, most of it wreathed in shadows. "Soon, Watson. Fucking soon, I'm gonna kill ya."

Chapter 31

The invading Russian force was on the correct road to Anchorage. They knew this thanks to the middle-aged woman they'd come across, who had told them so, right before she'd been used and abused by more than half the men under Varakov's command.

Over the long night, she was passed from one soldier to another. In the beginning, her cries had been strong, and she even tried to fight off the crude advances, but by the tenth man she had given up, and would just lay there, glassy-eyed, face blank of emotion.

Even when two men took her at once, one before her, another from behind, her face remained emotionless, the only movements of her body those created from the thrusting men.

When they had broken camp that morning, and began moving once more, the carcass of the woman remained behind, her entrails spilling out her stomach, her eyes open, but seeing nothing.

The Soviet force moved in pairs of two down the long road, each man's face hidden within thick furs and anoraks, to fight off the biting wind and frigid temperature. Many of the clothing and uniforms the men wore were splattered with dried blood. The pack animals moved slower than the horses, weighed down heavily with food and supplies, a lot of it taken from the plundered villages.

They had met no opposition that would prevent later forces coming over from Russia. No military presence at all had been found. Only the weak, cowering villagers from the few enclaves they had come across.

One thing Major Varakov and his men agreed on was that the women in America were slightly more comely than those of

Russia. In the Soviet Union, women were made of beefier stock, hardy in both body and mind. The women in America were softer, their bodies devoid of the layer of fat most Russian women had.

And they screamed more when being taken, much to the enjoyment of the men doing the taking.

Here and there, the snow was receding, and unlike the barren land of Siberia, Alaska had areas where life was thriving. Patches of green earth dappled with moss and stubby grass were everywhere the more the soldiers traveled inland.

But there had been casualties since leaving Russia, and not just losing men and horses to the treacherous ice.

Though opposition seemed nonexistent, that wasn't entirely true. One time, while ransacking a small commune of mostly old men and women, a sniper had taken shots at the men from a low slope, killing two soldiers with chest shots. Varakov had sent six men to find the sniper, and they had done so, but when the man had been cornered, he had taken his own life by putting the rifle in his mouth and pulling the trigger. His brain matter and skull fragments still dappled the white snow where he had fallen, the soldiers stripping the sniper of anything of value and leaving the corpse for the wolves.

A handful of his men dead already, and considering the timeline for the invasion and then return to Russia, no doubt many more of his men would perish before he stepped foot back in Mother Russia.

The journey was taking longer than expected, too. After a four day trek across the Alaskan interior, the invading force had come upon a large mountain range that needed to be crossed for their trip to continue.

So with no choice but to change direction, they began heading northeast, and eventually found a road leading south through the mountains.

An old highway sign hanging by one bolt to a large aluminum pole declared that they were on the proper road, the route they were on being the main highway connecting Anchorage to Fairbanks.

Major Varakov began to sing, a hardy ballad that would make young women blush. Soon, the rest of the men were singing as well, their voices loud over the deserted highway.

As they rode, the men laughed and sang; morale slightly better now that the mountain range was in their back trail.

Varakov looked off to the west, a gentle rise to the land making it blot out what lay beyond. He also made out the skulking shapes of a pack of wolves, their bellies low to the ground as they tracked the soldiers. Varakov smiled as he watched them, thinking they must be disappointed that there were no weak stragglers in his herd, much like there might be in a herd of buffalo or caribou. For stragglers could be dragged down and torn apart, while the rest of the herd escaped, relieved that only one of their number was enough to satiate the wolves for a time.

Later that night, as the men passed through a sharp ravine, where the highway had been cut directly through sheer rock, a small avalanche occurred directly before them, raining down ice, snow, and ice-coated boulders onto the beleaguered soldiers.

No one was hurt but if they had been just a little closer when it happened, they would have all been buried under the tons of snow and ice. Fortune was with them, however, and the men only received a small taste of the avalanche as the snow spread out far and wide.

The horses had become frightened as the ground shook beneath their hooves, and several of the riders, including Rhzhdestvensky, were unseated.

The rest of the men laughed at this, as they watched their comrades flail around in the deep snow.

Angered at this, Rhzhdestvensky got to his feet, grabbed his mount's bridle, and punched the horse in the head, the blow so strong the head was knocked to the side. The only reason the horse didn't go down from such a brutal blow was that the wound to the fat man's shoulder had eased the blow. Still, the animal was unstable for a few moments as it regained its wits.

Satisfied he had taught his steed some manners, he climbed back into the saddle, sitting taller now despite his bulk. Around him, the other soldiers clapped and cheered.

Varakov smiled at the fat soldier's display, and when the other men had regained their mounts, they set off again, having to leave the road to venture around the avalanche. It was slow-going, but eventually they made it to the other side of the highway, to then proceed onward.

Varakov was getting itchy for slaughter. It had been a while since he'd felt an enemy cowering beneath his heels, or felt the spray of blood on his face after decapitating a foe. He welcomed a true fight from the pitiful Americans, but as of yet no challenge had shown itself. He wondered if one ever would.

Perhaps Anchorage would offer an enemy worth fighting.

The wind shifted from the south, and he tasted salt on his tongue, which meant that the sea wasn't too far off. That also must mean he was getting closer to Anchorage.

A soldier rode up until he was abreast of Varakov, who glanced to his side to see it was Karamatsov, the explosives expert of their small army.

"Comrade Major, I would love to blow that up; have some fun." The man gestured to a large dam with towers to their right. The massive structure of concrete and steel dominated the entire valley the Russian soldiers rode through, the towers silhouetted against the deep blue sky.

Varakov looked more intently at the dam, studying it for a few moments. Finally, he said, "What would be the point? The water is probably frozen. There wouldn't be much of a show."

"Not so, Comrade Major. If you look up ahead, you will see there is a river with flowing water. Moving water does not freeze. Please, Comrade Major, let me blow it up. It would be a wonderful spectacle to behold. I promise."

Varakov considered the man's request for a few seconds, as he too could use something fun to take his mind off the tedious journey. Eventually, he decided it wouldn't be the right time. Later, they would need to return this way on their way home, and if the entire valley was flooded, then how would they manage to traverse the area?

"No, Comrade Karamatsov, not now. Perhaps later, when we head home."

"But, Comrade Major…"

"I said no! Do not argue with me!" Varakov placed a hand on his sword, the warning clear to the other man.

"Of course, thank you for considering it." Karamatsov quickly let his horse fall back so he was in the middle of the line. After angering his leader, he knew to be out of sight for a while was probably in his best interest. Still, he gazed longingly at the dam, wishing he could get a crack at it.

The next few hours passed quietly, each man keeping his own thoughts. Varakov gazed up at the sky as the sun began to set, knowing it would be time to make camp soon.

It had snowed a little during the past hour, and a light dusting covered the highway, making footing dangerous where ice had formed previously. The dam still loomed behind them, a towering form of concrete and steel.

"Look over there, Comrade Major," Streltsy said, pointing off to the far right.

Varakov's gaze followed where his second had pointed, seeing through the falling darkness several one-story buildings made of concrete, and a dozen large, saucer-shaped objects mounted on tripods, more than a hundred feet tall. Nearby, there were also three large ball-like structures around fifty feet in height, the outer surface looking as if they were made up of hundreds of triangles formed in complicated patterns. Both dishes and balls were white. It only took him a moment to realize what the objects were.

"Ah, radar dishes and arrays, Comrade Streltsy." Though he was still a distance away, Varakov didn't see any signs of movement. "It looks abandoned. That seems as good a place as any to make camp for the night. Let us go there."

"What if there are people there, Comrade Major?"

Varakov smiled as he returned his second-in-command's gaze. "Then perhaps we can have some fun after we make camp."

Chapter 32

"Shit," Henry said under his breath.

The engine of the jeep was turned off as it wasn't going any-where for a long time. Darkness surrounded the vehicle and the five people riding inside it. Cloud cover hid the moon, making visibility almost zero without outside illumination. Climbing out of the jeep onto the road, and standing a foot from one another, no one could see the other's face. It was a little over an hour before dawn, when it always seemed to be the darkest time of the night.

"What's wrong? Why'd we stop?" Mary's voice said from the surrounding darkness.

Henry turned his head, seeing nothing but blackness. "The damn transmission isn't working. The gears had been slipping for a while, but now it's to the point that we don't have any forward motion. Must have gotten damaged as we were driving over all that rough ground, or maybe a piece of shrapnel from those rockets hit it. There was a time for a few seconds when it felt like the whole planet was shooting up under it when we were driv-ing."

"Then fix it. We can't say here. Hopefully we lost those bikers, but if we didn't, they can't be too far behind us, even though we've got a good lead." This time it was Sue speaking.

"Don't you think I know that? But I can't fix a tranny out here in the middle of the desert, now can I?"

"No, I suppose you can't. So what do we do now?" Still Sue.

"Mary, you still got that map?" Henry asked.

"You know I do." It was Mary who answered.

Henry turned his head to where it sounded like she was, seeing barely a shape before him. "How far are we from Area 51?"

The sound of shuffling paper came to his ears, as if the map was being unfolded. "I can't see anything. I need some light."

"Okay, wait a second." Henry pulled out his Zippo lighter from a pocket and a heartbeat later, he could see the faces of all his friends, though Jimmy was still lying quietly in the back of the jeep. In the past hour, the young man had shown some signs of life, such as moaning once or twice. Henry hoped it was a good thing.

Mary moved closer to Henry. He had to move to the side slightly with the lighter or risk the edge of the map catching fire. "Careful," he snapped.

"Sorry," Mary replied, then laid the map on the warm hood of the jeep. Henry moved the light closer so she could see, as she moved her fingers across the lines on the map, studying it. "If I'm reading this right, we have about a half hour drive left. Longer if the jeep's not running."

Henry leaned over her shoulder, also scanning the map. "Well, we don't have time to study it longer. I'm pretty sure we're in the clear from Vincent, but better be safe than sorry. Once we reach the base there should be some shelter at least."

With the clicking of the upper half of the Zippo closing, the lighter flame was extinguished. He walked over and turned on the jeep's headlights. The light was weak without the engine running, and Henry knew the battery wasn't too strong. Even if the battery had been installed new just before the dead began to walk, it would now be near its life's end, as batteries like most things had ceased production due to the zombie apocalypse beginning almost five years ago. But it no longer mattered.

"Okay, let's gather what we can carry and then we need to rig up some kind of stretcher for Jimmy. Then we can take turns carrying him." He walked over to Jimmy, seeing the young man's sleeping features against the backwash of the jeep's headlights.

"Now we gotta carry you, pal. It's just like you to get shot so you don't have to walk."

Cindy joined Henry, while Sue and Mary got to work unpacking supplies. There was so much they wanted to take with them, but they knew only so much could be carried.

"Tell me he's going to be okay, Henry? Even if it's a lie."

Henry turned and cupped Cindy's chin in his hand, looking down on the pretty blonde warrior. He still remembered the first day he'd seen her. He was with Jimmy, the two getting a drink with the leader of the town, a man named Sam, at a local tavern in a town called Pittsfield. The instant Jimmy had seen Cindy, he'd fallen head over heels for the girl. Even then, Cindy had a fire in her, a willful spirit. Wanting to escape from her abusive uncle who ran the bar, she'd been excited to join the companions when they planned to leave the town. Of course, Pittsfield had fallen, overrun by zombies, so any semblance of her home remaining had been destroyed. But Henry was sure she would have come with them even if her home hadn't been destroyed.

"Sure, honey. He's going to be okay, and in a week or two it'll be like him getting shot never happened. So if it makes you feel better, yes. He'll be fine." He sighed and glanced at Jimmy's slumbering face once more. "We've been through a lot together, him and me. Don't tell me why, but I don't think this is the end of our story together either. He's young and strong, he can fight this. Now, don't tell me how I know this to be true, 'cause it's just a gut feeling, but I know he's gonna pull through." He gave her a gentle push towards the others. "Now you go help Mary and Sue, and I'll get Jimmy out of the jeep so we can get that stretcher made up."

She nodded and did as asked, and as she walked away, Henry leaned in close to Jimmy's ear and said, "Don't make me a liar, buddy. Wake up already."

* * *

Twenty minutes later, four people walked slowly down the center of the highway, carrying another of their group between them. The headlights of the jeep soon faded to nothing, either due to distance or the battery finally giving out.

"How come you didn't try and hide the jeep, but left it on the road where anyone can see it?" Sue asked as they walked together. Henry was holding the front part of the stretcher, Mary the other side, as she walked behind Henry so that Jimmy was lying prone between them, his feet near Mary, his head basically by Henry's butt. Two good thick branches had been found near the road from a long-dead tree, and spare clothing had been used for the material to make the stretcher. Henry didn't mind Sue asking questions. It took his mind off his sore arms, shoulders, back and so on. Man, he was getting old, he thought. Cindy would switch with Mary soon, but Henry so far had refused to let anyone else carry his half.

Henry tried to shrug but gave it up, the weight of Jimmy holding his shoulders from moving. The wound he'd received when fighting Foulmouth had reopened from carrying Jimmy, and he could feel a thin trickle of blood sliding down his back. "Didn't seem worth the trouble," he replied. "There was nowhere to hide it where we stalled and any time spent trying to push it off the road and figure out something was time we could spend walking. Besides, that damn thing is so covered in blood and crap from going through that deader mess back there that I didn't want to be near it any longer than I had to be. It smelled terrible. Gunk must have gotten everywhere: inside the fenders, the engine, around the gas tank. No, it's fine where it is; and if someone does come across it, at least we'll know about it."

"What do you mean?" Sue persisted.

"Never mind, it doesn't matter now."

For a while no one spoke, each of them keeping their thoughts private. Then once more there was sporadic conversation, such as what would be waiting for them at Area 51? Would it be inhabited? Would it be deserted?

Coming over a rise in the road more than an hour later, they were greeted to a welcome sight by the light of the false dawn.

"Well, will you look at that? Right where the map said it was," Henry said in awe.

"Looks quiet," Mary said as she walked beside Henry, who was still carrying Jimmy. Sue was on the other end of the stretcher, as she wanted to do her part to help.

In the distance, spread out before them, acres of land covered by low buildings and landing strips, was undoubtedly the fabled Area 51. Most of the concrete buildings were no more than one-story tall, square, with flat roofs, and painted white. Few had windows. A massive hurricane fence surrounded the entire base from what the group could see of it.

But there was something else there as well.

There were thousands of corpses lying around the base, where they had congregated near the hurricane fence near the gate.

"Looks like this place was under siege when the deaders took a nose dive," Cindy said as she studied the silent military base.

"Yeah," Henry agreed as he looked on. "But if you look closely, there are no flies over the bodies, and I don't see much animal activity. Do any of you?"

No one did, which they hoped was a good thing.

While they had been taking in the grand scope of the base and talking, they were walking, and as they slowly got closer, they were able to take in more detail.

There had been numerous fires on the base at one time in the past, and bullet holes could be seen in the walls of the guard shack at the main gate, more corpses lying before it, like some sort of grotesque carpeting.

The guard shack was behind a large, rolling gate with razor wire on its top. To the sides of the gate, the fence had bowed in a few places, but had still withheld the onslaught of bodies. Large klieg lights had been set up, probably to light up the place at night. Some lights had been shot out, the shattered glass on the ground reflecting the wan light of the coming dawn.

As the companions moved even closer, they were able to see a section of fence far to the left of the main gate, where the chain-links had broken under the awesome weight of so many bodies pushing on it. Through the hole and beyond into the base itself, bodies were sprawled everywhere.

"So maybe this place didn't get off as easy as we hoped," Henry said as he took in the hole in the fence. "At least we have a way in. If the power's off, it would be a pain to get that main gate open. I don't have any wire cutters on me, do any of you?"

The women shook their heads no.

"That's what I thought."

Jimmy moaned and then slowly opened his eyes, Sue letting out a shout of excitement that had everyone reaching for their weapons before realizing she was being slightly overzealous. No one could blame her, as they were all tickled pink to see Jimmy waking up.

They stopped walking and placed the stretcher on the road, while off to the east, the sun slowly began to rise, the sky a brilliant orange-red color on the horizon.

Gathering around the stricken man, all wore smiles of relief and happiness.

Cindy leaned over and kissed Jimmy, her hands going to his face, touching him lovingly. "Thank God you're awake."

"Water," he croaked.

Cindy pulled a bottle of Snapple from her pack and carefully let Jimmy sip some of it. "Not too much, you don't want to choke."

"Thanks, babe. What the hell happened?" he asked groggily, his voice hoarse. "Last thing I remember we were running from the bikers and then…"

"You passed out, buddy," Henry said, patting Jimmy gently on the arm. "You took a bullet in the thigh, but I managed to get it outta you. I was worried you lost too much blood though."

Jimmy managed a sneer, then winced in pain when he tried to move his legs. "Shit, Henry, you operated on me? Hope you're a better doctor than you are a marksman."

"Well, I must be, 'cause you're not dead, are you?" Henry smiled, taking the jibe in good cheer.

Mary leaned in and kissed Jimmy on the forehead. "He must be okay; he's already making jokes and insulting Henry."

Jimmy tried to sit up but realized it was a mistake. His head swimming, he put on his best smile, despite not feeling up to it. "Hey, it'll take a lot more than a biker gang to take out the great Jimmy Cooper. If a hundred thousand deaders can't do it, a bunch of pussies on tricycles sure aren't gonna do the deed."

More than five minutes had passed since Jimmy first opened his eyes, and that was five minutes the group hadn't spent walking. Five minutes they were going to wish they'd had when a moment later, from far behind them, the muffled sound of an explosion filled the air.

Everyone except Jimmy turned to look where the explosion had come from. Over the rise in the highway, a plume of black smoke was spiraling high into the lightening sky.

"I booby trapped the jeep," Henry said matter-of-factly, answering the question on the women's lips. "Stuffed a grenade with the pin pulled under the driver's seat, and left the key in the ignition. All it took was someone sitting on the seat and shifting the springs inside it to jar the grenade. Once that happened…" He closed his hands together and then pulled them apart. "Boom!" The grenade had come from the captured supplies taken from the cannies when the bodies had been stripped and the vehicles sorted. The grenade had been one of three taken off a cannie who had died long before he'd the opportunity to use them.

"So that was why you told us that no one could go back to the jeep once we left it," Mary said, thinking back to something Henry had said when they left with Jimmy on the stretcher.

He nodded. "Sure did. Figured it would be a good early warning system if someone was following us."

"Like Vincent and his cronies?" Cindy asked.

"Yeah, probably."

"But what if it was just some wanderer who found it?" Sue asked.

Henry looked at her, his eyes hard. "That would be terrible. I wouldn't want to kill some innocent traveler, but we both know the odds of that happening so close to us running for it is almost zero. It's gotta be Vincent still pursuing us."

"I bet he's pissed off now," Cindy said with a smile. "If he catches up to us…" She let the sentence trail off, everyone knowing what she was trying to say.

"Huh, so you mean making him madder at us is gonna make it worse?" Henry asked. "Cindy, we've done so much to that man and his people, it'll be a miracle if he doesn't kill us the second he lays eyes on us if given the chance. Trust me, there's no way we could get that guy any madder at us if we tried."

"Well, it's his own damn fault," Sue said, angry for everything that had happened. "He could have left us alone and let us leave that golf course. If he had, then none of this would have happened. Jimmy wouldn't be shot; his people would all still be alive. None of it."

While they talked, they had also begun moving again, knowing time was short. If it was Vincent and his gang of coldhearts who'd found the jeep, and it was pretty sure bet it was, Henry knew the man would be gathering his forces and would be on the move shortly, knowing the gang was gaining on its prey.

On foot, the companions were slow as molasses, and with Jimmy in the stretcher, they were even slower.

"Okay, no more talking; we concentrate on getting to that base," Henry said as the base loomed ever closer. They would be at the first of the corpses in ten minutes or less. They had made good time despite Jimmy being carried after leaving the jeep, and it would take anyone following them around the same amount of time to reach them from the location of the destroyed jeep.

As it was, seconds could decide the group's fate, and whether they reached the prospective safety of the military base or if they were caught out in the open. With no cover to think of and only their firearms and the two hand grenades, Vincent and his gang on their motorcycles could easily run down the companions, slaughtering them even as the group stood their ground.

Minutes later, the five friends reached the first of the corpses at the outskirts of the base. Stepping past them, it was clear to see that the only way through the bodies would be to walk right on top of them, as they were packed so close together.

But these corpses didn't look like the ones back in the ravine, that had been constantly saturated with water and were hidden from the harsh sun most of the day. These had been lying out in the arid desert, the sun baking them day after day, no water to be seen.

Basically nothing more than dried skin the consistency of leather, and clothing shredded and falling part, they resembled beef jerky wrapped in rags more than human beings.

Henry took a tentative step before the others, still holding the stretcher. Mary and Cindy held the other part, and by doing so, could move faster. Henry was still going strong due to his iron will, the long trek while holding Jimmy taking a toll on him. But when they'd set Jimmy down as the man had woken, it had given Henry a small respite, one that served him well now. With a second burst of energy, as well as a surge of adrenaline knowing Vincent was coming, they had reached the base quickly.

Henry stepped on the first unavoidable body, a puff of dust coming up from the corpse, the grinning skull falling to the side. The bones were brittle and dried as well, and cracked easily under Henry's weight.

The others soon followed, and soon there was a cloud of dust hanging in the air as the bodies were flattened into dust. No one breathed, knowing if they sucked in the dust, they would basically be inhaling pulverized people.

Slowly, they made their way to the opening in the fence, and just as they reached it, and prepared to enter the base, the sound of motorcycle engines filled the air, causing everyone to turn around while gasping for air whenever they felt they had a chance of breathing freely.

Coming up over a slight incline on the highway, with Vincent in the lead, rode what was left of the Skullfuckers, looking even from a distance like death incarnate.

Many of the bikers were covered in splattered blood, some of it the owners, but a lot of it from the explosion that had killed three brothers who had checked out the jeep to their misfortune. When the jeep had erupted in a firestorm, shrapnel had shot out in all directions, and the three brothers who had been around the jeep had been pulverized, their bodies turned into a pink spray that had washed over the other nearby bikers.

From a quick glance, Henry counted at least two dozen bikers still remained alive. The companions had managed to whittle away at a good chunk of Vincent's numbers, but there were still far too many to take on in a pitched firefight.

"Shit," Henry spit, "here they come. Come on, people, we gotta move. Now!"

Throwing caution to the wind, they began running into the base, heedless of the dust cloud they had made. The bodies were sporadic upon entering the base, more spread out so that it was easy for the group to avoid them.

Sue took one hand of the stretcher from Henry, so that all four of them carried Jimmy. One hand on the stretcher, the other hand holding a weapon, they ran as fast as they could into the base.

Coming onto a street, Henry slowed and looked around, seeing the pockmarked buildings, riddled with bullets, and one to his left that had entirely burned down, leaving nothing but the metal struts and cement pillars that had framed it.

"Well, we're here," he said quickly. "For all it's worth to us."

"Guys, let me walk, you don't have to carry me," Jimmy said, his voice barely above a whisper.

"Nothing doing, Jimmy. You're still weak and you'll only slow us down. Let us carry you, it's the best way right now," Cindy said, the others agreeing.

The motorcycle engines grew louder, and Henry glanced over his shoulder to see that the bikes were leaving the highway to cross the desert, the lead bike doing a beeline for the opening in the fence.

"They're almost here. We need to find that bunker." His eyes darted left and right, trying to figure out which way to go. The place was huge, and he quickly realized the idea that they would simply arrive at Area 51 and easily find the underground bunker was ridiculous. The entrance could be anywhere, and the egress was probably either hidden in one of the buildings or camouflaged somewhere else near the base.

Mary had pulled out the map with her free hand and was reading it. She was biting her lower lip in concentration as she studied the map, trying to make some sense of the numbers and words in the margin.

"Tick, tock, Mary," Henry said quickly. They needed to either make a run for where they needed to go or they had to find someplace else to make a stand. Unfortunately, Henry had a bad feeling that the stand he and his friends took would end up being a 'last' stand.

The biker gang had reached the first decayed corpses surrounding the base, and drove over the bodies, the air quickly becoming filled with the pulverized corpses, ash and dust suffusing the area, causing the bikers to begin coughing and hacking. They slowed down, unable to see, which gave Henry and his team a few more precious seconds to escape.

"That's it, we're out of time. Come on, we have to find a building we can fight off Vincent in," Henry snapped.

"But what about the bunker?" Mary asked, still holding the map as they began to run, Jimmy holding onto the sides of the stretcher with his hands or risk falling right out of it as he was being jounced around as if he was on a rollercoaster.

"It's irrelevant now, Mary. We don't know where the hell it is, and there's no time to begin searching. We need to prepare for our final stand against Vincent."

"But, Henry, there's too many of them for us to hold off with the armament we have?" Cindy said as she ran behind him.

"Yeah, I know. When we first ran for it after Mary killed those men, the plan was to reach the bunker before Vincent caught up to us." He glanced at Mary over his shoulder. "So, Mary, unless you can come up with an exact location where the entrance is in the next ten seconds, we're all probably gonna be real dead, real soon."

She frowned deeply as she took in the faces of her friends, each one looking back longingly in the hope that she would find the key to the hidden bunker. "Gee, thanks, guys, no pressure."

Chapter 33

The radar installation was devoid of life, only a few desiccated corpses found in one of the squat buildings to show there had ever been anyone human there at all.

The bodies had carelessly been tossed out into the snow like they were trash, to make room for the pack animals and horses, where they were stabled and fed, feedbags draped over their faces to give them a well-earned meal.

Another building was designated the mess hall by Varakov. Under his orders, a hole was hacked into the roof, to allow the smoke to escape from the cooking fire set up to roast the meat taken from the last village. It wasn't long before the aroma of roasting pig filled the air around the buildings the Russians soldiers were occupying.

Five buildings in total were commandeered by the soldiers, Varakov and Streltsy staying in the one closest to the radar dishes. Here, too, a hole had been made in the roof, and a warm fire was already burning, the fuel for it some old furniture found in a back room.

Major Varakov and his second-in-command sat in a far corner, their backs pressed against the wall, their coats over them like blankets, as they enjoyed being out of the cold air.

With a pot of coffee brewing over the fire, the smell filled the inside of the room, making Varakov salivate. He was hungry, so he pointed to the first man he laid eyes on, a thin, pasty-eyed boy of no more than seventeen. This was the first time he had even seen the boy, and when he thought back before leaving Russia, he couldn't recall the boy at all. But then there were many faces he didn't recognize, as the make-shift army of soldiers had been thrust upon him.

"Boy," he called to get the teen's attention.

"Yes, Major, sir?" the boy asked.

"I hunger. Go get me some of that roasting pig the cook is preparing, and be quick about it."

"Yes, Sir, right away," the boy replied as he stood up and began to leave the building.

"Get me some too, son," Streltsy said as an afterthought. He'd planned on waiting till later to eat, but decided he might as well dine with his commander.

"Yes, Sir, right away, Sir," the boy said as he paused at the doorway to answer Streltsy, then turned to scoot out into the snow. Upon opening the door, the cold air rushed in, many of the men yelling at the lad to close the door before he ended up getting a beating.

Varakov smiled at the jibes sent the boy's way, but said nothing to quiet his men. There were times when the men needed to let off steam, which was why he let them raid and pillage whenever possible. Of course, he also had needs he wanted to be fulfilled.

Thinking of those needs, and how he'd managed to fulfill them thus far, caused him to get an erection, and he shifted his position on the floor to become more comfortable. His coat covered his lower half, so no one could see his excitement.

The boy was still in the doorway, fighting to pull the door closed behind him, thanks to the strong wind that had begun blowing around the radar dishes. His body was silhouetted to anyone watching him outside, thanks to the firelight within the building.

With everyone yelling at the boy to close the damn door, the commotion within the building was rather loud, so at first no one realized what had actually happened, when the boy's head suddenly exploded, bone and brain matter painting the door pink and red, which then flew open as limp hands released it.

The door slammed into the wall behind it, the wind rushing in, causing even more yells and shouts as the cold air bit into exposed flesh.

The boy's headless body seemed to remain poised where it stood, but then the wind forced it to topple back into the building, blood still squirting from the jagged neck opening where a head once rested.

Half a heartbeat later, bullets zipped through the open doorway, peppering the wall opposite the opening with rounds, hitting a man in the arm before he ducked lower to seek refuge from the buzzing death.

The rest of the men inside the room moved away from the doorway, the bullets now ineffectual.

In the corner, safe from the barrage of gunfire, Varakov jumped to his feet, snapping orders instantly.

"We are under attack! Get your weapons up, you fools; we must repel the enemy! Get outside! Fight, damn you, or so help me, I'll kill you myself!" He pulled his sidearm and fired once into the ceiling, raining plaster down over his head. Shrugging into his coat, he prepared to charge outside.

If they ended up trapped within the building, there would be no escape. No, the only way to win would be to go outside and spread out.

He moved to the doorway, not afraid of being shot, but another man got in his way. It was a good thing, too, for the second Varakov was about to rush outside, the man was there, becoming a human shield for the bullets that peppered his body from crotch to neck, bullets that would have hit Varakov if he had been a little faster through the doorway. Varakov fell backwards, away from the doorway, as more bullets flew inside like angry hornets.

Tossing the dead soldier away from him without care, Varakov turned to Streltsy. "We must find another way out of here. Surely there is another exit."

Streltsy nodded. "There is, Comrade Major. Before we holed up here I made sure to have one of the men do a recce. There is another exit in the back room."

"Good, then let us use it." He pointed to half the men, six in total. "You men come with me, the rest of you stay here and send off a few shots out the door when you can. We need our enemy to think we are trapped inside. We will skirt around from the rear and when we attack, you come out shooting as well."

"Yes, Comrade Major, it will be done," Ivan the torturer said.

With Varakov leading the way, the men made their way through the building. After a brief pause at the rear exit, where Varakov waved his hat in the air on the tip of his sword out of the door, and nothing happened, no gunfire, no shouts of warning, the men charged off into the snow to circle around the area and come up behind the enemy.

Night had fallen since they'd entered the building, and as Varakov moved through the snow, he searched for the two guards he'd posted to walk the area, their jobs to make sure the exact situation that was occurring did not happen.

He made a mental note to have both men whipped within an inch of their lives, and then when they were teetering on the edge of death, he would decide if he should finish them off or let them remain alive. The only reason he wouldn't kill them outright was because he needed men to take over Alaska, and if he kept killing them himself, he would soon be out of manpower, and the journey to America would be a failure.

A few minutes later, as he, Streltsy and six others made their way past the building to the radar dishes, he realized his dilemma about killing the guards wouldn't be an issue.

Both men were lying in the snow on their backs, about four yards apart. The snow around them was dappled red with blood, and as he peered at the bodies more intently, he saw a pool of blood already freezing beside each man.

More gunshots sounded, and flickers of light could be seen from near the radar dishes. He counted six individual flickers, denoting six shooters.

"The fools are either too stupid to know they are showing their positions or they are overconfident," Varakov said. He gestured to each of his men, their faces clear in the moonlight as it reflected off the snowy terrain. "Each of you take a target and kill whoever you find. Show no mercy."

"Yes, Comrade Major," and "It will be done," and other replies came to Varakov as each soldier set out for a chosen target. Two men were going to go to the same target, but at the last second they realized this and stopped, conversed quickly, and then one continued on the same path while the other set off for a different shooter.

Varakov glanced over his shoulder at Streltsy who was by his side. "Finally we have a real fight, my friend. At last we battle real warriors and not cowards that hide under their mother's skirt and piss their pants the moment they see us coming."

"I agree, Comrade Major. If only we could take part in the killing, instead of remaining behind."

Varakov turned fully so that the two men were face to face. "What made you think that? No, my friend, we are not staying behind. Do you think I would let the men have all the fun?" He pointed to a flicker of light. "That one is our target."

"But one of the men is already going there."

Varakov nodded. "Yes, but if you see where that shooter is, our man will be spotted easily."

"So you sent him to die?"

"Yes, but he dies for the glory of Mother Russia. What more can a man ask for?" Varakov smiled in the cold air. "But with the shooter distracted, it will allow us to come upon him from another direction and kill him." He began to move. "Come, let us be moving, there is no time to waste."

As predicted, the man Varakov sent to his death did what was expected of him, even if the soldier didn't know it.

Though the soldier tried to be stealthy, he was spotted soon enough, the shooter stitching the soldier with bullets from crotch to neck, the man's body dancing a jig of death before falling to the snowy ground, dead before he hit the ice.

But the time it took the shooter to kill the soldier was more than enough time for Varakov and Streltsy to surround the sniper and take the enemy from behind with a bludgeoning to the head with the hilt of Varakov's sword. His Makarov PM had been ready for use in his other hand, but he was glad he hadn't needed to use it. A living prisoner always was better than a dead one when needing to extract information.

While the two of them had captured their shooter, a quick succession of gunshots could be heard, as each soldier found their prey and executed the enemy with extreme prejudice. Meanwhile, Ivan the torturer and two other soldiers fired from the doorway of the building, the gunfire keeping the shooters from returning fire in anything that would be considered an onslaught. The shooters had all been older men, not warriors at all, but simple men who had taken arms against the invading Russians, after hearing stories about the atrocities happening across the snowy plains. Evidently, Varakov's reputation was preceding him as he made his way through Alaska.

Thirty minutes later, with five new guards posted around the buildings being used as living quarters, and back inside the squat building, Varakov sat before the fire, warming himself. Streltsy had gone to the other buildings to brief the men there, all of them anxious for news as to what had occurred.

In one of the buildings that had been transformed into a barracks, the men within hadn't even known there was a problem outside, their singing and boisterous behavior so loud that the gunshots hadn't penetrated the thick concrete walls.

The corpse of the boy gunned down in the doorway of Varakov's building had been dragged away and dumped in the snow with a thin layer tossed on top of it as a grave, the blood from where he'd died in the doorway still there, where it would remain. The effort of cleaning it would be a wasted one, as the army wouldn't be there long enough for it to matter.

In the far corner of the room, where the pool of light from the fire barely penetrated, a naked man in his fifties with Asian features, was hanging by his hands with rope that led up to the ceiling. There, the rope was secured to a beam, the false ceiling removed for easy access. His feet were secured as well, and only by standing on his tiptoes gave him respite from the weight of his own body as he hung like a piece of meat in a butcher's shop. Drying blood covered one side of his face from a scalp would, the one he'd received from Varakov when he was captured. The captive's head hung low, his chin touching his chest, eyes closed, still unconscious.

A haze of smoke swirled around in the air, the remnants of what didn't escape through the hole in the roof.

From outside, coming from another building, the faint scream of a woman was heard. Varakov knew who the owner of that scream belonged to.

When his men had reported back after killing the shooters spaced around the radar installation, one man had brought back a prisoner.

An Asian woman.

Middle-aged with dark black hair and piercing green eyes, she had been wounded by the soldier that had been sent to kill her. A bullet to the stomach had knocked her out, and seeing she was still alive, the soldier had carried her back to the barracks. The woman had not awoken since being brought back however, so Varakov had given her to his men for some sport.

To the great appreciation of his soldiers, too.

Though gut shot, a mortal wound if there ever was one, as hospitals with surgeons on call were a thing of the past, it would take her hours to die. Even if she could have been brought to a working hospital, her survival would have been unsure. So still being alive, in that time she was to be used, over and over again. No doubt, when death finally claimed her, it would be a welcome mercy from her suffering under the hands of the merciless killers and rapists.

Varakov knew even after she died her uses would not end. For as long as the body remained warm, he knew there were less discerning men in his squad that would still feel no guilt in using the woman as they saw fit.

Sighing heavily, Varakov first looked at the prisoner hanging in the corner, then at Streltsy, who was sitting close by. "It seems these Americans are all soft, my friend. Finally, I thought we had a fight on our hands, only to discover it was a few peasants who happened to have decent armaments." He picked up one of the rifles taken from the dead shooters. It was an M16A, the metal polished, the clip still half full before the man who had owned it had been killed. "It truly appears there are no challenges here in America. Whatever happened to the great United States?"

"Perhaps, Comrade Major," Streltsy suggested, "the undead outbreak wiped them all out other than a few measly villagers we have already come across."

"Perhaps," the commander nodded, "but surely there must be some men who are not old and frail, and who know how to fight like real men." He dropped the rifle to the floor, where it clattered on top of the other weapons. "Why, if these people had been better strategists, we might have been slaughtered before getting off a single shot." He sipped his coffee, and realizing it was cold, tossed the contents of the mug into the fire, where the liquid hissed for a moment on the hot coals. "Time to have some fun." He stood up, crossed the room, and slapped the prisoner in the face, jarring the man from oblivion and back into the world of the living.

Eyes opened, glazed and surprised to be hanging like a pig ready for slaughter. The man began babbling in Chinese of all things and Varakov looked at Streltsy and the other men and shrugged. "It appears this man does not speak English, and I do not believe any one of us speaks Chinese or Japanese or whatever this fool's dialect is. Am I correct?"

All the men replied, some together, others separately, that no, they did not speak the language the man was babbling.

He pointed to Ivan the torturer. "You, go to the other buildings and check to see if someone there speaks this fool's tongue. Hurry back."

Ivan jumped up and was off, not even bothering with a reply.

Major Ishmael Varakov stood with his arms crossed as he watched his prisoner swing back and forth slightly as the man tried to move, then feeling pain, would stop and try to remain still.

Another female scream floated through the walls of the building, telling of the enjoyment his men were having with the captured woman.

"Speak English?" Varakov asked the man, using his schooling once more. "Hello, Sir, it is nice to meet you. Where are you from?"

The man shook his head, not understanding, then babbled some more in what to Varakov sounded like gibberish.

"Do you speak Russian?" Varakov asked in his native language, figuring it was worth a try, but once more the prisoner shook his head and said something in a language Varakov didn't know.

Disgusted, Varakov turned and walked back to the fire, warming his hands.

"Comrade Major, if the man does not speak a language you understand, what will you do?" Streltsy asked.

"Let us wait and see what Ivan reports. Then I will decide what to do next."

They didn't have to wait long. Ivan returned a few minutes later, having made the rounds of the other buildings. "Comrade Major, I am sorry to say none of the men speak anything other than Russian."

Varakov grunted in response, then waved a hand to dismiss Ivan, who rejoined his friends near the fire, where they were playing a game of dice. Muttering about incompetent fools, he turned and walked back to the prisoner, while drawing his sword from its sheath.

The captive saw Varakov coming for him and he redoubled his efforts to pull himself free of his bonds, now shrieking in Chinese.

Varakov ignored him, and as calmly as a man cutting a branch off a tree, stabbed the man in the throat, the blade slicing through the Adam's apple and larynx, before slicing into the spine and jutting out the back of the neck.

The man's eyes went wide for a moment, the mouth opening and closing like a landed fish, then he began spewing blood, which dribbled down his chin to splash onto his chest.

Varakov twisted the blade once to the left, then slid it out gracefully.

The prisoner choked on his own blood, dying noisily.

Turning to his men, Varakov spoke to all of them. "Get this useless piece of shit out of here. Throw the corpse out into the snow. Do not bother covering it, there is no reason to. Then throw some snow on the blood here, and when it is absorbed, scoop it up and toss the snow outside as well. Then clean up the blood by the doorway the same way. This place is beginning to smell like a slaughter house, and though we will only be here for one more day, I want it to smell better than it does now."

Streltsy got four men working on what Varakov ordered, and fifteen minutes later found Varakov sitting by the fire again, drinking a fresh cup of coffee, the killing from only minutes ago already forgotten.

Another cry sounded from outside, this time softer than before, telling that the woman wasn't too long for this world. He had sent Ivan to check on her and apparently she had never actually become conscious, but every once in a while, when she was treated particularly harsh, she would open her eyes and scream, before falling back into unconsciousness.

The woman being Asian as well, Varakov hadn't even considered trying to interrogate her, deciding it wasn't worth the effort to see if she could be revived. Besides, even if the woman did speak English for some reason, unlike the man, what information could she really tell him that he did not already know?

He idly wondered if the woman and the man had been husband and wife, but then figured it didn't matter.

Pulling out an old paperback book to read, one he'd taken with him from Russia, Varakov sat back and relaxed, enjoying the warmth of the fire while his men talked around him.

Before he turned in for the night, he heard a few more screams from the woman, but then it had gone silent. No more screams.

He found out the next morning that the Asian woman had lived the entire night she had been captured, and long into the morning, expiring just before dawn.

He hadn't asked for details about what happened to the body after her passing, though he had an idea.

There were some things his men did that even he didn't want to know about.

Chapter 34

Through the cloud of disintegrated corpses, the Skullfuckers roared onto the base, their engines reverberating off the nearby buildings, adding to the decibel level, until it was deafening.

Pulling the pin on one of the two remaining grenades Henry had, he tossed one at the oncoming bikers, then turned and continued running. The others were right in front of him, Mary in the lead as she scanned the buildings for possible clues as to the location of the hidden redoubt.

The grenade landed thirty feet away and began to roll across the ground before it erupted, just as a biker drove over it. The resulting explosion, magnified by the gas tank on the Harley, sent shrapnel and body parts flying off in all directions. Bone shards became gory projectiles that struck bikers and sent them sprawling to the ground, their motorcycles sliding out beneath them. Ten bikers in total were hurt in the blast, but only the one biker who had driven over the grenade was killed.

"Get the fuck up, you pussies!" Vincent bellowed. "They're not getting away this time!"

Ignoring bleeding wounds, the bikers did as they were told, once more roaring off after the companions. One bike wasn't in good enough condition to continue, so the man jumped onto the back of another one, willing to accept the indignity of riding 'bitch' to stay in the chase.

While the fallen bikers recovered, the rest simply drove around their brothers, not wanting to slow down and help them.

Henry cursed under his breath when he saw the bikers barely slowing down. He'd hoped the threat of more grenades coming would cause Vincent to be more cautious. But the man was relentless, and even the threat of death wasn't going to stop him from catching Henry and the others.

Henry hated using one of his remaining grenades, but then better to use one and survive then hoard them and die.

While they ran, Mary kept looking at the buildings and the map. The buildings were numbered, and there were letters and numbers scrawled on the margin of the map. Mary had always been a person who could think on her feet, and she had an above average IQ, so after a few buildings passed by her, she realized she might have figured out where they were.

Pointing down the street they were on, and looking to the right side of the road, she yelled, "This way! I think I know where we need to go!"

"Where?" Cindy asked as she carried Jimmy's stretcher, Sue also carrying him.

"We need to find Building 7. She gestured to the building they were passing. There's 20, so it's down this way but on the opposite side. They go even and odd on each side."

Henry had caught up to the others and he took the stretcher from Sue, then directed her to take one of the sides from Cindy so the two women carried one end, and Henry the other. Now they were moving faster, though not fast enough to outrun the bikers, who were even now reaching the first building at the beginning of the street.

The companions had just reached Building 10, and 7 was only three more away.

They were cutting it far too close for Henry's liking.

"Mary, take the stretcher so I can slow them down some more!" Henry yelled as he unslung Jimmy's shotgun. Anxious to kill the companions, a few bikers were shooting at them, though the bullets were going wide.

"But what about you?" Sue yelled.

"I'll be right behind you; just go!" Henry pulled away from the others as Mary took the stretcher from him. Jimmy said something but Henry didn't hear him, his attention focused on slowing down the bikers.

Standing in the middle of the road, he leveled the shotgun at the oncoming bikers. Like some sort of mythical warrior battling an army alone, he stood his ground, legs spread apart, jaw set tight, as the first bikers in line came roaring at him.

With a grimace to his features, he fired twice in quick succession, the steel-shot pellets spraying out in a six-foot radius, the penetrating power up to ten feet away. His ears rung with the report of the weapon but he ignored it. He'd timed it right, and the first bikers were about fifteen feet away when he fired; they were moving fast and drove right into the lethal barrage of steel balls. One man was blown clean off his bike, half his face becoming nothing but bloody hamburger. Another biker was blinded, and a third took multiple steel pellets in the throat, which tore out the left side of his neck, blood shooting from the severed carotid artery.

There was no time to move, so Henry stood perfectly still as the rider-less motorcycles came barreling right at him. Two missed him completely, but a third was on a collision course with him, the biker still in control as he bled out with a destroyed throat. At the last second, just before the front tire would have collided with Henry, he simply stepped to the right two feet, the biker whipping past him to then crash into a building. Going headfirst over the handlebars into the wall, the rider's neck snapped instantly, the skull becoming a bloody paste which painted the white wall red. Pink brain matter slid down the building like tiny snails in a race to the finish line.

Satisfied with the results, Henry turned and began running again, as more bikers came roaring down the street. Bullets zipped past his head and Henry ducked instinctively, though knowing it was a waste of time. He expected to feel a bullet strike his back any second but nothing happened, and in a matter of seconds he was back with his friends, who were gathered around a gray door with a large number 7 painted on it.

"The door's locked!" Mary yelled. "There's no way to get inside!"

"Get out of the way!" Henry shouted, directing the muzzle of the shotgun at the lock on the door. The report was deafening, and an instant later the lock and a large portion of the door were gone, leaving behind a smoking hole.

"Get inside, now!" Henry yelped as he swiveled on his heel's to see the bikers a heartbeat away. Bullets pockmarked the wall around him as he ducked into the building once the others had entered. Just before he was through, he felt a tugging at his left arm, but then he was inside.

Pulling the door closed behind him, he felt foolish for doing it, as there was no way to lock the door now that the locking mechanism had been blown out.

Pulling his Glock and letting the shotgun hang by its lanyard, Henry walked backwards, away from the door, ready the second a face appeared in the doorway.

He didn't have to wait long. When he was no more than ten feet from the door, it was thrown open and a biker stood in the doorway. Henry fired twice, a double tap that hit the biker in the chest, sending him flying back out of the doorway. Then another biker appeared and once more Henry fired, the bullet missing the Skullfucker but making the man duck back outside. Once more his ears were assaulted by the loud report in such a confined space. Henry's ears rung from the gunfire, but with nothing to do about it, he suffered through it. "That'll make them think twice before trying that again," he said as he caught up to the others, who were all standing in the center of the building, which from inside was basically a warehouse. As he gazed up at the walls of the structure, he realized it was made of nothing more than corrugated sheet metal on a steel frame. The building wasn't permanent, or didn't have that feeling.

It was empty inside, devoid of anything other than a small structure the size of a gardening shed that was directly in the center of the building. The shed was around ten feet by ten, with a flat roof as well. Made of solid cement, it had a solid steel door that when tapped on, gave back a sound that said it had to be inches thick if not more. Shooting through the lock on the door wasn't an option, and not even the last hand grenade would probably put a dent in it.

Another head appeared in the far doorway, and given that Henry and the others were now deep in the center of the building, there wasn't really a way to defend themselves from the bikers entering the structure as well.

"Quick, get on the other side of the shed," Henry urged, shoving everyone around the far wall of the shed, and by doing so they had at least some protection from the bikers, who had already begun shooting the instant they came charging inside.

Bullets rebounded off the shed, some coming close to the corner edge when Henry peered around it. He fired a few shots with his Glock. Cindy joined in as well with her M16, kneeling on the ground below Henry. Sue did what she could as well, poking around Henry whenever it seemed viable, but she knew her .22 wouldn't do much damage from the distance she was firing from.

Motorcycles began pouring in through the open doorway, the odor of exhaust fumes filling the air as the bikers began driving around, firing with their free left hand, while the other remained on the throttle. They manually kicked their transmissions into gear by using their feet, thus avoiding using the clutch. The noise inside the warehouse was deafening, a wave of sound that would not relent.

Henry searched for Vincent amidst the circling bikers, and he let out a roar of anger upon spotting the man. Stepping out away from the shed, Henry fired three times at the Skullfuckers' President. He saw Vincent go down, falling off his motorcycle, but then Henry had to duck back or risk being riddled with bullets sent his way.

"We're not gonna last too long here!" Henry yelled over his shoulder. "Mary, you figure out anything more?" A biker came screaming at the companions, firing a pistol, Cindy shooting the man in the chest, sending the body flying off the bike, the empty motorcycle veering off before falling over. The bikers cared nothing for personal safety, only wanting revenge for their fallen brothers. Henry knew they wouldn't stop until Henry and his friends were dead.

Peering cautiously around the shed, Henry saw Vincent getting back up, a dark spot of blood on his right shoulder, where he'd been hit; the man was still very much alive. Climbing back onto his Harley, he drove off to circle around to make another pass. Feeling like the cowboys, the bikers the Indians, in an old movie, Henry knew the outcome would be about the same. The bikers had vehicles to move fast and superior numbers. There could be only one ending to this fatal confrontation.

"Henry, I think I might have gotten it," Mary said as she studied the map from behind him. "Look for some kind of keypad near the door."

"Cindy, cover me while I go look. Make sure those assholes don't kill me."

"Got it, Henry, go for it." Sue stood up, spraying bullets every which way, burning through an entire clip in seconds. It was wasteful, and she didn't hit any of the bikers, but it got them to seek cover or risk being peppered with bullets. Henry's ears rang once more from the loud reports but he ignored it. Loss of hearing was the least of his worries at the moment.

Henry waited a heartbeat for Cindy to begin firing, to make sure the bikers had pulled back, then he stepped around to the front of the shed, his back now fully exposed to a bullet. His eyes roamed around the doorframe, and for a moment he spotted nothing, but then, painted the same white color as the cement shed, he spotted a small square outline around eight inches in diameter. Pulling his panga, he shoved the tip into the crack and twisted. A panel popped open, exposing a glowing digital keypad, set up like the numbers on a payphone.

"I found it, Mary, it's here! What do I do now?"

Ignoring her own safety, Mary ran around the shed, the map still in her hand. "Here, punch in these numbers," she said, pointing to a set of seven numbers scrawled on the side of the map in the margin.

Doing as instructed, Henry quickly punched in the numbers, but when he pressed the 'enter' button after finishing, nothing happened.

"Shit!" he shouted. "It didn't work!"

"Do it again," she urged. "And this time slow down. I think you pressed two numbers at once the first time."

Making an annoyed face and glaring at her, he did what she said. Though his adrenaline was pumping through his body, making him want to move as fast as humanly possible, still he forced himself to slow down.

"Hurry up, guys, I'm almost out of bullets!" Cindy yelled as she fired her third magazine at the bikers, keeping them from returning fire from the sheer volume of her bullets. Her muzzle was smoking, however; it was starting to glow red it was so hot. She knew the rifle would misfire if she didn't let it cool down.

"Damn it, I'm out again," she said as the last bullet in the mag cycled through. Suddenly, another magazine was passed to her from over her shoulder. She looked up, expecting to see Sue's face but it was Jimmy. He was as white as a ghost, dark shadows under his eyes, and he looked ten years older than before he'd been shot. But he wore the shit-eating grin she'd grown to love. She took the magazine and said, "You shouldn't be up, you need to lie down."

He shrugged, as he leaned against the shed wall for support, or else risk falling over. "If we don't get outta here, it really won't matter, 'cause we'll all be dead. Now give those fuckers some lead and let's hope Henry and Mary do whatever the hell they're doing over there."

She nodded, and soon was firing on semi-auto, taking slow, careful shots so as not to burn out the barrel. The bikers had no choice but to duck down or risk being shot, though a few still did their best, sending sporadic gunfire directly at Mary and Henry, who were exposed.

Henry couldn't help but duck his head as a bullet ricocheted off the wall close to his head, leaving a small crater in the cement block. Other bullets had left pockmarks where they had struck the wall wide of their mark. Henry tried not to think what one of those bullets would do to a human body.

He began punching in the code once more. He made sure to only press one button at a time, his finger making contact right in the center of the button before moving to the next. This time, when he pressed the 'enter' key, there was a soft 'click' and the door popped open an inch. Getting his fingers into the crack, he yanked it open, feeling the weight of the door, and seeing that the edge was at least four inches thick.

"Get the others," he snapped at her, as there was no time to celebrate. They were far from safe yet.

As Mary ran around the shed, Henry turned and began firing with his Glock, using up the rest of the seventeen round clip in a few seconds. He popped out the empty clip, shoved it in a pocket, and pulled another from a different pocket, then popped the new one back into place, the entire action taking seconds. As he was halfway through firing the second clip, the others appeared, Mary and Sue helping carry Jimmy, while Cindy walked before them, spraying her last magazine at the bikers, which was the only reason why Henry hadn't been riddled with bullets.

Vincent, upon seeing his prey about to get away, let out a yell to charge, the Skullfuckers obeying in their berserker fury, all of them abandoning the bikes they were hiding behind, and running directly at the shed and the retreating companions.

Jimmy, Sue and Mary were the first inside the doorway, nothing but darkness to greet them. Not that anyone said anything. Whatever was inside the shed couldn't be worse than the biker gang that was trying to kill them right now.

Once they were through, Cindy was next, and then Henry, who grabbed the door with his left hand as he continued to fire with his right, the Glock spitting bullets right up to the last second, the assault to his ears enough to make his eyes water. He shot the first three bikers in line as they ran at the shed, then he stopped shooting, needing both hands to finish closing the door. It had been years since the door had been opened, which was painfully apparent by the lack of grease on the large hinges.

Just before the door slammed closed, Henry spotted Vincent running at him, his face a mask of hate, his gun in his hand as he fired at the door. Henry and the biker President locked eyes for one brief second, and in that moment, Henry couldn't help but flash Vincent the most wise-ass grin he'd ever produced, one he believed Jimmy would have been proud of if he'd seen it. It said, "I beat you, I got away. I win, you lose."

Then the door sealed shut and almost all sound was muted to the point of being nothing but muffled echoes.

Jimmy was sitting on the floor, his back up against the wall, resting, the women gathered around him. The second the door closed, there was a soft click, and fluorescent lights came on in the ceiling. Overhead, the soft hum of ventilation could be heard. They were in a small, square room, around the same size as the diameter of the shed. The walls were devoid of anything, and the floor was just poured concrete.

On the opposite side of the thick metal door, the sharp, metallic sounds of bullets slamming into the metal could be heard. But no voices carried into the interior of the shed.

"Everyone in one piece?" Henry asked as he surveyed his people. They all looked exhausted, but no one looked to be bleeding from a wound they didn't know they'd gotten—not counting Jimmy of course, but he had no new wounds showing anyway.

Sue came over to Henry and touched his left arm just above the elbow, in the meaty part of his bicep. "Blood," she said softly.

He looked down at his arm, feeling where the blood was. His finger went through a hole in the front of the material, then found another in the rear. "Looks like I got hit," he said flatly. "But it only caught the edge of my arm. A flesh wound. It'll wait till we get wherever we go from here."

Sue tore off a piece of her shirt and wrapped it around his arm, ignoring his protests. "For now," she said simply, and he nodded.

Henry walked past the others, seeing another metal door before him, and another keypad as well. "Think it's the same code?" he asked Mary.

She shrugged. "If it's not, I guess this is as far as we go."

"Let's find out," he grunted and did the code again, remembering it easily. Five numbers and an asterisk, not difficult at all. When he finished, he stepped back, waiting for the door to open.

At first nothing happened. He was going to try again when there was a soft hiss of hydraulics and the door popped open.

"We going in there?" Cindy asked as she knelt by Jimmy, giving him another sip of Snapple. After Jimmy drank some, she finished off the bottle, suddenly very thirsty. Policing her area, she shoved the empty bottle back into her bag, either for disposal or reuse later.

Henry walked to the new door, peering inside what lay beyond it. At first there was only darkness, but as he put his head in a little more, he must have tripped a motion sensor for fluorescent lights flicked on, their low hum filling the long hallway illuminated before him. At the end of the hundred-foot plus hallway, he could see what sure looked like an elevator.

He told the others what he found, finishing with, "We can't go back outside, that's for damn sure, so that leaves only one way to go."

Deciding there was no rush, Henry propped one of the supply bags in the doorway to prevent the door from closing, then they sat and rested for a few minutes. This also gave them an opportunity to reload their weapons, making sure each of them had a full magazine, and not half of one.

While they rested and checked their armaments, every so often they heard something banging from on the outer metal door, though the sound was muted.

"Sounds like Vincent wants in here," Jimmy said, his voice still hoarse.

"Nothing short of a tank is gonna blast its way in here," Henry said. "He's like the wolf and we're the little pigs, only this time instead of a brick house, we're in something even stronger." He chuckled. "So let him huff and puff all he wants. He isn't gonna blow this house down anytime soon." He gestured to Jimmy's leg. "How you doing?"

Jimmy gingerly touched the bandage over his wound. "It hurts like hell but I'll live." He flashed Henry a grin. "Thanks, old man, for saving my ass, by the way." His grin vanished. "I guess I owe you one now."

Henry waved a placatory hand at Jimmy. "No you don't, pal. It's what we do for each other. We're family. We're all good." He stood up, getting antsy and wanting to be moving. Though the outer metal door was strong, he didn't want to be where he was if by some chance Vincent actually managed to open it, either by explosives or by hacking the keypad. He doubted the latter would occur, but then anything could happen.

"If everyone's had a good enough rest, let's get a move on," he said as he stood up and gathered his gear.

The others did so as well, and a few minutes later, Jimmy being carried between Henry and Cindy as if the man was drunk, the stretcher having been left outside in the haste to get into the shed, they began walking down the long hallway.

Mary took the lead, Henry and Cindy with Jimmy in the middle, and Sue followed last. Both Sue and Mary had their weapons drawn, ready if needed.

Eventually, they reached the end of the small hallway and Henry saw he'd been correct. It was an elevator. To the side of the elevator was a metal desk with a single chair. The desk was empty, and though there was no dust thanks to the ventilation which must have filtered air, it looked as if no one had sat there for a long time.

Pressing the call button, everyone waited as the elevator came to them.

Or at least they assumed this, as there were no floor numbers lit up above the elevator door telling the location of the elevator car like in an office building.

After a full two minutes had passed and nothing happened, Henry was about to say something when the elevator door finally opened.

No one moved, just stared at the interior.

The inside of the car was metal, the welds on the seams apparent to anyone who knew what they were. The elevator was for one job and one job only, and cosmetics hadn't been taken into account.

The door of the elevator began to close, and Henry stuck out an arm to prevent it, the door stopping, a warning alarm sounding somewhere overhead.

"Looks safe enough," Henry said as he held the door open. "Go ahead and get Jimmy in. I've got the door."

Jimmy, who had been leaning against the wall, was led inside with Cindy and Mary's help. Sue followed, carrying some extra supply bags.

When everyone was inside, Henry stepped in as well, taking his arm away from the door, the pack on his back brushing the frame. Immediately, the warning alarm stopped sounding and the door began to close.

There was only one button to push. No markings were on the white button, not that it mattered.

Being closest to the panel, Cindy's finger hovered over the single button. She looked at the others, her eyes landing on Henry last. Her facial expression asked if she should push it.

He nodded. "Go for it." He cast a furtive glance at the others, except Jimmy of course, who was still as weak as a newborn kitten. "Okay, everyone, get hard. We don't know what's waiting for us when that door opens wherever this thing is taking us."

Cindy pressed the button and immediately everyone felt their stomachs drop, like they were on an amusement ride. While the elevator moved deep into the ground, they each prepared their weapons, muzzles aimed at the elevator door for when it opened. Only the sounds of weapons being cocked, magazines checked, and clips re-checked, could be heard within the car.

It seemed like forever when the elevator finally began to slow and the door opened, but in fact it was only thirty seconds.

The door slid open silently on greased tracks, and if anyone had been waiting for the companions, they would have been in for one hell of a surprise, for a barrage of rounds would have peppered them before the waiting opponents knew what hit them. But the hallway was empty of human life, only the soft hum of the fluorescent lighting breaking the silence.

Once more an empty desk sat off to the side, the chair pushed in, as if the guard had stepped away for a smoke break and would return in a minute.

"Looks deserted," Mary said as she peered out into the corridor. Fifty feet down it dog-eared to the left, halting any more chance of a recce.

"Yeah, I agree," Henry said. Slowly, he stepped out of the elevator, his Glock leading the way. There was no movement, no guards appeared with guns, nothing. Turning, he waved the others to follow, and soon everyone was by the desk, looking every which way. The elevator door slid closed behind them, once more barely making a sound.

"This place has power," Cindy stated.

"Yeah," Henry agreed. "Must be nuclear."

"Shit, you think we have this place to ourselves?" Jimmy asked, his voice slightly stronger. He was sitting on the corner of the desk to take the weight of his bad leg. He was sweating profusely from the exertions he'd been forced into, though he didn't complain. "I mean, if there were people here, they sure as hell wouldn't just let us walk around like we own the place."

Henry spotted surveillance cameras mounted high on the wall, one aimed at the elevator, the other to the opposite end of the corridor.

He gestured to them with the muzzle of his Glock, the others following where he was pointing. "Well, if there is someone down here they sure as hell know we're here." He walked down the corridor until he was halfway from the elevator. His eyes glanced at the mounted cameras, seeing they weren't moving at all. If someone was in the security room, they weren't operating the cameras.

There was a map of the complex mounted to the wall. It was under plexiglass and framed, a red dot showing where he was now, compared to the rest of the installation. He studied it for only a moment before waving the others to him. "You gotta see this," he said, his voice hushed.

Mary and Cindy helped Jimmy walk, and with Sue bringing up the rear, they joined Henry in a minute, as Jimmy couldn't move too fast. When they were all together and clustered around the map, Henry pointed to what he'd been looking at, each of them taking in the map for themselves; mouths fell agape and eyes went wide.

"Holy shit, will you look like at the size of this place?" Jimmy said as he stood with one leg bent, the limb raised in the air to keep his weight of the wound.

"Surely this can't be correct," Sue said as she studied the map.

"Yeah, I think it is," Henry nodded. "It's hard to believe, but then in a way it isn't."

The map showed a massive complex, entirely underground. Three levels, hundreds of feet deep under the earth, had been built basically in secret. Though the buildings above ground had been used as well, the major part of the installation was located underground. The uppermost level seemed to be office space and living quarters, and some research, plus the motor pool. The second level was dedicated to only research, and the third level was only for the nuclear reactor and office space dedicated to the running of it.

"Maybe the Roswell aliens are here somewhere," Jimmy said.

Henry moved his finger around the map, finally stopping when he found the Medical Bay. "Forget about aliens for the moment, Jimmy. Right now we need to get you some antibiotics for that leg. You don't want to lose it, do you?"

"Fuck no. So let's go already." He made the women help him as he moved down the corridor.

"Stay sharp, we still don't know if we're alone down here," Henry called as the others moved away from him. Pausing longer at the map, he memorized where the Medical Bay was, then saw there were other elevator banks scattered across the complex. Apparently, the one the group had arrived in was only for shuttling people back and forth to the surface.

Turning, he began to follow the others, and with one last glance at the cameras mounted overhead which remained motionless, he was satisfied the group wasn't being observed.

As he walked down the corridor, he didn't see the invisible light beam sensor he and the others passed through, nor would he ever have known it was there.

Deep in the bowels of the installation, dozens of small red orbs flickered on, the glowing crimson eyes piercing the darkness. The light sensor/motion sensor beam had been tripped, and since the intruder alarm had been set more than a year ago, when the last living human had abandoned the complex to seek other humans topside, there should have been no one within the complex to trip it.

But in case it had been returning base personnel, a cancellation code was expected, so that nothing more would come of the alarm being tripped. Only, when a full minute passed and no code was transmitted, the original purpose of the creators of those red eyes continued.

With the sound of metal clicking on the concrete floor, the owners of those red eyes began moving to find the intruders and destroy the threat to the complex.

Chapter 35

A sign pointing the way to the Medical Bay was on the wall. It instructed Henry to go right, at a junction in the corridor. "This way," he said. "Stay sharp, we don't know what's around the next corner." The hallway went on for about fifty feet, then slightly curved to the left, the rest of the passageway out of sight. The air tasted stale, as if no one had breathed it for years. The ventilation was working, however, and as they passed down each new hallway, lights flickered on, though some didn't come on at all, the light bulbs burned out or the transformer for that circuit on the fritz.

The Area 51 redoubt was different from the one they'd been in when in Colorado. The previous one had been more compact, but this new one had more area that could be called 'dead space.' And by that meaning there were times when there were no doors opening off the corridors, only long and bare passages with nothing but white walls.

"No one seems to be home, Henry," Jimmy said as he hobbled between Mary and Cindy, using the women for support.

"I agree with you so far, but people who take chances end up dead. Until we know for sure, we stay on alert."

"How come the floors are clean of dust if no one's here?" Cindy asked.

Henry gave her one of his shrugs. "Who knows? Maybe they have some kind of cleaning robots that drive around sweeping or the air could be cleaned to the point there's no dust at all."

Another sign pointed to the Medical Bay and they followed it, eventually coming upon a set of double-swinging doors with the same name. Pushing the doors open, Henry led with his Glock.

The spacious room was empty, only the gleaming instruments and hospital beds to be seen in all directions. The room was huge, easily the size of a conference room in a hotel.

Hospital beds lined both sides in neat rows, stretching off for a good while, and in the center were large cabinets and desks; most of the furniture was made of heavy glass and stainless steel.

Henry pointed to a gurney near the front of the room. "Sit him over there and I'll see if I can find some penicillin or something similar. Sue, give me a hand, will you?"

"Of course."

The women helped Jimmy sit and he sighed as he hopped up on the table, finally getting to rest. "Man, that feels good." He winced when he moved his wounded leg to become more comfortable.

Henry and Sue were searching cabinets, reading labels on the bottles.

"You find anything yet?" he asked her.

Sue shook her head. "No, not really. I have to be honest, I don't really know what I'm looking for."

"An antibiotic," Henry explained. "Penicillin is the most well known but there are others like Cipro that'll work just as good. Oh, and anything in the Tetracycline family will work, too."

She raised an eyebrow in curiosity. "How do you know all that?"

Henry shrugged again. "Well, I know about other options to Penicillin because of Emily. She was allergic to Penicillin so she had to take Cipro instead, which was okay with her. Some people can't take either, which I suppose would be difficult now given Penicillin would be the easiest to find nowadays. After all, if you were hoarding medicine, you'd only stock what you thought people would need. Most of the complicated names would be ignored and the common ones would be what people would want, as most people don't have any medical training and only know what they've picked up from television shows."

"I never thought of it that way," she said.

He smiled at her, casting a glance over his shoulder to look at her. Sensing he was looking her way, she turned to lock eyes with him.

"Stick with me, baby, and I'll teach you all kinds of things." He wiggled his eyebrows and leered at her, making sure his innuendo got across.

"Yeah, that's what I'm afraid of, you dirty old man." She went to a glass refrigerator filled with bottles of medicine and began searching again. Then her eyes lit up and she called out, "Hey, I found that one you said, Cipro. Here's a full bottle of it."

"Fantastic, bring it over here." He grabbed a few wrapped syringes for giving shots, knowing he was going to need them.

She joined him and he took the bottle from her, reading the side. Then he frowned when he read the expiration date. "Shit, this expired more than two years ago."

"Will it work?"

"It might. Just 'cause it expired doesn't mean the medicine still isn't potent enough." He sighed. "Let's hold off and see if we can find something not that old."

Once more they began to search, and soon Mary and Cindy were helping as well, while Jimmy sat and waited. He passed the time singing to himself, which quickly became annoying to the others.

"I'm starting to regret saving his skinny butt," Henry told Cindy as they went through a double set of cabinets together.

Mary had the idea to use one of the computer consoles in the Medical Bay to search for the medicine, thinking maybe she could come across an inventory list. But the computer was password protected and she couldn't get in.

"It was worth a shot," Henry told her.

"Hey, guys, when we get through here, can we go and find some of the aliens they keep here?"

"What are you talking about, Jimmy?" Mary asked from across the room.

Jimmy sat up taller, enjoying the subject. "You know, aliens, like Roswell or on the X-Files. They kept them here, experimenting on them and shit. I even heard they got themselves a genuine flying saucer in this place."

"You're an idiot," Mary said with a grin. "There's no such thing as aliens."

"Oh really? Well, Mar', there was a time when there was no such thing as zombies for real, and you know how that shit turned out."

"He's got you there, Mary," Cindy said, smiling.

"Maybe so, but aliens are entirely different. Little green men running around. Please, I thought even you were smarter than that."

"You overestimate me, Mary. I'm not smart enough not to believe it. In fact, I'm just dumb enough to believe it all!"

Everyone stopped and turned to look at Jimmy.

"What the heck did he just say?" Sue asked the room. "I didn't understand any of it."

Cindy laughed. "Welcome to my world, he's my boyfriend! I hear that kind of stuff all the time!"

Everyone began to laugh and Jimmy, who'd been smiling, slowly began to lose the grin, until he looked rather sad. He'd slowly figured out he'd been the butt of a joke, but even then he didn't fully understand what exactly the joke was.

"All right, gang, enough looking. Anyone had any better luck yet?" Henry hoped someone would say yes, but they all shook their heads, not having found what he had explained to them.

"Then we use the bottle Sue found and hope for the best." He took it from the refrigerator where it had been returned and then crossed the room, while taking one of the syringes from a pocket, where he'd stashed them.

Jimmy began shaking his head vehemently. "Nah-ah, you're not gonna stick me with that thing." He eyed the syringe in Henry's hand warily like it was a knife about to cut off his arm.

"Oh, don't be such a big baby," Henry said as he moved up beside Jimmy. The syringe was in one hand and the bottle of Cipro was in the other. "It's just a pinch. Hell, I didn't hear you complaining when I was digging around in your leg to remove the bullet."

"That's because I was unconscious!" Jimmy yelled. "I fucking hate needles. No way, man. There's gotta be another way."

Cindy joined Jimmy, grabbing his left arm and holding him. "There isn't another way, lover. Now Henry's right. Quit being such a baby and let's get this over with."

"No fucking way! I hate needles! Always have, ever since I was a kid."

Mary came up as well, as did Sue, everyone surrounding Jimmy.

Leaning in close, Mary glared at him, her eyes locking with his. "Jimmy, if you don't let Henry do what he needs to, so help me we'll all hold you down till it's done. I will personally sit on your chest if I have to."

"You wouldn't dare," he said meekly, cowed by the force of Mary's tone. Her visage said she would brook no argument.

Hanging his head low, he closed his eyes and considered it all. Finally, he sighed. "Okay, all right, but I don't want to see it coming, though."

Cindy gestured for everyone but Henry to back off a little, then she moved in even closer to Jimmy. Pushing her breasts against his arm, she leaned in and nuzzled his cheek with her lips. Her warm breath caressed his face, and he could feel the softness of her breasts pressing on his arm. Immediately, he began to get aroused, and he had to sit a little differently to hide it from the others. Cindy wasn't finished yet. She began to whisper into his ear, then gently, playfully, bit his earlobe with her teeth. While she was seducing him, her right hand, hidden from Jimmy's view, pointed to Henry to do what he needed to.

Jimmy, fully involved with his beautiful girlfriend telling him what she was going to do to him when he recovered from the bullet wound, barely noticed when the needle was jabbed into his arm—or almost.

"Ow!" Jimmy yelled, pulling away from Cindy and turning to glare at Henry. "That hurt, you fucker."

"It's all over now, Jimmy," Henry said with a grin. "Relax. If I had a lollipop I'd give it to you and tell you what a brave little boy you were—which you weren't."

Mary laughed. "The big bad Jimmy Cooper. Scourge of deaders everywhere. Afraid of a little needle."

"Ha-ha, laugh at the wounded guy," he retorted. "You're just lucky I can't walk."

"Okay, that's enough, both of you," Henry was always playing the parent to them, as if they were two fighting siblings. "Let's have another look at that wound. My patch job on the road was pretty half-ass."

"Oh, that's comforting," Jimmy quipped but he let Henry examine him.

Henry unwrapped the old bandage and gently prodded at the wound, while cleaning it with antiseptic. Jimmy winced slightly but didn't say anything.

"Looks okay," Henry said with more than a little surprise in his voice while he wrapped the wound in a fresh bandage. "I guess I did a better job than I thought. There's redness around the wound where I sealed it but I would think that's normal. Hopefully, the antibiotics will punch out any infection that's setting in."

"And if it doesn't?" Jimmy asked.

Henry grinned slightly, deciding to have a little fun with Jimmy. "Then we'd have to amputate, I'd think."

"What!" Jimmy yelled. "You mean cut off my fucking leg?"

Henry nodded. "Yup. Hack that baby right off."

"No way, old man, you're not cutting off my leg. Why, if you even try I swear I'll…" He stopped talking upon seeing the wide grin on Henry's face. He frowned deeply. "Wait a second. You're fucking with me, aren't you?"

Henry nodded. "Yes, Jimmy, I'm just screwing with you. I'm not a doctor but I'm pretty sure your leg should be fine, as long as you rest and stay off it."

"Very funny, you bastard. Don't think I'm gonna forget this. Why, when I get better, I'm gonna make sure I…" He stopped talking again, then cocked his head to the side, as if he was listening for something.

"What's wrong?" Cindy asked, the others also curious.

He raised a hand palm out to stop them from talking. "I thought I heard something coming from out in the hall. Like a click-click sound."

Everyone remained silent, each of them also listening. A moment later Cindy's eyes perked up. "Wait, I hear it, too. It's like something metal is tapping on the floor somewhere down the hallway."

"Cleaning robot?" Mary suggested, the others shrugging.

The sound began to grow louder, and more and more little clicks could be heard.

"Whatever it is, it's coming this way," Henry said. "Everyone get hard. Maybe there are people here and now they're coming to say hi." He handed Jimmy his shotgun, the younger man taking it. "You got this?"

"Yeah, old man, I got it." He quickly began chambering shells into the weapon.

The sound grew even louder.

Clickety-clack.

Clickety-clack.

Cindy helped Jimmy climb off the gurney, then it was tipped over so it could be used as a shield, the others hiding behind cabinets. Desks in the room and other furniture wasn't an option, as most of it was made of heavy glass; after the first bullet hit the glass, it would shatter, rendering it useless for protection.

Henry was about to say something else, about only shooting if necessary. For all they knew, whoever was coming could be an ally and not an enemy. But still, not to take chances if it came down to it. None of that was spoken, and in fact, none of it would have mattered even if he'd had the chance to relay his words to the others.

Before the five warriors even had a chance to get comfortable behind their makeshift shields, the double doors were forced open, each one slamming hard into the walls on either side.

Everyone was looking high, around the five feet area, expecting human beings to come pouring into the Medical Lab, but there was nothing there. Then gazes moved lower, and continued downward until stopping when they were staring at the floor.

About a foot high, with eight legs a piece, and made of polished metal, two red, glowing eyes the only color in them, came over two dozen security droids.

"What the hell are those things?" Mary screamed as she stared at the rampaging security droids.

"I have no idea," Henry responded as he took in each gleaming chassis of the spider droids. They moved like insects, the legs seeming to flow in synchronicity. Upon seeing them, he didn't know what they might be for, but then the fluorescent lighting reflected the front of each droid, right where the mouth would be, directly below the gleaming red eyes. Two razor-sharp pincers, resembling on a crab, snapped the air as they moved. Five inches wide, the pincers could slice a leg clean off, bone and all if someone was unfortunate enough to get a limb caught.

Henry wasn't about to wait around any longer, as the spider droids were swarming into the room like giant silver beetles. "Take them out!" he shouted and began firing his Glock. There wasn't much need to take aim, the droids filling a large spot on the floor, as they all had to come together to enter through the double doors.

Instantly, the room was filled with the sound of gunfire, and the odor of cordite suffused the air as each of the group opened fire. Henry winced from the loud reports, the gunshots deafening in such a confined area, but there was nothing he could do about it. Already his ears were ringing so loudly he wondered if he would lose an eardrum.

Cindy fired on semi-auto, hating to have to waste what ammunition she had remaining, but knowing there was no choice. Bullet after bullet poured into the mass of circular metal, knocking some of the droids onto their backs, where the legs twitched and kicked before the things righted themselves.

Jimmy waited until they were closer, then fired two full blasts with the shotgun from no more than five feet away. He sent six of the droids scuttling backwards, their metal legs scraping the floor as they slid away from the pellet impacts.

But they were back in an instant, as if they had merely been pushed away by a hand that had retracted.

"Fall back!" Henry bellowed as the droids came at them. He could see half of the killer machines spreading out, flanking the companions, while the first half kept them busy.

Bullets weren't doing much good at all, and other than a few dents appearing in the polished domes, the rounds hadn't even stopped one of them.

"What the fuck are these things made of?" Jimmy yelled as he shot a trio that were trying to get over the gurney.

Jimmy's voice seemed muted, but Henry quickly understood it was because his hearing was compromised. "Some kind of titanium alloy would be my guess," Henry replied as he fired at one droid point bank. One red eye was shattered and the droid fell back, but was up in a moment to rejoin the fight. Henry shot it again, this time hitting it in the same spot. It fell away again, and though it returned immediately, it took a little longer to attack. Henry also saw that the droid was unsteady on its feet.

If they could be hit in the same spot more than once, the casing couldn't stand up to it, or perhaps the inner workings couldn't take the repeated impacts and the continuous blows scrambled the circuitry. Out of the corner of his eye, Henry saw Jimmy blow away five of the little bastards. They were back up almost instantly, but he'd managed to take off more than half the legs on the things. With legs broken or missing, the droids couldn't function at all, and tried pitifully to crawl across the floor.

So they weren't invulnerable.

There was a chance to overcome them, though it was an infinitesimally small one.

The droids surrounded the companions, who though not realizing it, had moved closer to one another, almost coming up back to back to protect each other.

Henry realized this and he frowned. The little bastards were clever, and had been herding the enemy into a tight little circle since they'd arrived.

One of them took a snap at Henry's leg, and he yanked his leg back, the material on his pant leg remaining in the droid's pincers. Air caressed his leg and he cringed inside, thinking what would have happened if he hadn't been fast enough to avoid the swipe. Another droid climbed up the cabinet beside him and tried to jump on him, while systematically trying to bite at his arm. Henry shoved it away. The droid fell away, landed on its back, then flipped itself over and returned for more.

Glancing around, Henry saw the others were in similar predicaments. They needed to get out of the Medical Bay, right now!

"Jimmy! Clear us a path with that room sweeper!" Henry bellowed. "Everyone, we need to get outta here now!"

"But the hallway is blocked off!" Cindy cried as she shot one in what she assumed was its face as it tried to take a bite out of her.

"Then we go the opposite way. There's gotta be another way outta here than the way we entered."

Jimmy swung around and fired at the area behind him, the steel pellets from the 12-gauge making an opening; the sound of steel pellets pelting the polished casings of the sec droids reverberated throughout the room.

"Now! Go!" Henry yelled, seeing the opening, and also watching it shrinking as fast as it was made.

Kicking out and shooting when possible, the five warriors charged through the path Jimmy had made and began running for the back of the Medical Bay. Cindy helped Jimmy, the younger man not able to move as fast as he wanted to.

The sec droids seemed to hesitate, as if microprocessors were readjusting for an enemy that was retreating instead of fighting, then the spider droids all turned on a dime, in unison, and began charging after the five humans.

Jimmy hobbled along rather fast for a wounded man, thanks to Cindy's aid. The risk of dismemberment gave him the motivation to move faster than he should have given his wound, but adrenaline pumping through him had that effect. Some blood had appeared on the bandage from his activity, but there was no time to do anything about it. He could feel a thick rivulet of blood trickling down his leg. He ignored it.

Henry was in the lead, followed by Sue, Mary, then Cindy and Jimmy.

Their combat boots slapped the polished linoleum tiles, overriding the clickety-clack of the steel legs of the spider droids.

Running like a marathon runner, Henry pulled away from the others, dashing to the far back of the room. It seemed to go on forever, but finally he saw the back wall. His eyes darted all over it, searching for an exit sign, anything that could be a means of egress.

Then he spotted it, a small metal door in the far corner. A non-lit sign was above it with the word EXIT. "This way!" he yelled and ran for the door. It had a cross bar on it, a standard emergency door if there ever was one.

His hand went out before him, the Glock getting repositioned in his hand so he could use both hands to push the cross bar. He planned on barreling through the door ahead of the others, holding it open, then slamming it closed when the last one of his people was through.

He was still moving fast, barely slowing when he reached the door.

His hands went out to press on the bar, and he didn't expect it not to give way when he pushed on it. After all, that was what emergency exits were for.

Only the door didn't budge when he hit it. Bouncing off the door like it was made of rubber, and dazed from the impact, he fell backwards and landed hard on his butt. Sue was there to catch him or else he would have fallen back further and cracked the back of his head open.

Stunned from the blow with the door, he shook it off and jumped up, running back to it as the others gathered around him. Pushing on the bar one more time, it didn't open, not even an inch. Shaking the metal bar hard, the door shook in its frame but didn't open.

"Shit! The damn door is locked!" he screamed.

"Who the fuck locks an emergency door?" Jimmy said anxiously. "That's what they're fucking for! Emergencies!"

The sound of clicking steel came to them, and as one unit the group of five spun around, weapons up, their backs pressed against the wall.

The droids seemed to pause for a moment as they took in their helpless prey.

Henry stared at the gleaming red eyes, the pincers that opened and closed, as if the droids were already tasting the flesh they were about to rend and tear apart.

He cursed inwardly. After everything he and his friends had suffered through over the past few days, the constant battles and running, the ever-present pall of Death hanging over their heads, only to reach the salvation of the underground installation, where they thought to be safe.

But it seemed they had only traveled here to die, something they could have done aboveground, where at least they could have seen the sun one last time.

"Take out as many of the bastards as you can," Henry said, realizing the defiance he felt was foolish. These weren't living enemies; they were robots, machines without feeling. Though the group could sell their lives dearly, in the end, it would all be for nothing.

Then, as if a silent command had been sent amongst them, the security droids charged.

Chapter 36

"Wait till they get as close as possible so we don't waste bullets!" Henry backed up as far as he could go, his butt pressed against the cross bar on the exit door. He didn't think about it as he put pressure on the bar, only about what was happening in front of him.

The droids had started forward en masse, their metal legs clickety-clacking on the floor, a sound Henry knew he would hear in his nightmares, that is, if he was still alive to ever have nightmares again, which wasn't a high possibility, as he would be dead momentarily.

The others were right beside him, guns aimed at the spider droids, ready to fire instantly. But all knew the wisdom in Henry's words.

Henry glanced at Sue, her .22 locked firmly in her hands, her face set hard in a tight grimace. Sue's blonde hair flowed around her face, a few strands sticking to her cheeks due to perspiration. He thought she'd never looked as beautiful as she did right then. He wanted to tell her he loved her, that he was sorry he'd gotten them into this mess. As leader of their group, ultimately it was his decision to come to the installation, a decision that was about to mean all their deaths.

The clicking grew louder as the sec droids picked up speed. Any moment he planned to give the order to commence firing, though hopeless as it would be.

He prepared to speak, to say the last words he would probably ever utter, when suddenly there was a soft click from behind and the bar his butt was pressed into collapsed, the fire door popping open. Henry just about fell onto his ass as the door opened, but he reached out and grabbed the doorframe with his left hand, his right holding his Glock.

"The door! The door's open!" he yelled in amazement. "All of you move, now! Through the doorway!"

No one moved, everyone too focused on the attacking droids, so he reached out and gripped Sue by the arm, and then roughly yanked her to him. She let out a yelp of surprise but he ignored it, and basically threw her through the doorway. He grabbed Mary next, shoving her through, followed by Cindy. Jimmy was last and the farthest away. The young man's eyes were locked on the spider droids, and that was all he could see or hear. Leaning as far as Henry could, as he didn't want to remove his foot from the doorframe and have it close on him, he grabbed Jimmy by the wrist and pulled the younger man to him. The act was so sudden that Jimmy fired the shotgun, squeezing the trigger involuntarily. The muzzle was pointed upwards, and plaster and ceiling tiles rained down to the floor, some of the debris striking the droids, but doing no harm.

The spider droids charged forward, heedless of anything in their path, but Henry was throwing Jimmy into the doorway, and then was following, diving through the air like a man jumping into water with his ass on fire.

Mary had recovered from being tossed into the doorway and was ready. She pushed the door closed the instant Henry was through, just as the first spider droids reached it. Muted clicking could be heard on the far side of the door, scratching too.

Picking himself up, Henry looked at the others.

"What the hell, old man?" Jimmy snapped. "What's the deal?"

"He just saved your life, Jimmy," Mary snapped. "So if that's the 'deal' you're talking about, that's your answer."

Sue gathered herself and went to Henry, hugging him. "But I thought the door was locked."

"Yeah, me too," Henry replied. "But all of a sudden it popped open. Luckily, I was pressed against the bar to open it or we may not have known."

Mary shook her head. "That door was locked, and then it wasn't. Someone must've unlocked it by some security remote, it's the only explanation."

"Then people are down here with us," Sue added. "After all, someone activated those robots, too."

"Maybe," Henry agreed, "or they might have been activated by some kind of motion sensor we tripped. Right now it doesn't matter how they got turned on. All that does matter is that they're after us."

A loud tearing of metal filled the corridor they were in, and all eyes went to the bottom of the exit door. A small hole had appeared, but it was quickly growing larger, the unmistakable gleam of pincers appearing.

"Jesus," Jimmy said. "The little fuckers are eating through the metal like rats!"

"Then let's get going," Henry ordered the others. "We need to find a place they can't penetrate, like the armory or someplace with reinforced doors and walls."

The hole grew ever larger, the entire *face* of a spider droid appearing, the twin crimson eyes seeming to glow with malevolence, while beside it, new holes were opening as other droids chewed into the metal to reach the humans beyond.

"Come on, this way!" Henry began moving, the others following on his heels. Jimmy hobbled along with Cindy helping him, the two keeping up well considering his wound.

They began traversing the corridor until it curved left, and just before the door behind them was out of sight, Henry cast a glance over his shoulder in time to see the first spider droid popping through the bottom of the door, the lower half now nothing but torn metal, looking like paper punched through by a child's hand.

Clickety-clacks filled the corridor and Henry knew their time was up before it had begun.

"Damn it, they chewed through the door like it was nothing. I thought we had more time. On the double, people, they're coming!" He considered throwing his final grenade but held off, figuring even if he managed to take out a few droids, there were still far too many remaining.

The click-click was even louder as the bottom of the door basically disappeared, the droids pouring in to continue the pursuit. Once more the companions were running for their lives, death nipping at their heels.

Henry searched for someplace they could hole up, but the hallway was devoid of doors, nothing but the recessed fluorescent lighting overhead, and every fifteen feet a ventilation shaft near the ceiling—only about a foot long and six inches wide. Far too small to escape into, even if they wanted to, which they didn't. The spider droids would be even deadlier in the confined space of the ventilation system.

Henry thought briefly how when it had just been himself, Jimmy and Mary, how the trio had sought refuge within the ventilation system of Pineridge Laboratories, when a gang of escaped prisoners had come to investigate the complex, in search of supplies.

Trapped in an office, there had been no hope of escape until Henry took the desperate chance of having them shimmy into the overhead ductwork. It had worked, saving them from discovery, though their loyal dog Blackie hadn't been able to follow them to safety. The dog would never have been silent for hours inside the duct, even if there had been time to get the canine into the ceiling with them.

The dog had fought bravely when a convict had broken into the office, but brute strength was still no match for hot lead. They had buried the bullet-riddled carcass of their trusted friend behind the building, along with Scott Peters, a traveling companion who had been killed by the walking dead.

Since then, there had been so many adventures, so many challenges, and though loved ones had been lost along the way, in the end, there were still five of them trudging on, forever facing the daunting future with guns in hands and a defiance of death.

But it was all over now.

The hallway dead-ended at a blank wall, the five warriors stopping cold in their tracks, each of them turning to face the silvery gleam of the approaching sec droids.

There was nowhere to go.

The security droids were only seconds away, and there would be no exit door that would pop open at the last instant to save the group from certain death. The corridor was devoid of anything remotely useful to save them.

Even the camera mounted on the wall near the ceiling was dead, the motionless eye seeing nothing.

"Here we go again," Henry said, pulling his last grenade, about to use it. If they were about to die, there was no reason to save it any longer; he might as well use it.

As if sensing their prey was trapped, the sec droids redoubled their speed, the clickety-clack sounding even louder in the confines of the passageway. Their red eyes seemed to glow brighter, exuding evil, as pincers snapped at the air in expectation of the coming slaughter. Their designation was to seek out all intruders and eliminate them, and they were about to do what they were programmed for, the only reason they existed—with extreme prejudice.

"Shoot the bastards!" Henry roared. Pulling the pin on the grenade with his teeth, his right hand holding his Glock, he began shooting at the oncoming wave of gleaming metal. His left arm went back in preparation of throwing the grenade. The noise in the corridor became even louder with the crack of the companions' firearms, the reports deafening without ear protection, the odor of cordite suffusing the air.

"I love you, Henry Watson," Sue said by his side as she fired her .22.

"What?" he yelled, his ears ringing so much he couldn't hear a thing. Even the firing weapons had become muted as his ears suffered under the decibel onslaught.

"I said I love you!"

Reading her lips more than hearing her, he replied, "Me too." That was all he had time to say, though deep down he regretted it. He should have turned to her, pulled her close and kissed her passionately, one last kiss before the pincers tore him and her to shreds, or when he shot her before the droids could reach her, and then if there was time, to put a bullet in his own head. But he knew he wouldn't do that, not to any of them. He knew they would use every last round to destroy their enemy, and when the time came to take the last train west, they would do it fighting until the last breath was exhausted from their lungs. He knew this without asking any of them, knowing his friends as well as he knew himself.

But all the posturing and pontificating wouldn't do a bit of good when death finally gripped their hearts and squeezed.

Ten feet away, nine, then eight, the spider droids came on, as bullet after bullet was pumped into them, sending some skittering away, only to right themselves and renew the attack.

They were unstoppable, unrelenting, wanting only one thing—the death of the companions.

Henry swallowed hard as he began moving his left arm forward to throw the grenade, one last defiant action in the face of certain doom.

"Well, guys!" Jimmy yelled over the booming of his shotgun, knowing death was a heartbeat away. "It's been nice knowing you." He looked at Cindy. "Love you, babe!" Then he cast a glance at Mary, who was firing her .38 by his side. "You too, Mar'. I love you, too!"

She read his lips as well, her hearing almost gone, and smiled, nodding, returning his gesture, then she turned and focused on finding a gleaming silver target to shoot. She managed to hit a droid in the right eye, the red orb winking out, but still barely slowing the machine down.

Then there was no more time for contemplation, no more time for regrets, or anything else, as the first droid in the onslaught began its leap upwards from the floor, its pincers already spread wide open to tear and rend exposed throats, while behind it, others were also lunging, their gleaming bodies reflecting the overhead fluorescent lighting, their ruby-red eyes sparkling.

Though it had been a hard road for Henry and his companions, the end had finally come.

To be continued in Dead Incursion
Available now.

If you enjoy the Deadwater series, check out this action-packed saga by A. Giangregorio

WARRIORS OF THE APOCALYPSE

No one knows who first dropped the bombs, or released the first nuclear warheads, and no one probably will.

Not that it matters.

In the blink of an eye, the modern world was destroyed, leaving behind a wasteland of death and destruction.

Electricity, cable television, and restaurants, all gone in an instant, to be replaced by a lawless planet filled with cannibals, slavers and mutants—the latter lost souls who were too close to the initial blasts and are now nothing but feral animals that walk upright, with seeping, open wounds that cover them from head to toe.

Hank Summers was one of the survivors, a hard man who adapted quickly to the new world. With his companions, Laurie, Stewart and Carl, they travel the nukescape, searching for something better on the horizon.

A new dark age has dawned with the hope that tomorrow may bring salvation to the survivors, but after the apocalypse, hope may not be enough.

Also available in the same series:
Warriors of the Apocalypse:
Dark Holocaust